WARLOCK HOLMES

The Sign of Nine

By G. S. Denning and available from Titan Books

WARLOCK HOLMES

G.S. DENNING

WARLOCK HOLMES

The Sign of Nine

TITAN BOOKS

Warlock Holmes: The Sign of Nine
Print edition ISBN: 9781785659362
E-book edition ISBN: 9781785659379

Published by Titan Books
A division of Titan Publishing Group Ltd
144 Southwark Street, London SE1 0UP

First edition: May 2019
10 9 8 7 6 5 4 3 2 1

A CIP catalogue record for this title is available from the British Library.

Printed and bound by CPI Group (UK) Ltd, Croydon CR0 4YY.

To Jill and Clifford McCloe
whose kindness I have repaid by ruining
Cliff's name forever.

CONTENTS

THE ADVENTURE OF THE NOBLE ARSE-FACE

DEAR READER, HOW LONG HAVE YOU KNOWN ME?

If you have followed this dreary tale from its start, you have now consumed the volume wherein my strange adventure began. Thence on to the volume in which I came into my own as an adventurer and detective (and learned something of the nature of the man who had started me upon my path). Most recently came the volume dominated by our foes—when Moriarty and Adler came back into our lives to bring us defeat upon defeat.

And now?

What fresh apocalyptic treat have I for you now?

This is the volume of my shame. Perhaps my own sun has never reached a very high zenith, but in this volume, it is at its dimmest and most flickering. So close to failure, personal defeat, degradation and dishonor. There is nobody to blame but myself. Nobody to thank for my deliverance except Holmes and—oh, I shudder to say it— the hated Mary Morstan. Part of this volume is not even the chronicle of my actions, but merely of my dreams. A strange inclusion, to be sure, but I would not have bothered you with them had they been at all… natural.

How this volume commences depends upon one's point of view. I suppose it could be said that it starts with me, poisoned by a kiss, splayed unconscious across the sweat-reeking sheets of my bed at 221B Baker Street. Yet, that is not how it seemed to me.

To me, it seemed, I was on a ship. And not just any ship, but the one Britain loved best: HMS *Victory*, on the finest hour of our nation's finest day.

Drawing a breath of the clear salt air, I raised the spyglass to my eye and squinted at the wall of wood, guns and sail that lay before me—the entire combined French and Spanish fleet. Poor bastards… I had them right where I wanted them.

"We should turn," said a miserable little voice from behind me.

"I will not!" I said, with a grim laugh. "You know the plan: we go straight at them. We break their line of battle. This is a new kind of tactic—one designed to guarantee a decisive engagement."

"But… we'll all be killed!"

"Your opinion has already been noted, Mr. Lestrade."

Through my glass, I could see my target clearly: the French flagship *Bucentaure*. I smiled. "Able Seaman Holmes?"

"Aye, Watson?"

I turned to the tall figure beside me, lowered my voice and said, "You are supposed to address me as 'Vice Admiral'."

"Aye, Vice Admiral?"

"Give me seven degrees starboard rudder; I want to come through just behind their flagship."

"Eh? Seven whats of what, what?"

"Look, just turn the helm that way a little bit," I said, pointing to my right. "See the big pretty ship over there?"

Able Seaman Holmes's reverent "Oooooooooooh" gave me to know he did.

"I want to come in right behind it. Her stern is weakest. She is commanding the entire enemy fleet. We're going to hit them right in the admiral."

"Aye, aye, Watson!"

Close enough. Scanning the deck for a moment, I located my over-aged, oversized cabin boy and shouted, "Mr. Grogsson!"

"Whut?"

"I know it is not your area of expertise, but I am placing you in charge of the gun crews. The ideal commander for this engagement, I feel, will have exactly your level of discretion."

"Disc-whut?"

"Exactly. Just down that hatch, if you please. Make ready the guns and await my order."

"M'kay."

He jumped down the hatch I indicated and assumed command with a few well-chosen words. "All right, boys! Dis is gonna be great! Stick da guns out!"

The bangs of the wooden gun-ports slamming open told me *Victory* was ready for battle. And just in time. Since our bow was to the enemies' broadsides, they were able to fire well before us. I grinned to see how disorganized and ineffective their fire was. Their fleet was already in disarray as individual commanders lowered sail or turned, trying to decide how best to cope with my novel tactic.

My drooping bosun gave a deep sigh from beneath his preposterously large sunhat. "You know," he said, "there may still be time to turn…"

"Mr. Lestrade!" I thundered. "This is not the hour for cowards! Now for England! Now for *Victory*!"

"Sure… But I'm just not comfortable—"

"Then here is a task that might suit you better. Get to the signal flags, Mr. Lestrade, and send the fleet the following message: England Expects Every Man to Kick a Fat Load of Arse!"

He paused. Blinked. Muttered, "I'm just not sure we have the proper flags to express that exact sentiment."

"We do," I told him. "I sewed them myself. Now off with you, Mr. Lestrade. Hop to!"

To my south, I could see the second column, led by Collingwood's *Royal Sovereign*, drawing near the enemy. He'd pulled well forward of the rest of his ships, straining to be first into the fight. *Not before me, Collingwood.* I looked behind me. *Temeraire* and *Neptune* were with me. England's wooden killers bore down upon their prey.

Below me, I could hear Grogsson's expansive bass, urging, "Steady, boys… steady…"

And, with a final swish of sail, we blew to our place. To our starboard, the middle section of the combined fleet, pulling up sail, desperate to avoid collision. To our port, the vulnerable stern of *Bucentaure*.

"Mr. Grogsson! Now!"

From belowdecks came a thunderous "GRAAAAAAH!" By which, one supposes, he meant "fire".

"G-doom!" went the first of our guns, followed by its fellows. The air filled with smoke and noise and flying embers. The French fleet were in utter disarray, cannonballs bouncing off them in every direction.

Yep.

Just…

Just *bouncing right off.*

Every single goddamned shot.

"Oh…" I said. "Oh, I see… erm… We're sure about that, are we? No holes in anyone's… No? No damage at all?"

My guns, now empty, fell silent. My sailors fell silent too, staring in disbelief at the perfectly intact fleet that faced us.

The French sailors were quiet as well, mouths agape at their good luck. But only for a moment—then their ships erupted with triumphant cheering, followed by an ominous creak as hundreds of cannons were aimed, pretty much, right at my face.

"I do think I warned you," Bosun Lestrade noted.

"No!" I cried. "My plan was sound! How could…? I mean…? *What kind of wood are they growing in France, nowadays?*"

Lestrade shrugged. "Are there any further futile orders you would like me to convey?"

"Um… reload?"

Apparently I intended to lay a second row of non–holes in the French ships. Yet, even as I despaired at my lack of reasonable recourse, I felt a jaunty tap upon my shoulder. Turning, I beheld the smiling face of Able Seaman Holmes, who piped up, "You know, it might be better if you don't. I know a little trick! Watch…"

Dragging me to the rail, he directed my attention down towards my useless, smoking cannons. He pointed his finger at the nearest of these and said, "Pop."

Instantly, the empty cannon jerked backwards, emitting a terrible squeal as if somebody were twisting 10,000 nails in half, just beside my ear. A brilliant bolt of purple fire shot forth, catching *Bucentaure* just above her rudder. The bolt tore through, into the interior of the ship, from which issued cries of dismay and pain.

"Pop, pop, pop!" Holmes added, joyfully. Three more of my guns sent howling purple hellfire tearing into the French vessel. I couldn't see exactly what happened inside, but it must have been bad, for we could see purple flashes of secondary and tertiary explosions through the remaining windows of her stern gallery. Sailors poured out, jumping from every deck and gun–port. A second later, her magazine went up and the great flagship sagged into the sea.

Holmes paid no attention. Looking down at two of my port guns, he said, "Frip, frip!" and the three-ton cannons effortlessly swung their muzzles, one fore, one aft. "Pop, pop!" Holmes added and both discharged a screaming hellshot. One hit a hapless frigate, just off our port stern.

The other arched up and across the battlefield, screaming past fifteen or twenty targets, until it smashed into the very first ship in the French line.

And so it went. "Pop, pop! Frip-pop! Frip, frip, frip, poppity-pop!" until all fifty-two guns on the *Victory*'s port side were empty. Or… *re*-empty. Then he traipsed over to the starboard side and did it again.

It took less than two minutes, I am sure. A hundred and four shots. A hundred and four hits. Ship after ship, burning with demonic fires while their crews screamed and threw themselves into the sea.

Able Seaman Holmes had just laid waste to the entirety of the combined French and Spanish fleet. Only one ship remained to them, *Redoutable*—a notable omission, since it was right off our starboard bow and bearing straight for us. Why she did not run, or strike her colors, I will never know. Perhaps she was commanded by some kind of French Grogsson. As she neared, I could see that her captain had lined her decks and rigging with musketeers—not a bad strategy, at such close quarters.

And, from somewhere far outside my dream, certain thoughts started to intrude. I was meant to be Nelson, wasn't I? But Nelson hadn't actually survived the Battle of Trafalgar, had he? No, I seemed to recall he'd been felled by a marksman sat in the rigging of… Oh! *Redoutable*, wasn't it? If memory served, he'd been shot in the shoulder. Just like me, in Afghanistan. However, unlike me, he'd also had his spine severed. So, I guess there was *that* to look forward to.

I believe I began to perspire.

"Um... Holmes?" I said, pulling at the helmsman's sleeve.

"Yes, Vice Admiral?" he asked.

"Er..." I pointed up at the big French warship.

"Oh, that?" he scoffed. "Never mind *that*."

Stepping back along the rail, he took up the handle of one of the tiny starboard swivel-guns. Holmes tipped the barrel down towards the sea and began rhythmically spanking the side of the gun, humming a happy little sea-ditty as *Redoutable* neared. From within the swivel-gun came a soft, rolling, grinding noise as the glorified musket ball within her started to slide forward. At last it fell from the muzzle and plopped into the sea. "Ah-ha!" said Holmes, then swung the gun upwards and added, "Pop!"

"Pop!" agreed the gun, then "Scrreeeeeeeeeeeee!" as a little ball of purple fire arched forth and caught the mighty French ship straight in the center of her bow. The tiny fire tore through and burst, somewhere deep inside. The entire forecastle of *Redoutable* sagged to one side and fell into the sea. On all three of her now-visible decks, we could see sailors running this way and that in confusion as purple flame ravaged every surface.

The day was ours. Unequivocally, completely, *costlessly* ours.

No cry of triumph broke from our ranks.

The air was swollen with the sound of five hundred and fifty mariners just gawping at each other.

Then a chipper voice called out, "Three cheers for Vice Admiral Watson!"

Nobody did. Instead, eleven hundred eyes turned to Able Seaman Holmes and silently wondered why anyone would suggest such a thing.

Yet Holmes's spirits were never so easily dampened. He slapped me on the back and piped up, "Congratulations, Vice Admiral! An inspired tactical maneuver! They never stood a chance!"

"Er… no…" I managed through parched lips. "I suppose they never did."

"Hurrah for Watson's victory!" Holmes suggested, to renewed silence.

"Yes. Well… I'm not sure we can call it entirely *my* victory, can we?"

"Of course we can! And we do! Right, everybody? Watson! Yaaaaaaaaaaaaaaay!" cheered Holmes, convincing absolutely nobody.

Through the foggy silence of my sailors, I heard a voice from far away, saying, "Watson, I need you!"

"Eh?" I said, turning to Able Seaman Holmes. "Did you say something?"

"Watson, yaaaaaaaaaaaaaaay?"

"No, no, it sounded like…"

And again, across the great gulf came a voice that sounded just like Able Seaman Holmes, saying, "Watson! Watson! Watson! Watson! I'm sorry to wake you, but everybody with a brain knows you're not dead. Now, I don't mind letting you sleep away a defeat—you know I don't—but a situation has arisen that requires diplomacy, and we both know I haven't got any! Please, Watson, please! I need you!"

And the ship was gone. I threw aside the heavy veil of my dream and opened my eyes to find Warlock Holmes leaning over my bed, repeatedly slapping my forehead.

"Watson! Watson! Watson! Watson!"

"Ow! Holmes! What are you…?" My voice was weak and hoarse—a barely audible croak. "Oh, I just had the most wonderful, vivid dream!"

"Of course you did. Remember how weird your dreams were after you accidentally smoked part of that sorcerer's mummy? Being exposed to great magic always causes prophetic dreams. Or shows great secrets. Or other stuff like that. And I don't know if you know it, but you've been flat on your back in a magical coma. I've no idea what put you there."

"Irene Adler," I said. "She had poisoned lip-rouge."

"Oh, did she now?" Holmes asked, raising his eyebrows. "Well done, you sly dog, you!"

"Not too well done, I should think. She's beaten me again," I muttered. "Wait! Holmes, you said *coma*? How long have I been out?"

"Oh, two weeks."

"*Two weeks?*"

"But never mind that, Watson! Get up and help me!"

"Get up? Just like that? Certainly not, Holmes! If I have been lying here, unable to take food or water for two weeks, why I must be practically…"

"Dead" was the word I had intended, yet as I moved

my limbs experimentally back and forth underneath the bedclothes, I found them to be… fine.

Just fine.

I was a bit thirsty, to be sure, but otherwise I had no complaint. Not even a headache. Gobstruck, I turned to Holmes and wondered, "How is this possible? What have you done to me?"

"Oh, do you want to see? It's wonderful! Wait right here!"

With that, he ran out of my bedroom and into the corridor. I couldn't see where he went, but a series of bangs and clatters testified to his energetic activity. Some moments later he returned, clutching a strange brass contraption and—bless him—a glass of water.

"Here," he said, handing it to me. "Now, drink up and look at this: a real runcible amphigory!"

The device he gave me was queer in the extreme. It was an oblong brass pot, suspended over a single-candle burner. It had an opening at the top, like a teapot, and a handle like one as well. Yet, where one would have expected the spout, there was only a coil of copper piping, from which dangled a rubber tube. A queer set of scales was suspended over the open top, with one side cleverly hinged so as to allow the user to tip its contents easily into the body of the pot. As an instrument for mixing ingredients, I admired the ease with which it allowed its user to achieve precision—admirable in any scientific device. Clearly, no small amount of thought and clarity of design had gone into the creation of… whatever this was.

Holmes must have seen my consternation, for he proudly declared, "What you are holding in your hands, Watson, is the absolute peak of seventeenth-century Moldovan medical and alchemical technology!"

"Indeed? Well, that's… erm… rather faint praise, isn't it?"

"Oh, no! It's marvelous! I saw it down at Brombert's House of Curios in Covent Garden some weeks ago and I'd been thinking of picking it up for some time. When you fell unconscious… well… I was almost happy to have the excuse. It's a most useful little device for keeping incapacitated people alive. You just drain some of the person's blood and pour it in here—"

"*What?* You've been draining my blood?"

"Me? No, no. I've no art for it. *Lestrade* has been draining your blood."

Holmes pointed. I shifted my gaze in the direction he indicated, pulled back the covers and beheld my right arm. The sleeve of my nightshirt had been messily torn away to expose the full length of my limb to the vampiric administrations of Scotland Yard's second-least-popular detective inspector. Dozens of horrific fang-marks lined my skin, from my biceps down to the tips of my fingers.

"Aaaaagh!"

"Always nice to have a specialist on hand," said Holmes. "Once you've got the blood, you get whatever you want to infuse into it and measure it in this little scale. Food, medicine, whatever is needed, although you can't go over seven percent by weight. Then you light the candle and boil the blood until the infusion is dissolved. When it's ready, it drips out of this hose here, and you just inject it back in."

Holmes now indicated the hollow of my left elbow, which—in my horror over the fate of my other arm, I had failed to realize—bore a grapefruit-sized swelling.

"*Aaaaaagh!*"

"Ah, yes… Sorry about that," said Holmes. "I went out to help Lestrade on a case, last night, you see, and we left you to Grogsson. It turns out that a seven percent solution is quite a bit more than is needed for most medicines, but it isn't much *food*. I'm absolutely certain we told Grogsson not to try to inject the entirety of the beef Wellington in one go. But you know how excited he gets. Still, no harm done, eh? Here you are, hale and hearty!"

"There's an entire beef Wellington in my *arm*?"

"Oh, I suspect Grogsson may have had a bite or two, but—"

"No, no, no! This is all impossible, Holmes! Blood cannot be made to dissolve beef Wellington. Nor can it be boiled and then returned—still functional—into the human body. And you expect my immune system to digest an entire dinner, which you insist has been inserted subcutaneously? Preposterous!"

He rolled his eyes at me. "Really now, Watson! After all you've seen in my company—all you've experienced— you've still no faith in me? Still no imagination?"

"You'll forgive me, I hope, if the state of my imagination does not command as much of my concern as the state of my *bloody arms*!"

"That isn't the point, Watson. The point is that you are alive and well and ready to get out of bed, because look who's coming at four o'clock and I don't know what to do!"

Holmes removed a card from his jacket pocket and held it in front of my face.

"Lord Robert St. Simon?" I asked. "Who is that?"

"He's this horrifyingly important fellow I've been working for," said Holmes, throwing up his arms in exasperation. "He's a lord! And apparently a saint. I've been helping with his wedding. Only, there seems to have been a bit of a mix-up with his new bride, who sort of vanished in the middle of the wedding breakfast. It's in all the papers. I've saved a pile of them for you."

I sighed. "What o'clock is it?"

"I don't know… about a quarter after two, I should think."

"We haven't much time. He'll be expecting tea."

"Why?"

"Because four o'clock is teatime, Holmes. I'll see if I can get myself cleaned up a bit. You run out for scones and a pot of jam, then make some tea, won't you?"

"But *how*?"

"You can keep a fellow alive for two weeks via the intravenous administration of beef Wellington, but you *can't make tea*?"

He shrugged.

"Fine. Just get the scones, all right?"

* * *

By "I saved a pile of newspapers for you", Holmes had apparently meant, "I have been reading the newspapers for the last two weeks and leaving bits of them everywhere. Oh, and I made hats out of some of them." The sitting room was in a dreadful state. Interspersed amongst the newspapers and plates of toast-crusts and soup bowls were numerous scrolls of a magical and distinctly waterlogged appearance.

"Holmes, what are all these?"

"Remember that sea monster who promised me information on soul-binding magics if I could save his wedding from Irene Adler?"

"Yes."

"Well, those are them. Or... those are they? Anyway, Watson, they are fascinating! Real magic, achievable within this realm, without having to call on the help of outside entities. Can you imagine? To be able to use magic without damaging our world! Wouldn't that be great? So I've been practicing and practicing with them for the last two weeks!"

Much as I dreaded the prospect of Holmes teaching himself new magics, I had other matters at hand. I dug into the pile of discarded newspapers, searching for background on my pending visitor.

The first thing I found was a column from a few Wednesdays ago, stating that Lord Robert St. Simon would wed Hatty Doran of San Francisco, California, a week from Saturday at the Church of St. George, Hanover Square. That was all. Given the illustrious parentage of the groom, the announcement was brief, to say the least. One might be tempted to say "clipped". One might also note the suspicious proximity of the announcement to the event itself. This, perhaps, was an attempt to stop the local wags from commenting on the possible motivations of the groom.

Which it had absolutely failed to do. The next bit I found was a rather opinionated opinion piece wherein the writer could not help but wonder what was wrong with England's ladies that our eligible titled must be forced to the act of importation. Were there not sufficient twenty-three-year-old beauties to please the forty-one-year-old, as-yet-unmarried second sons of our dukes? Might Lord St. Simon's particular choice have something to do with the rumors of his family's failing finances and the fact that Hatty's father—Aloysius Doran—owned about half the gold that had ever been found in California? The writer felt guilty for having assigned such a base motive to so illustrious a personage and had sought clarification from Lord St. Simon's father, the Duke of Balmoral. Sadly, the old fellow could not be reached for comment as he was otherwise engaged: selling off the family's art collection as fast as was humanly possible.

And then the papers fairly exploded. There was not a single London daily that did not hover—with salacious abandon—over the strange events surrounding Lord St. Simon's nuptials and the subsequent brevity of his wedded bliss. From what I could gather, the wedding was carried off without a hitch, St. George's being open to the public at the time (which may have said something about the state of the duke's finances). Following the service, the wedding party retired to a furnished house—rented by Aloysius Doran—for the wedding breakfast. Apparently, there were two signs of trouble. First, the bride—who had previously appeared happy and eager for the union—displayed considerable consternation once the vows had been exchanged. Secondly, the gates of the house were besieged by a mysterious woman of low character, who said she had some claim on Lord St. Simon. This lady was escorted away with considerable alacrity and the wedding breakfast began. Just a few minutes in, the new Lady St. Simon had begged a moment to freshen up, stepped away from the table, and disappeared.

Her long-time maid claimed to have seen her mistress slip upstairs, throw a duster over her wedding dress, pop a Stetson on her head, and jump out of the upstairs window. Then again, the maid was American so her opinion was disregarded, in accordance with the acknowledged best practice regarding all American opinions.

The English public was quite taken with the story and had joined in with careless abandon. The missing bride had been spotted several times, in locations ranging from a merchant steamer bound for Calais, to a shallow grave in Dublin. One overenthusiastic gentleman claimed to have found her disembodied fingers in a tin of pickled herring. He even displayed the proof. Yet, as the gentleman in question had three freshly missing digits, his evidence was regarded as little more than a desperate and medically inadvisable plea for attention.

I had got thus far when I was interrupted by an imperious knock on the door of our rooms and the voice of Mrs. Hudson, stridently shrieking, "Lord Robert Walsingham deVere St. Simon, scion of House Plantagenet and of House Tudor, wronged, slandered and *possibly* single, to see Mr. Warlock Holmes!"

From her tone, I could tell she had heard of Lord St. Simon's recent misfortunes, become just as obsessed as the rest of the general public, and was more than willing to personally assuage any loneliness his Lordship might be feeling. I rose with a sigh, went to the door, swung it wide and said, "Ah, Lord St. Simon, do come in."

Lord St. Simon was… well… one hates to say it, after only one brief glance at a person, but… Lord St. Simon was rather horrible. He had sallow skin and milky, lazy eyes brimming with judgment. His clothing was impeccable: a black frock coat, white waistcoat, yellow gloves, light-colored gaiters and golden spectacles dangling by a cord from his right hand with a particular air of moneyed nonchalance that I'm sure he must have practiced in the mirror. He had absolutely no jawline and no chin. It was as if these two features had one day declared, "We are traditional symbols of manliness and therefore wish nevermore to be associated with this awful, awful fop." They had then buggered off, leaving the featureless expanse below Lord St. Simon's lower lip to slope gently away, until that point—unique to each observer—where it must cease being "face" and start being "neck". He had that aristocratic habit of holding his head high, which would not have been so bad if he had not also possessed one of those short, piggy little noses that angles up at the bottom. The combination ensured that anybody who was speaking to him was forced to stare directly into his nostrils the entire time. He had a tangled, thorny profusion of nose hairs that bristled aggressively at me. I was almost glad for them; otherwise, I think I might have been able to see all the way to the back of his skull. He regarded me for the barest instant, then said, "Who are you?"

"I am Warlock Holmes's companion. My name is Dr. John Watson."

"And what exactly is wrong with your arm?"

Though I had managed to force my shirtsleeve over the unwanted Wellington-lump, I had no means of concealing it. The seams bulged and strained.

"A passing malady," I said.

He hesitated upon the threshold.

"And by 'malady' I mean 'injury'," I said. "It is assuredly not contagious."

He gave a snort of grudging acceptance, which made his nose hairs waggle straight out at me, and stepped inside.

"Will you take tea?" I asked.

"I will."

At this point, Holmes emerged sheepishly from his room and muttered, "Oh, Saint Lord! So good to see you again. Um… what brings you by?"

Lord St. Simon gave a sideways glance at the pile of crumpled newspapers and replied, "I believe you know."

"Oh yes! I heard about that," said Holmes. "Bad luck. Yes, just… bad luck, indeed."

"Luck, you say? Are you sure it wasn't the work of evil spirits?"

"What? Hey! Why would you think that? No, no, no!" Holmes stammered.

With a polite cough I wondered, "Lord St. Simon, do you have reason to suspect the involvement of evil spirits?"

"Only that I hired this buffoon to keep them away and he cannot seem to do *anything* right!"

"Yet why hire anybody to so strange a purpose, if there was no perceived danger?" I pressed.

"Oh, it is a family tradition. Always have a clever solicitor examine any addition to the family to make sure it is legally advisable. Always have your most trusted accountant make sure it is financially sound. Always have a sorcerer on hand to make sure no invisible forces are arrayed against you. Silly, I know. But my distant relative, Queen Elizabeth, kept John Dee about and if it was good enough for her, well…"

"Indeed," I acceded.

"The only problem is," said Lord St. Simon, with a wet, hairy sniff, "it's getting rather hard to find sorcerers! Not so many lying about as there used to be, are there? One is forced to make do with whatever second-rate refuse one can find!"

"Hey!" said Holmes.

"And you are now convinced evil spirits have crossed your marriage?"

"What other explanation is there?" he demanded. "I am a prize, sir. Everybody knows my older brother shall never marry. My father is elderly and will not live long. What is the result? Any who think to wed me know that they will presently be wife to a duke. Why should any woman chase such a prize, obtain it, and abandon it in the instant of her purest happiness?"

"Why indeed?" I asked, somewhat dryly. I'll confess that only a few minutes in Lord St. Simon's company had been quite enough to suggest one or two motivations for spousal withdrawal that Lord St. Simon himself perhaps lacked the perspective to observe. "And it is your intention, I presume, to secure Mr. Holmes's aid in discovering the fate of your wife?"

"It is my intention, sir, to see justice done!" He turned to Holmes and sneered, "I'll see you hang for witchcraft."

"Oh, no, no," I said. "Surely that law is not still on the statute."

"Sir," said Lord St. Simon, haughtily, "this is *England*!"

Holmes gave me a look of some urgency.

"Yes, well... it's so hard to prove evil demonic influence in a court of law, you know?" I said. "And there are so many mundane explanations as to what might have occurred. Perhaps the machinations of a jealous rival? Perhaps the severity of her sudden happiness overcame her wit and plunged her into madness!"

"I have considered that," Lord St. Simon admitted.

"Yes, I'll bet you have," I said. "You know, Holmes and

I have unraveled more than a few mysteries such as this. Would it not be wiser to see if we can determine the fate of your bride before we involve the courts?"

Our visitor hesitated, his nose hairs waving doubtfully back and forth.

"And of course we must consider the public exposure of your belief in evil spirits, which such a trial would involve. Imagine the mockery by the common rabble!"

Lord St. Simon went white.

Well…

Whit*er*.

"I am not accustomed to sharing the intimate details of my personal misfortunes…"

"Of course, yet these are desperate times, are they not? Here, just sit down, Lord St. Simon, and tell me about Lady St. Simon, née Hatty Doran. What kind of woman is she?"

"Not… not the type of woman I *expected* to wed," he said with an uncomfortable wince as he settled into one of our chairs. "And yet, not without her charms. Be assured, gentlemen, I would not have bestowed upon her the name it is my honor to bear if I did not think she were—at heart—a gentlewoman. Yet she is American, you know. The daughter of a mining baron. And her father's rise to prominence is so recent that she grew to adulthood in mining camps and the wilderness, rather than in a proper genteel environment. I have a picture of her here…"

Lady St. Simon's face could hardly have provided a greater contrast to her new husband's. Here was a woman in the flower of youth and happiness. True, the unrelenting California sun had placed a few premature wrinkles, yet they were clustered at the corners of her mouth and eyes and told that here was a woman who liked to smile. Indeed, she had eschewed the custom of staring dourly at the camera and had given the photographer a funny, one-sided grin. It was as if the camera had snapped just as she'd finished saying, "Hey, wanna play catch?" I found the lady irresistibly charming.

"And how did a person such as this come to your attention?" I wondered.

"Through our fathers," Lord St. Simon said. "You see, as a young man, her father, Aloysius Doran, was… well, he was named *Aloysius Doran*. It's rather a hard name to bear in a mining camp. All the other fellows were running about with names like Jack Bootstrap and Dick Puncher, from what I gather. Everyone always expected Mr. Doran to be a great deal fancier than he actually was, and once he'd made his fortune, matters got worse. He had the name and he had the money, but he had no manners, no breeding, and no connections. He needed to join his family to another so illustrious that his status would be beyond reproach."

"Enter your own father," I said, "whose money troubles are no longer concealable. He can trace his lineage to both the Tudors and Plantagenets. What he cannot do is promise he'll be able to pay for groceries next week."

"That is salacious and scandalous, sir!" Lord St. Simon thundered. His nose hairs lunged angrily towards me.

"Do the papers have it right that Hatty Doran's dowry ran considerably over six figures?"

"No more than is normal for my family," Lord St. Simon insisted. "No more than is called for."

"And—in view of the fact that the wedding was held—this much, at least, will be retained by your family?"

"Thank God, yes!" said Lord St. Simon, expelling a sudden, involuntary sigh of relief. "It looks like the courts are on our side, there. There's really no way Mr. Doran can get it back. But what of the rest of it? He isn't a young man, you know, and Hatty is his only heir!"

"Yes, well, I believe his Lordship has made his position clear," I said. "But tell me: the disturbance at the gate of Doran's house, the woman who had to be led away—what do you know of her?"

"Oh, that's just Flora; spare her no thought!"

"So you know her?"

"As we are being frank with each other: yes. I know her *rather well*. But what of it? She has no basis for complaint. I've been more than generous. Yet I have always made it clear that she who cannot have a child certainly cannot have a duke. And let's not even talk about the difference in social standing, shall we? No. Flora's not above making a scene—if she didn't have a theatrical streak, she wouldn't be in the theater, would she?—but she'd never hurt anybody."

Holmes gave an uncomfortable look as if he'd rather be helping Flora than Lord St. Simon. I couldn't say I blamed him.

"Did Hatty display any previous signs she might be averse to the marriage?" I asked.

"None! Why up until the night before, she was

chatting away about what we should do together in our future lives… places we should visit…" The disdain with which his Lordship spat that last part out made it pretty clear he had no interest in visiting anywhere at all, apart from the bank.

"When was the first time Hatty seemed reticent?"

"During the ceremony itself," said Lord St. Simon, throwing up his hands in exasperation. "Halfway through, she flushed bright red and started looking about as if something had upset her. By the time we were done, she was so nervous that she dropped her bouquet as we walked down the aisle. Fortunately, it was not damaged. Some gentleman in the first pew picked it up for her."

"Oh, disregard him," Holmes suggested.

"A gentleman?" I asked.

"I use the term as a politeness," said Lord St. Simon, airily. "If the man had any rank, it would come as a shock to me. He was nobody we knew. Probably a reporter. He'd been scribbling away furiously a few moments before."

"Disregard him," said Holmes, with a nervous laugh. "He's a reporter! What do reporters deserve? To be disregarded, everybody knows it!"

"Quite right," said Lord St. Simon.

"So you saw this 'gentleman' too, Holmes?"

"Oh? Er… yes. Well, I was sitting a bit behind him, you see. Warding off evil spirits and the like. He was directly between me and Saint Lord, so it's only natural I would have seen him. Hey, do you know what? Let's disregard the fellow."

"Mmm hmm," I said. "And after this, Lord St. Simon, you went to the wedding breakfast?"

"Yes and Hatty had hardly sat down before she went upstairs, and was never seen again!"

"Very well, Lord St. Simon. I feel that is sufficient information to begin my investigation. Do let me know if—"

"But, no! Are you sure you—?"

"Quite sure, yes. Holmes knows where to find you, I trust? Good, good. We shall call upon you the moment we have news."

I bustled Lord St. Simon out a bit faster than I should have, as chance would have it. If I had not let him forget his hat and gloves—which he had hung from the coat rack—the whole case might have turned out very differently. But, ah well… hindsight.

No sooner had I heard the Baker Street door close than I rounded on my friend and demanded, "Why did you do it, Holmes?"

"Do what?"

"You know perfectly well!"

"Yes, but… how do *you*?"

"Because I reasoned it out, Holmes, and it wasn't hard! Egad, you're practically transparent! You've got a face like a crumb-covered puppy next to an empty biscuit tin and if that were not enough, what about your words? '*Oh please, disregard him! Disregard him!*' Something happened with that man in the front pew, Holmes, and you know exactly what it is!"

"All right, but you don't!"

"Maybe I wouldn't, if I hadn't just spent the last hour tidying up all your notes on *soul-binding magic*! Why did you do it, Holmes? Why did you bind the soul of Hatty Doran to the gentleman in the first row?"

He wrung his hands and gave me a look of pure anguish. "I didn't mean to, Watson! You've got to believe me: I didn't! It's just... well, there I was sitting in the church, making 'oooh-ooooooh' noises and waving my hands about, as if I were banishing evil spirits. Only there weren't any. So I was bored. So I started looking at people's souls and the bonds between them. And there was Hatty, trying to put a brave face on things but it was clear she had no attachment whatsoever to the groom. And how could she? He's an absolute arse-face."

"*Holmes!* You cannot speak about a man like Lord St. Simon in such terms! His position is above reproach! He is noble—"

"Then he's a noble arse-face, Watson! Please, if that man is not an arse-face then there is no such *thing* as an arse-face!"

I wished I had grounds to refute him, but... instead, I fell silent.

Holmes continued, "Well, I thought Hatty might like it better if there was some kind of bond between the two of them. So I started looking around for the purple stringy things of his soul, so I could tie them to Hatty's. But it wasn't easy! You remember what a mess souls are! So many people in the same place with so many strands reaching out from them. It was like sitting in a room full of lavender spaghetti! Let me tell you it wasn't easy finding St. Lord Robert's strands—the little arse-face has barely got a soul at all. Well, at last I found some and I tangled them all up with Hatty's, but…"

"But as there was another gentleman seated *directly between* you and Lord St. Simon…"

"…I might have mistaken some of the other gentleman's strands for his…"

"And now Lord St. Simon's new bride finds her soul and destiny intimately linked to a man she'd never met before. Well done, Holmes. Really, just a whole new level of achievement for you, isn't it?"

"It wasn't my *fault*, Watson!"

"Well… it was."

"All right, but I didn't mean to."

I sighed and looked at my friend. "Regardless of your intent, Holmes, the damage is done. I suppose the best we can do is try to track the lady down and gauge how best to ameliorate the situation. Come on."

"Where are we going?"

"St. George's, Hanover Square."

My hope had been that someone at the church might know the gentleman Holmes had bound Hatty Doran's soul to. We asked around, but the only information we got was from the vicar, who had a vague memory of the man in the front pew. He'd been around a few times in the past two weeks, but had not been back since the day of the wedding. He was a handsome young man, the vicar recalled, but sad-looking, with a strong jaw and large, lonely eyes. They'd exchanged greetings only once. The man had had some form of foreign accent—Australian or American, probably.

"Could you understand even a single word the man said?" I asked.

"Quite easily," said the vicar.

"Then he was no Australian. Officially, Australia was begun as a penal colony, but I have long suspected this to be a lie. More likely, there was an extra question on the 1785 census: *Can you speak English?* Any man who responded, 'Of course I can,' was welcome to stay. Any man who said, 'Wolla! Ronza turolla rei,' found himself with a bag over his head, being trotted onto a prison transport with no recourse to further appeal."

So, we hadn't gotten far. Our man was likely American, and definitely in possession of a rugged jawline. But, really, aren't they all? I've often wondered who the saddest person in the world is: the only Eskimo girl who loves fancy shoes, or the only man in Montana with a normal, human jaw. Dejected and defeated, we turned our steps towards Baker Street.

As we opened the door, who should we find coming down the stairs but Detective Vladislav Lestrade. The stunted Romanian had traded his usual dour black suit for a blue pea-coat, white shorts, white knee socks and a jaunty little sailor cap. In his hand he had a sodden canvas bag and on his face he had his usual expression of tired hatred for the entire world. When he saw us, he exclaimed, "Hello, Holmes. And... um... hello, Dr. Watson. How's the arm?" He gave me the look of a young debutant who's just been discovered in a broom closet, snogging a handsome undergraduate: sorry indeed to have been caught; not at all sorry to have done it.

"Practically shredded by a vampire," I replied. "Yet, if the infection processes I'm sure are underway are kind to me, I might manage to keep it."

"Oh, no, no. There will be no infection. My saliva has not only anti-coagulating characteristics, but it's quite cleansing as well. You should remember that, in case you ever need to seek employment as anybody's blood doll."

I think he was on the very point of telling me I was delicious, and only the extreme iciness of my gaze stopped him. Finally, I drew a measured breath and asked, "And exactly why are we dressed like Bucky the Little Sailor Boy?"

He gave a sigh. "Because I am assigned to the St. Simon case. I've been dragging the Serpentine and Lord St. Simon insists that anyone with a nautical job dress the part."

"Nautical?" I scoffed. "He made you dress as a sailor to look in a pond?"

Lestrade gave a pained look. "I'll be glad when this is over. Speaking of which: let me show you what I've found!"

As soon as we got upstairs, Lestrade upended the canvas bag over our dining table and disgorged his treasure. A sopping-wet wedding dress, two bridal slippers, a veil, a bouquet and half of a soaked and torn note poured forth. Last came a gold wedding band, which pinged off our table and landed in the much-abused posies of the bridal bouquet with a wet thump.

"I think we can use these," Lestrade said. "I am building a case against Flora Millar, the woman who made the disturbance after the wedding."

"Why?" Holmes asked. "Is it your opinion she lured Miss Hatty away and did her harm?"

Lestrade gave him a sideways glance. "No. I have no idea what happened, Holmes, but I'm sure it will prove to be all your fault and I just assumed I'd need to have a scapegoat ready. Millar is harmless, but I'm sure the public will easily believe she was driven mad by jealousy of her lover's younger, prettier, richer new bride. Murder cases have been built on less. We've no body, but we've got the clothing and that's something."

"Well done, Lestrade! Bravo!" Holmes crowed.

But I shook my head. "No. It makes no sense. If this were the work of a murderer, why strip the body and hide the clothes separately? It would mean two incriminating bundles instead of one. And a woman in a wedding dress found floating in the river might have wound up there by accident. But a naked corpse, with all her belongings bundled up separately? Well... that's less likely to be coincidence, don't you think?"

"Of course I do," Lestrade agreed. "But judges never worry about such things, nor do bloodthirsty mobs. Really, the biggest problem is the note. I'd like to destroy it and pretend I never found the thing. Alas, two constables have seen it, so it must remain. Still, it's torn and the part we possess has no signature. Unless the other fragment should turn up and dash our hopes, my plan to hang Flora Millar can proceed, unhindered. That note cannot lead anybody to its author. As long as it is incomplete, it is untraceable."

Fortunately for Flora Millar, Lestrade was incorrect. I took the note in my hand and examined it. On the one side, it said:

> I must see you again! I must speak with you! Please, won't you come to th—

Turning it over, I saw it had been written on a fragment of a hotel bill. The hotel name was missing. All we had was a few fragmentary charges. 22 June 1883: rooms 8s., breakfast 2s. 6d., cocktail 1s., lunch 2s. 6d., glass sherry 8d.

"Ha! Wonderful!" I crowed.

"Eh?" said Holmes and Lestrade together.

"Don't you see, Holmes? The fellow in the front pew! What was he writing? This note! He must have flashed it at Hatty when she and her bridegroom turned to the congregation after the ceremony. She made sure she dropped her bouquet right next to the man, so he'd have a chance to slip it in when he handed the flowers back! Ha! I've got him now!"

"How?" asked Lestrade. "Just because you know he was staying at a hotel? There must be hundreds in London!"

"Possibly," I laughed. "Possibly. But how many are there who would dare to charge eightpence for a single glass of sherry? Four? Perhaps five? No, no, gentlemen. I intend to start my search at Northumberland Avenue, and I wouldn't be surprised if I conclude it there, as well. Holmes: please order a nice cold supper for you, me and two guests. We'll be expecting company at nine this evening. Cold pheasant and bisque might do."

"But what will I e—"

"Bisque is soup. You must wait here for it to arrive and make ready for guests. Lestrade: thank you for the help, but you must go."

"Why?"

"Because our visitors are likely to find your maw full of glistening murder-fangs off-putting. Or if not that, at least they might notice that you don't eat food. And now, I will bid you gentlemen adieu. This shan't take long."

It didn't. Luxury hotels are not afraid to charge grotesque fees for the most humble of items, but that does not mean they are in the habit of passing any of that money on to their employees. Thus, for a one-shilling bribe, the front desk clerk at the Hotel Northumberland agreed to show me the visitors' book. In no time at all, I found the 22 June entry that matched the fragment on the back of the note Lestrade had recovered. The items had been billed to a Mr. Francis Hay Moulton—an American visitor of notoriously strange habits. Well… he hadn't been, at first, but a number of days ago he had taken to his room and refused to emerge. His only contact with any of the staff had been his repeated orders of huge amounts of food. At this, I raised an eyebrow and asked the clerk if perhaps Moulton had anybody in the room with him. I was haughtily assured this was not that kind of hotel. After which, I counter-assured the clerk that there simply *was* no other kind of hotel, then asked him how else he could explain such large quantities of food. The man shrugged and gave me a better answer than I had expected.

"Well, he *is* American."

Begging the use of a pen and a sheet of hotel stationery, I dashed off a quick note, sneaked upstairs and slipped it underneath the door of Francis Moulton's room. I gave a quick little knock, then hid around the corner of the nearest corridor. The cry of alarm I heard a moment later gave me to know my impromptu invitation was unlikely to be disregarded. A minute later, I was on the street with my hand in the air for a cab. Two miles after that, I was back at Baker Street, happy to see that my orders had been carried out. Lestrade was gone and Holmes had successfully procured supper.

Nearly.

"Holmes, why are there five settings?"

"Because that is how many people are coming."

"Holmes, look: you and me—" I held up two fingers "—and two guests—" two more fingers "—makes four."

He frowned at this. "I must say, Watson, your mathematics seem sound. And yet… It's *five*, I'm sure of it!"

I had no time to argue with him, for other matters pressed. Though I had spent the day in pursuit of this case, I knew a portion of it must also be directed towards my own continuing survival. I went to my room, cleared my writing desk, fetched my surgical bag and undertook the task of ridding myself of one unwanted beef Wellington.

It was easier than I'd expected. Wincing and cursing Torg Grogsson, I made a small test-incision in my left arm. Probing inside with my forceps, I easily located my target. The whole thing felt squishy and gelatinous. It was so slippery I had trouble getting a grasp on it. Yet, when at last I did, the whole thing slid forth out of the incision in one gooey wad. I had hardly expected it to emerge in pristine and appetizing condition, yet still, I found its current state just… *weird*. I poked and prodded at it with great fascination. Though it was recognizable, its texture shared no trait with either pastry or meat. Clearly, its trip through the runcible amphigory had changed it significantly.

Still, I had little time for inquiry, magical or scientific. I pushed the disgusting thing aside and set to stitching my arm. I had just got myself cleaned up and had buttoned my shirt when the bell rang promptly at nine.

"Oi!" came Mrs. Hudson's voice from just outside our door. "Couple o' unescorted young people, lookin' somewhat pie-eyed and dehydrated, but who am I to judge, eh?"

With my customary sigh of distaste, I went to answer the door, saying, "Thank you, Mrs. Hudson, you may *go now*."

To say either of my visitors looked at ease would be utter falsehood. How they had ever imagined they wouldn't be caught is beyond me, but now they looked deeply uncomfortable.

"Um… Yes. Hello. We were invited to come here to dinner, I believe. I am Mr. Francis Moulton and this is Miss Hatty Doran."

"If only that were so, we would find ourselves in a much improved circumstance," I chided, "but in fact you are Mr. Francis Moulton and that is *Lady St. Simon*! Now, step inside, if you please, and let us find the way to handle this situation that involves the fewest deaths and incarcerations."

I was perhaps not the ideal person to comfort our guests. Holmes, as always, outdid me. He gave a dismissive snort and said, "Oh, don't mind him, he's always like that. That's Dr. John Watson, and my name is Warlock Holmes. He's right that you've got yourselves in a bit of a spot, though. It got me in a spot, too. But come have dinner and we'll put it all to rights. Look, there's soup and present, and I made everyone a big pile of toast!"

Sure enough, before I could even say, "*Pheasant*, Holmes," my friend whisked the silver cover from one of the serving dishes to reveal a towering wad of toasted bread. I threw my hand to my brow and shook my head. One simply does not present visiting millionaires a plate of twice-warmed bread. Yet Holmes's words—and even his pile of toast—proved to be just what was needed. Both our guests broke into broad smiles.

"Wonderful!" said Hatty. "Toast and soup is the best, but I've yet to meet the Englishman who'll serve it for dinner."

"Then I apologize for the ignorance of my countrymen," said Holmes, beaming. "But come, sit down and tell me all that has occurred since the wedding!"

Which they did. Francis and Hatty, scared as they were, seemed happy to have an ally. Their description of what had happened since the wedding was brief. And, I suspect, heavily censored. Yet the most interesting part of the tale, to me, was Hatty's description of what had happened *at* the wedding.

"There I was, standing at the altar with Lord St. Simon feeling… well… I'd already made my peace with it. Really, compared to what my fate should have been as the daughter of an uneducated miner, I was about to enter a world I'd no right to dream of. Yet… I just kept thinking, *Let it be anyone but him*. And then, as I was looking about at the congregation, there was—"

"Anyone but him!" Francis Moulton cut in, and the two of them laughed.

"Such a strange moment," said Hatty, with a smile and a shake of her head. "It was like a rush of familiarity, but not quite the same. Not the feeling that I *knew* this man, but the feeling that I *ought* to know him. That my love somehow belonged to this perfect stranger and my heart's true home was a place it was now forbidden ever to go."

"And you, Mr. Moulton?" I inquired.

"Well, I was just sitting there feeling down in the dumps. I wasn't even there for the wedding. I'm a Boston inventor, you see. I'd come to England because I've devised a new machine for weaving cotton into cloth, similar to your Raveling Nancy."

"Except it's three times as fast," Hatty interjected, supportively.

"And it doesn't break as much," Francis added.

"Or even cost as much."

"Or pull quite so many people's arms off. It's done quite well for me in America and I suppose I've already made my fortune. But… I don't know… Honestly, I thought it would do very well here, as soon as the English manufacturers saw how much better it is. But nobody wanted anything other than a Raveling Nancy and I was taking it a bit personal, I guess."

"I suppose we Englishmen can be a bit set in our ways," I admitted.

"So I was just moping in the church," Francis continued, "and I looked up and I saw this girl and I just… I realized that it didn't matter! My machine didn't matter! If I'd come all the way to England and didn't sell a damned one, that didn't matter. I should count myself lucky—count myself blessed—because I'd seen *her*! I didn't know who she was, but I knew she was perfect for me. But then I looked around a bit more and realized I was watching her get married. I didn't know what to do! So I grabbed a slip of paper out of my pocket and scribbled down a note. And she was looking at me, just like I was looking at her, so I waved my note a bit so she could see it."

"And when I came down the aisle, I dropped my bouquet."

"And I just slipped the note right in there and went back to my hotel to think of her. God, I was just on the edge of going crazy! I don't know what I'd have done if she hadn't come. But not two hours later, there was this knock on my door and…"

"And there I was!" said Hatty, beaming.

"Your souls had become entwined," I noted, then fired a rather hard look at Holmes and added, "Just *incredibly*, *powerfully* and—one is tempted to suspect—*irreversibly* entwined." Holmes gave me a guilty little shrug. "Well done, Holmes," I said. "Well done, indeed."

"What was that?" Hatty wondered.

"Never mind. The important thing now is to find a way for this situation to be corrected."

Hatty took Francis's hand in her own, gave it a firm shake and said, "No. This particular situation will not be *corrected*. It is correct, Dr. Watson, and I shall not allow it to be changed in any way."

"That's right! You tell him!" crowed Holmes, through a mouthful of toast. He looked quite happy to settle in and cheer on his chosen side. Which, it appeared, was not me.

"But, Lady St. Simon," I said—and Hatty bristled at the name, "Scotland Yard is treating this as a disappearance. They're on the case. There is simply no way to stop them revealing what has happened."

From the corner of her mouth, she growled, "All

this new education that's been thrust on me has taught me the value of investing in social infrastructures, so perhaps I'll just have to *buy* Scotland Yard and have them all arrest themselves."

"Madam, I have no doubt that in many countries, your money could solve this problem, but England is no such place. Propriety matters! The idea of what is right matters!"

"Not to me," she said. "At last I have found happiness and I am disinclined to surrender it so easily."

"She's right, by God!" Francis cried. "Lose Hatty? Never! I'll die first!"

"Well put!" Holmes cried, spattering the tablecloth in a light dusting of soggy crumbs.

"All right," I said. "All right. Clearly, something must be done. We simply need to take some time and find a way to—"

Yet time was to be a luxury we could not afford. At that moment there was a knock at our door, which—since I had failed to fasten it properly—slowly swung open. Just behind it stood Lord St. Simon, looking disinterestedly down at his shoes. "I hope you gentlemen will forgive the intrusion," he said, "but when I was here earlier, I left in such a hurry I fear I forgot my…"

He looked up, saw the scene before him, let his jaw dangle stuporously for a moment or two, then breathlessly concluded, "…wife."

"Ha!" shouted Holmes, leaping from his seat and triumphantly directing my attention to the empty place setting. "*Five!*"

Hatty's face lit to its most defiant red. "I am not your wife!"

"By God, you are!"

"She says she isn't and she's not!" Mr. Moulton thundered.

"She's really not," Holmes added and—to my chagrin—he had this peaceful, happy little look on his face as if all our problems had just dissolved.

What this sudden source of relief might be, I could not guess, so I leapt between our first two guests and our third and spluttered, "Wait now, everybody! I appeal for calm. Let's not say anything that might get anyone arrested or hanged or burned at the stake, shall we?"

"Quite right," Holmes agreed. "Hatty, Francis, I think we should be honest."

"Honest?" Francis wondered.

"Yes," said Holmes, and the hint of a victorious smile began to play about the left corner of his mouth, "about Hatty Doran's first wedding. Remember? In California?"

"What?" said Francis Moulton, Lord St. Simon, Lady St. Simon and I. Yet, after that first wave of surprise, I realized it was perfect. Just perfect. Yes, I could sometimes be dismissive of Holmes's intelligence but I could just as often fail to give him the credit he was due. From time to time my friend could be counted on to come up with the perfect whopper.

Hatty Doran's face flicked from an expression of perfect incredulity to one of sudden hope. "Oh!" she cried. "Oh, yes! That's it! We should... We should be *honest*."

I appeal for calm.

"Eh?" said Francis Moulton.

"About how you and I met in the mining camps outside Sutter's Mill," Hatty prompted, "long before I ever met Lord St. Simon. And how we got married."

Moulton's face lit up with joy. Lord St. Simon's expressed more than a little doubt. "This man," he said, indicating Moulton's rather costly clothing, "was a *miner?*"

"Oh, well… I mean…" stammered Moulton, who appeared to have little experience generating fabrications, "sure I look pretty put-together now, but… in my youth… *Grrr!* Pickaxes: I love 'em! Right?"

"But no," insisted Lord St. Simon. "Hatty was never married! Aloysius Doran was quite clear on the matter."

"Oh we never told Daddy," said Hatty.

"How could they?" Holmes interjected.

"Right, because, you see… well, Daddy had just made his fortune. And Francis still hadn't, so…"

"So people might think I was *only marrying her for her money!*" Francis said, shaking his fists and thrusting his enormous American chin a bit too close to the unfortunate array of features Lord St. Simon called a face.

I placed a hand gently atop one of his fists, pressed it back down to his side and said, "Which nobody would do, of course."

"Right," Hatty said. "So we got married in secret and agreed that Francis would go seek his fortune in Boston, then return to claim me."

"Which I totally did," Francis confirmed. "That's where I got these clothes and this accent and invented a really good machine for making cotton cloth that the stupid, stupid manufacturers around here ought to take a closer look at!"

"Sure," agreed Hatty. "Only then he never made it back to get me."

"Why?" Lord St. Simon asked.

"Er…" said Hatty.

"Um…" said Francis.

"On his return trip, he was captured by Apaches…" said Holmes. Hatty and Francis shot him smiles of relief and gratitude.

"…on elephants," Holmes added. The young lovers' features fell.

"*Elephants?*" Lord St. Simon bellowed. "But elephants are not native to Americ—"

"And a good thing, too," Hatty interrupted, "or the famous elephant raiders of the Apache nation would surely have crushed the entire USA before it even got started!"

Egad, she was a gifted liar.

"They were from a circus!" Francis declared. "The Apaches had previously raided a circus, you see."

"Right! And then cut a swathe of destruction from Philadelphia to Santa Fe!"

"Sure! Oh! It was bad. You should have seen it."

"The US Cavalry was helpless!"

"Because horses are afraid of elephants, you know."

"I have read that somewhere, I think," Lord St. Simon admitted.

"And after the raid, I thought Francis was dead," said Hatty.

"But... but wouldn't you check?" Lord St. Simon wondered. "Wouldn't you assume him to be alive, in the absence of a body?"

"In a normal raid, perhaps," Hatty countered, "but this was an *elephant* raid. Whole wagon-train smashed. Bits of bodies everywhere. So hard to tell which piece went to which person. Whole families reduced to gobs of dusty paste."

"So she thought I was dead, when in fact I was merely captured."

"But after a time, he escaped."

"Sure. Um... One night as the Apaches were preparing a scouting party, I attached myself to the underside of one of the... you know... *elephants*..."

"And then, that night he rolled off into the bushes by the side of the trail and made his way back to me," Hatty declared happily, then added, "Except I was already gone."

"Yes. She was here," Francis agreed. "So I tracked her down and caught up with her in the church."

"You can imagine my surprise, Lord St. Simon," Hatty said, placing her hand to her chest in well-fabricated distress. "So of course I had to sneak out and find out where matters stood."

"A situation which is, of course, all too clear," I said, laying an apologetic hand on Lord St. Simon's shoulder. "As a doctor and a person who pretends to know a great deal about matrimonial law, I can assure you that Hatty Doran's first marriage—though foreign and secret—is binding. Your marriage—through no fault of anybody's—

was never valid. Though it may have seemed so for a time, there is not, nor ever was there, such a person as Lady St. Simon. So sorry, old chap."

Lord St. Simon tilted on his heels a moment, then stammered, "Can... Can any of this be verified?"

"Oh, I suppose," said Hatty, nervously. "What we'd need would be a marriage certificate from a court in California, dated roughly two years ago..."

"Ha!" said Holmes, with a dismissive wave. "No problem! I know a fellow."

"A fellow?" said Lord St. Simon. "What do you mean? A fellow who can transport the documents from California?"

"Of course," said Holmes, smiling broadly. "That's exactly what I mean. Now, Lord St. Simon, did you notice there are *five* places set at the table? Doesn't that make me look awfully clever? Maybe you ought to sit down with us, have a civil supper, and we should all part as friends— victims of that same strange twist of fate that brought us to the brink of disaster, yet ended so well."

"Never, sir!" said Lord St. Simon, recoiling. "Stay? Here? Under the roof that has brought so much damage to my person, my reputation and my hopes? I have been injured, sir. I have been shamefully misused and I do not intend to tarry to... Is that cold pheasant?"

Holmes nodded. "I believe it is."

"Well, I am a bit peckish. It's been a long night, you know. Had to go see Flora down at the Allegro Theater and put things right. I may have forgotten supper in all the commotion. Yes, I might just… I think I'll try a bit of this…"

As he spoke, Lord St. Simon piled a plate high with pheasant and vegetables pausing only to mutter, "Oh, is that toast? Just the thing!"

"Right!" I said, slapping my brow. "Pheasant on toast! That *is* a dish. Well, propriety is satisfied."

Yet Lord St. Simon did not construct the aforementioned delicacy. Instead, he thrust two slices of toast into his pockets, turned from the table and declared, "No, I will not stay in this house of insult! You will be hearing from me! There's the damage to my family name to be considered. And, of course, the matter of the dowry."

Hatty gave a little smirk. "Well… as this was all the result of an unfortunate misunderstanding, perhaps the dowry might be left with the St. Simon family as reparation for their misfortune. Provided, of course, my previous marriage is recognized and no further claim is placed upon me."

My eyebrows went up and I muttered, "A bit expensive for a near miss, isn't it?"

Holmes placed a hand upon my shoulder and said, "Watson, hush."

He was right, for Hatty's words seemed to have a dramatic effect on Lord St. Simon. "Oh?" he said, hopefully, then caught himself and blustered, "I mean, if it lies on that footing, perhaps I must be the better man."

With a gigantic smile of fiscal relief on his face, Lord St. Simon better-manned down our steps and out onto

Baker Street, meal in hand. I could not help but notice that he set off not in the direction of his home but of the Allegro Theater, where Miss Flora Millar's late show would soon begin. Holmes watched him go with a knowing grin.

"Well," he said softly, "we shan't be getting that plate back, I would think. But never mind. Watson, fetch down that bottle of Tokay, won't you? I think it's time to raise a glass to new hopes and fresh prospects. I hope you won't take it amiss if I don't join you. You three have a toast and I shall have… toast."

And that is where the matter came to rest. Or… it would have. If I'd been a wiser man. If I hadn't been about to make one of the worst decisions of my life.

You see, a number of clues had been presented to me that day that had nothing to do with the adventure at hand, but with one I cared about a great deal more.

Where was Adler? Where was Moriarty? What were their true natures, their goals? I'd sought this information time and again, but had little success. Perhaps it was time to try a new tactic…

What had Holmes said? Prophetic dreams? Revealed secrets? My recent bout of vivid dreaming had come because Irene Adler had dosed me with a magical toxin. And—in my previous adventure of My Grave Ritual—I had accidentally induced visions by smoking part of a shredded Persian sorcerer. But now… If magic worked in any way like common drugs, would the effect not be more potent if the compound was introduced directly into my bloodstream? And had Holmes not showed me a device capable of that exact function, only a few hours before?

Perhaps it would all come to nothing. I was no magician, after all. But it was worth a try, wasn't it?

After our guests had left, I went to our mantel, to the old Persian slipper filled with the shredded remains of the sorcerer Xantharaxes, and helped myself to a teaspoonful. Then I went to Holmes's door and—as casually as I could manage—inquired if I might borrow the runcible amphigory. It had captured my curiosity, I explained, and I wished to examine its workings. He was delighted I'd taken an interest. After discreetly closing the door to my room, I put the amphigory on my writing desk, opened my surgical bag, and removed my trusty hypodermic needle.

Holmes had said a seven percent solution was ideal…

I rolled up my sleeve, found a vein, and got to work. In no time at all, I had an ounce of my own blood heating over the candle. I watched in fascination as the shreds of Xantharaxes I threw in lost their shape and disappeared into the liquid. Then I sucked the solution back up into my needle, gritted my teeth, and stepped into a strange new world.

I still remember my dream, that first night. Amazing. But not particularly useful.

I dreamt I was a cow. There was a moment of panic when I discovered I had hooves instead of feet and four legs rather than two. I almost toppled until I realized I knew how to balance. It was an indwelling knowledge, born of simply *being who I was*. By the time I awoke the next morning, I had a fairly complete idea of what it was to be another creature, although not a creature I'd ever wondered much about. Still, I had found strange comfort in the slow and rolling progress of bovine thought. How wonderful the sensation of hooves sinking into soft loam. How satisfying the experience of belching up half-digested grass from my reticulum, chewing for a bit, then swallowing it down into my omasum for further processing.

Most of the dreams were like that, in those nights of experimentation. Vivid. Illuminating. Rather useless. I was hardly hot on the trail of Moriarty and Adler. Not until the third night, when I at last caught a glimpse of the knowledge I desired.

On the third night, I beheld the toymaker.

THE TOYMAKER

FROM THE DREAM JOURNAL OF DR. JOHN WATSON

THE SHOP IS DANK AND UNFINISHED. NO TILES UPON THE floor, no carpet, only worn planks of untreated wood. There is only one window, through which London's dirty afternoon light is cast upon the rows of shelves and—though I have not seen it—the dream comes with a knowledge of how this shop advertises itself to the world. A simple sign above the door with a single word carved into it: TOYS.

And there *are* toys. Tops and velveteen plushes and wooden blocks, piled with no particular care upon dusty shelves. But then, as one steps further in… clockwork figures. Magnificent automatons, crafted with exquisite care—their gleaming metal gears cut by hand to precisely the proper shapes. Here is a bear that will beg for food, when his key is wound. Here is a shining metal queen who dances with a grinning goblin. And then, a strange rush of familiarity! Here is my circus tableau! The one Holmes and I took from the rooms of Percy Trevelyan on our second adventure together. I had often wound its spring and admired the mastery of its workings. Now, I behold its maker.

At the back of the shop is a worktable, lit by three lamps—a circle of light in the gloomy confines of the shop. At the table is a man. He is old, but not so old as he seems. His work has aged him. Countless hours of bending over that table have left him stooped. He has the papery white skin of a man who rarely sees the sun. On his head is an apparatus of brass arms and lenses that can be pulled down before his eyes. Through two of them, he is peering with masterly interest as he squeezes a few final gears into the back of a tin soldier. With a final "*Ha!*" he places the soldier on the table, winds it and lets it go.

It marches across the surface. *Properly marches!* There is no wheel around which two pinned legs pivot, like pedals on a tricycle. Only legs. The little soldier balances on two feet, just as I do. Five steps into his march, his little booted toe makes contact with a wooden block that the old toymaker has placed in his path. The soldier teeters. The boot bumps again. And slowly, experimentally, it starts to raise.

In the dream, I am naught but a disembodied observer. I have no mouth. If I had, I'm sure it would be hanging open in gobstruck wonder. That little toy is going to step over the block! Does that mean it could feel it? Is it figuring out how to defeat the obstacle? Has the strange old man behind this dusty bench managed to make a collection of gears and springs capable of reason? Is that toy… *learning*?

If it is, it's not learning fast enough to please the old man. "*Ach! Nein!*" he mutters, then picks the tin wonder up, pries the hatch off its back and digs in with his tweezers, to pull out some offending gear.

There is a gentle tinkling from behind me. The little silver bell over the door. The old man sighs and complains, "Irene! So late! Why do you make your grandfather worry?"

But it isn't Irene.

It's a corpse.

I mean... it is walking. Moving of its own accord. And yet, to my doctor's eye, there is no way that it can be a living creature. Once it was a man, but it is impossibly aged. On its back is a tremendous iron boiler. From this emanate four long brass and steel appendages, like the legs of a spider. On these, much more than its two wasted human legs, the corpse man walks slowly towards the toymaker's worktable. He holds an elegant, silver-topped cane in one hand. He's wearing a sensible black frock coat, a top hat and a smile of absolute mastery. Leather bellows on the top of his boiler pump air through the corpse's chest and in hollow, somewhat mechanical tones, it says, "*Guten Abend*, Herr Adler."

The toymaker gapes for a moment, then draws a breath and croaks, "Sir... Sir, are you... a *toy*?"

The corpse pauses, rocks back on its spidery mechanical legs. Suddenly the bellows on its back pump with unexpected vigor. The dead man throws back his head, opens his cadaverous mouth, and laughs. The whole apparatus shakes so horribly that, if he isn't dead already, I fear this overexertion will finish him off. Finally, and with great effort, he controls himself, draws a breath and says, "Ah! Forgive me. I have been called many things but nobody—*nobody*—has ever thought of me as that. No, no,

Herr Adler, my name is Professor James Moriarty. I've brought a challenge for you."

The spider legs grind forward, propelling the visitor towards the place where—it seems to me—I am standing. Yet, he passes right through me, goes to the table and reaches inside his coat. From one of the pockets within, he draws forth a curious wooden cylinder and places it gingerly on the worktable.

"Something precious lies within," Moriarty says. "Can you open it?"

The toymaker leans in, scrutinizes the thing first with his naked eye, then with a few of his lenses. He purses his lips and mutters. "Not so easy. This catch is false, you see. Look inside. It is meant to look like a pin for a hollow key, but it isn't. Almost like… a needle?"

"Indeed. The box is trapped," Moriarty confirms.

"And there is a second trap, too," the old man says, with a nod. "Here and here… See? If you thought you were clever to avoid the catch, it seems you could twist the ends and this might release the lid. But… something comes out through the cracks."

"Little poisoned blades. It's killed three this week."

The toymaker looks up at his guest in disbelief. "Your toy is very dangerous."

The corpse gives a little smile. "Most of my toys are, Herr Adler."

Which, of course, would be the absolute, final warning for a reasonable man. What sane individual would dare to touch this corpse-man's deadly toy? But that's just it:

Herr Adler is not a reasonable man. He is a *genius*. Self-preservation and societal expectation are not nearly so important to him as his art. And this is a rare moment—he is being asked to examine a device whose craftsman's skills are equal to his own. Could you imagine bringing Mozart the composition of a worthy rival, and expecting him not to play it?

The two men stare at each other for a moment. Something plays across the toymaker's face. "Please… My granddaughter will be home any moment."

"Then I suggest you hurry, Herr Adler."

The toymaker sighs. "Well, it has a weakness. There is a hinge. We go in the back way, *ja*?" He takes a punch so fine it might almost be wire in one hand, a miniscule hammer in the other. With careful taps, he drives the punch against one side of the hinge-pin until it protrudes from the other side. Then, with fine pliers, he draws the pin clear. "There are no further traps?"

His visitor shrugs. "Nobody has made it this far."

The toymaker nods. Best not to use his bare hands. He picks up a pair of pin awls and works them gently into the cracks by the side of the hinge, then pries. There is a gentle pop as the cylinder lid separates from the base and sides. Still… caution… He works the awls forwards along the curved sides, separating and lifting the lid. Finally, he slides it forward and free of the false catch on the front. He gives a sigh of relief. Within is a worn slip of paper, covered in some strange writing.

James Moriarty leans in with a satisfied nod. He lifts the

delicate paper from the cylinder, slides it into a prepared case and says, "You are as good as your reputation, Herr Adler. I am going to keep you."

"Eh?"

"You were recommended to me by one of those foolish tinkers I mentioned, who fell for the trick of the blades. Trevors was his name. Always a bit of a disappointment, to tell the truth. No, I think you will do better. Gather your tools and say goodbye to your little home. We shan't be needing it more."

"But… No! This is my shop. It is my life."

Moriarty's tone is suddenly cold. "Then you have built yourself a very grubby little life, haven't you, Herr Adler? All this talent and no customers? What good is skill if it goes to waste in a dusty corner? Admit it: you love the work but only tolerate the customers—when you get them, that is."

"I was toymaker to the Emperor of Austria!"

"And now look at you. You can hardly care for yourself and you certainly cannot care for that granddaughter of yours."

"I will!" the old man cries. "I am all she has!"

"No longer."

"When my son left for America, I had nobody. And now he is gone… But at least I have her! We are together!"

"Together? Then where is she?"

The old man's eyes flick to the clock. He blinks.

"That's right; it's after four already," Moriarty confirms. "Where is she?"

"Well… She is willful…"

Moriarty concurs with a groan. "She certainly is. She ran six of my men halfway around this city. I'll swear she lured two of them right into a pack of constables on purpose. Now I find myself two men down. Who knows how many bribes I'll have to pay to hush this all up? And what do I have to show for it?"

The toymaker stares at his guest. His mouth is open, but he's silent. I can see the fear growing in him.

"Don't you see?" Moriarty asks.

The toymaker is silent.

"You. The answer is: you."

"You cannot do this."

"I have to," says Moriarty, with a cadaverous shrug. "Don't you see, Herr Adler? I cannot risk my person, exploring devices like this. The pursuit of immortality is not well served by such hazards. Happily, I have been directed to you. It is clear you have little care for money, but you do care for your granddaughter and your work— so I am assuming control of both."

"You are a fiend!"

"Many people feel so, but you have no reason to. Come now, what would have become of your granddaughter without my aid? When this shop finally failed? When you could no longer shield her from the fate London affords to its female poor? But if you are loyal to me, Herr Adler, Irene shall flourish. Under the tutelage I can afford her, who knows how far she can go? And you will get to see. I will make *sure* you see, so that you continue to work for me with zeal. So hard to force true talent, you know. Easier to inspire it."

The toymaker stares up with an expression of horror.

Moriarty grunts his frustration. "Don't you understand what I am giving you, old man? This is your *life's dream*! Every day, I will show you wonders! And every day, you will show me how they work."

THE ADVENTURE OF BEPPO VS. NAPOLEON (A FIGHT IN SIX ROUNDS)

OUR NEXT LITTLE ADVENTURE BEGAN AFTER, I SHOULD think, five nights of my magical experimentations.

Or eight. Was it eight? Those days are such a haze, I cannot recall. Though the true effects of Xantharaxes exposure had yet to trouble me, I was already feeling the early signs. Most notably, that any sleep found while wandering in the realm of mystic dreams can hardly be considered sleep at all. I stumbled into our sitting room, eyes black and bagged, moustache drooping, with only one thought on my mind.

Tea.

I needed tea.

And I needed to *remember*. The other problem with obtaining one's magical education through dreaming is this: the lessons are dreams. And—like any others—they seem so vital and important while one slumbers, only to flee the instant wakeful reason begins to chase them.

My dream the night before had been utterly preposterous. I dreamed that the telegraph had been perfected and miniaturized to the point that everybody could carry one in their pocket. They had no wires and yet their transmissive powers were so vast, one could even send pictures. Can you imagine such a world? Military mishaps would be a thing of the past, each commander in constant contact with all his units. How could there be civil strife, religious discord, even crime, if all humanity could instantaneously be informed and turn the combined weight of our problem-solving capacity against them? But no… In my dream, people mostly used these miracle devices to send each other updates on what they'd eaten for breakfast.

Preposterous.

As I fumbled about making tea, I became vaguely aware that Lestrade was sitting in one of our chairs. He and Holmes were discussing something and he had—I think—made some greeting that I'd ignored. As I began to stammer one out, Lestrade noted, "Are you quite well, Dr. Watson? You look…"

"He says he has a cold," Holmes said—which indeed had been the excuse I'd given him. "But to answer your earlier question, Lestrade, I think the strangest thing I've ever seen was the blind cobbler of Bangladesh. Fascinating fellow! He'd touch your forehead, you see, then have some sort of epileptic fit. When he emerged he'd run to his bench and start feverishly assembling you a new pair of shoes. Not just any shoes, mind, but the absolutely perfect pair for you. Right color. Right fit. Just perfect. And for the service provided, I found his rates to be most reasonable."

"Ha! This is nothing!" Lestrade scoffed. "As a child, I beheld wonders stranger than this. Why, I once met a dolphin stockbroker!"

"A *what*?"

"Yes. He lived in a large glass tank. Every Tuesday, his trainer would show him the financial section of the paper, turning each page until the dolphin got excited. Finally, Chip-Chip—that was the dolphin—Chip-Chip would surge to the top of his tank and shoot just a few drops of water from his blowhole. The stock on which these drops landed would unfailingly return twenty percent within three months."

"*No!*"

"Yes. Always. Twenty percent. Three months."

"Well… that *is* pleasantly outré, I must admit," Holmes conceded. "It does not have that element of the grotesque that I treasure, but… I say, Watson, how about you? What is the queerest thing you've ever seen?"

I let the question roll back and forth through my foggy mind as my tea stewed to a pleasing tar-like quality. Finally, I mumbled, "I once surprised a vampire and a wizard in my sitting room, discussing which was the most difficult thing to believe in: dolphins or shoe salesmen. Does that qualify?"

Lestrade gave me a sour sort of look, designed to say that he did not think it should. And even if it did, the dolphin was still better. Yet Holmes's face lit with admiration. "I say, Watson! That is fine! I hadn't thought of it until now but… can you *imagine* the chain of events that must have occurred to bring such a moment about?"

"But—" Lestrade began.

"No, no! I have decided! Watson wins," Holmes declared, but then his face broke into a mischievous little smirk and he added, "Unless, of course, this weird little case you're bringing us can best it. What do you say, Lestrade? Tell us of this latest problem upsetting Scotland Yard!"

"It is a matter of no importance," said Lestrade with a shrug, "but passing strange…"

"What is it? Tell me, tell me, tell me!"

"Very well, stop shaking me! It began three days ago at the shop of Mr. Morse Hudson in the Kennington Road."

"Aigh!" Holmes cried. "Any relation to our Mrs. Hudson?"

"No. Hudson is a common name."

"Oh, I know, but I still get a fright every time I hear it. So what about this Morse Hudson fellow?"

"He sells pictures and statues—fripperies for the middle class. Nothing special. Mr. Hudson's assistant was watching the shop but had stepped into the back for a moment when he heard a loud crash. He ran into the shop and found that one of the statues had been broken—a plaster bust of Napoleon, worth eleven shillings or so."

"That was all?" I asked.

"That was all," said Lestrade. "There was nobody in the shop, so the assistant ran out into the street to see if he could spot the vandal, but saw no one of particular interest. The case was reported to the neighborhood constable."

Holmes shifted in his chair, gave Lestrade an apologetic look and confided, "Well… I was hoping for better."

"Oh, don't worry, it got better the next night. You see, also on Kennington Road, just a few hundred yards down from Hudson's shop, lives Dr. Barnicot. The doctor has something of a mania for Napoleon—worships the little blighter."

"Ah! Perhaps it is he who smashed the bust," Holmes volunteered. "Perhaps he felt such cheap replications did no great justice to his idol. His love of Napoleon makes him a possible suspect!"

"No," said Lestrade evenly. "It makes him the second victim. You see, Dr. Barnicot had bought two copies of the same bust from Hudson's shop, some months ago."

"Two?"

"Yes, one for his home on Kennington Road and one for his surgery, which is in Lower Brixton. Yesterday morning, he awoke to find he'd been burgled, the thief gaining entry through the window of his upstairs study. Barnicot has a successful practice, so his home contains several items of value. Nonetheless, only one object had been taken."

"The bust of Napoleon?" I asked. Lord knows I wanted nothing else than to get my cup of tea and retreat back to my waiting bed, but I knew Lestrade would not have brought this case to our attention if my guess had not been right. And when one thought about it, the case was already a strange one. No great harm had been done, perhaps, but the motive for such bizarre actions was mysterious and compelling.

"The bust of Napoleon," Lestrade confirmed, with a slight smile—enough to let us know he was smiling, reserved enough to hide his maw of fangs. "It was found just six houses down, in the garden of an empty home, smashed to fragments."

"That is strange," said Holmes.

"Yes, Dr. Barnicot thought so, too. He was even more of that opinion when he arrived at his surgery at noon yesterday to find his second bust had received the same treatment."

"*What?*" said Holmes and I together.

"Well… not stolen, per se. Smashed where it stood, on a decorative table as one enters the surgery."

Holmes pushed back his chair and gave a low whistle. "My, my… Some sort of petty burglar who's got a personal grudge against Napoleon?"

"It is unlikely someone would have a *personal grudge* against Napoleon," I noted.

"Perhaps the man is an ex-soldier and blames Napoleon for the death of his comrades."

"The war against Napoleon ended nearly seventy years ago, Holmes."

"Really?" said my friend, bunching his brow. "Seems like only yesterday…"

"The Battle of Waterloo was fought in 1815. For your supposition to be correct, we'd have to be looking for a ninety-year-old cat burglar with a military background."

"Ye gods, I hope it's true!" said Holmes, leaping to his feet. "I hope he still wears one of those feathered shakos! Oh, what a fellow! Can you imagine him?"

"Holmes, control yourself," Lestrade urged. "I don't think you'll be finding any nonagenarian house-breakers. I think it is much more likely we are dealing with a simple madman. Don't you agree, Doctor?"

"Hmmm… I suppose we might be looking for a man who suffers from monomania—the fixation with a certain person, item or idea. It is possible the subject has some hatred for Napoleon, or that the sight of his face brings back some unhappy memory, such that he cannot stand to leave an image of him intact."

"There you are," said Lestrade. "Solved."

But I shook my head. "No… You said one of the statues was upstairs. That means our man could not have seen it from the street. This fellow knows where his targets lie. There is method in this."

"Brilliant! Wonderful!" cried Holmes. "Lestrade, we are on tenterhooks! You must keep us informed as the investigation progresses."

"What? No, no. There will be no progress. I told you about the case because I know your taste for strange occurrences, not because Scotland Yard intends to waste its time on a case that amounts to no more than three cheap statues and one window latch. We are not investigating."

And that is where the matter came to rest.

Until seven o'clock the next morning. Unlike the previous day, I found myself awake and alert. I had not partaken of a Xantharaxes injection the night before. Not because of any moral rectitude, of course, but simply because I'd fallen asleep before I got the chance. At least I was fresh and ready when a red-faced messenger boy charged up our stairs and delivered a telegram, which read:

```
NOPE. NO. I WAS WRONG. WE ARE
INVESTIGATING. 131 PITT STREET, KENSINGTON.
COME INSTANTLY. LESTRADE
```

Alighting from our cab an hour or so later, Holmes and I beheld that familiar gaggle of chattering constables which indicates something very serious has occurred. The first victim was apparent. Just under the streetlamp, by the railings of no. 131, lay a pile of plaster fragments that—I had to assume—had recently borne the visage of the terror of Europe. On the steps to the front door of the house lay a dead man.

Just…

Really dead.

He'd been bludgeoned about the head with such violence that the impressions of the device used to murder him were quite clear. Perfectly round indentations spotted his face and scalp—most of them deeper on one side than the other. They were too large to indicate the head of a regular hammer.

"It appears likely the victim was bludgeoned to death with a walking stick," said Lestrade, striding up to me.

"What? No! A walking stick? Why does everyone assume…? That is *not a weapon*!"

"Tut, tut, Watson," Holmes remonstrated. "It is the single most British weapon anyone can name."

"Even if it were, the indentations it left would be more rounded—spherical. These have a flat bottom, you see? The weapon that made these was cylindrical. I think what we are looking for is some sort of wooden mallet or maul."

"Oh…" said Holmes with visible disappointment. "That's not very British at all."

Even more disturbing than the victim's cranial trauma was… well… the rest of him. His head lay on the top step, with his body sprawled down the stairs below. I saw no more of the cylindrical markings, yet his torso, arms and legs had suffered repeated blunt trauma. If it hadn't been for the lack of shoe marks on his clothing, I'd have thought someone had been jumping up and down on him for several minutes. So many bones had been broken that the shape of the victim's body corresponded with disgusting exactitude to the shape of the stairs. Near the victim's outstretched right hand lay a bone-handled knife.

"Ah-ha!" Holmes cried, pointing one accusatory finger at it. "*The murder weapon!*"

Lestrade gave him a resentful look.

"No, Holmes," I said. "It looks as if he was holding it."

Holmes made a queer face. "So he was walking up to this man's door with a knife in his hand? What do we think, some sort of pre-dawn knife salesman?"

"Well, that's one possibility. Any idea who he was, Lestrade?"

The question was met with another of his dour little shrugs and a somewhat unhelpful, "Italian, by the look of him. See the cut of his suit? Very nice, despite the workman's quality and the wear. And look at his hair— jet black and so slick it looks like he's been combing it with butter. His pockets were nearly empty. He had a screwdriver, a picture, and some sort of pulpy white mess I can only assume was an apple. He had no wallet or identifying papers of any kind."

"Because the murderer took them?" Holmes wondered.

"Possibly," said Lestrade. "Either that or because he

was up to the kind of business where he didn't wish to be identified."

"You say he had a picture in his pocket?" I asked. "A picture of what?"

"A fellow Italian, from the look of him," said Lestrade, producing a bent and battered photo from his notebook and handing it to me. The subject of the photograph was male and rough-looking, with a jutting, simian mouth and lower jaw. His brow ridges were prominent, but his forehead sloped back to a shock of black hair that rather resembled a cheap wig. The front of his face was adorned with a large black moustache that had been clearly—just *clearly*—glued on.

"Italian?" I cried. "No, no, no! This is a chimpanzee! A shaved chimpanzee!"

"Well, you said it, not me," Lestrade replied, raising his eyebrows in that you-know-it-and-I-know-it-but-it's-usually-not-said-in-public way.

"You misunderstand me," I said. "This is an *actual ape*, I am sure of it."

"Quiet, Doctor!" Lestrade hissed. "Some of the constables have Italian ancestry—"

"That should have nothing to do with this primate!"

"He's only joking!" Lestrade called to the assembled constables. "Very funny, Doctor. Now come along inside, won't you? I think you and Warlock should meet the owner of the latest shattered bust, don't you?"

And so we did. Just inside the door, we encountered a slim young man in his late twenties, leaning against a wall and looking positively green. When Lestrade introduced Holmes and me, our host looked shakily up, announced, "Buh—bhn. Uh… Buh…" and teetered dangerously backwards.

"This man requires medical aid!" I cried. Pausing only to fling my new patient into the nearest armchair, I dashed to a side table, seized a brandy decanter, sloshed a healthy dose into the first glass I saw, then ran back, shouting, "Here: medical aid."

He gazed at it for a moment, took the glass in his trembling hands, and sipped.

"More," I said.

He took a healthy gulp. Then came that medically questionable moment where we all waited to see which it would affect first—his wits or his stomach. Finally, he breathed a sigh of relief and said, "Ahh… thank you."

"Pish, tosh," I scoffed. "What else are doctors for? Now, when you feel up to it, why don't you tell us who you are?"

"I am Horace Harker, of the Central Press Syndicate—a reporter, by trade. By God, to think of it… I spend my life chasing stories like this, but as soon as one happens to me, I find myself so rattled that… well… I wouldn't be surprised if today's evening edition finds this story in every newspaper in London except mine!"

"Oh dear," said Holmes. "Before we go, you must tell us which paper it is, so we can all make sure not to buy it."

Our host gave Warlock a less-than-generous look.

"What? Sounds like it will be missing the day's best story," Holmes said, with a defensive sniff.

"And just what is that story, Mr. Harker?" I prompted.

"I was up very late last night, working on an article. Some time after three in the morning, I heard a noise. I thought it came from within the house, so I was very alarmed. I grabbed the poker from beside the fireplace and went down to have a look."

"Very wise," said Holmes. "If it had been a misbehaving fire-demon, you could have poked him."

"Holmes!"

"It's one of the only weapons they fear, Watson."

I rolled my eyes. "And *did* you find a misbehaving fire-demon, Mr. Harker?"

"No," he said, looking somewhat mystified. "Nothing seemed to be out of place at all. But I did hear small noises coming from the hallway, so I made my way slowly towards it. I heard the gentle click of my front door closing, and then…"

He paused and his eyes went wide with fear. "Oh, and then! A terrible screech! A yell of alarm! The sounds of a fight! I can hardly describe it! Yells! Shrieks! Thumping and thumping and thumping and screaming! I was only on the other side of the door, gentlemen, but I could not open it. I was paralyzed with fear! Well, finally the noises abated and all I could hear was gentle moaning. I gathered my courage and peeped out. There I discovered… well, you saw him."

"Moaning, you say? So he was still alive when you found him?" I asked.

"For a moment," said Mr. Harker, nodding. "When he saw me he said, 'What a fool I was! The knife was in my hand. The apple, in my pocket.' Then his eyes rolled up, he coughed out a great gout of blood, and died! I ran back to my study and grabbed my police whistle—"

"Wait now," I interjected. "You are a *reporter*, not a constable. Why would you have a police whistle?"

"My job takes me often to the Liverpool docks. I keep the whistle always on my person, in case someone should try to force himself upon my virtue."

I gave him a questioning look.

"Clearly, you have never been to Liverpool," our host blustered. "Everybody there ought to have one. Anyway, I opened the door and just blew and blew and blew the whistle until a constable came and then… I don't know… I think I've just been sitting here ever since."

"You seem quite shaken, Mr. Harker," I said. "It is probable you will require further aid. Holmes, grab that bottle."

"No, no!" Harker cried. "I must focus! I must gather my wits and write the story, only… by God, I've no idea how to start! I've no mastery over myself." He stared helplessly at his own shaking hands.

"Hmm, yes, I see," I said. "My training leads me to suspect that perhaps one more glass of medical aid and a quick nap might be required before that mastery is restored. But first, tell us about the bust. When did you discover it was missing?"

"Not until one of the constables mentioned it. There has been a spate of similar trouble, from what I gather. Honestly, I hadn't noticed it was gone."

"And where was it kept?"

Harker gulped and wiped some of the sweat from his brow. "In the corridor upstairs. Just outside the door to my study. Egad, when I think of that murderer being mere inches from where I sat working! Why, I don't know— I don't know—"

"Holmes, could you…?"

"Yup! Medical aid!" Warlock said, popping a full glass of brandy into Horace Harker's grasp.

"Now, Mr. Harker," I continued, "do you remember where you got that bust?"

"Yes. I got it at Harding Brothers—just two doors down from the High Street Station. I just needed something for the hallway, you know, and it was cheap."

The young man was beginning to look rather green again, and his eyes rolled back and forth with nervous energy.

"Lestrade, does the official force have any further questions for this man?" I asked.

Lestrade shook his head.

"Good," I said. "Now come on, Mr. Harker. One more glass of medical aid and then it's off to bed with you."

"But…"

"No, no. Doctor's orders. Come on, Holmes, help me get him up to his room, won't you?"

Three minutes later, Horace Harker was sprawled unconscious across his bed.

"What do you make of it?" I asked, as we descended the stairs.

"By the gods, it's wonderful!" said Holmes.

Lestrade was less enthusiastic. "It seems to me we are looking for an Italian—probably accustomed to violence—who kills by hammering his victims, or jumping on them. Oh! I've just remembered! We had such a case, a few years back. A pair of brothers, as I recall. Plumbers. But most of their violent urges were directed against turtles and crabs they found in the sewers."

"How do you intend to proceed?" I asked.

"I have sent a message to Inspector Hill. He frequently works amongst London's Italian population, so I was hoping he could help identify the victim. I thought I might show him the photo, too, but what is the point? They look so similar, it could be any of them."

"Any chimp, you mean?"

"*Keep your voice down!*"

I sighed. "Well, if you don't feel it will be helpful to you, Lestrade, might I borrow that photograph? I may have a use for it as I track down the busts."

"You're going after the *busts*?" said Lestrade, incredulously.

"Why not? They seem to be the unexplained bond holding all three cases together. We know that Morse Hudson is not only the first victim, he is a seller of such statuary. I thought Holmes and I might go round and see where he got them. That is, if you think it's worth our time to investigate, Warlock."

"Are you joking?" Holmes shot back. "If I follow your reasoning correctly, Watson, it seems you are forming the opinion that someone has trained an anti-Napoleon murder-monkey! Of *course* we are investigating! Ye gods, I've lived two hundred and fifty years and there's every possibility this may be my very best day!"

Morse Hudson was a red-faced, small-minded tradesman of the sort that forms the very backbone of English mercantilism. His opinion of who had smashed his cheap plaster bust of a dead French emperor was as strident as it was predictable.

"It was red republicans, sir, you may count upon it! Socialists! Anarchists!"

"So… let me get this straight, Mr. Hudson," I said. "In an attempt to destroy our system of social order, 'red republicans' walked into your shop during business hours and destroyed just one statue?"

"*But they won't win!*" he confirmed, waving a pudgy finger in my face.

"No, I don't see how they could," I agreed.

"A thousand tiny victories, such as these! A million slight acts of disobedience and sedition!"

"Why, soon we should have no plaster statuary of our greatest national enemies at all!"

He gave me the sort of look that gave me to understand he *might* be beginning to realize I was making fun of him. I changed my tactics immediately.

"Tell me, Mr. Hudson, do you make the busts yourself?"

"What? Of course not! I am a merchant, sir! I would

not dirty my hands with such labors! My place in life is to buy things from one person and sell them to another. As such, I am entitled to live in a large house with plenty of servants. Everybody knows this."

"Do you recall who did make those particular busts?"

"Well, I don't know. Do I? No! I do! It was Gelder's place in Church Street, Stepney. I recall I bought a batch of three from him, oh… must be a year ago, now. Sold two fairly quickly but the third stayed on the shelf."

"Until it was destroyed by 'red republicans' trying to undermine our social order?"

"*But they won't win!*"

"Of course not. One more thing, Mr. Hudson: do you know this… um… fellow?"

I held up the picture we'd found in the dead man's pocket only an hour or so before. Morse Hudson squinted at it, puffed some air through his pendulous lips and opined, "I don't know, some Italian. Oh! Wait! I do know him! That's Beppo!"

"*Beppo?*" said Holmes and I together. My expression—I am sure—was one of extreme skepticism. Holmes's was that of pure joy.

"Yes, yes! He comes around the shop sometimes and makes himself useful. Oh, we love Beppo! Such a happy, funny little fellow!"

"Little?" I said. "I don't suppose you mean he's short, with overly long arms?"

"Longest you've ever seen! And a mute, you know. Tragic. But he makes it known what he wants. Works all day on whatever we set him to and all he ever wants in exchange is a shilling or a few pieces of fruit. 'Beppo, fetch down that reproduction Vermeer,' we'll say, and he hauls himself up to the highest shelf and takes it down for us. By god, he's good at climbing! Handy with a hammer, too. Always smiling at us with those funny lips of his. Atrocious teeth, though."

"Mr. Hudson, has it ever occurred to you that your part-time worker, Beppo, might be a chimpanzee?"

"What? No, no, no. Italian! He's got that black moustache, doesn't he?"

"Do you know his last name, Mr. Hudson?"

"Oh, I don't think he has one. Italians often don't, you know."

"And when was the last time you saw Beppo?"

Morse Hudson pursed his lips and considered. "Just the day before the bust was smashed, I suppose. Yes he'd been in helping out for an hour or two. He seemed distracted, though. Kept leafing through our sales books in that funny little way of his. My assistant, Jacob, said he saw Beppo carrying one of the books towards the back window, but when I looked for it later, it was in its proper place."

"I see… Well, thank you, Mr. Hudson. You have been most helpful. Good luck with the anarchists."

"And you as well, sir! *We won't let them win!*"

"No, indeed."

"*Rule Britannia!*"

"As you say."

On the way down the steps, Holmes leaned in towards

me and whispered, "Really? Italians don't have last names?"

"Oh, they emphatically do, Holmes. Great, sweeping, classically beautiful ones with lots of vowels. But do you know who doesn't have them?"

"Battle monkeys?"

"Well, I was going to say 'apes' but... yes."

Mr. Bertram Gelder of Gelder & Co., Stepney was a saggy sort of fellow. He had saggy brown hair that sagged over saggy eyes with great bags under them that sagged onto the saggy cheeks he tried to hide with a saggy moustache. As we entered his shop, he blinked at us and wondered, "I don't suppose you're here to buy something?"

"Er... no," I told him.

"Thought not," he sighed.

"We were rather hoping you might help us with a question about busts of Napoleon. You make them here, do you not?"

"Indeed."

"Could you tell me how?"

He shrugged. "It's fairly simple. We've got a copy of Devine's *Head of Napoleon*, done as a mold, in two pieces. You fill both sides with plaster, then when they're dry, you glue them together with extra plaster, sand down the seam, and you're done."

"Have you ever sold any to Morse Hudson?"

"Not for a year or so."

"And Harding Brothers, of Kensington?"

"Yes, but I haven't had any lately. I usually have the Italians whip up about a dozen a year, but it's been some time."

"Ah, so you work with a lot of Italians, do you?"

"If you need works of art produced quickly, they're rather good. Oh, I mean... nothing compared to a proper British tradesman, you understand, but..." Gelder gazed at the floor a moment, trying to muster up some national pride. But no. Truth welled up in his heart and crushed whatever jingoistic sentence he was attempting to concoct. "...*rather good*."

I showed him the picture we'd gotten from Lestrade and asked, "I wonder if you know this fellow."

His response was instant. "That's Beppo! He's not supposed to come back here!"

"Oh? And why is that?"

"Well, there was that whole mix-up with Benito Marinetti, last year. A man got stabbed! And... well, I suppose none of it was Beppo's fault, really. But he's always going about with Marinetti. The two were almost inseparable. They always worked together, and Beppo was fiercely protective of the old man."

"Meaning Benito Marinetti? What can you tell me about him?"

"He was a nice enough old fellow. Used to live in America. From what I hear, he'd been an organ-grinder in Philadelphia, as well as Venice."

Holmes gave a scandalized gasp. "Organ-grinder? Is that some kind of demon?"

Gelder just gave another of his droopy little shrugs and muttered, "I always thought he made sausages. He was a good craftsman. Never drank, like some of the others. Strange, though. Whenever he met another Italian, he refused to talk to the man until he'd pulled back the other fellow's shirt and had a look at his chest."

"Odd choice," I noted.

"He was in trouble with a gang of theirs, from what I gather. Call themselves the Red Circle, or the Scarlet Ring, or something like it. I think he had something they wanted. That's what all the fuss was about. A year ago, somebody came after Marinetti, right outside my shop. Usually everyone was afraid to give him trouble, because of Beppo, but Marinetti was alone that day. There was a fight. Benito Marinetti stabbed his assailant and fled in here. Well, I refused to shelter him, of course. I called the police and turned him right over."

"And what happened?"

"The other fellow lived, so they gave Marinetti a year in prison."

"A year? Seems a bit light for knifing a man, doesn't it?"

"Oh, no, no. Knifing an *Italian*."

I reeled back and stammered, "Oh. I suppose, I… I just didn't realize how deeply this prejudice runs. Is that how everybody feels about Italians?"

"Why not?" asked Holmes. "It's the same way you feel about Canadians."

"Well yes, but that's because they're *Canadian*."

Mr. Gelder gave a serious shake of his head and confirmed, "Oh no. We wouldn't hire Canadians."

"Hmmm," I reflected, scratching my chin. "You say Benito Marinetti got a year's imprisonment. And you haven't sold any busts in that time? I wonder, is there any possibility he may have been released by now?"

"I'm not sure," said Gelder. "We could ask the boys in the back, I suppose. Come on."

He led us into his workshop where eight or nine Italian craftsmen were doing their utmost to remind everybody just who'd started the Renaissance. The army of back-room Botticellis went to their tasks with third-rate materials—plaster instead of marble, cheap wooden frames they constructed by hand—but the art they produced ranged from the attractive to the gobsmackingly gorgeous.

"Oh!" said Holmes, gazing about at the works around him. "The colors!"

"That's just the problem!" Gelder shouted, and suddenly all the droop had gone out of him. It was replaced by a militant and familiar British zeal. "Too many damned colors! Look at this landscape painting of Castello Estense! Garbage! A red-stone fortress, surrounded by sunny vineyards? Ha! That is not a castle, sir! Chillingham! Now there's a proper castle! Gray and wet, like a castle ought to be! These Italians have got it all wrong. And their food! So many tomatoes! So many herbs and spices! So light and yet so zesty! Where is the decorum, I ask you? Where is the restraint? They should learn from Britain! Yet they cannot fathom the simple truth: that proper cuisine is gray and wet!"

"Um… sure," said Holmes.

"Even their portraiture," Gelder continued, gesturing angrily at one of the half-finished pictures on his back wall. "Too vibrant. Too energetic. It spoils the whole thing! With good, proper British paintings there's always something in the subjects' eyes, you know? A certain restrained propriety that lets you know that the soul that resides within is more…"

"Gray and wet?" Holmes volunteered.

"There you go! Yes! Exactly!" Gelder bellowed, then settled into a nearby corner to cry a bit.

Three minutes of interrogation gave us to understand that the local Italian position was that Benito Marinetti had been released from prison, but had not been seen since. Additionally, anybody with information as to his whereabouts might want to come forward and say so because they knew a number of very bad men with very big wallets who would readily pay for that information.

Now, at last, I was getting somewhere. "Mr. Gelder, is there a way to tell where the last batch of Napoleon busts was sent, before Mr. Marinetti was sent to prison?"

There was. A quick check of the books indicated that—in all likelihood—six such statues had been in the process of being made on the day of Marinetti's knife-fight. Of these, three had gone to Morse Hudson, and three to Harding Brothers.

"Now we are getting somewhere, Holmes!" I said. "Quickly, we must hasten to Kensington!"

Holmes puffed with annoyance. "But, Watson, why?"

"To track down the two final busts."

"We're going to go somewhere else and talk to someone else and get more information and blah, blah, blah?"

"Well… yes."

"I don't want to."

I gave him a hard look. "What do you mean you don't want to?"

"Look, I don't know if this is the sort of thing a gentleman is supposed to say, but…" He leaned in very close to me. "I want to fight a battle monkey! I've never done it before!"

I stared at him.

"Please, Watson? Please? I know I'm supposed to pay attention to all this sneaking about and clue-getting, but… Gads, all I can think about is fighting that monkey! Do you suppose it will be close?"

"*No!* You fight demons and sorcerers! I've no idea how a simple chimpanzee is supposed to hold his own against—"

"He's got a hammer, Watson. Don't forget."

"You've got a *demonic soul-blade*!"

"Well, I still think it will be fun. And I'm losing my patience with all this driving about London, talking and talking! When do I get to fight a monkey?"

"Oh… very well. I suppose I can solve the whole thing with a couple of telegrams. Let's head for home."

"Yes, excellent! I'll have some toast and soup and rest up for my monkey-battle!"

I suppose it was no worse than any other big game

hunter's desire to bag their first rhino. Nevertheless, I stopped by the fruit stand on the way home to purchase alternatives, should they be wanted. Once at Baker Street, I began a furious campaign of telegram writing while Holmes retired to his chamber to draw pictures of fierce apes with hammers fighting big-chinned, sword-swinging gentlemen of—*ahem*—unknown identity.

My first telegram went to Harding Brothers. I sat in agony for almost two hours before I had the reply. Hearing that their customers' lives might be in danger, they happily provided the names and addresses of the gentlemen who had purchased the last two busts. I sent each of the purchasers a telegram. My final missive went to Lestrade, begging him to join us at our lodgings when the sun went down. We hadn't long to wait, for my flurry of activity had taken most of the afternoon. Barely half an hour after sunset, he knocked on our door.

"What news, Lestrade?" I asked, as I ushered him in.

"Some," he mumbled. "The dead man on Horace Harker's doorstep has been identified. His name was Pietro Venucci, a Sicilian by birth, but he had spent much time in America. He'd recently arrived in London but was well known to the Italian community here. It seems he was a knifeman for the Mafia—that's a little gang the Italians have. Bless me, they do try, though lord knows they will never match London's gangs for toughness, fearfulness or organization."

"Ha! Of course not," I agreed.

"Recently, Venucci has been affiliated with a splinter faction called the Red Ring, or something like it. They're an extremist Italian-nationalist secret society. Well... secret, I say, but Pietro Venucci had a red circle tattooed on his chest above his heart. Apparently it is required of all full members. So they must have a new definition of 'secret' I was previously unaware of."

"And yet, it corroborates the story I've formed to explain this bizarre rash of crimes. It explains why Benito Marinetti checked the chests of every Italian he met."

"Benito who?"

"I think I've figured the whole thing out, Lestrade. Let me tell you what I know."

Holmes tilted his head to the side and said, "Eh? That's not like you, Watson. Usually you make us wait until the end."

"Well this time I'm not going to. It all begins with an organ-grinder, named Benito Marinetti, who worked with a chimpanzee named Beppo."

"An organ-grinder?" said Lestrade quizzically.

"A kind of demon," Holmes explained.

"Really?" Lestrade wondered. "Because most of my homes are underneath slaughter-houses and I've always thought—after they've taken the muscles of the cow for meat and the skins for leather—there must be somebody whose job it is—"

I cut him off. "Organ-grinder is carnival slang; it denotes an entertainer who works with a hand-cranked calliope and a trained primate. The man plays music while the monkey dances and begs the audience for coins."

"I have heard of such things," Lestrade reflected. "Yet, aren't the monkeys usually quite small?"

I had to admit that they were and that I had no idea what a full-grown chimpanzee might be doing in such a role. Holmes was wiser. "Ha!" he scoffed. "Perhaps it might be easy to deny your pocket change to the average capuchin, but what if you knew he could snatch you up and throw you over the nearest fence?"

"Good point," I admitted. "Organ-grinding was Mr. Marinetti's trade in Italy and America yet, upon his arrival in England, he took new work, shaved his ape, stuck a false moustache on its face and passed him off as a fellow Italian."

"That would never work," said Lestrade.

"You'd be surprised," I told him. "Now, why did Marinetti need to hide? Because he was in possession of an item that was sought by this Red Circle gang, or whatever they're called. Unless I miss my guess, the item must be fairly small—probably no bigger than a man's fist and possibly much smaller. What do you say, Lestrade, do you know of any items stolen roughly one year ago that are connected with Italy?"

Lestrade barely had to reflect at all before leaping to his feet and crying, "The Black Pearl of the Borgias! It went missing from the prince of Colonna's bedroom at the Hotel Dacre, just over a year ago. Suspicion fell on the princess's maid—a girl named Lucretia—but nothing was ever proved."

"Perhaps now it may be," I said, smirking. "You see, one year ago, Benito Marinetti found himself in possession of a small item desired by the Red Ring. He was accosted outside Gelder & Co. and badly wounded his attacker with a knife. He knew he had only a matter of minutes before he was killed or taken into custody. What should he do with his treasure? He fled into the wholesaler's where he saw just the expedient he needed: six freshly cast busts of Napoleon, drying in the molds. He thrust his treasure—probably the Borgia pearl—into the wet plaster before the constables came for him. Can it be coincidence that—just after Marinetti's release from prison—busts of Napoleon started getting smashed all over London? And not just any busts! Holmes and I have traced every single one to the particular batch made at Gelder & Co. on the day that Benito Marinetti was arrested."

"Only four have been smashed!" Lestrade cried. "Quickly, we must track down the last two busts!"

"Already done," I told him. "Both were bought and subsequently sold by Harding Brothers, near Kensington High Street Station. One went to Josiah Brown, of Laburnum Lodge, Laburnum Vale, Chiswick. The other to Mr. Sandeford of Lower Grove Road, Reading. I have dispatched telegrams to both men, warning them to expect attempts on their busts, urging them not to confront any intruder as he is quite dangerous, and offering to purchase the busts if they will bring them to 221B Baker Street tomorrow morning."

"Well done!" Lestrade crowed. "Have you had any answer to your inquiries?"

Just at that moment, the bell rang.

"I was about to say 'no' but perhaps I'd better hold my tongue until we see who is at the door."

Sure enough, it was a messenger boy with a telegram from Mr. Sandeford, promising to hide his bust of Napoleon that night and bring it to Baker Street the next morning.

"Well, that simplifies matters," I said. "It leaves only one bust vulnerable this evening. Gentlemen, I suggest we hurry to Chiswick and lie in wait outside the house of Mr. Josiah Brown."

"Yes, perhaps we shall capture this Benito Marinetti," said Lestrade.

"No, I shouldn't think so. Marinetti has gone into hiding. Nobody has seen him since his release. He has a well-trained confederate who has been breaking into the targeted houses and smashing the busts."

"And who is this well-trained confederate?" Lestrade wanted to know.

I handed him back the picture we'd taken from Pietro Venucci's pocket only that morning. "His chimpanzee, Beppo."

"But no," said Lestrade. "This is just some random Italian fellow."

"He's not!" Holmes declared, in strident tones. "He's an anti-Napoleon battle monkey! And he's wonderful! And I'm going to fight him! Oh, it will be a sight to see!"

Lestrade gave Holmes exactly that same disbelieving glance I'd used earlier that day. "No it won't. You'll kill him in an instant. He's only an ape. Or maybe an Italian, but either way…"

"All right, but he's got a hammer! Did Watson tell you that? He's *armed*."

"So?" said Lestrade. "Holmes, I'm not sure there's any such thing as a god, but if there is, and if you were going to fight it, I really wouldn't know where to place my bet."

And then a strange light lit up in Lestrade's eye. He did have a bit of a mania for gambling, after all, and putting this thought into words helped him realize that—at least in the case of this night's festivities—he knew *exactly* where to place his bet. He turned to me and shouted, "Five pounds on Holmes!"

"No! I'm not taking that."

"Five pounds on Holmes in five seconds! Monkey dead in five seconds from the first blow or the initial challenge!"

"No bet, Lestrade."

"I'll give you two to one!"

I gave a heavy sigh. "Very well. But I tell you this: I intend to win. I know it will disappoint Holmes terribly, but it's the right thing to do. For Beppo's sake, I'll take that bet."

We shook on it and Lestrade gave me one of his rare smiles. "Done! I suppose we'd best head for Chiswick, eh?"

"Yes!" Holmes cried. "To battle! To greatness! To Chiswick!"

If there's one thing I regret about my career as a criminal/magical investigator, it is this: just how often I wind up standing about in the cold and dark, waiting for mischief to start. If only criminals would publish their timetables in advance, the whole job would be eminently more pleasurable.

We took up position in the front garden of a vacant house, just down the row from Mr. Josiah Brown's front door. Though I repeatedly urged my companions to silence, a thousand primate-slaying tips and observations passed between the two of them. Though—to his credit—Lestrade insisted that if there was any question of our foe being an Italian and not a chimp, Holmes was forbidden from murdering him. In such a case the bet was off, of course. Though, if I were any kind of gentleman I must own that the mistake had been mine and pay the forfeit anyway.

Such was the stealth of our foe and such the strenuousness of my friends' discussion that I had no warning until it was nearly too late. A sudden, joyous shriek split the night. Popping up over our garden wall, I beheld the shadowy form of Beppo jumping over Mr. Brown's front gate. He wore blue overalls over a bright red shirt. A jaunty little red cap rested atop his (clearly simian) head and the glued-on moustache waggled back and forth as he bounded down the street towards us. No sooner had he reached the first streetlamp than he raised one of his hands up over his head.

A plaster bust of Napoleon gleamed in the gaslight.

With a second screech, our foe flung the bust down upon the pavement and jumped on it twice, with great violence. Then, he treated the unfortunate emperor to three lightning-quick blows from the wooden hammer in his other hand, then one more jump. He bent over the dusty wreckage and—with some diligence—sifted

Apple, Beppo? Apple?

through it for some moments. At last, he gave a frustrated "ook" from which I inferred that the object of his search must not be present.

By this time we were all approaching him at a full run. Holmes was well in the lead, enjoying the advantages of both the longest legs and the greatest zeal. I was just behind, pointlessly urging caution. Lestrade brought up the rear, stopwatch in hand, eager to claim the spoils of his bet. As we neared Beppo, Holmes threw his left hand back and cried, "Melfrizoth!" No sooner had he spoken the name of the blade than it materialized in his hand—black and gleaming, curved like a serpent's tooth and burning with demonic green flame. Those same otherworldly fires lit in Holmes's eyes as his voice dropped an octave or three and he cried out, "Battle monkey: face me!"

If Beppo was slightly taken aback I think none of us could blame him. Then again, we also could not fault his courage for, after reeling back in surprise for only an instant, he raised the hammer above his head and shrieked a battle cry. He came at Holmes with that mixture of fear and ferocity that only a true savage can muster. Holmes dropped into a low crouch, sword at the ready, which allowed me to catch up and come between the two combatants. My hands feverishly searched my pockets for my alternate solution. One hand closed around it—my only chance.

Well… *Beppo's* only chance.

I pulled it free from my coat pocket and shouted, "Wait, Beppo, wait! Look! Apple, Beppo? Apple?"

Beppo's gaze swung my way, then doubtfully back to Holmes...

And then to me!

Because really, given the choice between certain death at the hands of a flaming soul-blade and a nice, fresh apple, which of us wouldn't take the apple? He knuckle-walked cautiously over to me and held out his hand.

"Here you go, Beppo. Good job!"

He took the apple, gave it a skeptical sniff, then an exploratory bite. Finding it just what he'd hoped, he gave me his battered wooden hammer, still filthy with smashed plaster and the dried remains of Pietro Venucci's scalp. With both hands free for his new task, Beppo began to devour the apple, turning it round in circles as he chomped, until only a core remained. This, he tossed over his shoulder into the smashed remains of the great French emperor.

"Awwwwww," said Holmes. "Cute little fellow, isn't he?" Then, with just a hint of guilt, added, "Ves, Melfrizoth," and the burning blade vanished from his hand.

I turned to find Lestrade standing dead still in the middle of the street, his fang-lined maw hanging open in disappointment and disbelief.

"Dead ape within five seconds of the initial challenge, wasn't it?" I said. "I believe that's ten pounds you owe me." A light tug at the hem of my coat caused me to turn back. "What's that, Beppo? Oh, you think I've got more, do you? Well you just may be right. Come along, now."

* * *

This narrative would be incomplete, I suppose, without a word as to the final fate of Beppo the chimp. Scotland Yard held him for a time on suspicion of the murder of Pietro Venucci—and not without reason. If the circumstances were not damning enough, there was the matter of the murder weapon, retrieved by Inspector Lestrade from the hand of Beppo himself (or so we told them). There was also some question as to whether he was wanted by the French authorities regarding some unpleasantness on the rue Morgue.

Then again, the British legal system had little precedent for trying apes. To our more conservative judges, such an idea was distasteful—nearly an admission that Charles Darwin had been right all along. Besides, Venucci had been a known killer and had been found in possession of Beppo's picture, as well as a knife. Who was to say the little fellow's actions had not been mere self-preservation? He was held in custody, in the hopes that Benito Marinetti would come out of hiding to claim him. No such luck. Mr. Marinetti was never found and I fear some evil may have come to him. Nevertheless, the Marinetti family eventually did come for their grandfather's trusted helper, Beppo. And I was forced to make an apology. It seems that—as he was born in a circus just outside Venice—Beppo technically *was* an Italian.

But still…

The next morning, William Sandeford arrived on the 10:15, bearing a carpet bag containing the final bust. Holmes, Lestrade and I were all on hand to greet him. He was a red-faced, grizzle-whiskered old man who chewed his moustache with nervous apprehension as he stepped through our door.

"I had your telegram," he cried, despite the fact we were four feet from him, "and I don't know why any man's so keen to steal a thing like this! Nor do I know why it's worth ten pound to you! But I don't care! Ten pound is ten pound and that's the heart of the matter!"

I don't think Mr. Sandeford was deaf, but it seems as if he assumed the three of us were. The sheer volume with which he conducted business had us wincing.

"Now I don't know where the church stands on the matter, so I tell you straight," he continued, "this Napoleon's not worth ten pound! I put it to you gentlemen: is it a sin to take ten pound for a statue that's not worth ten shilling? I don't want it weighing on my soul!"

"No, no, Mr. Sandeford," I protested, "we think the price is fair. We do not want just any bust of Napoleon; we want *this* one. We are happy to compensate you for your good fortune to have acquired it in the first place and for your good stewardship while it was in your care. I am sure the church would have no objection."

"Well… as long as you're sure it's no foul deed…"

"Not at all, Mr. Sandeford."

"All right, then!"

"Excellent! I have a contract drawn up right here, if you would be so kind as to—"

As I spoke, Mr. Sandeford reached inside his bag, withdrew the bust and put it on our table. And my words… they just… stopped.

Everything stopped.

Holmes recoiled from the thing, his face a mask of amazement. Even Lestrade stared distrustfully at the statue.

On the one hand, there was nothing wrong with it. It was only a cheap plaster-of-Paris bust of Napoleon. And yet... I had never before stood in the presence of such an aura of command. Honestly, I think the three of us were waiting for orders. The little emperor's stern countenance stared up at us, as if demanding our obedience. And I'm sure we would have given it. If he'd ordered us to charge Wellington's batteries at Waterloo, we'd have done it. If he'd ordered us to turn and kill each other, we'd have done that, too. Perhaps Holmes could have withstood the influence, but Lestrade and I were mastered the second we looked at it.

Holmes gave a low whistle. "This is... not as we expected."

"No," I agreed.

Slowly Holmes's hand moved to the contract of sale I had drawn up. As I considered it likely the bust contained an item of extreme value—albeit an illegally obtained one Mr. Sandeford had no right to keep—I had been careful to phrase it in such a way that the seller released all interest in the bust and its contents.

"I think I'll just be making a few changes to this contract, Mr. Sandeford," Holmes said. "For safety's sake. Firstly, you shall not be selling this to Watson, but to me. Second, I will not give you ten pounds in notes, as in essence, a promissory note is nothing more than a stranger's promise to deliver value if ever you should present him this note. No. In matters of magi— er... in matters such as these, ownership is too important. I must pay you in metal. I trust ten guineas is acceptable?"

"Well, certainly!"

"Very good, Mr. Sandeford." Holmes leaned in to make the necessary changes to the contract. As he did, he sighed, "And yet... here where it asks you to sign your name... I don't suppose you know your true name, do you?"

"What do you mean? Of course I do!"

"No, no. Not the name you gave us. Nor the name your mother gave you. It would be only a few syllables long, but would proclaim everything you are and everything you have done to any who heard it. Well... any who know of such things."

"What are you talking about? Secret names?"

"We all have one, Mr. Sandeford."

"Well, what's yours then?"

Holmes straightened up. "My name," he said, in even, factual tones, "is Warlock Holmes. And if I am one of only a handful of beings in this world who goes about using its true name to conduct its daily business, it is only because I know I have naught to fear." But his eyes drifted from Mr. Sandeford to the bust, and he added, "Generally. In any case, Mr. Sandeford, I'm afraid a standard signature simply will not do. I need a mark that represents the very essence of you. Earwax, I think. Yes, just dip your finger in your ear and leave a little dollop on this line, here. That should suffice."

"Are you mad?" our guest demanded.

"Many say so," replied Holmes, with a sigh. "Look, I know it's an unusual request. Perhaps if I were to change this figure here to fifteen guineas…?"

William Sandeford stuck his little finger in his ear so fast I feared he might puncture his brain. As soon as he'd made his disgusting yellow smear on the line indicated, Holmes gave a great sigh of relief, wrote his name on the line below, said, "Excuse me for a moment," and went to his room. He returned with a handful of gleaming coins.

"It's practically a fortune!" Sandeford declared, looking down at his newfound wealth.

We bid him adieu, then stood around the statue, staring. Two of us dumbstruck. One curious.

"What was your plan now, Watson?" Holmes asked.

"Well, I *was* going to smash the thing open. But that was before. Now that I see it, perhaps… um… perhaps another plan is warranted."

"Perhaps not," said Holmes. "I find you usually know best."

He went to the fireplace, swept up our poker, and with a single blow he smote Napoleon's head in twain. Plaster dust filled the air. I nearly cried out in dismay, but then a kind of invisible veil fell away from my wits and I found I had no desire to continue. There, amongst the white shards, a small black item caught my eye. Gathering my self-mastery, I strode forward and picked it up, declaring, "Gentlemen, behold: the Black Pearl of the B—"

But it wasn't.

In fact, besides color, the item in my hand had nothing in common with the item I'd expected. In my hand lay a tiny bundle of black iron sticks, bound together with wires of the same material. I blinked at it. There was no question it was the source of the power we'd felt earlier.

"Watson!" Holmes cried. "Put that down! Do not do anything else. Especially, do not *say* anything else. Remember: that belongs to me."

Slowly, I dropped the object on the table. It fell with a dead, metallic clunk. As I drew back, I dazedly reflected, "I know this thing… Holmes, you used to draw it, remember? You drew it all up your arm once."

"I did," he confirmed, lifting up the tiny totem. "And now here it is in my possession… in my home…"

As he walked into his bedroom, I heard him add, "Damn it all." He closed the door behind him without a word of explanation.

A month before, I would have been furious. But that day, I could only smile. *Go on, Holmes, keep your secrets. I don't need to beg knowledge from you anymore. I have my own methods now.* How I looked forward to that evening's dream. How I craved the next revelation.

Or maybe I just wanted that needle in my arm.

THE DEVIL AND THE NEOPHYTE

FROM THE DREAM JOURNAL OF DR. JOHN WATSON

THE LOUDEST THING THERE IS, ACCORDING TO PEOPLE who claim to have heard it, is the voice of God. It will carry across continents, with a force that cannot be disobeyed; when God speaks, all must hear.

Not so the devil. In fact, the devil does not speak at all. The devil sings.

And not intrusively. If you've ever heard the devil's song, it is because you wished to. The devil sings soft. Slow. Adagio.

The wisest thing is not to listen. Yet those who choose to chance their soul should heed, at least, this warning: *listen well*.

Tonight I'm going to hear the devil. For the first time, my dream is infused with a special urgency. This is happening right now. It is nearly four in the morning in London, where my body lies in tussled sheets in 221B, its heart beating feebly. That makes it almost nine at night in Deadwood—too early an hour for real mischief, but a perfect time to start it. And just the spot—the Gem Saloon.

The air is full of smoke and sweat. It's a rainy night

and people come in shaking water from their collars and hats. It's as crowded as it gets. Anyone who wants a drink is gonna have to wait a spell. But that doesn't matter. Nobody would miss the show tonight. There's a special treat—a singer come all the way from Olde London Towne. And the word is: she's a real corker!

In the back corner sits a man, alone at a table. He's well dressed, in as much as any American ever is, in a dark gray suit with less fluting than his countrymen generally glue on to their jackets. His waistcoat is black and the carnation in his buttonhole is purest white. He has one of those grand, sweeping moustaches they wear out West, but instead of a Stetson he wears a gray bowler, to make him look more continental.

It isn't working; he looks like a gunfighter.

Which is apt, because he is one. This is a man accustomed to taking life and to risking his own. He was a bad man once, though now reformed. He has only one small revolver on his person, and in his pocket is a wallet with a badge: an all-seeing eye, above the words "We Never Sleep". He's a Pinkerton detective. And he's here tonight to work.

He's just not sure what kind of work it will be.

He checks his pocket watch. Nine exactly. Near the stage there is a muted clamor in the audience, a whispered debate as to whether the show has started. Then the room falls quiet.

But not silent.

There is one sound. A single note. Hovering pure and sweet, just at the edge of hearing. It is only one human voice, yet with an almost inhuman quality. So small a thing to command so large a room. You have to strain to hear it.

If you've ever heard the devil's song, it is because you wished to.

The tattered red curtain rattles open, and there she is: my murderess. The Woman. Irene Adler. The light plays on her simple white dress and her outstretched arms. Her eyes are closed as she pours herself forward into that one quiet note. Her accompanist shakes himself from his trance, leans over his battered piano and plays a few chords of introduction. Poor fool, he's well out of his depth. And he's not the only one. As Irene launches into her song—an Italian ode to the silent swan who sings only once, as she knows herself to be dying—the Pinkerton man sits frozen at the back, a glass of whiskey halfway to his lips.

This is his foe?

She's just like in the briefings, in a way. The old man himself, Allan Pinkerton, took him aside before he left, to urge him to remember the importance of his mission and the excellence of his opponent. They taught him all about her. And yet they did not prepare him.

He's been told that she is foremost a mastermind—both at a strategic and tactical level—always two moves ahead. Her second level of significance is as a sorcerer. They *think*. The level of art she possesses is unclear, but as she grew up as a ward of James Moriarty, she is to be treated as if she were amongst the world's most dangerous practitioners of the magical arts. Third: she is a beauty. And she knows it. She dominates with it. Fourth: she is a singer. As the agent sits with his mouth just slightly open, listening to Irene Adler leap from one note to land daintily, perfectly at the next…

By God, if this is the *fourth best thing she does*…

Her green eyes are open now. She is smiling out at the audience as if to say, *I'm so glad you all came here tonight, to give your hearts and wills to me*.

Can she be beaten? The agent swallows his whiskey. He's going to try. He's going to put his life on the line again, tonight. It's going to be a close-run thing, but she has something the old man wants. Two things, if intelligence is to be believed: the Heart and the Cruciator. In short, should things go badly for him this evening, they could go very badly indeed.

She sees him sitting at the back of the room and gives him a shy smile. What a lie! Irene Adler? Shy? I know her well enough to realize it's not even a real smile; it is an opening move—an invitation to her foe to come and play against her. I wonder how the game will go.

But the dream is shifting me away. Why? Damn it, why?

This is all I want to see: her. And I suppose I even want to see him. Or, no. To *be* him. He's about to cross swords with the foe I most cherish, to enter into that dance of tricks and lies and—damn it—*probably seduction* that forms the most addictive game I know. Why can't *I* play?

Why is she so far from me?

Now I'm looking at a youth, not even twenty. He has a shock of forgettable brown hair over a splash of freckles. His clothes are more suited to the age of Elizabeth than Victoria. He's holding a candle in one hand and a broken feather in the other. With careful purpose, he holds the feather above the candle. As the air fills with the stink of singed barbules, he says, "Demon, I have done your bidding."

He's not talking to anybody, just a shadow on the wall.

Though… it *is* a bit of a deep, palpable, twisting shadow, if I'm honest. From the empty corners of the room comes a voice—soft and distant and audibly displeased.

"Not to my satisfaction."

"I care nothing for your satisfaction," scoffs the youth. "I have fulfilled the word of our contract, if not your intent. Now I claim my fee: I will live the life of another being. And then, when that is over, I shall return to the life that is mine, having lost no moment of it."

"But you have not helped me," the voice insists. "I cannot long endure upon this world."

"And from what I gather," says the young man, with a smirk, "that time will be even shorter if you try to withhold payment. I have done my part and I now demand my due!"

The demon is quiet a moment. "Very well. I shall render first the payment I would have given, had you pleased me…"

And the world shifts and skews. The young man and I are swept away, into the body of another living thing. We have no power to control its actions, but we feel as if we are the creature; we think its thoughts.

The world is a deep, brown haze. A stretchy membrane contains me and I begin pushing against it. It gives way.

I am climbing free—free from my shell and the mud that cradled it—out into the light. As I stand, dazed and stupid, letting my newborn eyes accustom themselves to the new input of sight, instinct takes over and I spread my wings in the sun. They are wrinkled and weak, but as they dry they stiffen. My six legs can move me back and forth along the surface of the mud. I hardly even notice when my wings begin to vibrate, then to beat. I'm flying! Up into the air—a clumsy circle, then back down. Around me, more and more of my fellows are emerging.

I spend the whole day flying above the mud and the cool surface of the pond. My eggs are fertilized—that's a bit of a surprise. But it's all right. I know it is something I'm supposed to do. I deposit them in the cool water. The day is almost over now, and the mud has become dry and cracked.

I can feel my body slowing down. That's all right. My eggs are laid; my job is done. My wings can no longer lift me. My legs won't hold me up. I let myself fall into the mud. The sun is going down. So am I. A buzzing confusion grows in my simple little mind. I can hardly move at all anymore. I can't even breathe.

And then, with a sudden wrenching wave of nausea, I'm back with the boy. I have ridden along as the demon gave him an entire second life.

The life of a mayfly: one day in August.

"But that was hardly a life at all," says the youth. "You planned to cheat me."

"And you, it seems, have succeeded in cheating me," replies the demon. "I am fading. My powers wane. There is no point in spending them to sustain myself, so I shall set them to another purpose. I gave you the life you would have had for serving me well. Now here is one more, because you have served me so cruelly. Goodbye, James Moriarty. Since you have left me no way to save myself, I shall ruin us both."

Oh, thank whatever gods may be that my dream does not show me the entirety of James Moriarty's second payment. Yet I see enough to understand why Moriarty becomes the man he does.

He goes through the agony of being born. Human, this time, or something very like it. The eyes are bigger, the fingers longer. His kind have very spare frames and no hair at all. By God, the things they've invented! The wonder of their cities! The strangeness of the vehicles that take them to the stars!

The babe Moriarty is too young to understand exactly what happens to his mother and why he finds himself suddenly in the care of people who… don't. His race has a factory-like method of raising children. He grows to near-adulthood in a loveless system and it is no surprise to me when he lashes out against it—when he finally performs the transgression his society was waiting for. At last, they have an excuse to punish him. At last, they can give him a job everybody wants done, but nobody wants to do.

His schooling takes on a new focus. He is taught how to fly a spacecraft and how to maintain it. He is taught how to focus his attention and he is given a series of drugs and operations to ensure that he cannot help but do so. He is taught about loyalty and duty. He's promised that he will be provided for and one day retire with the thanks of his people. Then, when they think he is ready, he is loaded into a small craft and launched into space.

The shuttle flies for six years.

Any wonder I feel at the accomplishments of his race dims, day by day, as we pass through the empty void. As the months go by, the stars outside the windows shift. The view is constantly changing and yet, always horribly the same.

Then finally comes that happy day he docks with a vessel bigger than any building I've ever seen. The woman who meets him is ancient, and so excited she can barely speak. Indeed, she hasn't had much practice—she's the only creature that lives here. She shows him the captain's chair and how to work the controls. She tells him how to aim the solar sails and how to feel the pull of a new star as you leave the push of the old. She shows him the strange turbines that power the thing when the stars are too distant and cautions him not to allow this too much. She shows him the machines that give him food and air and water and warmth and hold physical atrophy at bay. She speaks of their quirks and what must be done to keep them working. She tells him the day will come when he will not *want* them to keep working, when he hopes they will break or thinks of breaking them himself.

But this is expressly forbidden. He has a job to do.

When she steps into the six-year shuttle, she seems so happy that I fear her ancient heart will fail. Whether it does or not, I will never know. The craft flies away, with either the smiling old woman or her corpse. The creature that is now Moriarty is alone, in command of his ship.

The society he is from has discovered something called "sub-actuality quantum transfer". They've discovered a way to move energy—even mechanical force—from one atom to another. This is accomplished slightly outside reality—just "underneath" the known fabric of the universe. The kinetic force of this huge, heavy ship is being robbed from it, to power the view-screens and vehicles of thousands of people back home.

This technology has only one flaw: intent. The energy used by all those people back on the surface of their planet will be purposefully used, therefore it must be purposefully generated or the transfer will fail. Otherwise, I am sure they would be robbing motion from some faraway moon, dragging it slowly back until it crashed into the planet it orbited. Hence, the strange work sentence Moriarty received. Hence the surgeries to hone and focus his will. Day after day, for fourteen-hour shifts or more, the Moriarty creature sits in his captain's chair, turning the great ship this way and that. He anchors his path to one star, then the next, his razor-sharp attention focused on the blackness before him and the points of light all around. With intense purpose he flies the ship back and forth, all around the galaxy. It doesn't matter where he goes, only that he does not stop and that he never travels anywhere he doesn't mean to go.

Day after day, in the captain's chair, eating the same food—designed for nutrition, not for taste, with nobody to keep him company and nothing to hope for but the day he can return home to enjoy some of the energy he's producing. The ship's computer does its best, but despite possessing medical technology that dwarfs my own, it cannot possibly keep him alive for as long as the other members of his race.

Probably not even three hundred years.

Slowly, those years creep by. Back and forth, through the blackness, as the stars grow slowly familiar. His eyes lose their focus and his skin becomes a wrinkled, pallid coat over protruding bones.

Until finally, the six-year shuttle returns and a nervous young man steps out.

The love and happiness the Moriarty creature feels is so overwhelming it almost breaks my heart. It is not only that his duty is done—not only that this youth is his deliverance—it's much more than that. He looks with the eyes of one who has sinned and repented, upon the face of one whose sin is new. He does his best to help the lad. He uses all the cogent thought he can muster explaining how the food-replicator works and how not to overtax it. This ship is the only world he knows and he explains the entirety of that world to the creature that must now inherit it. Only then, when the last shaking bit of advice is drained from his enfeebled mind, does he finally make his farewells and step away from his captain's chair.

The craft flies for six years.

He finds himself staring forward, day after day, willing himself to fly in the direction he is going. It is habit. He's not used to the fact that his intent does not matter anymore.

How happy he is to set his trembling foot on the orbital station. He returns with the air of a conquering hero. He expected gratitude—and it is delivered—but the pity that alloys it is a surprise to him. He has a little cabin waiting on the planet below, to ease his twilight years. It's on a mountainside. There are trees.

They tell him not to go there yet. Not until his body is accustomed to the gravity. Not until the countless pathogens he's been sequestered from for the last few centuries can be safely reintroduced to his tissues.

He doesn't listen. None of them ever do.

As soon as he can, he's bound for the planet's surface. He wants to know what fresh air is like. He wants to feel water made not from his own recycled sweat, but from melting snow that fell from an open sky.

He cannot help himself.

If he had been more careful, his wasted old body might have afforded him a decade or two of comfortable decline to pay him back for all his long hours of labor. But nobody returning from a captaincy on the quantum fleet ever has the will to wait. It's why the company only has to keep four cabins. The rewards afforded to the returning workers are lavish, and yet the cost of providing them is never high.

He's dead within the month.

And with a sickening lurch, James Moriarty is back inside James Moriarty. He stumbles and falls. He's not accustomed to his thick, strange fingers and his own bizarre, unnecessary hair. This nineteen-year-old lad has just lived 338 extra years. No time has passed in the reality he left, yet he has existed long enough to have forgotten he ever was another creature before the one that just died. He doesn't remember himself or why the deepest, strangest shadow in the room is using its final breath to laugh at him, as nothingness creeps in to claim it.

Though he is my enemy, I cannot help but pity James Moriarty. It's clear the demon's double payment was a gift of exceeding cruelty. Moriarty knows better than any living man what time really means, and how it swallows us. Every night he reads, feverishly striving to understand even one of the millions of human lives that have been lost to time. He can't do it. He can't feel what they felt, or know what they knew. But he understands this: someday his life will be lost in the fog of ages, too.

The demon has ruined him.

Yet it has also made him. It has instilled him with a purpose. Every trick he's learned in the three lives he's lived will be applied to the same problem: the finality problem.

Though it could not possibly have known or intended it, the demon has given humanity exactly what it most fears: one lonely human mind, capable of destroying our world.

THE ADVENTURE OF BLACK PETER BLACKGUARD MCNOTVERYNICE

I CANNOT, IN ANY HONESTY, CLAIM I WAS ASLEEP.

Then again, the deplorable state in which my mind languished can in no way be compared to wakefulness. I hovered in that silken twilight I'd come to love so well as the seven percent solution suffused my blood. Each beat of my enfeebled heart sent a new rush of wonder against my senses, like waves lapping some unseen midnight shore.

I was sure I heard the crying of birds and the whish of fleshy wings in the darkness above my head. But no, I came to realize. Not birds. Dinosaurs. With long beaks in conic heads, screeching with avian stupidity from one to another. It made me want to laugh. Instead I drifted off to something like sleep again.

I heard a friendly voice say, "Well, go on then. Let's see if you can do it. Transfix the pig," followed by a grunt and a thump, a cry of dismay and a burst of laughter. Several more thunks and thumps and outcries followed, I think. I can't be sure, because I was distracted by six phantoms of smoky light who were trying to tell me their secrets. Only, they had no voices. The dead seldom do. Yet I could not help but be moved by the strange earnestness with which they leaned towards me and failed to make themselves heard.

"It is impossible," moaned a gloomy voice. "That is solid brick. It is not reasonable to transfix a pig in such a manner."

"Ha!" a hearty voice replied. "Torg can do it! Grrrrrah!"

There was a sudden crash, so violent I would swear it made my bed jump off the floor for a second.

"Well done!" the friendly voice cried. "I say, you've transfixed the hell out of it!"

This was followed by a roar of triumph and a series of other thumps, each more violent than the last. My bed bumped and skipped this way and that. Judging by the supportive cheers, each thump must have signified a successful transfixation. Transfixion? Transfixment? I could not bring the proper term to mind. I didn't care.

There was this ancient queen, you see, and I *think* she wanted to kiss me. But whenever she leaned towards me, we drifted apart faster than we came together. Through the diaphanous haze of my dreaming, I could hear that the miserable voice was disappointed it hadn't managed a successful transfiction yet.

"Try another wall, Lestrade," the friendly voice suggested. "Only the front one is brick. The inner ones should be easier, eh? Let's start you off small and work up to the challenge. Here…"

I had the impression that the owner of the miserable voice did not crave lesser successes and did not care to be pandered to. Nevertheless, he must have agreed to make an attempt, for the next thump was accompanied by the squeal of nails pulling free from the wall above me, the crackle of splintering wood and a sudden deluge of shattered plaster. I opened my eyes just in time to see two feet of blood-slicked steel slide through the wall above my head. Sudden, unwelcome sobriety intruded itself into my mind—a fact I chose to protest in the only manner available to me.

"Aaaaaaaaaaiiiiiiieeeeeeee-aaaaagh!"

"Ha! Sounds like Watson's up," noted Holmes, from the other side of the wall.

"Well…" said the ponderous yet thoughtful voice of Torg Grogsson. "*Maybe*…"

"By the gods! I hadn't thought of that!"

A few moments of silence followed, then tentative footsteps could be heard in the corridor. My door creaked open and Holmes peered in, gave a sigh of relief and announced, "No, it's all right! It's gone through straight above him. Good morning, Watson! Sleep well?"

"Not particularly. What the deuce is this, Holmes?"

"Harpoon," he replied, matter-of-factly.

"And why have I been nigh-on murdered with it?"

"Don't be dramatic, Watson. That was never our intent. This is merely an experiment to assist Grogsson and Lestrade in the solution of a case. We're transfixing piggies! All very scientific, you know. All very deduction-based. If you take a moment to reflect on it, I'm sure you'll want to offer your congratulations on how clever we're being."

I was less sure. Wriggling out from under the shaft of Holmes's wall-piercing weaponry, I threw on my slippers

A successful transfixation.

and bustled down the corridor to see what my friends had done to my sitting room.

I was not well pleased.

The bloody carcasses of two pigs hung pinned to the front wall by a pair of ancient harpoons. The act had clearly been carried out more than twice, however, judging by the series of jagged holes that looked down onto Baker Street. It seemed that not only was Torg Grogsson capable of powering a pig-laden spear through a solid brick wall, he was also capable of pulling it out again and repeating the process—partly to demonstrate that such an act was possible and partly because it was the single most fun thing he'd ever been asked to do in the pursuit of police work. A third pig hung from a still-quivering harpoon against one of the interior walls, next to the somewhat sheepish-looking Inspector Lestrade.

"Ah…" he said. "Yes… well… Good morning, Watson."

"Really? *Is it?*"

He shrugged. "Compared to some people's. For example, you're having a much better morning than Captain Peter Carey."

"True, Lestrade, very true," said Holmes. "Of course, Watson was only six inches away from having a somewhat similar one. Still, a miss is as good as a mile, eh? Now that you're up, you should join us, Watson. Hurry now! Get dressed! We're off to Woodman's Lee!"

"Where is that?" I inquired.

"Near Forest Row, out in Sussex."

"And why are we going?"

"New case," said Grogsson.

"An *exciting* new case," Holmes agreed. "Now, while Watson's getting ready… is anybody in the mood for bacon?"

We drove out to the house of Peter Carey, but did not go inside. Apparently, the man himself had rarely done so either. Though it appeared comfortable, Carey had preferred to spend most of his time in a small brick shed he'd built for himself. He called it "the cabin" and had decorated it in nautical style. It was towards this small building that we directed our steps.

My first impression of Captain Peter Carey was not a favorable one. I swung open the door to his shed to find him staring directly at me with an expression of perfect rage, as if he'd like nothing better than to pick me up and hurl me across the lawn. Not that he was going to. He was, after all, stone dead. He'd been impaled through the chest by a ten-foot whaling harpoon and pinned to the wall behind him. His feet dangled just a few inches above the floor.

Incredulous, I ducked under the harpoon and went up on my tiptoes to examine him. In life, he'd been an utter brute; that much was clear. He was a man of prodigious size and, though he had a large paunch, his physical strength must have been profound. Nor did he look like he was unaccustomed to employing it. His teeth were bared in a furious grimace, which—even in death—seemed to imply he was about to lunge forward and grab you. He had wiry black hair, shot with gray at the sides. He was one of those people who made one eyebrow do the work of two; a thick, bushy line of black hair shaded both eyes and did little to dispel his thuggish air. He wore leather boots, a Greek fisherman's hat, a sailor's sweater and tough canvas trousers.

Vladislav Lestrade stepped forward to make the introductions. "Dr. Watson, meet Peter Carey, ex-captain of the steam sealer *Sea Unicorn*, better known in the sea-going community as Black Peter. To those who know him well, he was Black Peter Blackguard. To those who were forced to endure his company on a daily basis, he was Black Peter Blackguard McNotVeryNice."

"Ah," I said. "So, his character was…"

"About what you'd expect from looking at him," Lestrade confirmed. "As a captain, his reputation was that of an utter tyrant. His tempers were famous, especially when he'd been drinking, which seems to be…"

Here Lestrade paused to indicate the table just before the corpse. It was still set for two. Or… no, let me say, there were two *glasses*. Between them stood so much liquor, it might be fair to say the table had been set for twenty. Only a bottle of cheap rum had been opened, lending the room a stink of sickly-sweet inebriant, which mingled with the smell of recent death. On the side of the table farthest from Black Peter, a half-wrapped parcel lay upon a battered ledger. Amongst the many bottles I spotted a cutlass, a flensing knife, a gaff hook and a heavy belaying pin. Here were half a dozen tools for nautical-themed murder, interspersed with enough liquid inspiration to virtually ensure it.

"…most of the time," Lestrade concluded.

"It's a wonder anybody would sail with him," I remarked.

"Well he wasn't all bad," Holmes chirped. Grogsson, Lestrade and I turned dubious glances at him. "I only mean he had a reputation for success," Holmes sniffed. "If a man of the sea found himself in need of coin, he could do a fair deal worse than signing on for a berth with Black Peter Blackguard McNotVeryNice. Was he a bit hot tempered? Yes! Did he often return to shore with a few mysteriously empty bunks aboard his ship? Of course. But he always turned a profit. Whether whale or seal, he always knew which hunt would fetch the best market price and he always came back with his hold full. His command was absolute. Not only was he capable of inspiring fear in others, he was utterly devoid of it himself. On his very first voyage as captain, he became famous for an encounter off the frigid coast of Greenland. It seems a killer whale was trying to knock a clutch of seals off an ice floe, but Black Peter wanted the seals for himself. He grabbed a harpoon, dived into the water, speared the whale straight through the head and then punched it in the face until it died."

"Preposterous," I declared.

Holmes cleared his throat politely, then indicated the wall just behind me. Turning, I beheld a huge orca skull, mounted on a plaque with a weathered harpoon driven through its left temple, then out through the right. Plus, one broken cheekbone.

"*Oh!*"

"I don't blame you for doubting the tale, Watson," Holmes confided. "Yet apparently anybody who sailed with

Black Peter Blackguard McNotVeryNice came to regard such occurrences as commonplace. It is possible to respect a person and yet to revile him. Almost everybody did, it seems."

"Which presents us with our first difficulty in solving his murder," said Lestrade. "A wide field of suspects. It seems everyone who met him wished him ill."

"Perhaps not *everyone*. Let us not give in to hyperbole," I suggested.

Lestrade raised his eyebrows at me, then turned to Grogsson and said, "Torg, why don't you read Dr. Watson the statement you took from Mr. Carey's daughter?"

Grogsson produced his battered notebook and read, in a halting monotone, "He was a bastard and a crook. I am glad he's dead. I wish I killed him. I wish I speared him. Would it be all right if I speared his body? Like, maybe in the face?"

"Little Ophelia turns eight next month," Lestrade informed me. "She likes ponies and tea parties."

"Very well, I concede the point," I said. "Nevertheless, it seems unlikely she is our prime suspect. Unless little Ophelia has unusually developed musculature, I find it unlikely she is the one who drove this harpoon through not only her father, but the brick wall behind him."

"Ah! Therein lies our second difficulty," Lestrade agreed. "Though there seem to be a wealth of people who *would* have killed Black Peter, there is a distinct shortage of people who *could* have. Not like this, anyway. The funny thing is that if any of his acquaintances were asked who might be capable of such a thing, Black Peter himself is the one they would name."

But Holmes shook his head. "I don't know, though... It just doesn't *seem* like a suicide."

"I should think not," I said. "I suppose this explains your little porcine-transfixion experiment this morning. I gather Grogsson was the only one with the physical strength to pull it off."

"And there you begin to hint at our third difficulty," said Lestrade. "This case is neither mine nor Grogsson's. It has been assigned to our colleague, Inspector Stanley Hopkins."

"I don't believe I've heard of him," I said.

"Nor would you, if his wife's father had not been a retired chief inspector. Young Hopkins is not well suited to this line of work, I fear. Though he is technically of equal rank to Grogsson and me, he has yet to solve a case."

"A blow to the safety of the average Englishman, surely. Yet I cannot see how this presents any particular difficulty to us."

"Because when Scotland Yard has somebody who cannot perform his duties—and whom they cannot fire—they assign a mentor to that person," said Lestrade.

"A sound practice, I would say."

"They assigned Inspector Lanner."

I groaned. The last time we'd dealt with Lanner, he'd been trying to get Grogsson hanged for tearing two men's ears off and boxing them up to give to a pretty girl. Though, in all fairness to Lanner, he'd been absolutely right. Torg had done that. "So now we fear Hopkins has become nothing more than an inexperienced extension of Lanner's will and that Lanner will try to find a way to blame Grogsson for this crime?"

"Well done, Watson!" said Holmes. "You've deduced our third difficulty. It's the worst one."

"It is," Lestrade agreed. "Especially as Grogsson happened to be staying at the Brambletye Hotel, barely two miles from here, at the time of the murder."

I looked over at Grogsson, who shrugged and mumbled, "Had a case there."

"I see," I said. "And did you happen to transfix this particular little piggy?"

"No," Grogsson said and blushed with shame. One must not assume that this action belied his words. It absolutely confirmed them. Torg Grogsson never lied. Then again, he had a particular love of battle and feats of strength. For him to realize he'd been idle, less than two miles down the road, while someone else was up here being more Grogsson-like than Grogsson himself must have been galling indeed.

"So though there is no direct link between Grogsson and this murder, circumstance is our enemy," said Lestrade. "There may be no other man in Sussex who is even physically capable of this crime. Also, Peter Carey was known for bringing out the worst in people. Anyone who spent five minutes in his company might have been moved to make an attempt on his life and Grogsson—as we all know—is famous for his temper."

"Hey!" the hulking detective protested. "Talk nice or Torg will kill you!"

"And there is a witness," said Lestrade. "A stonemason named Slater was walking down the lane last night. He says he heard raised voices—though they sounded merry—and saw the silhouette of two very large men in the window."

"Yes but that could have been anybody," Holmes scoffed. "Or anybody *large*, anyway."

"Not in Lanner's eyes, I would think," I said. "And, by extension, not in Hopkins's. I think it best if we could solve this one quickly."

Shaking the last of the mystic cobwebs from my mind, I began my investigation. Of particular interest to me on Black Peter's table were the partly unwrapped parcel and the ledger it lay upon. As they were at the opposite end of the table from Black Peter's corpse and the book was turned away from him, I judged it was most likely they belonged to the other man who'd been present. Yet the first item gave me reason to doubt that supposition.

Within the parcel lay a sealskin tobacco pouch, emblazoned with the initials "P.C." It was filled with fresh tobacco and tied up with its pull-cord. It seemed new, the skin being lately tanned with no signs of wear.

"So," Holmes reasoned. "Whoever sat at this side of the table was in the process of opening a gift for the man tacked to the wall, eh?"

"Unlikely," said Lestrade and I together.

"But it's new. And it has Peter Carey's initials on it."

Holmes was right—though those facts baffled me, they could not be disputed.

The second item—the ledger—proved more promising. According to the inscription, it had once belonged to John Hopley Neligan, and it contained a long list of negotiable financial securities. Each entry had space to record the sale of the security in question, but these were all blank. Nevertheless, several of the entries had checkmarks by them. The ledger drew a worried expression from Lestrade, who paced the floor looking vexed and confused for a few moments. Suddenly he snapped his fingers and cried, "Dawson and Neligan!"

"Eh?" said the rest of us.

"Dawson and Neligan! Don't you remember? They were West Country bankers. They failed for a million and ruined the fortunes of many of the great families of the region. Neligan left for Norway with a number of valuable securities, but he never arrived. Of course, the bank could not withstand the loss and it went under. A few of the securities have come back through the London market over the last few years, but Neligan has never been caught."

"Well, here's his ledger, anyway," said Holmes.

Yet the true prize was still to come. On one of the shelves in Black Peter's cabin we found a battered tin box, with the initials J.H.N. upon the lid. Though it had once been locked, the latch had since been forced. Inside lay a pile of stocks that must have been worth hundreds of thousands. Sure enough, they exactly matched the unchecked entries in Neligan's ledger. Those securities with checkmarks beside them were missing. My companions swelled with triumph at what we'd found, but I will confess I had a certain gnawing discomfort at what we *hadn't*.

No pipe. No ash. No lingering scent to tell us this cabin was the haunt of a man who smoked.

And if the gift was intended to be Peter Carey's new tobacco pouch, there was certainly no sign of his old one.

I even looked at the dead man's teeth. They weren't pretty, but I could not detect the telltale yellowing of tobacco stains, or the notch some fellows have in their teeth from habitually clutching a pipe stem.

Of course, I was the only one to worry of such things. The other three were ecstatic with their find, noisily trading theories as to what it all might mean. So distracted were they that none of us heard the tread of feet on the path outside, until a shrill voice in the doorway declared, "Oh, look, it's Grogsson! Just as Lanner said: the murderer always returns to the scene of the crime!"

Holmes and Grogsson gave little cries of surprise. Lestrade snarled, turned towards the doorway and said, "No they don't, Hopkins. That is a myth."

There in the doorway stood an exceedingly wiry young man. He looked as if he might weigh no more than a hundred pounds. His hair was black and straight-cut, exactly as per regulations, and he had a well-groomed black moustache that I could already tell he must be fiercely proud of. He began feverishly scribbling in a notebook: *Ah-ha! Found Detective Grogsson at the scene of the crime! A clue? Seems highly indicative!*

"If it's clues you want," said Lestrade, with a close-lipped scowl, "there are plenty of real ones. I wonder, Inspector Hopkins, have you heard of Dawson and Neligan?"

"Dawson and Neligan? What's that?" Hopkins wondered.

"In this case, a motive," said Lestrade, and began

explaining what we had discovered. I found myself impressed by the earnest interest the young detective displayed as he leaned in to learn from the seasoned veteran. True, Hopkins could likely be used as a tool to discredit, perhaps even to cause the execution of Grogsson, but he seemed also to be possessed of a curious and eager personality. He was an honest-seeming fellow, and diligent. Also to his credit, he was the first to realize that if John Hopley Neligan had been making his way to Norway by sea, he must surely have found himself in waters frequented by Peter Carey's *Sea Unicorn*.

"Yes! Of course!" cried Lestrade, so loudly that he nearly showed his teeth.

Lestrade and his new nemesis-in-training spent the rest of the day working together, with Grogsson following them about. The only other clue of worth at the cabin was the lock to the door, which was scratched all over, as if somebody had been trying to force it. Hopkins thought Carey himself might have done the damage—being as famously powerful as he was famously drunk. Yet it seemed too extensive to be accidental and likely resulted from an attempt to force the door. But why so *much* damage? The lock was so cheap it could have been forced with almost anything. I tried it myself with a stick and had no trouble.

Next, we interviewed Peter Carey's widow and daughter, neither of whom seemed overly concerned at being bereft of his company. Indeed, his wife appeared fiercely proud of the fact that he'd been murdered. She declared that whatever hand had ended Black Peter's life was surely the hand of a friend. I was tempted to ask why she'd remained married to him so long if these were her feelings, yet something about her eyes stopped me. They were sunken with long wariness and the stress of misuse. One glance was enough to tell that she considered herself less married to Peter Carey than trapped with him.

As for little Ophelia, she was mostly just curious to know if there were any life insurance payments forthcoming and whether there might be sufficient surplus to furnish her with a pony.

Our trio of detective inspectors then searched the house to see if any more clues might be gleaned, or even information on how Peter Carey had lived when he… you know… *lived*. This left Holmes free to pursue his new hobby—staring queerly at me and pursing his lips. I'd caught him at it several times that day already. As we were now alone, I had the opportunity to hiss, "What are you doing, Warlock?"

"I was just wondering… are you quite well, John?"

"I… What? Me?" My hand flew instinctively to my arm, to cover the multitude of black and blue needle marks. Of course, the touch of fabric reminded me that I owned sleeves and had already tasked them to that purpose. Relieved but guilty, I stammered, "No, I am… I'm quite well."

"Are you sure? Because you're looking a bit green about the gills, if you don't mind my saying. I mean, I expected you'd be less than your best after two weeks flat on your back, knocked out by poison lipstick. But that was weeks ago, Watson. I thought you'd look better by now. So why do you look worse?"

How hard it is for me to describe the dread his words engendered. Of course, it had not escaped my notice that the seven percent solution was destroying my body. I could feel how poisonous my blood was becoming to me. I seemed to spend a good portion of every morning vomiting some of it up.

"Well… perhaps I still have that cold, you know?"

"And what about all this doom you've got?" Holmes continued. "True, you were rather rife with it when we faced Miss Adler. But then instead of killing you—which would have been the easiest thing—she kissed you into a coma and buggered off to America. Quite charitable, I thought. Now, common sense would seem to dictate you'd be significantly less doomed with her gone, and I'll swear you *were*. So why are you so very doomed now, John? You haven't been doing anything doomy while I wasn't looking, have you?"

"I don't know… um…"

"You've got to be careful, Watson. Promise me you'll be *careful*."

"Yes. Fine. I'll be careful. Look, can we talk about Inspector Hopkins?"

"Why? Is he dooming you?"

"No, but Inspector Lanner clearly intends to use him to doom Grogsson."

"Yes but Hopkins seems like such a fine fellow, don't you think? Take it from me, he'll go far in the force."

"I'm not so sure of that, Holmes," I said. "Remember, he has yet to solve a single case."

"Ha! A formality," Holmes declared. "Why, I'd say his

investigative prowess is every bit the equal of my own!"

"Yes… I'm not going to comment on that," I decided. "What I *am* going to suggest is that if we could hand him his first victory, he might prove more friendly to our cause, mightn't he? Look at him hanging upon Lestrade's every word. I think his loyalty might easily be turned."

"So be it!" said Holmes. "Inspector Stanley Hopkins shall remain one of our company until we help him to solve his first case!"

Just the tiniest bit of green fire lit in Holmes's eye.

"Holmes… you didn't just cast a spell, did you?"

"Did I? I don't think so, Watson."

"It's just there was this little… pop…"

"Oh, I shouldn't worry about that. Come on, Watson, let's see what the others are up to, eh?"

Very nearly nothing. It seemed Scotland Yard had exhausted the available clues. They puttered about for a while longer, but to little effect. Once or twice I caught Holmes twiddling his fingers at Hopkins or me, although he always stopped as soon as he realized I'd seen it. I'd have asked him what he was doing, if I had not feared the conversation might veer towards what I'd been doing with Holmes's irreplaceable slipperful of shredded sorcerer. After half an hour of fruitless searching, Lestrade suggested we head home for the night and hope the case might develop further.

Which it did—rather sooner than any of us expected.

As we left the Carey home, we saw a man standing in the lane, periodically engrossed in a newspaper. That is to say, when he thought himself unobserved, he would gaze nervously at us or hungrily at the door to Black Peter's cabin. Yet the instant any of us turned to look at him, he whipped the newspaper up in front of his face, as if it was no strange thing to wander out onto a country lane, half a mile from anywhere, to read your daily papers in the failing light. He was even thinner than Hopkins and sweated with such alacrity that his newspaper was getting soggy where he gripped it. Lestrade gave Hopkins a meaningful glance, then marched straight up to the stranger.

"Hello there," said Lestrade.

"Um… yes… good morning," the man replied.

"*Evening*," said Lestrade.

"Oh. Yes. That. Good evening." He turned his back to us, raised his newspaper and thrust his nose right against it, folding it back as far as he could, in an attempt to shield himself from our gaze.

"Riiiiiiiiight," said Lestrade. "Well, I think we're done here. Don't you, gentlemen?"

"But shouldn't we…?" Hopkins wondered, indicating the stranger with a finger.

"No. There is no point," Lestrade assured him and guided Hopkins away down the lane, in the direction of the village and the train station. Forty yards along, Hopkins leaned towards Lestrade and hissed, "Didn't he seem a bit… suspicious?"

"Oh, more than a bit, but I want him to think we're gone. Once we're around that bend in the road, let's get into the woods. We'll come up behind Black Peter's cabin. Clearly, that's where our man is heading. I think he may be waiting for darkness so we've less than twenty minutes."

If there was one thing you could count on, it was Inspector Vladislav Lestrade's uncanny certitude regarding when the sun was due to rise or set.

Thus it was that we made our way around one bend, through the woods, and right up behind the worst thief I'd ever encountered. We stood half concealed, some fifteen feet behind him as he struggled and grunted with Black Peter's feeble lock. He must have scratched at it for five or ten minutes with his little silver penknife before it finally opened. His cry of triumph was quickly followed by a scream of terror, when he beheld the impaled body of Peter Carey.

"We should probably take that down," Holmes reflected.

As soon as he mastered himself, the thief began casting about inside the cabin until—with a second triumphant cry— he came across the box. He tore it open, beheld the securities within and gave his third, and loudest, cry of triumph.

"Theefs shoon't yell so much," said Grogsson.

"True," I agreed. "Yet there he is, with the evidence in hand. Shall we? As the case is Hopkins's I think it would only be proper to allow him to make the arrest."

Stepping from our feeble concealment, we walked to the door of Black Peter's cabin, whereupon Inspector Hopkins declared, "Sir, I place you under arrest for the murder of Peter Carey."

The intruder gave a squeal and turned to run. He made it around Hopkins, but effected no more than two steps across the threshold before Grogsson caught him by the collar and hoisted him, shrieking, into the air. His skinny little legs continued to pump furiously—though none too effectively—as the disgusted detective marched him back inside. Grogsson threw the prisoner down in one of the chairs, hard enough to knock the wind out of him, and demanded, "Who you?"

"Just a moment, Grogsson!" Hopkins interjected. "Let me first caution this young man that anything he says to us is admissible testimony and may be referenced in court!"

"Whutever," said Grogsson, rolling his eyes. "Now… who you?"

The young thief stared up, visibly terrified by the array of official-looking faces looking sternly down at him. With one quivering finger, he pointed at the ledger.

"You are John Hopley Neligan?" Hopkins wondered.

"Junior," our prisoner replied.

"Ah-ha! Son of the absconding banker!"

This drew a flash of anger from the young man. "No! Never! Papa would do no such thing! I know that's the first thing everybody thinks—and who can blame them, with the sums involved—but you don't know him like I did! Something must have happened to him!"

"He became a thief and his son became a murderer?" Lestrade suggested.

"I tell you, he would never! His reputation is much maligned and I have made it my life's work to uncover the mystery and do right by his creditors!"

"That does not explain how you come to find yourself at Peter Carey's cabin," Lestrade pointed out.

"Simple," replied John Jr. "Father was not without his

friends. As soon as it was reported that one of the missing securities had appeared on the London market, Mother and I heard of it. I spent all my school holidays and much of our remaining money tracking it back to the source. It had been sold by this man, Peter Carey!"

"So you killed him!" Hopkins roared, eager to show he'd been the first to figure out the crime.

"No! No, I wouldn't!" Neligan insisted, then furrowed his brow and muttered, "Or… I *think* I wouldn't, but I never found out. Look I… I may have come here two nights ago and forced open that lock—"

"Which would explain the inexpert scratches we found," I whispered to Holmes.

"—but Mr. Carey was not here. Neither was the box. I came back last night, but I heard two scary voices arguing so I ran away. Only tonight did I learn all my searching has not been in vain! At last, I have the means to repay my father's creditors and clear my family name!"

"Ha! Or maybe you killed Peter Carey last night and, in your passion, forgot to rifle his possessions!" said Hopkins. By God, he did have Lanner's love of premature accusation.

"Are you sure you aren't being a bit hasty, Inspector Hopkins?" I asked.

"*Hasty?*" he scoffed. "He has a motive! He admits he's broken in here before! His father's ledger was found at the scene of the crime! What more evidence could we possibly require?"

"I do see your point," I conceded, "but there are two other factors I would ask you to consider. Firstly, even though Mr. Neligan thought himself unobserved, he cried out in surprise when he saw the corpse of Peter Carey. Do you suppose he murdered the man last night and then forgot he did it?"

Hopkins's indignant glare wavered for an instant, but he maintained his skepticism. "And the second?" he demanded.

"Only this…"

I placed one foot behind the back leg of John Hopley Neligan Jr.'s chair, grasped him by the lapels, and tipped him backwards. He screamed. Once I had him flat on his back, I placed two fingers on the center of his chest and pushed down as hard as I could.

"No! Ouch! What are you doing? Eeeee! Eeeeeeee! Eeeeeeeeeeeeeeeeeeeeeeee!"

He squealed and thrashed, slapping at my wrist, yet, try as he might, he could not free himself from my two-fingered pin.

"It is your contention, Hopkins, that this gentleman forced a harpoon all the way through Peter Carey and the brick wall behind him, in a single blow?"

"Oh…" said Hopkins, turning somewhat red. "I hadn't thought of that."

"Clearly."

"So then, what did happen? Why is he here?"

"It is just possible Mr. Neligan is telling the truth," I said, allowing the man up. "Whatever business he and his father had with Black Peter Carey may indeed prove to be incidental to his murder."

"Well, I can't count on that," Hopkins said, stamping

his foot. "Look, even if he isn't under arrest, John Neligan Jr. is a person of interest in this case and is not to leave town until this matter is resolved!"

"Yah! Dat's right!" said Grogsson, giving Hopkins a congratulatory poke on the shoulder that nearly bowled him off his feet.

"Very prudent," Lestrade added.

Stanley Hopkins colored from the tips of his toes to the roots of his hair. I smiled. Yes indeed, it seemed it would not be hard to win him to our cause if we could bring him his first victory.

"So… erm… what should we do now?" Hopkins wondered.

"Tonight? Very little, I should think," I said. And oh, it was horrible, how tired I felt. "I suggest we return to London. You can investigate further tomorrow."

Before we parted company, I took Lestrade aside and told him, "Keep me abreast of the case, won't you? I've thought of a promising avenue to chase in London. Give me a few days and I think I may be of some service…"

I did not inject myself with Xantharaxes that night. My body needed time to heal. And yet it frustrated me deeply to miss a night of dreaming. I'd learned so *much*! The secret magics that underlay our familiar physics, the thoughts and hopes of demons, cows, grass, stars and clouds had all been made known to me. By God, it was thrilling! Thus, every night I faced a choice: heal or hurt. Yet, what if I missed the dream I needed? Any night might bring the final piece of the puzzle I needed to move against Adler or Moriarty. It was becoming ever rarer for me to abstain, and ever harder.

At least I was in good shape to be useful the next day. I needed to know how a man might go about setting himself up with a crew for a seal-hunting voyage. I knew a seafaring nation such as Britain must have well-established practices for such things, so I went down to the docks to enquire. Before noon I had my answer: shipping agents. But they had no wish to speak to you unless you were a captain with berths to fill or one of the unfortunate saps who would end up filling one.

Two hours and twelve telegrams later, I'd set myself up in business as Captain Basil, a seasoned and trustworthy old whaler, even if he was a bit fictional. Britain's sea trade is so vast, I feared I would never find the fellow I needed, until a casual word from one of the agents put me on the trail of a man named Sumner, on Ratcliff Highway. It seems he'd worked with Peter Carey several times before and was in a unique position to help me. By the end of business that day, I had things so well in order that I sent a further fan of telegrams, apprising Hopkins, Lestrade and Grogsson of my plans and inviting them to Baker Street on the morrow.

That night I injected myself with some Xantharaxes-infused blood. Sadly, it was a waste, for I sickened and the dream I had was useless; some rubbish about a ship that traveled under the water.

I'd rather have seen Irene.

I awoke weak and nauseous, to find Holmes standing

by my bed with a fistful of telegrams that gave me every expectation of bringing our case to a satisfying conclusion within only a few hours. Grogsson was first to arrive, chewing on an enormous crumpet. Apparently he'd helped save a baker's child from kidnappers some years ago, and the man never failed to have at least one Grogsson-sized baked good available every morning at a very reasonable rate.

Next came Hopkins and Lestrade, together. The former was most confused by my telegram and told me so, as he stepped into our sitting room. "What's this I hear about me cracking the case?" Hopkins asked. "I haven't done anything! I spent yesterday chasing shadows. If John Neligan Jr. didn't do it, then... well... I just don't know!"

"Ah, but what you did do is help me clarify my thoughts," I told him. "When you placed the blame on Neligan, I demonstrated why he could not possibly be our man. This inspired a chain of reasoning that may very well lead us to the killer. It begins like this: how was Peter Carey murdered?"

"With a harpoon. You saw it," said Hopkins.

"And who tends to be very adept in the use of harpoons?"

"Er... harpooners?"

"Exactly. Now, was Black Peter Carey in a position to know many harpooners?"

"Oh! Of course!" Hopkins cried. "He captained a ship that hunted seals and whales!"

I raised a finger and said, "Ah! In fact, you have just touched upon the next important fact. He captained *a* ship. The entirety of his captaincy was spent on one vessel: the

Sea Unicorn. The balance of probability therefore dictates that Black Peter's killer is most likely…"

I paused to let Stanley Hopkins figure it out. In half a blink, he clapped his hand to his brow and cried, "A harpooner who worked with him on the *Sea Unicorn*!"

"There, you see?" said Lestrade, laying a hand on the young man's shoulder. "You *did* figure it out. When Lanner asks what your line of reasoning was, you must tell him exactly that."

"But, no! I didn't solve anything; Dr. Watson did," Hopkins spluttered.

"It doesn't matter," Lestrade said, in his most soothing tone. "Holmes and Watson do not want credit. If ever they should be of use to you in a case, the kindest thing you can do is to claim you thought it all out by yourself."

"But that's not right!" Hopkins protested.

"Oh, I'm sure you'll solve many cases on your own," I told him. "But Lestrade is correct. Anonymity is all we crave. Holmes, what do we say about anonymity?"

"Sweet, sweet anonymity: it's better than strawberry jam!"

"Just so. Now let me tell you what I did next, Hopkins, and why I've asked you here. As Black Peter has quite the reputation in seagoing circles, it is reasonable to expect news of his death to be the talk of that community. I therefore presented myself as the first vulture to pick his corpse. I contacted several shipping agents and told them my name was Captain Basil. I was a whaler myself and had often been jealous that Peter Carey always came home with such a fine catch and a huge profit. The reason for this, I was sure, was the excellence of his crew. I was therefore willing to pay high wages to any of his former men and, of course, high commissions to any agent who could send them my way. Mr. Sumner is confident that he can produce at least three of Carey's former harpooners to speak to me today, and they are coming at nine, ten, and eleven. Now, I do not say this will definitely provide us with his killer, but it's the best trap I've been able to devise."

"Brilliant!" Hopkins crowed.

"Let us hope so."

Promptly at nine, Mrs. Hudson ushered up the first arrival, banged her bony little fist against our door and trilled, "Got a salt-smellin' seal murderer out here, what wishes to talk to sum'un named Captain Basil! That one o' your aliases, Warlock?"

Clearly, my landlady was going to need some coaching on the finer points of the morning's deception. Indeed, if that first visitor had been Peter Carey's killer, she might have blown the whole show.

He wasn't. What he was, was a grizzled old man of the sea with half a face. Apparently there had been an ill-advised wager one night, involving rather a lot of rum and a disagreement over whether a grown man could swing three times around the starboard hoist, with one foot in a shark-sized fishhook.

The answer: two and a half.

His name was James Lancaster, though, so he was of little interest to me. We told him the berth had been filled, gave him half a sovereign for his trouble and took his name and information "in case something should open up". In truth, we wanted to know where to find him if my guess as to the murderer's identity should prove false.

Speaking of murderers: the second applicant almost certainly was one. His name was Hugh Pattins and he didn't want to say exactly why, but if we could have him on board a ship and off English soil before the day was out, that would suit him just fine. The only thing to foul him as a suspect was this: he was the only person on earth who had both known Peter Carey and also liked him. It seems the two men had seen eye-to-eye on the subject of whether it was appropriate to spear a man in the face while he slept for saying something mean about you. Having just lost his sole supporter on this point, Hugh Pattins was shocked and saddened to hear Carey had been taken from this earth. We gave him his half-sovereign, took his information and sent him on his way.

Hardly twenty minutes after we'd seen him off, there was a kick at the door and Mrs. Hudson called, "Got another 'un out here to talk to *Captain Basil*! Wink, wink!"

Well, I can't say she wasn't improving.

The third harpooner was... most interesting. To start with, he was huge—not quite Grogsson-sized, but not far from it. He was blubberous, as if it were only his clothes that gave him human shape. Yet despite the jiggly blobbiness of him, he moved with obvious strength. He had close-cropped graying hair and a beard to match. His nose was bulbous, his eyes dark and close-set. He looked about the room nervously and twisted a battered fisherman's cap in both hands as he greeted us.

"Good mornin', sirs. I'm… er… here about the berth?"

"Have you your papers?" I asked, trying to keep my surprise at his appearance from creeping into my voice.

"Yes, sirs."

He withdrew a wrinkled sheaf from his belt and threw it upon our sitting-room table. My eyebrows rose.

"Your name is Patrick Cairns?"

"Yes, sir."

"Then I believe you are exactly the fellow we want." I took a good step back and added, "Grogsson, get him."

In a blur, the hulking detective was past me, with his hand on his man. Which, if Patrick Cairns had turned out to be an actual *man*, would likely have been the end of things. Instead he gave a pinnipedial bellow and fetched Grogsson a backhanded smack that rattled our windows. Grogsson responded with a quick jab under the ribs that I'm sure would have knocked the wind out of a buffalo or two, but Cairns—to everyone's amazement—remained on his feet. The two of them set to in earnest while Holmes, Lestrade, Hopkins and I leapt and darted about the room in a generalized effort not to be crushed to death by nine hundred pounds of quarreling bully. When they hit the wall near our little writing desk, Cairns swept up a marble ink-blotter and flung it. Grogsson ducked it easily, leaving it free to careen across the room towards my face.

Time seemed to slow, almost to a stop. I could see the ink-dappled face of the blotter as it neared. *That needs a clean,* I remember thinking. Yet, at the same time I knew: I would have no such chance. I'd never clean anything ever again. Here was finality. Here was the end of me, flying towards my face.

Funny... I always thought the reaper would use a scythe.

And then, at the last minute... it just... *didn't*. An almost imperceptible bending of the space within the room—or of fate—carried it just past my head. I remember the sudden sting as it nicked my left ear, then whistled past me across the room.

And smacked Stanley Hopkins straight in the face. It struck him right between the eyes and sent him reeling back against the wall where he collapsed, insensible.

With a grunt of rage, Grogsson seized Cairns by the scruff of his neck and thrust his face against the corner of our mantelpiece, shattering it. Between that and the piggy-transfixings, Grogsson was running up a daunting repair bill for Holmes and me.

"Ork! Ork!" howled Cairns, in a none-too-human-sounding cry of protest. Yet the fight had gone out of him, and he collapsed to the floor. In a second, the rest of us were on him. We got his hands behind his back and snapped Lestrade's cuffs around his wrists. Then, because it was laughable to think that might hold him, we got Grogsson's on there as well.

Then Holmes's.

Then Hopkins's.

At last, satisfied he wouldn't break free, we all heaved a mutual sigh of relief. "Let's get him flipped over and see what we've got, eh?" Holmes suggested.

"I don't think he's quite human," Lestrade opined.

Grogsson nodded and rubbed at the massive red mark on the side of his face where Cairns had slapped him. "Not reg'lar," he agreed.

"I don't suppose he is…" Holmes mused and began a close examination of the old sealskin coat Cairns had tied around his waist. Holmes unwrapped the sleeves and pulled it free. As he held it up, I realized it was less well finished than I had originally thought. Less of a sealskin coat and more of a… well… just a skin.

Behind Holmes, Cairns stirred, saw what Holmes was holding and gave a frantic, "Ork! Ork! No, please! That's mine! Give it back!"

"And what if I don't?" Warlock wondered. "Would you be bound to my will for eighteen years? Could I even force you to marry me?"

All the color drained from Patrick Cairns's face. He looked quite aghast.

"Gentlemen, I think what we're dealing with, here," said Holmes, tapping his lips thoughtfully with one finger, "is a selkie."

"Eh?" Grogsson grunted.

"Seal folk. Do you mean to tell me you've never heard of them? By the gods, Grogsson, if you're going to keep on being a policeman—and a monster yourself—don't you think you ought to read up on your mythical creatures? A selkie is a shape-shifter. They mostly take the form of a seal, but they can remove their skin and walk about as a man. Any who finds the coat while they're in human form has power over the selkie for eighteen years. Folk tales are full of sailors who force beautiful selkie women to marry them. I strongly suspect Mr. Cairns here to be part seal. Or… judging by the size of him…" Holmes gave the skin he was holding an exploratory sniff. "…Yes. *Sea lion*, I should think."

"Whaaaaaaaaaaaaaaat? That's mad! Do you know how crazy you sound right now?" Cairns asked. Yet, it was clear the man was a better harpooner than liar. His wide, nervous eyes betrayed him. Seeing he'd fooled nobody, he gave one of our chairs a vicious kick and shouted, "Here now, give that back or I'll kill you!"

"Like you killed Peter Carey?" Holmes suggested. "I don't know how Watson figured it out, but the more I see, the more I suspect Black Peter Carey was the last fellow to hold this skin. Am I wrong?"

"It's no business of yours!" Cairns insisted.

"No? But as we've caught you dead to rights—and even more to the point, as I'm holding this coat—why don't we discuss it, eh?"

Patrick Cairns looked as if he wished to protest, or even simply refuse to answer. Yet he could not. After just a moment of shaking—fighting the words that strove to escape—he burst forth with a sudden cacophony of self-incrimination.

"Not *my* coat! In all the years I knew him, Black Peter Carey never managed to get my coat off me. No. It was Juuuhgh-juhyor's!"

"Who?" Holmes wondered.

"You know her as *Mrs*. Peter Carey."

"Oh dear," said Holmes. "Just like in the tales, eh?"

"She was the love of my life! My favorite bride out of all my harem!"

"Your *what*?" I cried, rather taken aback.

Holmes waved me down. "He is a sea lion, Watson. Different folk have different customs. Now, Mr. Cairns, tell me: did it come off as in the tales? Peter Carey found Juuuhgh-juhyor out bathing in her human form and seized her skin?"

"And brought her aboard his ship—naked and dripping—to amuse him!"

"Oh dear. I fear this story has taken a bit of a dark turn," Holmes reflected. "I mean, I expected a certain amount of *murder*, but this is quite another thing entirely."

"I followed them all the way back to London," Cairns continued. "I took off my skin and walked the land. I found Carey and begged him to return Juuuhgh-juhyor to me. I won't lie. I won't say I didn't threaten his life, but he said he'd hidden the skin where I'd never find it—that Juuuhgh-juhyor would never return to the sea if I didn't do as he said."

"So you obeyed him? For eighteen years?"

"I had to! Would you trust a man like Peter Carey? Even when the time was up and the spell was broken, what would he do? Would he give Juuuhgh-juhyor back her skin and let her return to me, or would he keep it hidden? He told me he'd only give the skin back if I served him. So, I did. I went aboard the *Sea Unicorn* and took up that hated harpoon. For eighteen years I betrayed my kind; I led that bastard against the seals and the whales, and made sure his ship was stuffed with my bloody kin. It was I who really paid for that grand house where he kept my love a prisoner! Where he kept the daughter that should have been mine!"

"Yep…" Holmes reflected. "Bit of a dark turn, indeed."

"Now the eighteen years is set to end in less than a week," said Cairns, "but there was a dark edge to my hope. I feared Peter Carey would not be true to his word. As a mystic creature, I had no power to go back on my promises. But he did. And wouldn't he? He was a blackguard if ever there was one, with a soul rotted by drink. Yet, I hadn't spent eighteen years in his damned company without learning a thing or two. See, I remember a night about eleven years back… We'd come across a yacht in storm-tossed seas earlier that day. The crew had abandoned her, for there were only one soul left."

"John Hopley Neligan?" I hazarded.

"That's right. An' the captain took him on board. One old box and a tattered ledger—that's all Neligan had. Now, I don't know all your human ways, but I think the papers in that box were worth a fair amount."

"Indeed they were," I said.

"And Captain Carey knew it," said Cairns, with a grim nod. "Being a creature of the sea, I don't mind a storm as much as most. I like to take the air, even when it's blowin'. So I was out on the deck that night, when John Neligan come to the rail, lookin' somewhat green. There he was, lettin' his dinner out into the sea, when Peter Carey come up behind and tipped up his heels. Over he went, into that black water, and nothing ever got said about that box and that ledger. Then again, if Black Pete had somethin' to hold over my and Juuuhgh-juhyor's heads, maybe we had somethin' to hold over his!"

"Ah," I said. "And that's what you were doing in the cabin, the night of his death. You were negotiating your continued silence for the return of your mutual wife's seal skin?"

Cairns nodded. "He were pretty well along with drink when I showed up. And he had a lot of weapons within easy reach. I didn't mind. I knew if he came at me, I could kill him pretty quick. But then, could I find the skin? That's the only thing that worried me. He sat me down, poured me a glass of rum, talked about old times. Then... then he said he had a gift for me..."

"Which an uninformed investigator might have thought was a gift for *him*," I interjected. "And that is why I set Grogsson on you the moment I learned your name. After all, it only made sense for that gift to be from Peter Carey if he happened to be presenting it to someone with the *same initials*. It seemed unlikely that Carey—a non-smoker—had been given a brand-new tobacco pouch made of..."

"...made of...

"*Oh*."

Holmes gave a sympathetic little cluck. "I do remember thinking Mrs. Carey seemed to be a rather put-upon sort of person. But I'll admit, I hadn't recognized the extent of it."

"And now she can never come back to the sea!" said Patrick Cairns, and burst into tears. The four of us stood for a few moments, watching this confessed murderer— oh, how I hope the reader will forgive the term—*blubbering* in the middle of our floor.

"All right," said Holmes after a time. "Raise your hand, everybody who thinks Peter Carey was a right bastard and anybody who's willing to cut up his imprisoned bride's seal-skin so she can never return to the seal-life and seal-husband she loves, then presents a tobacco pouch made of that same skin to the seal-husband just to gloat about it, deserves anything he gets."

Four hands went up.

"Now, raise your hands if you think Mr. Cairns should be punished for what he did."

No hands.

"Very well, it's unanimous," said Holmes. "Of course, we're still going to have to turn you in. Hopkins needs credit for solving this case and Scotland Yard needs someone other than Grogsson to blame. We're going to have to see justice is done."

Patrick Cairns howled, "I don't care what happens to me, now that—"

"I said 'justice' not 'a hanging'," said Holmes. "I don't think this will be very hard to put right. Fortunately for us, this entire conversation has occurred while the only non-monster representative of Scotland Yard is conveniently unconscious. Strange how well these things work out, isn't it?"

"Um… I'm not so sure, Holmes," I said.

"Eh?"

"I'm just looking over at Inspector Hopkins now and… does anybody else see him… *breathing*?"

"Really?" asked Holmes, his face a mask of horror.

I knelt down and pressed two fingers to the side of Hopkins's throat. My heart sank. In a hoarse croak, I told my companions, "It's as I feared. This man is dead."

The four of us exchanged horrified glances. Actually the five of us, if one includes Patrick Cairns and—seeing as he'd just been informed he was responsible for the death of a detective inspector of Scotland Yard—one probably should.

"All right," said Holmes, beginning to sweat. "All right, but he's not *very* dead."

"What do you mean?"

"Well, it's not like his head's off!"

"It might as well be, Holmes. The man has no pulse! He isn't breathing!"

"But if he were, he'd be fine, right? I mean, it's not like someone's run a sword through him or anything!"

"Holmes," I said, in my darkest, most warning tone, "you're not thinking of *doing anything* are you?"

"But it's my fault, Watson!"

"How?"

"Well because you were so doomed, two days ago. And I got to thinking about Hopkins who was so fresh-faced and eager and not-at-all-doomed and I thought, 'What if I took just one strand of Watson's soul—the one with all the doom on it—and tied it to Hopkins? That might take a bit of the pressure off Watson, eh?'"

"You bound my soul to Hopkins?"

"Just the doomy part!"

"Holmes, no! Look what you've done!"

"Well it's your fault too, Watson! You promised you'd be careful."

"I was!"

"Oh? Were you? Were you just *super careful* today? Or did you happen to start off a Grogsson fight *in the middle of a crowded room*?"

"Er… well… I um… I did do that, I suppose."

"Well then," said Holmes. "It seems we are all agreed."

There was a flash. And a world-shaking boom. And the sun went out. And the air filled with the voices of a thousand demons, shrieking with triumph.

Hopkins jerked bolt upright and drew a panicked breath.

Lestrade went even paler than usual. "Holmes, no," he said. "Death is final. Death is important."

"Oh, pish-tosh. Not to me."

Cairns, Grogsson, Lestrade and I exchanged worried glances as the sunlight slowly returned through the windows behind us.

"What… what happened to me?" Hopkins asked.

"That depends," said Holmes, brightly. "What do you remember?"

"We interviewed Mrs. Carey and her daughter and then… and then… there were a thousand voices laughing at me as I spun away into an infinite nothing."

"Don't worry about that last part, eh?" Holmes encouraged. "The important thing is: you've solved the crime!"

"Have I?"

"Yes, and we were all *very* impressed. Don't you remember how you reasoned it out?"

"Um… no."

"Well, I'm sure we can remind you…"

It was not difficult to ensure that Inspector Lanner be the one to arrive in Scotland Yard's Black Maria. Indeed, when he heard his protégé was claiming to have solved his first case—and the company in which he had accomplished said feat—it might have been quite the task to stop him. Lanner and two constables listened while Hopkins told all he "remembered" about his pursuit of the case. Lestrade stood by, hanging his head in shame that he had not beaten this promising new detective to the critical deductions. Torg, of course, had been dismissed. His inability to sustain even the most innocent fabrication dictated in no uncertain terms the necessity that he be elsewhere.

We modified the story as little as we could. Clearly, Cairns wished to blackmail Carey with the knowledge that Carey had killed Neligan and absconded with the securities. The fact that the non-smoking Carey was presenting a tobacco pouch to someone with the initials P.C. seemed to make the case against Patrick Cairns fairly inescapable.

Congratulations were in order for catching one murderer, who had slain a second murderer and for clearing the name of an innocent (if somewhat dead) country banker.

The details of Juuuhgh-juhyor's skin and the fact that Patrick Cairns was in some sense her husband and spent half his time wandering about as a sea lion were the only details omitted.

Lanner helped Hopkins load his very first criminal into the back of the big black carriage. A criminal who was wearing—and this was a key detail—only Hopkins's set of handcuffs. And wouldn't that seem fitting? Lestrade, Grogsson and Holmes had all reclaimed theirs and had no intention of informing Lanner that one set was likely to be insufficient. Hopkins might have had some notion of that fact, but he'd been… er… *indisposed* for most of the encounter that proved it.

As they prepared to pull away, Holmes came down to the street to offer his congratulations, and something more. "Here you are, Lanner," he said. "These were the only other items in the prisoner's possession: his sailing papers and his coat."

Lanner took them with a grunt, opened the door of the Maria, and shoved the bundle unceremoniously into the back with his prisoner. The Black Maria trundled off down Baker Street.

Though it was in many ways a success, I have several regrets regarding the adventure of Black Peter Blackguard McNotVeryNice. I regret how thoroughly I had allowed my Xantharaxes habit to overcome my mind, body and will. I regret the loss suffered by Juuuhgh-juhyor, for it is always a tragedy to hear of a creature bereft of its place in the world. I regret the death of Stanley Hopkins, and now—in the unfaltering light of hindsight—I regret his resurrection.

Mostly though, I regret that I was not on hand at Scotland Yard to watch Lanner and Hopkins open the back of that police van to retrieve their prisoner, only to discover a *whacking great sea lion*.

The two detectives were so shocked that the beast managed to barge past them and escape down the lane. All London was on alert for the wayward animal by the time that evening's papers were released, yet strangely, all sightings of the beast seemed to have been limited to within a few streets of Scotland Yard.

One happy occurrence followed these events, at least. Patrick Cairns and the widow Carey realized that—even if she was never able to return to the sea—perhaps the two of them might make a go of it together on land. Though it might be necessary for Cairns to change his name first. Yes and also, he was absolutely not allowed to keep a harem in a country house in Woodman's Lee. The third condition was this: in order for the two reunited lovers to have any chance of happiness whatsoever, the loyalty of a certain member of that household would need to be purchased. Luckily, it was for sale.

At the very reasonable price of one pony.

THE GANG

FROM THE DREAM JOURNAL OF DR. JOHN WATSON

IT MUST HAVE BEEN A HOTEL ROOM ONCE, BUT THE OLD man on the bed has stayed so long it's his room now. He's not looking well. His breaths come in harsh wheezes; his skin is even more papery and frail than it was the last time I saw him. Still, there are enough of his toys scattered about—and enough of Moriarty's too—to quash any doubt. This is Adler, the toymaker.

He's propped up in bed, wearing—somewhat to my surprise—a stethoscope. Though he looks as if he ought to be receiving medical treatment, he seems to be administering it, instead.

To a demon.

The creature has three legs and three arms. His skin is brown and his stature is all wrong. He's shorter than a man, and narrower at the hips and shoulders, and he's... deeper. He runs too far front to back. His eyes shine with a golden light, but he shakes as he moves. His six limbs have no strength.

Herr Adler shakes his head. "It isn't working."

"Impossible. This creature was immortal!" the demon

173

retorts. I recognize him. Not the voice, that is new. But the tone, which is incapable of hiding its own intelligence or its imperiousness.

That is James Moriarty, without a doubt.

"Do you know how long this creature has endured?" Moriarty continues, indicating his borrowed body with one hand. "Its powers of prophecy are sewn deep into human history. The Greeks knew it as the truth that seeped from the fissures in the rock, inhaled by the priestess at Delphi! The Chinese know it as the words of I Ching!"

"Perhaps," says Adler, with a shrug. "But that was before you trapped it here. There is a right way to play with our toys, Mr. Moriarty, and there is a wrong way."

"No! It should have worked! I gave up my body! I blended our souls! Do you understand, Adler? I gave this creature a part of my *self*. I have diluted myself in exchange for—well it should have been at least another thousand years of life. At least!"

Adler shrugs again. "It's dying."

Moriarty opens his mouth to retort. Who knows what he might have said? "So are you," would have been apt. Yet we will never know, for the body he is riding in interrupts him. The eyes shine with sudden light as a voice as deep as the earth rumbles forth.

"Poor is the mind that thinks its wisdom wards off folly. Brothers are they. When one grows great, so too the other. Wise men make the greatest fools. All his life, this one has laid out traps, and now gasps to find his foot in one! *Rache! Rache!* Justice comes upon the wicked!"

And *that* voice, I know. I have several times heard it from the lips of Warlock Holmes, when he was host to James Moriarty. What a strange partnership it must have been. Like a nesting doll. The essence of a prophecy demon, trapped within that of James Moriarty, trapped within Holmes. Until the moment when Irene Adler's bullets and Charles Augustus Milverton's arts had set all free.

Moriarty doesn't tolerate the creature's departure any better than Holmes did. As soon as the voice is gone, he sags forward, just catching himself by bracing two of his arms against the nightstand. In the non-prophetic voice of his new body, he mutters, "Damn."

What is that? A knock at the door? I can hardly tell. The dream is shifting. Yes, I think there is another man here. He's telling Moriarty something, but I can't hear what. Something unwelcome, that much is clear. Moriarty's face is pure rage. Adler rocks forward in his bed and cries, "I knew this would happen to her! I knew it!"

"Careful, Adler! Your heart!" says the demon Moriarty.

"You told me you wouldn't let it happen! You promised!"

"Careful, I said! Calm yourself!"

But it's too late. The old man's face twists. A sweat breaks across his brow.

And the dream shifts.

It must once have been a ballroom in that same hotel. It's a throne room, now. And upon that throne, on a raised dais, sits the demon Moriarty.

Looking rather put out.

Behind him stands Irene Adler. Younger than I've ever seen her, not yet twenty. Her face is bruised and puffy. She looks angry. Hurt, embarrassed, ashamed, but mostly just angry.

Three men drag a prisoner before the demon. I know one of them—Moriarty's short little killer, Sebastian Moran. Moran kicks his prisoner in the back of the leg, to help the other two force him to his knees.

The demon Moriarty issues an annoyed, paternalistic sigh. "Clifford McCloe, I thought I had been quite clear."

The prisoner looks up, but his eyes do not seek Moriarty's. They look for Irene's. There is desperation there, and hurt. There is apology—and I think it's sincere, but it's not enough. A fool can see he's in love with her, and just as clearly, she does not feel the same about him. It's not hard to see what's happened: Clifford McCloe has found himself in one of animal-kind's oldest troubles: unrequited love. And he has elected to deal with the situation in animal-kind's oldest, cruelest, most wrong-handed way. He tried to force himself on her. He nearly managed it, too. If it had been anybody less willful, less able than Irene...

But no. The suffusion of bruises that cover the two of them testify to how poorly Clifford McCloe chose his prey. He gives Moriarty a one-sided smile. "Come on, boss. I made a mistake. How about a little mercy, eh?"

"Why should the master show mercy, when his man shows none?"

"But think about all we done together! Think about

how much more we could do!"

"Oh, I am thinking of it. It is particularly irksome. You, Adler and Moran were my most trusted compatriots. Your foolish actions have cost me two of my three lieutenants, this day!"

The general murmur of confusion and the sudden look of fear that flickers across McCloe's face remind Moriarty that nobody else yet knows what has passed in the toymaker's room. Moriarty leans towards Irene and adds another layer of loss to the worst day of her life.

"It's your grandfather, I fear. He took the news rather poorly."

Shock crosses her features, but only for a moment. The next instant it is chased aside by a look of redoubled fury at Clifford McCloe.

"Don't worry, my child," says the demon Moriarty. "First I shall deal with this one. Then we shall find a way to put things right."

"No," she says, with a firmness nobody else in this room would dare use against the thing in the throne. "I'm leaving."

And there's just a flicker in those otherworldly eyes of Moriarty's. A thing I did not expect to see. *Pain*. In as much as he cares about anything besides himself, this is how he can be hurt. Today, his family—such as it is—has suffered.

He could forbid Irene to go, of course. But he does not. "Very well. Jenkins will give you funds for your travels. And…" He pauses. There's that pain again, deep and raw. "You may take one item from the vault. Do not tell me what it is; I do not wish to know."

Irene Adler licks her swollen lips. She hadn't expected her chance to come this way, but she's damned if she's going to let it slip by. She was supposed to be a daughter to these men of vice. That's what makes McCloe's trespass so vile, even in the eyes of these assembled murderers and thieves. She was the heart of the gang. And that's exactly what she's going to take: The Heart. The next time Moriarty enters that vault, he'll know. And that is the day Irene Adler is going to have to start running.

Actually… no. *Today* is the day she's going to have to start running. She'll need the head start.

Moriarty turns his gaze back to the man who kneels before him. "The creature whose body I inhabit has an irksome love of justice," he says. "Its failures today, as well as your own, have disposed me to *show it some*."

He raises his eyes to McCloe's captors. "Bring him to the workshop. Moran, I think I shall require your assistance. Fetch the Ephronian Cube."

"The cube? That's one of Adler's toys, boss."

"And yet Herr Adler finds himself in no condition to be helpful. Come along, Moran. I'll show you what to do."

And so they go their separate ways. Irene to the vault. Moriarty, Moran and McCloe to the workshop. Moran locks the doors. If any of Moriarty's gang had anything they'd intended to accomplish today, well, it's going to have to wait. They crowd around the workshop doors, listening.

It's a long time before the screaming starts, and it doesn't go on as long as any of them expected. There is silence within, then the sound of muted voices. The doors open. Moran steps out, then locks up again.

"Hey, what's—"

But Moran waves the question aside and walks away.

From within the workshop, more silence. Then the sound of Clifford McCloe's voice. "Hmm, hmmmmm, hmmmmmmmmmm. Mum, mum, mummmmmmmmmm. Now, let's see… The luscious ladies of Lindholm laugh with languid lips. No… not quite… The luscious ladies of Lindholm laugh with languid lips. Well… it will pass."

The door opens again and McCloe steps out. There's hardly a mark on him—just a little smear of blood at the inside corner of each eye. The gang stands, aghast. Finally, one of them thinks to ask, "What'd they do to you, Cliff?"

The bloody eyes turn to him. "That is not my name. There is no such thing as a man named Clifford McCloe. Do you understand?"

"*Boss?*"

But the creature only turns and walks away. In the room behind him is a sad little pile. It looks like a discarded leather suit, with three arms and three legs. As the new Moriarty leaves, he mutters, "Surely most of you must have some work to do, don't you?"

The dream begins to fade. It has only one more gift for me—one more jab at the series of bodies that calls itself Moriarty. He thinks he's bought himself some time. He thinks he has half a human lifetime to calculate his next step.

He's wrong.

That shiny new body of his is about to have Warlock Holmes's black blade lodged through its chest as it falls, spinning and spinning, into the depths of a mineshaft. Moriarty is going to come as close as he ever has to experiencing true mortality. Only a last-second gambit will save him.

He and his greatest nemesis will soon become one body, two souls.

THE ADVENTURE OF
THE RING OF RED FACTION

BANG! BANG! BANG! BANG!

"Oi! Warlock 'olmes!"

Holmes's voice drifted from the confines of his bedroom, across the corridor and through my open door. "Ugh. Mrs. Hudson seems to want something. Get the door, won't you, Watson?"

I gave my arms an experimental flex. No good. I could hardly move them. And Holmes proposed I should rise and walk? All the way to the front door?

Preposterous.

"Er… well… she's asking for *you*, you know."

Bang! Bang! Bang! Bang! Bang!

"Oiiiiiiiiiiiiiiiiiiiiiiiiiiiiiiiiiii!"

"That's true, Watson, but… I'm somewhat indisposed."

Well did I know it. The day before, Holmes had mixed himself up a batch of his special brew. Arsenic, this time, with a side order of strychnine, cyanide and bleach. Then he'd popped open a copy of *The Times* and sat in his favorite chair, sipping and reading, until he was effectively dead. This he would do from time to time to silence the thousands of voices that filled his head at all hours—and indeed, though it wreaked a certain level of havoc upon his physical form, he always seemed much more relaxed afterwards. The habit had horrified me the first time I saw it, but daily life with Holmes had taught me to accept as mundane a thousand peculiarities that I would previously have found incredible.

And in this particular instance, it came with a bonus. Over the past week or so, Holmes had become ever more suspicious of my persistent sickness and my rising level of doom. He'd been watching me carefully. I'm sure it was only his patent lack of observational prowess that kept him from realizing that I'd been injecting myself with bits of his shredded Persian mummy every night.

He wasn't wrong to be concerned, either. The doctor in me knew I had been poisoning myself far beyond the threshold a sane man would tolerate. But any night I did not give myself to the seven percent dream was a night I missed a chance to learn more about James Moriarty and Irene Adler. True, most of the dreams were useless, but any night I chose to forgo my injection was a night I might miss the piece of information that could have saved the world of men. So you see the risk my abstinence might bring?

Thus, as soon as Holmes had slumped over in his chair from obsessive self-poisoning the day before, I had dragged him to his bed and indulged in my intravenous ruination. All of which meant that, as Mrs. Hudson stood outside pounding the varnish from our door, there was little I could do besides croak, "Yes, I know. Sorry to say it, Holmes, but I'm a bit indisposed myself."

Bang! Bang! Bang!

"Oi! Warlock! Get up, y' bastard!"

Holmes gave a resigned sigh. "What's to be done, do you think?"

"Perhaps she might hear you if you shout."

"Oh, I don't know… I'm really not at my best. Do you think you might manage it, Watson?"

"Perhaps we might try it together?"

Bang! Bang!

"Oiiiiiiiiiiiiiiiiiii!"

"I'm sorry, Mrs. Hudson, but we are currently—"

"Go away!"

Bang! Bang! Bang! Bang! Bang!

"I know you boys is in there!"

"Perhaps another time might be more felicitous, Mrs. Hudson!"

"Bugger off!"

This went on for another ten minutes or so, as Holmes's and my voice grew ever weaker. I cannot remember which of us stopped first. I think I slipped into unconsciousness before the other two fell silent, but cannot swear to it. Whoever Mrs. Hudson was trying to introduce to us— and whatever fresh crisis—would have to wait. The two mystic detectives, helpers of London's magical victims, were simply in no state to make themselves useful.

I woke some hours later, refreshed and invigorated…

Well, no. Not really. But *functional*.

As I found myself able to rise, I recognized I probably should. I needed some food. By God, the grocer's seemed impossibly far away. But might the walk not do me some good? That's just what I needed. Good food and fresh air— or at least the closest approximation London could furnish.

As I walked, I began to feel better. Still, my progress was ponderous. Though I had convinced myself this was exactly the therapy that was required, I nonetheless had to stop every few minutes to vomit a great gout of discolored blood into the gutter. I always made a point to raise my hat and apologize to any passers-by; I am a gentleman, after all. It can be difficult to make one's way through London's crowded streets but on that particular day, I found I had all the room I required. Quite by accident, I had discovered a fine method for clearing a path through the gray city's multitudes. Assuming one could tolerate all the screaming, of course.

I had a nice little sit-down in Regent's Park. A few pigeons came up to see if I had any breadcrumbs, but then they'd get a look at me and there'd be this uncomfortable little silence. Then they'd coo some form of apology for having disturbed me and a supposition that the person on the next bench down might be a better place for them to… yes… well… good day to me, and… um… well, good day.

When I finally reached the grocer's, I bought everything that looked good and asked that it be carried to 221B Baker Street, because I *just couldn't possibly*. The man behind the counter looked somewhat wary, but I kept shoveling coins at him until he decided that—despite my appearance— this actually was a good idea. When he turned to shout to his least-favorite shop boy that he had a job for him, I knew everything would be all right. I took a single apple to eat as I went and turned homeward.

By the time I dragged my weary legs up the steps to 221B, I was nearly too tired to speak. This was especially unfortunate, as I could hear the sound of muted conversation from behind my door. Holmes, it seemed, had managed to rouse himself in time to answer Mrs. Hudson's second door-assault. As I let myself in, I saw Holmes slumped on the couch looking set-upon and miserable. To my horror, the guest was a second, equally formidable landlady.

"…so you've got to help me, Mr. Holmes. He's always in there, and he never comes out and I can hear him pacing about and it's driving me mad. Come on, Mr. Holmes! I have nowhere else to turn!"

"Yes, but, Mrs. Warren, I'm a very busy man and this really isn't the sort of thing I usually deal with."

"You'll deal with this, by God!"

Spying me in the doorway, Holmes brightened and slurred, "Watson! Thank heavens. Come and lend a hand won't you? This is Mrs. Warren and she's quite insane."

"Quite *disturbed*, is what I think you mean," said Mrs. Warren, defensively.

"Time will tell," replied Holmes and gestured to the couch beside him.

I staggered over and sat down with a thump. So violent was my descent and so feeble Warlock's state that the sudden impact of my posterior on the couch tipped him towards me. I waited for him to pull himself upright, but when he rested his head upon my shoulder, I recognized he had no intention of doing so. I was going to protest, but I realized how heavy my own head felt and let it sag down on top of Holmes's. And I'm not embarrassed to say I did it. Good friends support each other.

Sometimes structurally.

"Hello," I said. "M's Dog-der Wosson. I sometimes arm… help-y."

Mrs. Warren gave me the sort of look designed to communicate that she found this hard to believe. Undaunted, I asked, "Wossa problem?"

"From what I can gather," said Holmes, "Mrs. Warren is upset because she has let a room to a gentleman, and now he is in it."

"*Whaaaa?* Can't be right."

But it was. Mrs. Warren stamped her foot and shrilled, "He never comes out! Not once in the ten days I've had him! He rings when he's hungry and we leave his meals on a chair outside the door and he rings when he's done and it's time to take the tray and he leaves notes to say what he wants and he's always up there, pacin' back and forth and it's creepin' me out and I won't have it!"

"Ehr, Gerd… she irs unsane…" I mumbled.

Mrs. Warren gave me an uncharitable look. Silently she rose, walked to our little pantry alcove and filled a glass with water. She stalked back over and held it out to me with an air of stern, matronly expectation. Chastened, I took the glass and drank it down in three gulps. She was right; I felt much improved. She then took the empty glass, filled it a second time, returned once more and threw the damned thing in my face.

"Bleaghra! No, I'm better! Thank you, I'm better!" I cried.

On my shoulder, Holmes gave a little whine of protest.

"Now, help me!" Mrs. Warren insisted.

"What I do not understand," said Holmes, "is how you even come to know of me or why you seem suddenly convinced that I can be of service."

Mrs. Warren raised a conspiratorial eyebrow. "Years ago, I had a boarder, name of Mr. Fairdale Hobbs. He had a little matter you helped him out with, Mr. Holmes."

"Well, I think I recall the name… Fairdale Hobbs, eh? Yes, I think I brought his case to a satisfactory conclusion, didn't I?"

"No. He's dead," said Mrs. Warren. "Blown up, all over me upstairs curtains. By God, I had to scrub the walls and floor for two days!"

"Then why ever would you want me to—"

"Because *you owe me*, Mr. Holmes. And I know from Mr. Hobbs—God rest 'im—that you're the man to see when there's strange work afoot. Now, I ain't afraid of getting blowed up! What I am afraid of is living in uncertainty of what's going on under my own roof!"

There was a moment of silence.

Holmes cleared his throat. "Well, if I do take your case, Mrs. Warren, I know what my fee will be. If I am able to be of service, you must promise you will re-evaluate your list of things that scare you."

"Deal!"

"Oh, very well," Holmes grumbled. "What is this mysterious lodger's name?"

"Don't know."

"Eh?" said Holmes and I together.

"See, he came to us late at night. We was just about to put out the lights, my husband and me, when there comes a knock at the door. And there's this fellow with a bushy black beard and moustache and sharp dark eyes and he says he saw the sign for the room-to-let and he thinks he'd like it, because there's a bathroom and a sitting room. Really—and I don't tell him this—but it's pretty much the whole top of the house, for there's just my husband and me and Molly, the maid, and we don't go up there. But I don't like the look of him, so when he asks me how much for the rooms I tell him sixty shillings a week which—God help me—is a fair sight more than they're worth. He says he can't count that high and that our money's confusing. He wants to know if it would be all right to give me five pounds a week and I says that—yes, between friends—that would be just fine."

"So already he's managed to cleverly bargain himself up to a hundred shillings a week," I observed.

"And he whips out a ten-pound note and says he'll pay me the first two weeks in advance," Mrs. Warren confirmed. "But he's got some conditions, see? First, he wants a key to the house. Well, that's no problem. Lots of lodgers get those and for five pounds a week he might be in his rights to ask for a key to Molly's room. He also says he wants to be left totally alone. Nobody is to come into his rooms, under any circumstances. He'll ring for his meals and write us notes for what he wants. And for the price, I say that's just fine. So he gives me the tenner and goes outside and brings up two huge bags—strangely frilly ones—and hauls them upstairs. Not so much as a word to me husband or Molly. But we've got ten pounds, so we don't mind. Later that night, he goes out. *Very* late. In the small hours I hears him come back in, and that's the last time he's left his rooms. It's been ten days now. Ten days!"

"So your chief complaint, as I understand it," said Holmes, "is that a stranger came and gave you a great deal of money for a certain living arrangement, under certain terms and then—and this is the part that upsets you— *abided by those terms?*"

"Yes, but he also said I weren't to go poking about, trying to find out anything about him."

"Which you are presently doing."

"Because it's driving me mad!"

"Another word for which, I believe," Holmes whispered, from my shoulder, "is *insane*."

I gave an almost imperceptible nod.

"Now, starting on the morning after his arrival, our guest had been leaving notes, telling me what he wants. I've been keepin' 'em."

"Of course you have," said Holmes.

"Here's the first one," said Mrs. Warren, handing us a card that said SUBSCRIPTION TO DAILY GAZETTE.

"A reasonable request," said Holmes. "If I were going

to spend my life locked in rooms I'd rented from a landlady who secretly hated me, I'd want something to read, too."

"Sure, for what he's payin' me, no problem getting him a paper every day. But then, two days later, we got this." Mrs. Warren gave us a second card that said MATCH.

"Hmmm…" I said. "Note the lack of a plural, Holmes. And the slightly different appearance of the handwriting from one card to the next. Now, block print in capital letters is probably the simplest writing style to copy. Nonetheless, I'd say it was possible this was written by a different person. A person with substantially limited vocabulary compared to the first individual as the note is only one word and omits the plural. Either that or he wanted exactly one match, for some reason."

"Yes, and I weren't about to go buy one match, so I got 'im a box and much joy may he have of it. And then just days and days and days of nuffin' but listenin' to him pace back and forth up there, bringin' him meals and *Daily Gazettes*, until he leaves a final note with his breakfast this morning." At that point, Mrs. Warren turned to her oversized handbag and began digging about inside. Tired though I was, the sound of utensils clanging against glass spurred me to mental clarity. And to disbelief.

"Wait… you brought the *whole breakfast*?"

"Maybe it's a clue?" said Mrs. Warren, disgorging her mysterious lodger's dirty plates and discarded bits of egg onto our sitting-room table. Amongst the food scraps lay two used matches—just barely burnt down—and the stubs of two cigarettes, which had been smoked to within about a quarter inch of their ends. Apparently Mrs. Warren's lodger was not one to waste tobacco. Also in the wreckage lay her lodger's most recent note, which simply said: SOAP.

"Hmmmmm..." I said, perusing the pile of refuse. "Much as I hate to admit it, this evidence certainly does raise a peculiarity. Can you spot it, Holmes?"

"The fact that the strange man has been locked in those rooms for ten days and is only now requesting soap?"

"By God! I hadn't even thought of that!"

"Probably beginning to smell a little close in there, eh?" said Holmes.

"I shouldn't wonder. However, I was thinking of something else. Look how far down these cigarettes have been smoked. It's a miracle the person didn't burn their lips. Now, would any man with a full beard and moustache dare to smoke a cigarette so far down? He'd have lit himself on fire."

"Ah! And we know this did not occur," Holmes crowed, waving his I've-just-made-a-staggering-deduction finger about, "because the note he subsequently left says SOAP, and not REPLACEMENT FACE."

"Do you know something, Holmes, I am forced to concur. Personal hygiene is unlikely to be the primary concern of someone who's just scorched off all their facial hair. Well done."

I could feel his cheek tighten against my shoulder as he beamed with pride.

"We are now left with two possibilities," I continued. "Either Mrs. Warren's lodger met her while wearing a false beard—which would not be out of character, considering

193

his desire for anonymity—or the person now in residence is not the original lodger at all. Recall that he went out late that first night, returned when the rest of the household was abed, and has not been seen since. Recall also that his luggage was strangely 'frilly'. Finally, observing the difference in both writing and diction in the first card, compared with the last two, I am inclined to believe that Mrs. Warren now has an altogether different lodger."

"Ooooooh!" said Mrs. Warren, balling her fists in anger. "What should I do about it?"

Holmes and I both had our mouths open to offer an opinion, when Mrs. Warren raised a finger to interrupt. "What should I do that *won't* stop the five pounds a week?"

I raised my eyebrows. "Honestly, if that is your prime concern, I think the best answer is: nothing at all."

"I can't do nuffin'," she protested. "Not with my husband gettin' abducted and all."

"Wait, your husband was *what*?"

"Well, see, he's got this big black bushy beard, like my lodger. And this mornin' as he steps out to go to work, two big fellows whops him over the head with a blackjack, pops a coat over his head and shoves him in a carriage."

"Why on *earth* did you not begin your story with that?" I demanded.

"I don't know," said Mrs. Warren, crossing her arms defensively. "Maybe because I'm a landlady and not a student of narrative structure!"

"Have you heard from the kidnappers? Have they made any demands?"

"Oh, no, no, no. My Warren's back home safe and sound."

"Your... *Warren*? You call your husband by his last name?"

"No, that's 'is first name."

"His name is Warren Warren?"

"And if I tell you his father were a right cruel bastard, maybe you'd be inclined to believe me," said Mrs. Warren Warren. "Mr. Warren weren't gone all that long. He says they drove him about, shouting at him in some foreign language for a time, and when he couldn't answer, one of 'em took the coat off, took a look at 'im and started swearing up a storm. Well, they stopped the carriage, gave my Warren the boot, and sped off fast as you like. He came stumbling home less than an hour after he left."

"Well this paints the entire affair in quite a new light," I admitted. "It would seem the assailants mistook your husband for your lodger. If they and the person secreted in your upstairs rooms happen to be foreign, that would not only explain why your husband's kidnappers tried to interrogate him in a strange tongue, but also why your guest's notes are monosyllabic. I'm sorry to say it, Holmes, but it seems as if Mrs. Warren was right to bring the matter to our attention; there seems to be some real mischief afoot."

"How should we proceed, Watson?"

"I think we should try to sneak a look at this mysterious lodger. Mrs. Warren, what time does your guest usually take supper?"

Mrs. Warren shrugged. "Six or so."

"Then be so kind as to jot down your address and we shall call upon you just before that hour. Good day, Mrs. Warren; rest assured that Holmes and I shall give the matter our utmost attention."

As I rose to see her out, I was reminded of how absolutely exhausted I was. True, I had rallied while sitting, but even the trip from the couch to the door was taxing.

"Ugh. I'm not at my best, I fear," I told Holmes as I returned.

"Nor I, Watson. I can't even move my legs."

"Then how did you make it out here?"

By way of answer, Holmes raised his arms to show me his palms and elbows.

"You *dragged* yourself?"

"Needs must when the devil drives, they say," he replied, "and Mrs. Hudson is pretty much the same as the devil if you leave her unanswered on the doorstep twice on the same day."

"True enough," I agreed. "Yet I fear she is the next person I must consult in this case."

"Mrs. Hudson? Why?"

"Because she never throws anything away until she absolutely has to, and because she is one of the few people in London gullible enough to subscribe to the *Daily Gazette*."

"You want her old papers?" Holmes asked.

"Indeed. I can think of almost nothing to recommend the *Gazette* over the dozens of other papers our mysterious gentleman may have selected. It is utterly devoid of fact—

unless you happen to be one of those people willing to believe that 'Duchess Gives Birth to Goblin Triplets' is real news."

"You can't prove she didn't!" Holmes shouted.

Disregarding him, I continued, "But the *Daily Gazette* does have this going for it: almost nobody finds themselves in sufficient agony to use their agony column."

"Eh?"

"Thus, anybody who wants to march into the *Gazette*'s office at lunchtime and drop two coppers can probably get anything they want printed in the evening edition and very few people would notice it. So perhaps Mrs. Warren's strange guest is interested in the progress of London's goblin babies. Or perhaps—as it seems the original lodger has spirited somebody else into the rooms and has had no direct communication with them for ten days—someone has actually found a reasonable use for the *Daily Gazette*."

The good news was that Mrs. Hudson did indeed possess an impressive pile of cast-off copies of the *Gazette*. The bad news was that she claimed she wasn't done with them yet. She made me purchase her pile of as-yet-undisposed-of rubbish at full price. Happily, this proved to be money well spent. In the agony column from two days after Mrs. Warren's mysterious lodger's arrival, I found the message: "Be patient. Will find some sure means of communication. Until then, watch this column. G."

Three days later: "Am making successful arrangements. Patience and prudence. The clouds will pass. G."

And finally, in the previous day's paper: "The path

197

is clearing. Remember code agreed—one A, two B, and so on. High red house with white stone facings. Third floor. Second window on your left. Nine o'clock tomorrow night. G."

"Ah-ha!" I shouted, waving the paper at Holmes. "It seems that we are to have two missions this evening. First, to observe Mrs. Warren's current lodger and see whether they are the original one. Second, we are going to intercept and decode a secret message intended for that person. Whoever has been communicating with them through the agony column of the *Daily Gazette* has foolishly put the time, location and cypher for the message all in one place. Indeed, judging by the particular code they have selected—a favorite of schoolchildren the world over—I imagine this 'G' is a man of no very great intelligence."

Then again, the men who contrived against him— Holmes and I—were currently men of no very great *ability*.

I think it took us twenty minutes to get down the stairs. By the time we did, we were already a sight, our clothes in disarray, our brows slicked with sweat, leaning on one another to stay upright. Holmes had recovered some of his strength, but not much. Still, when one considers the state of most fellows who'd drunk what he had the previous night, it was a miraculous achievement. I was… wavering. Though the trill of intellectual challenge energized my mind and body, I was still rather used up. The urge to lie down—even if only for a moment—overtook my every thought.

We hailed several cabs but each of them seemed to be engaged (even if they were clearly empty) or just going off duty. *So sorry, guvnor*, said the waves of every cabby who didn't just pretend not to see us.

"Come on, Holmes," I said, struggling under my friend's weight. "Great Orme Street. It's just by the British Museum. We can make it!"

"What? No we can't!"

"But… try?"

"Watson, I couldn't possibly."

Fortunately, Blind Harold—one of the local knife grinders—was passing with his cart. By "cart" I mean "some old, stolen wheelbarrow with a grindstone set in and held in place by nothing but gravity and the luck that attends beggars and scoundrels". Still, never one to look askance at the gifts of providence, I gave Harold four shillings, told him his mobile service model was settling into a permanent location for the day, lifted the grindstone out of the barrow, and set my friend in its place. Then, with a tip of our hats, Holmes and I were off.

Though, not at any great pace. The wheelbarrow did better than might have been expected, but I did not. At the start, I was trundling. Two streets later, I was staggering.

"Turn left here," Holmes said.

"Ungh," I agreed.

"No, no! *My* left!"

"But… we're facing the same way, so my left *is* your left and…"

"Well then, shouldn't it have been even easier to get it right?"

"Um… right?"

"No! *Left!*"

By the time we arrived, six o'clock had just passed. Fortunately, dinner had not yet been delivered to Mrs. Warren's mysterious guest. She told us she had a disused box room we might secrete ourselves in, just across from the door to the lodger's rooms. And perhaps that was true, but do you know what else she had? Stairs. There was simply no way I was getting Holmes up there. In truth, I was glad to have him as an excuse because I rather suspected there was no way *I* was getting up there.

Instead, at my direction, Mrs. Warren set her full-length mirror in the corridor, so it might reflect the lodger's door. Then she set Molly's mirror at the top of the stairs to reflect the first. Then we borrowed a third from the next-door neighbor and set that at the bottom of the stairs, reflecting up so that Holmes and I might look in from the street—and our convenient wheelbarrow parking area—and get a roundabout view.

Molly brought the lodger's meal upstairs on a serving tray, carefully dodging mirrors all the way. She knocked at the door and retreated down the stairs. No sooner had she reached the bottom than the door opened and two bare white arms reached out to retrieve the food. Though my view was somewhat compromised by our less-than-ideal arrangement, I could nonetheless see that they were slender and delicate and certainly not well matched to the bearded brute Mrs. Warren had described. Between those arms, I could just make out a feminine face. Though it was hard to tell for sure, it seemed as if the face's owner might have been somewhat surprised to see a mirror outside her room.

Then, more surprised to discover that she could see a second mirror, reflected in the first.

Then even *more* surprised to catch sight of a third, reflected in the second.

And finally, just a bit put out to see two weirdos slumped over a wheelbarrow, staring at her, reflected in the third.

To say she closed her door with some alacrity might be an understatement.

"Definitely not the original lodger," Holmes noted. "I don't care if he did shave; that's not him."

"No," I agreed.

"What do we do now, Watson?"

"Well, that must be her window, up there, eh? Let's see if we can spot the house described in the *Gazette*. I believe it said: 'High red house with white stone facings. Third floor. Second window on our left.'"

Indeed, I had no trouble identifying the window in question. The front of the building was on Howe Street and thus obscured from our view, but the window described was plain.

"Very good, Watson," said Holmes, "but we've still got over two hours until nine o'clock. What shall we do?"

"Food?" I suggested.

"Oh, yes! Oh, by the twelve gods, food!"

Just around the corner, we found an unimpressive eatery which—and this speaks well of the proprietor's better sense—absolutely refused to seat us. One look at us was enough to convince him that we were drunk, suffering from some horrible form of plague or—most likely—both. I convinced the man to at least sell us some food we could enjoy outside. I had to pay him enough to cover the loss of his crockery (and then promise to return the plates anyway) but at last Holmes and I found ourselves outfitted with victuals. For Holmes, a few slices of bread toasted golden-brown and a bowl of chicken soup. For myself I got the biggest jug of water the kitchen could provide and a sandwich of wilted vegetables and… well… the fact that the waiter called it "beef" proved nothing aside from the fact that the waiter was a bald-faced liar. To this day, I cannot tell you what unfortunate animal provided the gristly scraps I swallowed as I sat on the pavement, leaning back against Holmes's wheelbarrow. I earnestly hoped it was not one of the street urchins whose numerous comrades still stared at us from the nearby alleys.

Though, if it was, he was *delicious*.

And it was just what I needed. Sometimes there is nothing quite so rejuvenating after an evening of self-poisoning than gnawing a terrible sandwich, sprawled in exactly the sprawl your body needs to feel at rest and just not giving one bloody damn what anybody thinks of you.

Apart from a quick trip to return the plates, I did my best to focus on the window and not fall asleep. Through good luck and diligence, I even managed to keep my wallet.

Just at the stroke of nine, Holmes and I beheld

a strange sight: a figure, obscured in shadow, began erecting some sort of machine at the third-floor window. It appeared to be a large metal cylinder atop a tripod. We watched as it was carefully aimed at Mrs. Warren's upstairs window.

"Any guess what that thing is, Watson?" Holmes asked.

I had none. But if my military service had been with the navy rather than the army, I'd have known better. Sixteen years ago the Royal Navy had finally abandoned the flag-based system of signaling so beloved by our aging admirals, and had adopted the modern signal lamp—a device designed to emit a beam of light visible for more than three miles, even in broad daylight. I had no idea I was looking at just such a machine, until its shutters swung open and threw out a single, retina-scorching blast.

"Aaaaaaaagh!" I screamed, falling back and clutching at my eyes.

"A single flash: the letter 'A'!" cried Holmes as the orphans around us ducked and scuttled for the cover of the alleyways.

"Erm… yes," I said, wiping away my tears. Then, taking up my notebook and pencil, I wrote down "A" and turned my attention back to the window, where the signaling beacon had undertaken a feverish barrage of flashes.

"That's twenty," said Holmes. "What letter is that?"

"'T'," I said, writing the same.

"Twenty more! 'T' again!"

"Again? That's curious…"

"Now five! Let's see… A, B, C, D… E! It's E!"

The next blast of fourteen flashes gave us "N".

"At ten," I said. "Perhaps something is going to happen an hour from now."

"Maybe he'll finish his sentence," Holmes opined. "I'll say, it takes quite a bit of flashing to get one's meaning across, eh?"

He wasn't wrong. Twenty more flashes gave us yet another "T", then a single one gave us "A". Then the light went dark for a few moments.

"Attenta? That makes no kind of sense, does it?" Holmes wondered aloud. "Ah! Perhaps that's the name of the lady we saw in the mirror! Miss Attenta! Oooh, it's got an exotic sort of ring to it, eh, Watson?"

"I shouldn't think so, Holmes. More likely it is one of the Romantic or Germanic tongues' version of 'attention'. They are closely related. Let us see… *attenta*… I want to say… Italian?"

"He's starting up again!" said Holmes. "Look: 'A'… 'T'… 'T'… 'E'… What the deuce? He's doing the same word *again*?"

Indeed he was. And as soon as he finished it, he let the light fall dim for just one moment, before beginning the same word for the third time.

"*What?*" Holmes and I cried together.

"That's two hundred and forty-three flashes, just to get someone's attention?" I said, shaking my head.

"I'll bet he has it, if he hasn't blinded her," said Holmes.

"It may be a good thing it's as bright as it is," I noted.

"If he'd been using a simple candle, she'd have fallen asleep by now."

"Here he goes again, Watson!"

P. E. R. I. C. O. L. O.

Holmes screwed up his face at that and wondered, "Er... do you suppose that's his name?"

"I do not. I think my earlier supposition was correct, Holmes. If I recall, *pericolo* is Italian for 'danger'."

"Are you sure? I seem to remember it as a name... From a play, wasn't it? Ah! Yes! The famous love story: *The Tragedy of Attenta and Pericolo*!"

"I don't think so, Holmes."

"But look: he's starting up again!"

P. E. R. I.

"Egad, is he going to do this all night?" Holmes wondered, but his thought was interrupted by a sudden scream from the signal window. A series of grunts and cries of protestation broke across the night air and the signal lamp suddenly tipped to the side and disappeared from the window with a crash.

"That's a relief, if I'm honest," Holmes remarked.

I was already on my feet, unsteady as they were. "Holmes! Something is wrong!"

"What do you think, Watson? Shall we investigate?"

"Of course, Holmes!" I cried, taking up the wheelbarrow's handles.

"Ha ha! Onward, to battle! Giddy-up, Watson!"

"*Giddy-up?*"

"Yes, it means: get going, quickly."

"And it is a term generally directed towards horses," I panted as my feeble legs pumped us towards the corner of Howe Street. "I will thank you not to address me as if I were a horse!"

"Even if you sort of are, right now?"

"*Especially* because I sort of am, right now!"

"Well what ought I to say, then, to you, my good friend and noble steed?"

"Don't call me that!"

"Hi-ho, Watson! Awaaaaaaaaaaay!"

"Stop it."

But the argument had reached its end, for at that moment we turned the corner onto Howe Street and beheld...

"Stanley Hopkins?" we both said.

There stood the diminutive inspector, leaning against the gate of the house, looking downcast and bored. When he heard his name, he looked up and said, "Mr. Holmes? Dr. Watson? What are you... *doing*?"

"There's trouble, Hopkins! Right there, in that house behind you!" roared Holmes.

"I know," he said. He made a miserable face and kicked a pebble into the gutter. "I'm supposed to watch the door and not go in."

"Who says?" I asked.

"Mr. Leverton. He's an American. Scotland Yard is working with the Pinkertons on this case. But it's really theirs, you know, not ours. So... I have to wait outside."

"While crime and mystery happen just behind you?"

Hopkins gave a meek shrug.

"Now look here, Hopkins," I said, wagging a finger at him, "if you are ever, *ever*, to become a true detective and solve a case on your own—"

"I thought you said I solved that other one!"

"—you mustn't allow yourself to be so easily cowed! You must develop a tireless thirst to know what's really going on! Do you think Inspector Grogsson would stand by, doing nothing, while criminals and Pinkertons battled behind him?"

"Er…"

Holmes leaned forward in his wheelbarrow to say, "The answer is 'no', Hopkins. No, he would not."

"Now, Holmes and I are going up those stairs to find out what's happening! Are you coming with us?" I thundered.

A sudden resolve broke across the young detective's face. He balled his fists and cried, "I am, by God!"

"Good," I said. "Because I rather need someone to help me carry Holmes. Just get your arm under his other shoulder, won't you? There's a good lad…"

As we began dragging the world's most powerful magical being upstairs, Holmes asked, "So, exactly what do we know, Hopkins? What's going on up there?"

"Three days ago, the Pinkerton Detective Agency contacted Scotland Yard. It seems they've been hunting a hired killer who works with a particularly dangerous splinter group of the Italian Mafia in New York. His name is 'Black' Giuseppe Gorgiano and he's killed at least fifty men. Apparently he's here in London, hunting another Italian, named Gennaro Lucca."

Holmes and I exchanged a look.

"Are the English and Italian alphabets different," Holmes asked me, "or does his name start with a 'G'?"

"The problem is, Holmes, that *both* men's names do."

Hopkins continued, "The Pinkertons sent one of their top men, Mr. Leverton, the hero of the Long Island Cave Mystery. Scotland Yard assigned me to follow him about and act as liaison. From what I gather, I'm just supposed to make sure he doesn't do anything too bold. Only, it seems to me—" Hopkins lowered his voice to a conspiratorial whisper "—Mr. Leverton seems a bit more interested in Black Gorgiano's prey than he does in Gorgiano himself."

"So the Pinkertons have crossed the ocean and neatly marginalized Scotland Yard in their own territory, so that they might hunt either an Italian-American killer, or an Italian-American kill*ee*, is that what you're saying?" I asked.

Hopkins nodded. "We followed Gennaro to this address an hour ago and watched him carry some form of large machine upstairs."

"Yes, Holmes and I may have seen it."

"We picked a spot in the alley across the street and waited. About twenty minutes ago, Black Gorgiano and a group of six or seven others went in. Mr. Leverton went after them, and told me to hold the door. Since then, I've been listening to them do—" A fresh barrage of frenzied screaming came from the floor above us. "—whatever that is."

Dragging Holmes up the last flight of stairs, we emerged into an empty corridor.

"To the right," I hissed. "It should be the second door from the end. Come on."

When we reached the door, we could hear strangled screams and a series of muffled thumps. I looked at Holmes.

"Careful, Watson," he whispered.

Oh, how I wish I'd listened. Instead, I gave a nod to the newly emboldened Hopkins. He set his jaw and nodded back. Then, we each drew back one leg and kicked open the door.

Oh, God… the things we saw…

Sprawled on the floor against the far wall of the room lay what had to be Mrs. Warren's original lodger, a fellow with a big bushy beard. He seemed to have been clubbed and stabbed a few times and—though I'm sure he must have deemed it unfortunate when it was happening—he was probably only alive because he'd been unconscious when the *real* trouble broke out. His arms were locked about the chest and throat of another Italian-looking gentleman, who was quite dead. A bone-handled knife protruded from his chest, and his neck was bent at a grotesque angle. It seems Gennaro Lucca had managed to take down at least one of his attackers. Compared to most of the other fellows in the room, these two seemed to have gotten off rather easy.

Seven other bodies lay scattered about—presumably Black Gorgiano and his gang. Some of them were still moving, banging their heads feebly against the floor, or trying to drag themselves away from the two figures who stood at the center of the room.

Mr. Leverton looked unworried and untouched by the violence around him. I was surprised by the darkness of his skin. After all, only twenty years ago he might have been deemed "property" in his home country. He did not look like property now. He wore rose-tinted glasses and a self-satisfied expression. His clothes were fairly normal—only slightly... American. His left hand was clad in a jagged gauntlet of blackened iron.

Beside him stood...

...a *thing*.

It was the same basic shape as a man and clad in black clothes. But it was impossibly tall. Hard to say its height, exactly   probably seven and a half or eight feet—because it was bent and crooked. Its skin was pale and crackly, like ancient parchment, bleached to a light gray. It had no face really, just crude holes for a mouth and eyes. As the door swung open, it turned its gaze to us: first Hopkins, then Holmes, then me.

Hopkins screamed. And not just a little bit. It was one of those horrible, wrenching screeches that make it clear that the screamer is not planning on using their vocal cords for anything else ever again. Hopkins howled until his air ran out, then clawed his face. Rather badly. His left hand worked so many knuckles into the socket of his left eye that, as a doctor, I could not help but despair of its future function.

Not that it mattered.

Because it was clear to me—and I don't think very much medical training was needed to come to this assessment—

that Hopkins's heart had just burst. Or stopped. Or something. You know that instant when something very important inside a person—some vital organ, or their soul, or very likely both—just breaks and they scream their life out in a single breath and fall down dead?

Well, I do. Because I watched it happen to Stanley Hopkins.

Next, the creature's gaze fell across my friend, Warlock Holmes. Holmes made a bit of a face, like he wasn't altogether comfortable with the present situation, and reached out to close the door. Unfortunately he was still a bit unsteady on his feet, so he didn't do it as fast as I might have liked. Because by then the monster's absent eyes had fallen on me.

How can I describe it?

Can you imagine the moment a gazelle sees the cheetah spring and turns to run, though it knows it is no match for the killer at its heels? Or the instant the condemned man feels the floor drop away beneath his feet, knowing only the rope around his neck can stop his fall? I felt as if I were frozen in that moment—that onset of perfect and primal fear. If I'd been able to calculate coolly, I'd have realized I was dying, just like Hopkins and Gorgiano's gang before me. And that would have come as something of a relief. But no, I could not imagine anything ever saving me from that terrible fear, not even the cold release of death. It seemed as if that initial horror would continue forever—the only thing I would ever feel.

His left hand was clad in a jagged
gauntlet of blackened iron.

Luckily, there was one form of salvation available to me: Holmes shut the door.

Suddenly, I could feel how empty my lungs were. I'd screeched all the air out and was trying still to scream, though I had no power to. My nails had sunk into the skin of my face. My heart, seized and useless, refused to pump. I realized I was on the floor, though I couldn't remember falling.

Then Holmes was on me, slapping my face and shouting, "Ponies, John! Think of ponies. One of those wonderful Shetland kind with all the hair hanging off it. Doesn't she look silly, John? Remember Christmas, with your family? Wasn't it wonderful? And what about puppies? What about a big-eyed puppy licking your nose because he wants a biscuit? And who's got all the biscuits, John?"

I could do nothing but writhe on the floor, grasping at my chest. Warlock raised his hand and gave me a slap so hard it would likely have knocked me off my feet, if I'd still been on them.

"*Who's got all the bloody biscuits?*"

He was too strident to be ignored. With supreme effort, I drew a breath. I felt a shock as my body remembered its vital functions. With an agonizing wrench, my heart beat once, twice, then resumed its familiar rhythm. I used that first, awkward breath to stammer, "Uh... *I* do?"

"Ha! Yes!" Warlock crowed. "*You've* got all the biscuits, John, yes you do. Oh, by the twelve gods, that was close."

I shook my aching head and wondered, "Holmes, what was that thing?"

"I've no idea," he said, then got a guilty sort of look and

added, "I... er... I feel I really *ought* to. Yet, if I'm honest, I absolutely cannot bring it to mind. But whatever it is, it's clearly got to be dealt with. I can't be weak, Watson. I must be strong. Gods, of all the days to have taken poison..."

As he spoke, an expression of agony and deep concentration broke across his features. Green fires lit in his eyes. He grunted and rose to his feet. He must have been using no small amount of magic to help him regain his strength, for blood began to run in rivulets down his face, as black goat horns curled forth from his scalp.

"Can't be weak..." he repeated, then shouted, "Melfrizoth!" and the burning black blade appeared in his hand. He turned to me. "I'm going in there, Watson. You must not look at what lies beyond that door. And no matter what you hear, you must not come in until I say it is safe. You stay here and take care of Hopkins, all right?"

"But... but Hopkins is dead."

Warlock's shoulders slumped. The fierce green flames dimmed just a bit and I'll swear those new-grown horns actually drooped.

"Seriously?"

"Yes. His heart stopped. I mean, I haven't examined him, but..."

"Damn it," Holmes mumbled. He stepped over to Hopkins's corpse, waggled the tip of his demonic sword in his face and said, "I'm getting a bit tired of this nonsense, Hopkins! Now stop being such a ninny and get up."

There was a sound like ripping canvas and the color red ceased to exist. All the droplets of blood where Hopkins had clawed himself and the burst vessels in his eyes turned suddenly gray. And—as red is a key component of other colors—the world looked quite queer for a few moments. The tasteful brown wallpaper around us turned a hideous shade of green. Fortunately, this lasted only a few moments. As the colors slowly reverted to normal, Hopkins took a deep breath and began screaming.

"Eeeeeeahghuah! Aaaaaaaaaagh! Mr. Holmes? Mr. Holmes, what has happened to you?"

"Oh, um… costume contest?" Warlock said with a shrug. "I've got a masquerade ball after this, so I… pretty good, eh?"

Hopkins sagged back in disbelief, but this seemed good enough for Holmes, who mumbled, "Right. Now, where was I?"

"You were going to go in there and do battle with that… thing," I reminded him.

"Ah yes, that was it. Botheration…"

I scuttled over to Hopkins, held his quaking head against my chest and tried to soothe him. I made sure to turn his face so he could not see into the room where the beast stood. Holmes stepped to the door, put on the most resolute face he could manage, and swung the door wide.

The beast was gone.

There stood the man in rose-colored glasses, smiling amiably. The black iron gauntlet hung from a hook on his belt.

"Well, hello there," he said in a smooth, companionable tone. "You must be Mr. Warlock Holmes. My name is

Nathaniel Leverton of the Pinkerton Detective Agency. I want you to know that my employer and I deeply regret any unpleasantness that just befell your two companions."

"They'll be all right," said Holmes, through tight lips.

"Oh?" said Leverton, leaning around Holmes to get a look at Hopkins and me. "Now, that is a piece of luck, isn't it? I don't suppose that's got anything to do with what just happened to the color red?"

"Who can say?" Holmes replied.

Leverton's smile broadened. "I imagine *you* could, if you wanted to. But men like you and my employer are careful with their secrets, aren't they? And that's as it should be, Mr. Holmes. That's as it should be." He leaned around Holmes again. "I'm so glad to hear you're all right, Inspector Hopkins. When I saw the door open, I was afraid it might be you, though I *think* I asked you to wait outside, didn't I? But, so long as there's no harm done…"

"No harm?" said Holmes, directing his burning gaze around the corpse-filled room.

"No harm to friends," said Leverton. "These men were murderers and thieves, Mr. Holmes. Only look at their hearts and you'll know what they were."

Slowly, without taking his eyes off Holmes and the burning blade, Nathaniel Leverton leaned down towards the nearest corpse. He pulled open the man's shirt, sending two or three buttons clattering across the floor. Emblazoned upon the skin beneath was a scarlet circle.

"They call themselves the Ring of Red Faction. They wish to see Rome returned to her former glory, with the nations of the world at her feet. But we have other business that requires our immediate attention." His eyes fell on me. "The Pinkerton Detective Agency's files regarding the recent defeat of Agent Burnwell lead me to suspect you might be Dr. Watson. Is that correct?"

I hesitated a moment, unsure if I should give this man any information. My only previous association with the Pinkertons was when I'd conned the Beryl Coronet from one of their members, used it to resurrect Holmes, then returned it spent and useless. I was sure they couldn't be all *that* happy with me. Finally, I gave an uncertain nod.

"The man against the wall is Gennaro Lucca. I'd very much like to ask him about a powerful magical artifact that went missing from a Pinkerton man's possession in New York City some years ago. Thing is, Gorgiano's boys treated him pretty rough. I don't suppose you'd have a look at him?"

Leaving Hopkins, I went over to the fallen stranger. Though he did seem to have been used as a combined punching/stabbing bag by Gorgiano's men, I had every hope for him. There was no sign that his skull had been fractured and the knife wounds were superficial. I mean... *awful*, but superficial. He must have put up a good fight, twisting and turning as the assassins struck, for he had a number of ragged gashes but no deep penetrations. As I began tearing up his jacket to make bandages and padding, he woke enough to struggle against me.

"No, no, Mr. Lucca! It's all right. I'm here to help," I said. Then, as I realized Holmes was commanding most of Mr. Leverton's attention, I leaned close and asked, "I don't suppose you'd know the Italian words for *come here* would you?"

As I worked, Mr. Leverton used the time to make overtures of alliance towards Holmes. Bless him, Warlock possessed the wisdom to display that certain reticence that is demanded every time somebody surrounded by a pile of fresh corpses says, "Hey, let's be friends." The green fire had cooled in his eyes and he'd put his sword away. Even the horns had begun to retract into his scalp, but it was clear he was far from enamored with our new acquaintance.

"You're on the side of the angels, that much is clear," Leverton was saying. "That's what my boss always says about you. Now, Mr. Pinkerton is a social thinker. He believes it is the responsibility of men of great power to change the world for the better. And he has. Do you know what I was when I met him? I was contraband. Now, Mr. Pinkerton is a little disappointed, Mr. Holmes, that you have effected no change yourself. But—he says—when you do act, you are a man of integrity and kindness. And do you know something, I think the two of you would get on pretty well."

As he spoke, I crawled over towards the window and righted the signal lamp as quietly as I could. Not quietly enough, it would seem, for Leverton turned and pointed a finger at me, demanding, "Now, what are you doing over there? You stop that."

"Watson is doing what he thinks is right," said Holmes. "Something very clever, I shouldn't wonder. You just deal with me, Mr. Leverton."

"No. The Pinkerton Detective Agency is in control of this case and no actions will be taken until they are cleared—"

"You will deal with *me*!"

But Leverton did not. He turned away from Holmes and shouted, "Dr. Watson, stop where you are!" His hand hovered threateningly over the gauntlet that dangled from his hip. A poor plan, as it turned out, for the entire room filled with the booming voice of Holmes.

"If you *touch* that talisman, Leverton, if you summon that friend of yours, I'm afraid I shall have no option but to slay you both."

I could see Leverton's mouth twist into a grim and bitter smile. "Make no mistake, Mr. Holmes, that thing is no friend of mine. No friend of any man's. And you could no more kill it than you could kill the wind."

Holmes gave a wry laugh. "Mr. Leverton, I absolutely *could* kill the wind if I put my mind to it. Then again, the wind has never offended me. You, on the other hand, are beginning to. And if you Pinkerton fellows know the first thing about me, you know what would happen if you and I came to blows. Watson, do carry on."

I turned my back on the two of them and spent the next few moments carefully flashing out: V. I. E. N. I.

Behind me, Nathaniel Leverton continued to argue his position. "Now, Mr. Holmes, what could I have done to offend you, eh?"

"Do you know the criminal charge I've always been most afraid of?" said Holmes. "Not witchcraft. Not murder. *Consorting with demons*. Given the company we found you in, you'd be wise to worry about it, too. Now, why don't you just sit down quietly on that chair over there while we wait for… whatever it is that Watson just did."

Holmes then whispered to me, "What was it, Watson? I hope it's clever because if it isn't we might look a bit foolish in front of the Pinkertons."

"Nothing too clever, I would think," I said. "Yet it's clear to me that Mr. Leverton may have a vested interest in painting Giuseppe Gorgiano and Gennaro Lucca in a certain light. As neither is currently capable of refuting such characterization, I thought fit to summon somebody who can: Mrs. Warren's current lodger."

"Very judicious, Watson."

"She is a criminal and a liar!" Leverton insisted, waving a finger at us. "You'd be fools to trust a thing she says!"

"We'll be the judges of that," said Holmes. "Oh, and since I deem it unlikely that you'll sit quietly and let us…"

The shadows at the corners of the room suddenly snaked forth, wrapped themselves around Nathaniel Leverton's arms, legs, and mouth, pulled tight, and solidified. His cry of protest was choked off the instant he began it.

"Holmes!" I hissed, and waved a hand at Hopkins. I needn't have concerned myself. He hadn't noticed. He sat outside the door, staring at the wall opposite him in pure, catatonic stupor. Being killed and resurrected twice in as many weeks will do that, I suppose.

"Well, I'm sorry, Watson," said Holmes. "But, by the gods, this Pinkerton fellow is tiresome. What do we do now?"

I shrugged. "We wait."

And so we did, but not for long. In less than two minutes, the sound of running feet came to our ears and, a moment later, a lithe young lady leapt over Stanley Hopkins and burst in through the doorway. "Gennaro?" she asked. Then, spying him on the floor at the far side of the room, cried, "No! My Gennaro!"

"He'll be all right!" I told her. "I am a doctor and I've seen to him. His wounds are not serious."

"Who are you?" she demanded.

Holmes answered. "We are friends to the hunted, the peculiar, the displaced and the vulnerable, which I strongly suspect makes us friends of yours."

She looked from Holmes, to me, to Leverton, to the corpses that lay all about. Her eyes went wide when she recognized Black Gorgiano amongst them. "What has happened here?" she cried, but then gave a gasp and added, "No! I see it! Gennaro! Oh, my brave Gennaro! They came at him, even as he was signaling 'danger' to me for the second time out of the three he likely intended. Like a knife in the darkness, they came to take his life! And see? He has slain them all!"

Holmes and I exchanged glances.

"Yep," said Holmes. "You guessed it. That's just what happened."

"And who," said our guest, stepping in front of Leverton and gazing down at him with a wary scowl, "is this?"

Leverton gave an earnest shake of his head, but despite that—or no, now that I put it to paper I am certain *because* of that—Holmes said, "His name is Nathaniel Leverton. He's a Pinkerton detective. He claims he's here hunting Black Gorgiano, but according to our somewhat stuporous friend Hopkins, he's shown rather an interest in that fellow. What did you call him?"

"Gennaro, my husband," the lady said, "and I am Emilia Lucca."

"Warlock Holmes, at your service. This is my colleague, Dr. John Watson."

I bowed my head and she bobbed a curtsey.

"Please," she said, "please, you cannot give Gennaro and me to the Pinkertons. They've been following us since New York."

"Watson and I are not working with the Pinkertons," said Holmes, in soothing tones. "Nor are we working with Scotland Yard. We are independent operators, concerned only with justice. Madam, if you think your cause is just, you would be wise to tell us all. Perhaps we may be of service to you."

She gave us a hard, appraising look for a moment, then reached up and pulled down the front of her dress.

"*Madam!*" I protested.

There, just above her left breast was the now-familiar crimson circle. Yet hers was different. A red line had been struck through its center. She ran to her fallen husband and tugged at his clothing until she revealed the same sigil upon his chest.

"See? See? This is where our loyalties lie. Or… where they *did*. We repented of it and ran, but the Ring of Red Faction does not tolerate dissension. They swore to kill us."

"I hate it when people try to kill me," said Holmes. "So tiresome. You have my sympathies."

"Mrs. Lucca," I said. "I wonder if you can tell us how you fell in with this Ring of Red Faction, how you fell out and why the Pinkertons are so interested in making your acquaintance."

"I am the daughter of Augusto Barelli, of Posillipo, near Naples. Gennaro worked for my father. I came to love him, but my father forbade the match. We married in secret and fled to New York. But life there was hard—we found ourselves lost in a sea of penniless immigrants. Then, one day, Gennaro saved a fellow Italian from a gang of Bowery toughs, only to discover the man was Tito Castalotte, of the famous fruit-importation firm of Castalotte and Zamba. Gennaro had just saved the life of the most powerful man in New York."

"Hmmm… the power of all that *fruit*, one presumes?" I asked.

"Look here," said Mrs. Lucca, stamping her foot, "not all wealthy Italians who happen to live in America are connected to the Mafia!"

"Of course not, madam," I conceded. "But, Mr. Castalotte…?"

"Oh, gods yes! *He* was. And he suggested Gennaro should come work for him, which was not an offer we were in a position to refuse. My Gennaro did good work for Mr. Castalotte. He might not have been very good at lying—he never could pass himself off as a legitimate businessman—but even his victims found his honesty refreshing. He became loved in the community and Tito Castalotte came to view Gennaro almost as a son, his real son having recently perished in a not-at-all-suspicious horse explosion. As it became increasingly assumed that Gennaro would inherit a great deal of control in the… ah… *fruit empire*, many people began to court his favor. One such group was a consortium of Mafiosi who had originally called themselves the Red Faction."

"Not the Ring of Red Faction?" I asked.

"By the time we met them, but not at first. Gennaro liked them. They cared not only for crime, but social right. They wanted to stop the world from spitting on our countrymen—to find a way to make governments respect us. At first they were dedicated to inventing a gun that worked not only on people, but could shoot away walls and scenery, as well."

"Did it work?" Holmes wondered.

"Sort of, but it wasn't very satisfying. So they changed their name to the Ring of Red and decided to build a huge, armored war-machine that walked like a man."

"Oooooooh!" said Holmes, alight with appreciation. "Did that one work?"

Mrs. Lucca shook her head. "They had one foot and

part of a leg, before their funds and the genius of their engineers failed. So, at last, they changed their name to the Ring of Red Faction and—"

But I cut her off, wondering, "They felt the need to change their name each time they tasted defeat? A strange compulsion, to be sure. But what strikes me as most peculiar is this: why should they continue to select such similar names?"

She pointed to her chest. "Because that way the same tattoo could…"

"Ah. Yes, of course. Do continue."

"In their third iteration, The Ring of Red Faction at last came across a weapon worthy of their cause. It seems that one of Pinkerton's former operatives had become disenchanted with his organization's methods and had fled. He must have been quite highly ranked, for he had in his possession a terrible weapon. Either he was a man of conscience or did not wish to be pursued abroad by Pinkertons looking to reclaim their property. As such, he stopped in New York just before leaving the country and attempted to mail the Pinkertons' property back to them."

"He tried to *post* a doomsday weapon?"

"What else could he do?" said Emilia Lucca, with a shrug. "If he went to see them in person, they would likely have detained him. He wanted to make sure the package got there safely, so he tried to impress upon the postal clerk how powerful and dangerous the contents were. Fortunately, he did make that impression. Unfortunately, the postal clerk was an Italian gentleman who owed money to Black Gorgiano."

"Ah…" I said.

"So of course he stole the package and brought it to the Ring of Red Faction. But it was years before they began to understand how to use it. When Gennaro and I met them, they were still somewhat harmless. They had noble goals, we thought, but had yet to turn to dark means to achieve them."

"What kind of doomsday weapon?" said Holmes. "That's the good part! Tell us about that!"

"This Pinkerton man here could likely tell you more than I," said Emilia. "It was only a small thing—a model of an ancient Roman symbol of power: the fasces. It was a bunch of black iron sticks, bound together with wire of the same black metal. In the time of Caesar, they were made larger, with rods of wood. You see, one rod—alone—can break, but many rods together become inflexible and strong. It is a symbol of unity. It seems that whoever held this black iron fasces could command unity of thought and action amongst his fellows and force their wills to join his. He could turn his followers against anybody who dared to stand apart—the strength of the many against the fragility of the one. It was said that there was a guardian who might be summoned by the man who held the fasces, but this was never accomplished before the fasces was stolen."

"Stolen?" I asked. "By whom?"

"Gorgiano had continued to rely on the postal worker who first brought it to him—a kind old man named Benito Marinetti. In the old country, he'd been an organ-grinder; all the children loved him. But the Ring of Red Faction became ever more violent, ever more intolerant of those who did not think as they did. Marinetti could not forgive himself for helping such men come to power; he stole their weapon and ran."

Well did Holmes and I know it. Though we had never made the acquaintance of Mr. Marinetti, we'd come to know his friend Beppo fairly well. Moreover, we knew the location of the item that Marinetti, Beppo, the Ring of Red Faction, and the Pinkertons sought so earnestly: it was currently in Holmes's bedroom. Warlock and I exchanged a nervous glance.

"So... um... what happened then?" Holmes asked.

"We all thought the Ring would dissipate—they'd been three times defeated and were running out of names to adopt. But no! In the years after Marinetti left, Gorgiano became worse and worse. Finally, he murdered Castalotte and tried to assume control, using my Gennaro as a puppet. But we knew his heart! We got new tattoos, striking out the rings of red upon our breasts, and ran. We hoped to flee home to Italy, by way of London, and tell the Cosa Nostra how Gorgiano had betrayed them. It was no good! Word reached Italy that we were coming. To set foot on our home soil would mean sure death. Gennaro took a room at Mrs. Warren's and secreted me there while he worked out safe passage. To make matters worse, Benito Marinetti had fled to London as well, and everybody assumed my Gennaro was in league with him! Black Gorgiano and the Pinkertons chased us all the way here, trying to reclaim the fasces, but—" she directed the final part of her statement at Nathaniel Leverton "—we *haven't got it!*"

Leverton rolled his eyes and gave the sort of look designed to communicate that he was absolutely willing to believe that statement—once he had interrogated Emilia and Gennaro to death, searched their luggage, searched the inside of their corpses, and offered similar treatment to anybody they'd spoken to in the last year, of course. Not before.

I turned to my friend and said, "What must be done, do you think?"

Holmes pursed his lips. "I can't say Gennaro Lucca has his hands entirely clean, you know. But his wife seems nice. And I've never liked people who hunt people with the help of Scotland Yard under false pretenses. Mr. Leverton is likely to find himself bound until exactly midnight. What do you think, Watson, could we have our married fugitives on a ship by then?"

"Absolutely not. This man is badly injured. Midnight is less than two hours off. Even if we had time to make travel preparations, he needs to be seen to."

"Oh," said Holmes. He furrowed his brow and concentrated for a moment. There came the strange, creaking sound of shadows tightening and Nathaniel Leverton gave a little grunt of discomfort. "What I mean to say is *next* midnight. Now do you think we might manage it?"

"I think… yes. If we hurry. First, we must find a way to convey Gennaro Lucca to safety."

"Luckily, we do have a wheelbarrow," said Holmes.

"Watson, Mrs. Lucca, why don't you see to it. Don't forget to help young Hopkins as well."

As we struggled to get Gennaro up, Holmes leaned in close to Leverton and said, "Allan Pinkerton cares about the social good, you say? Well I care about whoever needs my help. That is why I've inflicted this minor setback upon you today."

Nathaniel Leverton's expression gave us little doubt that he considered this a bit more than a minor setback.

"And I want you to tell Mr. Pinkerton that it is only because of my high regard for him that I do not turn this into a major defeat."

Leverton rolled his eyes. It was clear he thought Holmes's words were pure bravado. Yet they were not.

"After all," Holmes added, "what is to stop me from peeling that black iron gauntlet off your belt and ensuring you and your employer never see it again?"

Leverton's eyes went wide with terror.

"I am trusting you. I am trusting Allan Pinkerton. Pray do not make me regret my decision. I bid you good day. Which... um... which is not to say you will actually *have* a good day. I fear the next twenty-six hours are going to be... well... allow me to apologize in advance for the state of your trousers."

Getting Gennaro Lucca patched up and safely to Italy with his wife in the time available was no small feat. There was no possibility that the news of Black Gorgiano's death would precede them, so there was every chance the loyal members of the Ring of Red Faction would intercept and murder the two travelers. What hope had Holmes and I of negotiating the subtle and complex web of criminal politics in a land we knew so little of?

Luckily for us, when subtlety failed we had other options.

We sent Grogsson with them. If any of the local Mafiosi felt obligated to test his mettle against Torg... well... we wished him luck.

To Mrs. Warren, we could only extend our condolences on the loss of five pounds a week. Then again, that's what one gets for being nosey.

Personally, I was rather pleased with the outcome. It felt good to rub the Pinkerton Detective Agency's nose in it for a second time. I held this view for three more nights. Until a long-dead Persian taught me how unspeakably dangerous were the waters into which I had just thrust my toe. And how wrong I had been to do it.

THE DETECTIVE

FROM THE DREAM JOURNAL OF DR. JOHN WATSON

THE AIR SMELLS STRANGE. CITY AIR, TO BE SURE, BUT NOT London's. It's cleaner. Drier. Almost dusty. It gives the impression of summer, though I cannot feel the heat. In the center of this basement room stands a circle of nine lawmen.

Black Stetsons rest on their heads, probably seven feet from the soles of their black leather boots. The overcoats they wear are black, too. Or, they were. They are aged and weathered; one can hardly imagine the years and miles they've traveled. The eyes of the lawmen are dim and haggard above their black moustaches.

They stand in a circle, looking down at a man who stands in the middle of the ring. Their hate for him is palpable. They'd kill him if they could. Which—I realize—means they *can't*. All they can do is stare at him with impotent rage.

"Well now, here we all are, eh, boys?" says the man. He's American, though there's just the hint of a Scottish brogue to his speech. He's balding, with a dark beard in a severe cut. He must be in his forties, and yet there is a boyish quality to him, not unlike Warlock Holmes. His tone is jovial. "I'll bet you fellers didn't think anyone'd wake you up from that sleep of yours and put you to use. But that's what we're going to do, yes indeed! They're havin' a hell of a war, back east. And half of them is fighting for a cause you boys'd know a good bit about: they're trying to keep men enslaved. And I guess that's what you fellers're for, eh? But here's a bit of a catch: you're meant to *be slaves*, too. Yep, you were supposed to help some dead Frenchie rule us all. Now, it's too late for that, but I reckon *I've* got a use for you. You see, slavery needs new ground to flourish, or the Civil War's gonna wipe it out. So the ten of us, we're gonna make the West poison to the slaver. We're gonna hold it over there, where it can't live long. Yep! How 'bout that? Damned if Abraham Lincoln don't bless the day he met me! All right boys, let's get you presentable. Show me your 'badges'."

The nine lawmen's left arms move stiffly, as if against their will. Their pale hands reach forward into the circle and present black leather wallets. Each opens to reveal a gleaming badge in the shape of a triangle. Inside the triangle is an all-seeing eye, above the words *We Never Sleep*.

The dream is pushing me forward now, into the circle. I have no idea why, until I break into the center and all the lies that have been woven around these creatures fall away. I see them as they truly are. Those nine things aren't men. Had I thought them pale-skinned? That isn't skin! It's… more like… have you seen a wasp's nest? Their gray spittle dried to papery solidity? They have no eyes, no mouths. Just gaping holes into their empty, papery heads. They are not men, but made to fool men. Tall, slender, crooked lies with dried, crackling skin in black robes.

I know these creatures! One of them nearly killed me, just three days ago.

I'm so shocked to learn their true identities, it takes me a moment to notice that their badges are not exactly as they appeared, either. They hold no wallets; each of the nine fiends have been *branded* with marks of ownership. Their left palms have been scorched with the eye in the triangle.

I've seen that before!

I've *done* that before!

I once cut the hand from Alexander Holder, guardian of the Beryl Coronet, and burnt that symbol into his disembodied palm to try to save him from Moriarty. I drew that triangle and those words: the slogan of the Pinkerton Detective Agency.

My eyes fly to the man beside me in the center of the circle. That's Allan Pinkerton! By God… What has he done?

Holder's words come back to me. I remember how he scoffed at the thousands of men in Pinkerton's employ. He'd invited me to disregard them. Allan Pinkerton—he had said—had only nine true agents. Nine riders, clad in black. And woe to him that sees one.

What has Allan Pinkerton *done*? And how? And why? To end slavery? Of course it's a noble goal, but doesn't he understand what he's set loose? I am standing in a circle of mankind's worst nightmares. Pinkerton seems to have control over them for now, but what if he slips? What if he dies? He's only a man, as far as I can tell.

But what an audacious man. It seems he's Holmes's

equal for that, as well. Anybody who can behold the true visage of the nine can see the extent of Pinkerton's daring—can see just what steps he's taken to make his new agents "presentable". They aren't men and they aren't marshals and they certainly don't have facial hair—how could they; they don't have faces. What they do have is playful little curlicues of black paint just above where they ought to have lips.

Allan Pinkerton has painted *goddamned moustaches* on the greatest and most terrible magical beings this planet has ever known. I bet if I could see the tops of their heads, I'd find little doodles of cowboy hats.

To borrow a phrase from the locals, the man's got *balls*!

I feel the dream beginning to slip from me. No! Not yet! I need time to look on the nine: time to know them.

There is the least of them: Force, symbolized by the Sword. He is hardly more than an aspect of the other nine—a supporter and a catch-all.

Next comes Unity, the Fasces. He is duty. Propriety. If we know what is expected of us, and obey that expectation, it is his touch we are feeling. As a soldier and an Englishman, I know this fellow all too well.

There is Secular Command, the Crown, standing beside Religious Command, the Hieroform. The two are often at odds, yet how often have they come together to change the destiny of this world?

Pain, symbolized by the Cruciator, stands beside Fear, the Gauntlet—that's the one who nearly ended me, just a few days ago.

Wealth, the Coin, needs no companion. Because, really, what else do you need but wealth?

And here is the strange thing about the hearts of men, and what drives them to commit terrors upon each other: the softest forces are the strongest. Here stands the prince: second of the nine. He is the Heart. He is Love. He stands at the left hand of their king, the greatest of them. It's hard for me to know what his symbol is—it's stranger than the others. A little black tableau. A family? I think it must be.

He is taller than the others, and much, much stronger. He's the biggest, blackest liar of them all.

Hope.

And with that glimpse of Hope, humanity's strongest and most pernicious predator, the dream is over.

Which is not to say I wake from it.

THE SIGN OF NINE

1

HONK, HONK!

Ah, that familiar bane to nocturnal regularity: Holmes's accordion. The reader will forgive me, I hope, that I have not chronicled each and every instance when it stirred me from slumber. Neither have I seen fit to write of each barking dog, arguing cabman or overzealous sparrow that did the same. Yet all those secondary annoyances put together had not racked up nearly the score of Watson-wakenings as Holmes's damned accordion could boast.

To be fair, he had warned me. On the day we met he'd listed his flaws as a living companion and had dutifully included this predilection. He had certainly forgotten to mention a couple of other key traits (for example, the fact he was *riddled* with demons) but he'd been as good as his word on the accordion. He would often launch into honking, squealing song at whatever hour he felt he must. I'd learned not to mind it much, for I loved Holmes and he was always sorry to be a disturbance; he seemed as much a victim to this habit as I was. Yet that morning, he gave me a selection from my least favorite section of his repertoire: his incomplete tunes.

You see, it wasn't so bad when I could hear the whole song. True, "Davey, Get You Up and Kiss Me" was far from my favorite ditty, but at least I had the consolation of hearing its entirety whenever Holmes played it. Yet sometimes he played only tiny snatches of song, disembodied honks and chords that formed no cohesive melody. I'm sure anybody who has ever roomed with the second bassoonist for the Vienna Philharmonic could tell you what it's like—to have their living companion constantly playing tiny parts of the world's finest compositions. The man who can enjoy Wagner, having only heard the second bassoon part, has an infinitely superior musical ear to my own.

Until that fateful morning, Holmes's orphan honks had been much more vexing than his complete tunes. Yet, that morning I had failed to truly wake from my Xantharaxes-powered dream. The veil was yet over my eyes when I emerged from my room, sometime between four and five in the morning, bidden by Holmes's intermittent honking. Conscious choice had not yet displaced the strange felicity of imagination unfettered by waking reason. And so, with the secrets of magic burning in my blood, I heard Holmes's song for the first time.

The *whole* song.

Honk, honk! went the accordion. And from a thousand other realities, a multitude of demons screamed out, in perfect unison, "*O Freunde, nicht diese Töne!*" (Oh, friends, not these sounds!)

Though the words were the same, the meaning was

different for every creature. Some sang because they felt hate. Some because they were trapped in a realm of constant pain. Some boasted of their powers. Some only wanted to express that they were hungry and wished they could get to where Holmes was so they could eat. How was it that these thousands of different creatures—who could not possibly have known each other—had chosen to sing of their troubles in exactly the same syllables, at different pitches but in perfect harmony?

"*Sondern lasst uns angenehmere anstimmen und freudenvollere.*" (Let us make more pleasant and more joyful noises.)

Honk, honk!

Beneath us, I could hear the worms of the earth—the barely cohesive strings of thought and hope native to our world. They told of their fear of Holmes and the voices that sang in him. They pleaded for him to keep them out, for they were helpless to nurture the beings who lived on the planet they embodied, should the outsiders break in. They spoke in a rumble deeper than the shaking tones of whale song.

Brrrmmmm-hmmmmm-hrummmmmmm—

Honk, honk!

"*Freude! Freude!*" (Joy! Joy!)

—hrmmmm-bmmmmmmmmm-bmmmmmmmm!

Honk, honk!

"*Freude, schöner Götterfunken, Tochter aus Elysium!*" (Joy, beautiful, divine spark, Daughter of Elysium!)

And above it all, the all-but-inaudible trilling of the

stars, as the celestial bodies above us spun in infinity. I could hear the changing tones of the invisible bonds of gravity that pulled them together as momentum swung them apart. How great the force that flung them through the void!

Yet the thing that struck the most awe into me—and the most terror—was the fact that I knew that song. I had heard it at a concert not a year before.

Brmmmmm-hmmmmmm.

Honk!

"*Wir betreten feuertrunken, Himmlische, dein Heiligtum!*" (Divine being, we enter your sanctuary, drunk with fire!)

Beethoven's Ninth, the "Ode to Joy".

It was not the power of the thing that brought me to my knees, but the familiarity. Even the intoxicating grip of my dream could not shield me from the horror of it— could not stop me from understanding the ramifications of thousands of demons singing Beethoven. My eyes filled with tears. I knelt behind Holmes and held my hands up towards him. I don't know if I was pleading with him to stop or simply overcome by the power of the song, but I trembled uncontrollably. My arms—pocked with innumerable needle-marks—had hardly the strength to raise themselves.

Why couldn't they sing something else? If I didn't recognize the song, I could maintain ignorance of my true situation: that thousands of beings of immense power were fascinated with my world. My *home*. Why were they not fixated on their own weird little worlds? *Why were they singing bloody Beethoven?*

The answer was plain.

Holmes.

That's why: *Holmes*.

At last, I understood. And that is why I wept.

All these sounds I had never heard, Holmes *always* had. These were the constant truths and unwanted secrets that intruded into his mind at every hour of every day, usually as a cacophonous wall of noise. And, of course, he had no power to silence them. Silence reality? *All* the realities? No. He couldn't.

Or at least he had the grace not to.

What he could do is pick up that damned old accordion and bully them. If they would not be silent, they would at least be harmonic. Why not put a happy smile on his face? And—with just a few accordion honks—why not throw his will out across all existences and force the discord of the multiple cosmoses to yield to him.

Ode to Joy.

Why not?

I let loose a wracking sob. Holmes stopped with a jerk and spun around. "Oh! Watson! I'm sorry, did I wake you?"

I made no answer. How could I? I just knelt there, my palms stretched pleadingly up towards him as I wept the tears of the helpless and the damned.

"Well, you needn't be so dramatic about it, John!" he grumbled. "I'm finished now and you're welcome to go back to bed. Or here, look: I've put the kettle on. Tea always helps you forgive me. You do forgive me, don't you?"

He reached down and gently pulled me to my feet. "What's wrong, John? You look terrible. By the twelve gods, you seem even more doomed than when you went to bed! Has something happened?"

I had no power left to lie to him. In the face of the things I'd just learned, I had no wit to hide my deeds. All my worries and sins burst from my mouth in a flood.

"I stole it, Holmes! I stole your amphigory and I stole your Xantharaxes! I've been using it for dreams. Oh, Warlock, I've learned so much! I can tell you about Moriarty! And Irene! I've seen my Irene. But she's off kissing some Pinkerton bastard, I think. Oh! And, Holmes, I saw *Allan* Pinkerton! You won't believe what he's done! We're all in danger, Holmes! We're in such terrible danger!"

Holmes recoiled from me. "Wait, you've… you've *what*? You've been putting shredded mummy into the amphigory and injecting it? Why?"

"To know what you do, Holmes! To know enough about Moriarty that I'm not so helpless next time! To see her! I want to see *her*!"

"And that's why you've been looking so wretched lately, John? Egad, I thought it was the flu!"

"The flu? *The flu?*" I cried, and waved my needle-scarred arms at him. "How could *this* be the flu?"

"Well, I don't know. Chickenpox, then," he said, furrowing his brow. "It seems I have been somewhat remiss. I should have paid more attention, I suppose. Yes… I'm sorry. Please excuse me."

He walked past me with the saddest expression on his

face and went into my room. The muted brassy clangs that emanated from therein gave me to know he was reclaiming his property—that bizarre instrument of self-torture that had become so precious to me. I heard him deposit the runcible amphigory on his alchemical desk. Soon he emerged again and walked past me to the mantelpiece. He looked down into the Persian slipper and recoiled when he saw how much Xantharaxes was missing. He pulled the slipper free from the nail that held it in place and walked back to his room.

I had no idea what I should do. Then again, my doctor's training should have told me what I *would* do.

Sleep.

When you pull a bullet out of somebody, they sleep. As soon as that foreign irritant—the source of all their discomfort—has been removed, they cannot help it. The relief they feel is so profound, nature takes over.

In a sense, I was in exactly such a state. My lie was gone. The object of my addiction was stripped from me. I was still in pain, yet there was just enough relief to tinge the feeling, and there was nothing else I could do. I let myself sag to the sitting-room floor.

I woke some time later to find Holmes had pulled one of the overstuffed chairs next to me. There he sat, with his hands clasped in front of him. He knew I was awake, for his eyes locked on mine, but he made no move and offered no word. Nor did I. I just stared up at him, for as long as he stared down. Some minutes passed. Finally, he drew a melancholic breath.

"It has to end, Watson. Our partnership has run its course. It is time for you to find new lodgings."

"No!" I cried, my voice hoarse and cracking. "I don't want new lodgings. I don't want a new life. I want to stay with you and have adventures."

He shook his head. "It's killing you. I've been selfish. I let it go too far. You are not a sorcerer, John. Not a warrior. Not a monster. You're a doctor. From now on, that is what you must be."

How can I describe the panic and fury that arose in me? Had I expected my life to take its current course? No. Yet hadn't I done well? Hadn't I solved a few cases, triumphed over a few monsters, perhaps even saved Holmes? And now I was to be dismissed like some underperforming clerk? I would not accept it. My mind reeled through possible defenses and settled on a feeble technicality.

"No," I said. "On the day we met you said if I gave you a sovereign, I might stay here however long I please. Well, I gave that sovereign and I still want to stay!"

Holmes recoiled in horror. "Oh no! Oh, no, no, no! I *did* say that, didn't I? Well, but… This is no good! This cannot be allowed to stand! We have to find a way to change what you want. We must modify your desires, because otherwise…"

As he rose to pace, I stared up at him with defiant exhaustion. *That's right, Holmes: you are bested. How dare you try to get rid of me? Do you have any idea who you're dealing with? John-Bloody-Heimdal-Bloody-Watson, that's who! This is my right place and my right life and I will not let you take it from me! Ha!* In a paroxysm of triumph, I slumped forward onto my face and slept once more.

The next time I awoke, it had nothing to do with Holmes, but with my preeminent domestic antagonist, Mrs. Hudson. An ear-pounding door-pounding shook me from slumber. Luckily, the assault was quick. Our door latch—which had been a bit derelict in its duties of late—chose to give way. My eyes popped open to reveal the blurry form of Mrs. Hudson standing in the now-open doorway with a female visitor.

Perfect! Just what was needed: a case to prove my worthiness to Holmes and distract him from this preposterous John-you're-in-danger-and-we-must-stop-adventuring-together thing he'd concocted. I rose to greet our guest.

Well… I *tried* to. As I'd slept I seemed to have worked myself into an awkward head-down, bottom-up position, which was practically optimized to highlight… well… not my finest aspects. My right cheek was pressed against the floorboards in a manner that held my mouth slightly open, resulting in a fairly impressive puddle of drool. As I tried to rise, using my face as leverage, I slipped in this self-manufactured water hazard and tumbled sideways. I tried to stand again, but my legs were weak and I crashed down upon my rump.

"*That* is Warlock Holmes?" our guest asked.

"Nah," said Mrs. Hudson, reassuringly. "That's the other one, Watson. He's a medical doctor, would you believe? Usually, he ain't the scary one, but… Cor, blimey, Dr. Watson, what have you done to yourself?"

"You'll have to forgive Watson; he's a bit indisposed at the moment," said a voice from behind me. Warlock Holmes strode past, straightening his sleeves and fiddling with those cufflinks I'd stolen for him. Damn him, he looked impeccable. In a tone of languorous detachment, he asked, "Now, who is this you've brought to see us, Mrs. Hudson?"

"Mary Somefin-or-other. She's got a problem."

"Well, why don't you step inside and tell us all about it, Miss Mary. Perhaps I might be of service."

"Me too!" I insisted, from my spot on the floor. "Imma help!"

"I very much doubt that, John," said Holmes, then— in a tone of condescending charity—added, "I mean: I'm sure there will be no need for you to trouble yourself."

Damn him! He was helpless at this sort of thing without me, and it galled me that he didn't know it. I shook my head a few times to clear it, and focused all my observational powers on our guest.

It was as if she were being average on purpose. Her height was normal. Her build, perhaps just on the slim side of utterly nondescript. She had a face that could only be described as face-ish and hair exactly the color of... you know... *hair*. Her dress was of an unremarkable cut and—I swear this is true—of a *grayish beige* material. Someone must once have walked into a fabric shop and declared, "I am going to make a dress. My goal is to never have anybody remark that it is attractive, that it is ugly, or that it is anything except just a dress. Now, what sort of material can you show me?" Indeed, the only thing that stood out about her was her expression. It was disapproving, bordering on contemptuous. Which—now that I put it to paper, I realize—is precisely what I deserved.

Nevertheless, she presented me with a chance to prove my worth—a chance I had no intention of wasting. With Herculean effort, I drew myself to my knees and crawled towards our kettle. It was time to get this pinch-faced shrew onto the couch and find out what her problem might be.

2

AH, TEA! HOLMES HAD ONCE TOLD ME ABOUT THE GIFT the goddess Hestia had given him: whenever he ate toast and soup, it brought him some relief from the fact that he was an outsider to the human experience and that everyone he loved had died two hundred years ago.

Never had I received any such boon. The closest thing I had was my profound connection to tea. By God, it was nearly a panacea to me. Each sip brought with it just a tiny swell of sanity and strength. Thus I sat, seeking my lost humanity in the bottom of a Hammersley cup, as our visitor began her tale.

"My name is Mary Morstan. My father was Captain Arthur Morstan, an officer in one of Her Majesty's Indian regiments. My mother being deceased and my father abroad, I spent most of my youth at boarding school. Just before my seventeenth birthday, I had a letter from my father. He seemed excited, as if our lives were about to undergo a great change. He gave me few details, but said he had a furlough of twelve months and I must meet him in London. I hastened to the address he gave—the Langham

Hotel. I found he had secured us rooms, but was told that he had left the night before. Sure enough, his luggage was in his room, but there was no sign of my father. I found this paper on the desk. It seems he must have laid it there before he went out."

On our table, she placed an old map—fragile and oft-folded. It appeared to show a section of an old fort. "The Sign of Nine" was written in the lower corner, followed by the names Mahomet Singh, Dost Akbar, Abdullah Khan and Jonathan Small.

"What a strange phrase, 'The Sign of Nine'. Can you make anything of it?" I asked Holmes.

"Erm… perhaps none of these four men knew how to write the number nine?" he offered.

"You know, Holmes, I actually can't think of a better explanation. Well done, I suppose."

Still, I must confess that—after the previous night's dream—any reference to the number nine made me uneasy.

Mary Morstan cleared her throat, pointedly, to make it known that she'd like our attention again. "Gentlemen, my father never returned. There was some thought that he might have gone to the home of his old compatriot, Major John Sholto, who lived in Norwood. Yet Major Sholto was contacted by the police and they were convinced he had not seen my father. Nor did he even know my father had returned to London."

"Ah, I see," said Holmes, "and you wish us to see if we can find out what became of your beloved dad!"

"Of course not," said Miss Morstan, brushing aside

familial love as if it were a troublesome gnat.

"No? Then what do you want us to—"

"Perhaps you should *listen*. Then you might find out," Miss Morstan suggested, adding, "It is very rude to interrupt. Now, that was ten years ago. With my father missing and probably dead…"

I boggled at the casual callousness with which she said it.

"…my own prospects were greatly diminished. I had enough money to finish my studies but after my education concluded, I was forced into a life of drudgery and servitude. I settled at the home of Mr. and Mrs. Cecil Forrester in Lower Camberwell, to be governess to their wicked little children. There I remain. Seven years ago, an advertisement appeared in the pages of *The Times*, inquiring if anybody knew the whereabouts of Mary Morstan."

"Did you?" Holmes asked, forgetting our guest's injunction against interruptions. She reminded him with a withering gaze.

"Mr. Cecil Forrester—who has been against me from the beginning—took the extraordinary liberty of replying to the article. No doubt he hoped that the person who wished to know my whereabouts might effect my removal from his house. I tell you, the man has absolutely no regard for the fact that I am an orphan, with nothing to shield me from this wicked world."

"Except the fact that you were an educated and self-reliant adult, at that point," I wished to add, but did not.

To the more discerning reader, it may be telling that, in only the fifteen minutes since I'd met her, Mary Morstan had already cowed me sufficiently that I dared not give voice to such thoughts. It seems she'd overmastered me nearly as quickly as she had the Forresters.

"Well, it turned out against him!" Miss Morstan scoffed. "For, the very day his reply was printed, I received this box in the post. You have my permission to look at the contents, but you must not touch!"

She held a rather plain and battered cardboard box out towards Holmes and raised the lid so he could see inside. I could not. Yet, whatever lay within caused Holmes to give a low whistle.

"I have had it examined and appraised. It is a pearl of the highest quality. Ever since that day, I have—on the anniversary of the first pearl's arrival—had another box each year, containing another pearl to match the first. I have them here, in case you need to see them."

She withdrew a second box, set it upon our coffee table, and pulled away the lid. Within lay five small chicken eggs.

Damn it.

My heart sank. What I'd needed was a real client with a real case, not some addle-brained unfortunate with a wealth delusion. Why had I let her get my hopes up? Well… not that it was her fault, of course. She couldn't help it if she was a simple madwoman. Poor thing. I struggled to find some polite way to tell her she was crazy and her story was nothing but the fabrication of a diseased mind. As I searched for the proper words, my eyes chanced across the box a second time and I realized:

No, those actually *were* pearls.

"*Holy God!*" I cried.

Mary Morstan turned to me and narrowed her eyes. "Dr. Watson, are we *interrupting again*?"

I felt the accusation somewhat unfair, for the dual reasons that I had not been the fellow to interrupt the first time and because nobody else had actually been speaking. Yet my shock was such that I could only mutter, "So… you own all six of these pearls? And you are still a governess?"

"Why not?" said Miss Morstan, with a shrug. "The children are older now. Since they are all away at boarding school, my duties are light."

Ah. So less a governess and more of a person who continued to live with the Forresters, doing no work, drawing a governess's wage, and trading on the fact that they would not *dare* to put a poor orphan girl out of their house, despite the fact that the orphan in question was twenty-seven, and quite capable of purchasing the entire neighborhood. Or perhaps New Zealand. Yes, the situation was becoming clearer.

"So…" Holmes reflected. "You wish for our help because you are terribly wealthy and… er… Help me out here, Watson. Why does she want us?"

"Because today I should have received the seventh pearl! And all I got was this!"

Miss Morstan slammed a wrinkled letter down upon our table beside her box of gigantic pearls. It was written in loopy, self-important script in—oh how I hate to say it, given my personal history with this particular affectation, but—violet ink. A cursory comparison of the handwriting and the address that was still visible on the first pearl box gave me the firm conviction that the two had been sent by the same person. I leaned in to examine the letter, which read as follows:

> To the estimable Miss Mary Morstan,
>
> You do not know me, but I know you. You are a wronged woman! I regret the misfortunes you have suffered and blush when I think of my family's role therein. Will you meet with me and allow me to repair the vicissitudes of fate?
>
> If you will be so good as to go to the Lyceum Theater at seven this evening and meet my representative at the third pillar from the left, we can try to put right some of the wrongs you have suffered.
>
> I know this is an unusual request and must seem suspicious. Therefore I invite you to bring two companions to ensure your safety. My only injunction is this: given the sensitive nature of the matter we must discuss, they must not be police. My representative will ask for such assurances before he brings you to me.
>
> Yours with an eye to a future, superior to our past,
>
> A friend

I think I became a little smug. I looked over at Holmes and noted, "*Two companions*, eh? Perhaps my services might be required, after all."

"Not necessarily. I could always bring Lestr—"

"No police," I reminded him.

"Well then, Grogsson is—"

"*Also* a policeman."

Holmes opened his mouth to offer a third suggestion, but I gave him no chance.

"And so is Hopkins," I said. "Face it, Holmes, just about everybody else you know—or have the least amount of trust in—is associated with the police."

Holmes grimaced.

"It seems you must tolerate my help a little longer."

"Hrmph! Very well, Watson! But I'm going to have to insist you put some trousers on!"

"Your terms are acceptable," I said, "though it seems like a condition I would have been more likely to ask of you…"

"And therein we see how far you have let yourself slip," Holmes said acerbically. "Miss Morstan, please return no later than a quarter past six this evening. Watson and I shall be ready to accompany you then."

"Bring guns!" Miss Morstan urged. "If this fellow has my pearl and tries to get out of giving it to me, you may need to shoot him!"

"All right," said Holmes.

"What? No!" I cried. "Miss, we will not be murdering anybody just to secure you some mysterious jewels we don't even understand your right to."

"Then what good are you?" Mary Morstan growled at me.

"Well, I'm a doctor. I can prescribe medications and—"

"*Interrupting!*"

"I wasn't! You asked me a question!"

When at last we got our visitor on her way, Holmes urged me to spend the time until her return making myself presentable.

"Regrettably I cannot, Holmes. I have other plans."

"Erm… are you sure?" he asked, gesturing at me. I went to the mirror.

"Eeyugha! Well… I can't spend the *whole* time making myself presentable. I have business to attend to."

"What business?"

"The kind by which I might prove my worth! I shall be back before Miss Morstan returns and I hope to bring news that may illuminate her situation."

It is an advantage of my personal and family history that I know a few helpful facts about the military. I know, for example, that the two most universally popular topics of conversation for old men who used to serve in the army are how old they are getting, and the fact that they used to serve in the army. Several gentlemen's clubs exist where doddering military coots can go to drone on for years and years about these two subjects, and no others. Given that Miss Morstan had said her father's friend kept a house in Norwood, I resolved to head in that direction and ask after old Major Sholto. Being a retired officer myself, I could be reasonably sure I would find myself invited into any club I cared to inquire at, for a healthy dose of brandy and gossip.

I hadn't even cleared Brixton before I had what I needed.

I returned to Baker Street just after five that afternoon with a spring in my step, though my body was still weary from the treatment I'd given it last night. My bruised knees were aching, but my heart was full of triumph. Setting my hat and coat upon their hooks, I called out, "Success, Holmes; I believe I've plumbed this mystery nearly to its bottom. It shouldn't be too complex a matter, I think."

"Oh? What have you found out, Watson?"

"That the now deceased Major John Sholto was quite the character. He was a famous curmudgeon, and for the circles he moved in, *that* is saying something. He was never one to part with a shilling, though he was quite wealthy. Loved playing cards, but never for money, which disappointed those who knew him abroad; when he was stationed in India he had not only a reputation for gambling, but also for losing. Once back in England he seems to have sworn off it for good. He had two sons he viewed as utter disappointments and a wife he was terrified of, to the point he could hardly be drawn to speak of her. His health was never very good and it seems he passed away of natural causes. Here's the key fact: he died seven years and four days ago."

"Hmm," said Holmes. "Why is that important?"

"Why? Holmes, the whole narrative hangs on it! Look here, just a few days after this man's death, an advertisement appeared in *The Times*, asking for the whereabouts of Mary Morstan. As soon as it is answered, she begins receiving treasure by post. Now, the same person who has been sending that treasure wishes to contact her and describes her as a 'wronged woman'. What wrong can they be speaking of but the untimely loss of her father? I would say that the overwhelming balance of probability is that John Sholto knew a great deal more than he let on about the disappearance of Arthur Morstan. His sons or wife must have known about it and feel their family is culpable, as the letter Miss Morstan received today implies. While the old man was alive, they dared do nothing. But as soon as he died, they placed an advertisement and began sending a king's ransom to her. It is unclear what further financial gains our client may receive tonight, but I think it is plain she will know more about her father's mysterious fate. I mean… not that I'm sure she'll *care*, but there it is. That is my assessment."

"Well done, Watson," Holmes crowed. "And I am pleased to say the day has not been wasted here while you were gone. Behold! I have made us paper hats!"

"Holmes… *Why?*"

"To wear on our trip to the theater tonight!"

"To help us really blend in with the crowd?"

"Well partly, John, partly. But they do a great deal more than that. Have you asked yourself what would happen if it rains tonight?"

"Then my own, regular hat would do a fine job of holding the drizzle at bay," I told him. "As a special bonus, it would not then turn into a soggy lump of newsprint dripping down my face."

Holmes put both hands on his hips and grumbled, "I've said it before, Watson, and I'll say it again: you have much to learn of gratitude!"

3

WHEN MARY MORSTAN ARRIVED THAT EVENING, WHAT A strange trio we made. I suppose I was the most mundane-looking of the three. Though pale and trembling, my appearance was generally acceptable for the theater and it might easily be assumed I was naught but a London gentleman suffering from some minor infirmity. Of course, hidden beneath my clothes was the truth: I was a London gentleman suffering from mystic self-poisoning, who stood on the very brink of irreversible damage to almost every one of his internal organs.

Mary wore the same nondescript dress she'd been in earlier. However, she must have taken to heart my warning that Holmes and I might be unwilling to shoot her mysterious benefactor, even if she commanded it. Miss Morstan seemed to have grown suspicious bulges in both sleeves, one in her right boot and an alarmingly huge one in her handbag. My personal suspicion was that she had gone straight back home and ransacked her employers' house for whatever weaponry she could find. Let no aspersions ever be cast upon Mary's resourcefulness: she seemed to have dug up half an armory and strapped herself for battle.

So, there we were. I was sick, Mary Morstan was prepared to kill and kill and kill, and Holmes had a paper hat.

We hailed a cab.

On the drive, I think I must have seemed distant and desultory. In truth, I was simply exhausted. Mary seemed distracted. She didn't know what situation she was walking into, but she was resolved to walk out laden with loot. Holmes was chatty. He kept holding forth on the virtues of used newsprint as the basis for haberdashery, and how—given the unknowability of the night's events—certain people might feel better about things if they held hands.

I gave him a warning look. I think he was unsettled that I had not expressed my usual interest in our female client. And… well, I confess it was a failing of mine. As Holmes peppered his conversation with observations that the road was bumpy, and wouldn't the carriage handle better if Mary and I were to sit a bit closer, I thought I read a dueling uncertainty in his features. I think he was wondering if my lack of interest was due to my feeble physical state, or my agitation that he had tried to turn me out of 221B. Indeed, either of those two might well have explained it, but Holmes was overlooking a third, overriding motive.

Mary was just awful.

I had no desire to spend an extra instant in her company, more than the evening's business demanded. True, I was glad she'd sought our help, for I needed something to distract Holmes from my expulsion and a chance to remind him that he could not manage these little affairs without me. Yet my only desire was to bring the mystery to a satisfactory conclusion as quickly as I might.

Preferably without allowing Mary to murder anybody.

No sooner had we alighted outside the theater, than a street urchin gave a loud whistle to a shadowy figure who sat waiting in a four-wheeler directly across from us. The man said something to his driver and—in only the time it took to make an inadvisable U-turn in evening theater traffic—the carriage pulled up in front of us. The door opened to reveal a hard-looking man in his late thirties. He was not particularly large, but had a deformed cheekbone, two cauliflower ears and enough facial scarring to prove to even the most inexperienced observer that he must have had quite the career as a prizefighter.

"Miss Mary Morstan?" the man asked.

"I am," she replied. "And these are my two escorts, Dr. Something-or-other and Warlock Holmes."

"*Holy Hell!*" the man screamed, jumping back into the depths of the carriage. "Johnny, get us out of here!"

"Now just a moment, my good man," said Holmes, raising one finger. "Miss Morstan has broken none of your injunctions. I am not a member of the regular police force, nor have I ever been. True, I may have aided them in their investigations a few times. And... er... I may have been the *subject* of their investigations a number of times as well. But, so long as no harm is threatened to

Mary Morstan, I shall act as a simple observer."

"Promise?" asked the ex-fighter, wide-eyed and gripping the carriage door with white-knuckled fingers.

"I promise," said Holmes.

The man licked his lips and glanced around, nervously. "Well… all right, but I'll have my pistol drawn and on you the whole time, so don't try nuffin' funny."

"Fair enough," said Holmes. He climbed up into the four-wheeler, sending our mysterious contact shuffling back into the far corner. Holmes made sure to sit on the same seat with him, leaving the rear one for me and Mary, hoping—no doubt—that we might feel the need to snuggle.

As we settled in, the ex-fighter fumbled about in his pockets, then produced a small revolver, which he pointed at… well, *mostly* at Holmes. His hands trembled so badly that he waved the thing back and forth across half the compartment. He also took the opportunity to feebly knock against the roof and bleat, "Johnny! You got to… get us home… Move, Johnny… Johnny, please!"

I raised my eyebrows at Holmes. "Your reputation precedes you, it would seem."

"Well," he said, with a little shrug, "I've been operating in London for some time, so word has gotten about in… you know… *certain circles*."

It was not the most jovial carriage ride I have ever enjoyed. I tried to engage our mysterious escort in conversation, if only to calm his nerves. I had the distinct impression that somebody was sure to be accidentally shot if I didn't. We got a little information out of him—for example, that his name was Williams, he was the former lightweight champion of England, and he had never done anything wicked, so there was certainly no need for Holmes to punish him—yet he insisted that he was under strict orders to let his employer explain everything.

The evening traffic slowed us, until we cleared Vauxhall Bridge. From there we headed southeast at a good pace, through Stockwell, finally stopping outside an ornate house on Coldharbour Lane. Williams practically kicked the carriage door open and indicated, with a squeal, that we should disembark.

We made our way to the door, Mary in the lead and Williams hanging back a dozen feet, his eyes locked warily on Holmes. There was no bell, but the door had a corroded brass knocker, which Mary used to deliver a firm, businesslike rap. Almost instantly, the door was swept open by an aging Indian servant in a yellow turban. An overwhelming miasma of stinking vapor rolled out from behind him, stinging our eyes and sending us into fits of coughing. For an instant, I thought I was being poisoned. A good deal of my mistrust was due to the man's yellow headwear, which I knew to be the identifying mark of the murderous Thuggee gang. Yet, even as my lungs became accustomed to the initial onslaught of the house's atmosphere, I realized his turban wasn't so much yellow as *yellowed*—perhaps the natural reaction of any white fabric to such foul air. Indeed, the man himself seemed to have suffered the same. His eyes were bloodshot, yellow and dark-circled with stress and fatigue. He was just opening his mouth—whether to offer welcome or explanation, I will never know—when a high, whining voice from deep within the house called, "Ah! Hew! They are arrived at last! Oh, *khitmutgar*! *Khitmutgar!* You must show them to me at once! No delays, now! No delays! Mew, hew, hew…"

4

THE HOUSE WAS MOSTLY EMPTY. THE FIRST TWO ROOMS we passed had no furniture in them, and the third had only a small wardrobe and a simple bed—probably where our guide the *khitmutgar* slept. However, when we ascended the staircase to the first floor we suddenly found ourselves on a lavish carpet—thick and pleasant. Fine paintings lined the walls, although I noted they were of limited provenance. It was as if someone had told the owner of the house, "Look here, when it comes to world-class paintings, trust none but the Dutch, the Italians and the French, in that order."

Not bad advice, when one comes to think of it.

As we ascended to the next floor, our surroundings became even more opulent, with marble busts and tapestries all about. At last, the *khitmutgar* stopped before a carved wooden door, swept it open, and motioned for us to enter.

The smell was even worse. And there—seated on an enormous pile of silk-brocade cushions on the far side of the room, was our host. I don't think he was quite five feet tall. His skin was doughy white. He had a tall, bald head, strangely pointed at the top, but rounder and thicker at the bottom, like a misshapen gumdrop. His hands were in a constant state of motion, incessantly fidgeting with whatever came within their reach. Chiefly they toyed with the mouthpiece of a hookah-like contraption that rested just beside him, venting a foul, thick smoke. As we entered he was making a long, quiet "eeeeeeeeeeeeeeeeeeeeeeeeeee, mew, mew" sound. A few moments in his company was enough to suggest that this was the result of physical deformity. It seemed he could not exhale without making some sound, and was therefore forced to choose between speaking or simply emitting random noises. There was a brief moment where I imagined trying to sleep in the same room as him, and was stricken by a sudden revulsion.

As we entered, Holmes said, in a tactful whisper, "Well… there's no way *that's* human."

"Nope," I agreed.

Drawing a deep, excited breath, our host exclaimed, "Eww, Miss Morstan! The estimable Mary Morstan! It is an honor, madam. I am Thaddeus Sholto, your servant. Forever your servant. Ah. Mew."

"He says his name is Thaddeus," Holmes whispered. "Got to be a demon."

"No, Holmes. Thaddeus is a human name."

"What? Can't be!"

Mary Morstan was staring at our host with open expectation and strained patience. It was clear she was waiting—rather baitedly—either to be offered a seat, or a preposterously expensive pearl. Do you know, now that

I put it to paper, I have become fairly certain: both. She wanted both.

Yet Thaddeus Sholto did neither. He turned to Holmes and me and said, "And your servant, too, I am sure. Yes. Mew. Do tell me, Miss Morstan, who are these stalwart fellows who have agreed to safeguard you?"

Mary gave an impatient sigh. "This is Mr. Warlock Holmes—he has a reputation for helping people out when things get weird. That's Dr. Whatsisname. I can't remember."

"Dr. John Watson, at your service," I told him, but it was clear Thaddeus Sholto didn't care what my name was either. His eyes locked excitedly on my medical bag. I had grown in the habit of carrying it with me; if adventure should break out, it was a damned useful thing to have along.

Not least because there was a pistol in it.

"A doctor, eh?" he cried, much excited. "Have you your stethoscope? Might I ask you—would you have the kindness? I have great doubts as to my mitral valve, if you would be so very good. The aortic I may rely upon, but I should value your opinion upon the mitral. Hmm. Mew."

With a nod, I drew the stethoscope from my case and stepped over to our host. Now, there are certain specialists for whom the subtle clicks in the lub-dub of the human heart paint a clear picture, but I was no such authority. Nevertheless, the habit of my profession drove me to pretend I was. Nearly half of general practice is pretending you know what you're doing. The other half is referring your patient to somebody who actually might. Assuming an expression of competence, I leaned in and touched the bell of my stethoscope to Thaddeus Sholto's chest.

Lub d-spweeeeeeeeeeeeee, krickik, fwub, fwub, fwub, kik-kik… dub.

Eager to resume the business of the evening, I straightened and told him, "Sir, you have nothing to fear. I am sure…" Yet, as I still had some modicum of professional honor, the lie died upon my lips. "Actually, no. You might want to get that looked at. Tomorrow, if you're smart."

His eyes widened with the thousand innate fears of every hypochondriac and I gave him a curt nod to say that, yes, they were *all correct*. His mouth fell open in horror and a soft "eeeeeeeeeeeeeeeeeeeeee" sound began to escape. To quell this, he shoved the hookah's mouthpiece between his lips and took a deep breath. When he spoke again, puffs of stinking smoke leaked out left and right.

"It's no surprise, really. No surprise. I have always been a great sufferer. Mew-hew. Perhaps we had best hurry to repair Miss Morstan's fortunes, before my internal infirmities overcome me and I perish."

"Yes," said Mary, somewhat coolly. "Let's do that."

"We must go and confront Brother Bartholomew, I fear," said Thaddeus, with a shake of his pendulous head. "He suffers from our family failing. He is greedy. Mew. Oh. Greedy. From the day Father gained the Agra treasure—even before Brother Bartholomew and I were born—he always said half of it must go to Arthur Morstan. Yet, he and Mother—and now Brother Bartholomew too—were never able to give up so much as a single jewel. Eew. Terrible of them…"

"And is that your brother, Bartholomew, up there?" I asked, directing everybody's attention to the family portrait that hung above Thaddeus Sholto's nest of cushions. The painting portrayed a graying military man, dressed in a major's uniform with two medals pinned to his chest. Upon his lap sat two smiling boys. Two revolting, white, doughy, smiling, shapeless, hideously mutated boys. As there was no difference in their shape or size, I deemed Thaddeus and Bartholomew must be twins. Either that or the artist had been an inexcusably lazy sort of fellow. Upon the major's shoulder rested the claw-like hand of his wife, who must once have stood behind him in the picture. Once, I say, for the canvas was torn away, leaving a gaping hole. Little clue remained of her, save that the amount of space allotted was rather large and the hand had a greenish-white tint.

"All of us, yes, mew," Thaddeus confirmed. "How happy we were! Yes, those were better times. Better times. That is Bartholomew, on the left. Or… I think it is. Maybe it's me. Little difference, really. That is my father, John Sholto, whom I think you must have heard of, Miss Morstan. And… well… Mother used to be there. Sadly, we have no picture left of her. Eww, oh… just before his end, Father went a bit funny about her likeness and destroyed them all. She didn't seem to mind."

"How sad," said Holmes, supportively.

"Why would your father do that?" I asked.

"Who can say?" said Thaddeus, with a shrug. "Theirs was a peculiar courtship. Hew. I suppose I can speak of it, as it bears upon the business of the day. My father and Miss Morstan's father worked together to find a large cache of jewels—the Agra treasure, it was called. It was my father who went to claim it, but when he got to the hiding place he found it guarded by my mother. She refused to surrender it unless he agreed to marry her. Isn't that strange? Ha. Mew. A funny way to meet. But they were happy enough most of the time, you know. When we were growing up... mew. Yes."

As he spoke, Holmes leaned towards me and said, in a guarded undertone, "You know, Watson, it may just be your deduction thing rubbing off on me, but... do you suppose what we are hearing is the tale of an unguarded treasure, discovered by a wayward greed demon?"

"An interesting theory, Holmes."

"As an outsider, she would need to anchor herself to an object capable of inspiring immense avarice in the mortal heart, or she probably could not sustain her existence here."

"Especially because—" as subtly as I could, I cocked a finger at Thaddeus's reeking hookah-like contrivance "—in her native world, I suspect she may have been a methane-breather."

"Brilliant! Yes! Then one day John Sholto shows up and says he's taking her treasure. Now, she's probably got no real way of stopping him, being as weak as she is. Believe me, no greed demon would willingly part with its hoard."

"But she must have had enough leverage to ensure that part of the deal was that he'd marry her. Which is fairly clever, as it still gives her some claim to the treasure. Of course, the marriage would not be valid unless consummated…"

"Eww," Holmes noted. "But it must have been, at least once, because: twins."

"And they all lived happily ever after, until Arthur Morstan reappeared and… I don't know… what do you think happened?"

Fortunately, Thaddeus was entering exactly that part of the story.

"…but, of course, Mummy had always known that Arthur Morstan would come one day to claim his portion of the treasure. Ah-hew. She did not care for the idea, I assure you. Mew. Yes. And finally, he did come. Father greeted him as a friend and showed him the treasure, but that's where it all turned sour, you see."

"They murdered him," said Mary coldly, but more matter-of-factly than I might have imagined. It seemed she had accepted the fact of her father's death long ago and the fresh injury was not that they had taken his life, but that they had withheld his legacy.

Not to Thaddeus. He seemed utterly horrified by the idea. "No, no, mew!" he cried. "They would never! Arthur Morstan had a weak heart—everybody knows it."

"Did *you* know it?" I asked Mary.

She gave me a grim shake of her head to say it was news to her.

"Well, Father said everybody did," Thaddeus retorted, "and I well believe him, for as soon as they showed Captain Morstan the treasure, it gave out on him! Or…" Thaddeus paused and sucked uncertainly at his vile hookah. "Or perhaps he just fainted, we shall never know. The treasure, you see, was kept in a large iron box. Mew. As your unfortunate father fell, Miss Morstan, his head hit the corner."

"That'll make a dent," Holmes noted.

"Oh indeed—ah-hew!—a terrible wound," Thaddeus agreed. "My parents were horrified. They tried to stand him up, but he collapsed once more. Sadly, as he fell, his head hit the c—"

"—corner of the iron box, yes," I finished.

"Just so, just so! My parents tried to stand him up at least a dozen times more, but each time—"

"Yes, yes. Corner of the box."

"Until there was practically nothing left of the man's head, just a shapeless pulp. Oh, mew, it was the worst luck! Just unbelievably bad luck!"

"Funny that you should choose the word 'unbelievable'," I said, "as I was just reflecting on what a very difficult time your parents were likely to have in convincing a judge that luck was the culprit."

"Hm. Mew. Yes. We had an old Indian butler named Lal Chowdar who thought so too," said Thaddeus. "Or at least so my parents tell me. It's odd that Brother Bartholomew and I don't remember him, for we were well into our teens at the time, but my parents both insisted he was real."

"And what did this entirely non-fictional servant have to say about the matter?" I queried.

"Well apparently, he burst in on them and said, 'I heard you kill the guest, sahibs!' Of course they protested that they had done no such thing."

"Of course."

"But he would not believe them, impertinent fellow!"

"Oh, the cheek of him!"

"And my parents began to realize that if even their trusted servant—"

"Whom you do not remember…"

"Ah-hew, yes. If even he did not believe them, how could they prove their innocence to a judge?"

"How indeed?" I agreed.

"Luckily, Lal Chowdar said he knew a way to dispose of the body where nobody would ever find it."

"Always a useful thing for a butler to know."

"It was. Mew-hew. My parents trusted him with the sad task. And so—though they were deeply aggrieved and ashamed—at least they were safe."

"And then the loyal Lal Chowdar died, or disappeared somehow, leaving your parents' innocence perfectly intact."

"I am told he moved to Chicago," said Thaddeus. "Which seems right. Father always said that anybody who knew where to hide a body would eventually wind up in Chicago."

"Fairly salient point, actually," Holmes reflected.

"Now, Thaddeus, I have to ask," I said, "did your father

ever give any indication of how he and one of his old army buddies should have happened to come into possession of a mysterious foreign treasure?"

"Oh, no, no, no! Mew! No, I hardly dare to think of what Mother would have done if he ever spoke of such things. She always had trouble giving anything away, did Mother, even information. Hew. No. I always thought it might have something to do with Agra, in India, since it was called the Agra treasure and I know he spent some time stationed nearby. Yet he was chiefly in the Andaman Islands. Oh, and however he got it, I know it was somehow tied to his irrational fear of one-legged men and the number nine."

My eyebrows rose. "Did he ever happen to mention the phrase 'the sign of nine'?"

"Oh, yes. Frequently. If anybody ever mentioned the number nine, he always made them draw the figure, just to prove they could. Ah-hew. He always said if anyone ever wrote 'the sign of nine' instead of the digit, he would kill them where they stood. He hated the number. Why, when the local dairy delivered our milk—Brother Bartholomew and I were raised almost solely on milk, so delicate were our constitutions—he used to make sure the first two bottles were emptied at the same time. The crate held ten bottles you see, and he could not bear there being nine full ones."

"Peculiar," I noted.

"Hew. Yes. But not nearly so inconvenient as his feelings towards one-legged men. He once fired his pistol at a one-legged tradesman, in public."

I raised a finger and interjected, "This tradesman, what did he look like?"

"Oh, I don't know... poor? Hopeless?"

"Light-skinned or dark, Mr. Sholto?"

"Fairly light, I suppose. Average for an Englishman. Oh, but mew-eww, it cost us a fortune to hush it up. Mother was furious."

"More furious than she was at the death of Captain Morstan?" I hazarded.

"Oh infinitely more so! Mother never seemed to have much sympathy for him, though Father seemed quite broken up about it. But then, that's no surprise. Hew. He never had many friends, you know, and he always spoke fondly of Arthur Morstan. From birth, I knew his friend—and his friend's unfortunate daughter—must one day come for their share of our fortune. I would often reflect how unfair it was that this had not been done. I used to write about it, especially as I was composing verses. Um... hew... I could show you if you like."

He shot a guilty sidelong glance at Mary. The shadow of a blush lit his pallid cheek and the truth of the situation hit me in a sudden wave of recognition.

Of course. He was in love with her.

Only by reputation, I suppose, but was that not enough? What must youth have been like for a half-demon, half-human hybrid, who wheezed and mewed with every breath and was forced never to roam far from his methane hookah? From the moment Holmes had mentioned his probable heritage, my doctor's mind had begun to wonder whether—like many hybrid animals—Thaddeus Sholto might be infertile. Then again, the aesthete in me had put in a quick appearance to point out that—as a *particularly hideous* hybrid animal—he was unlikely ever to have the opportunity of finding out. It had not been difficult to imagine his family's motives for not sharing the treasure. Yet why was Thaddeus so insistent that Mary must be given her due?

Because he'd been planning it since adolescence. On his darkest day, he must have had only one thought that brought him comfort: that somewhere out there, was a girl. An innocent, kind girl, suffering in poverty. Bound to him by the shared destiny of their fathers' treasure. If he could only save her, could he not prove himself a worthy creature? Someone who did not deserve the crushing loneliness that had been his birthright?

For Christ's sake, he had just volunteered to show Mary Morstan his poetry, which—could there be any doubt of it—must be absolutely packed with dreamy idealizations of her.

For the first time in our long history of adventuring together, I felt as Holmes often did. I did not care if murder had been done. I did not care if there were a greed demon running loose in London. *I cared about our client.* It was not Mary Morstan, though she'd brought us the case. It was Thaddeus Sholto. By God, I felt *so terrible* for Thaddeus Sholto. I needed to help him. But how?

As I pondered how to unravel the terrible net nature and chance had woven around the young de-man, I became conscious that Holmes was staring at me with the most quizzical expression on his face.

"Right! Erm... right..." I spluttered. "Where were we? Ah, yes! Mr. Sholto, it has been years since the events you describe. In all that time, there has been no direct contact between your family and Miss Morstan, only the extraordinary gifts she received by post. Am I right in assuming it was you who sent the pearls?"

Thaddeus colored even more deeply this time and gave me a grateful little smile, as if he were rather glad someone had brought the subject up.

"Mew, hew... well... I did no more than honor demands, you know. I used to harry Father on the subject, and he always admitted that Arthur Morstan's orphan was entitled to his share. But he never let me act on it. The closest I ever got—ah hew!—was the one day he called me to his bedside. He was quite sick by that time. His liver, you know. Mew. And he showed me a golden goblet, set with pearls of extraordinary quality. There were tears in his eyes as he confided that he had resolved to send it to Miss Morstan a thousand times, and yet he could not bring himself to surrender it. He showed me where he had once pried out one of the pearls set in its base, thinking he might be able to part with just one of them. Yet he could not bring himself to do it. Hew. He wept and beat his chest and cursed his weakness. He knew I was the good son—ah-hew—and that I would have the strength to do what he could not. He forbade me to do it while he was alive, yet the instant his wicked heart ceased, he said, I must follow my conscience and make amends."

"Which you have," said Holmes, with a warm smile.

"Well, hew, *partly*," Thaddeus replied. "Father didn't make it easy. You see, he had always kept the main body of the treasure hidden, which was perfectly in keeping with his paranoia. Mew. Brother Bartholomew and I despaired that he was likely to go to his grave without telling us where it was. Yet one night he called us to his bedside. He said, 'My dear boys, my time is come. I bequeath to you all I own. My two earthly responsibilities must now be yours as well. One of you must care for your mother. One must do what is right. I will trust you both to know which is which. Now, in order to do so, you must know where the Agra treasure is. You must bear the weight of it, the weight that has crushed my soul for so very long. Boys, I have placed it—'"

We were all leaning in to hear the story, Mary Morstan most of all. Thaddeus gave a shrug.

"Then—ah-hew—he died."

Mary was across the room in a second, waving her finger in his face. "You've got to be bloody kidding me!"

"Madam! Hew!"

"Mid-sentence?" I asked. "He died *mid-sentence*?"

"Very nearly. He was looking at me as he spoke, but suddenly his gaze shifted to just over my shoulder. His hand flew to his chest. His face stiffened into the most horrible visage of pain and fright and he shrieked, 'The one-legged man!' For an instant, I thought he was delusional, but when I turned to look—oh! Mew!—There in the window! Such a horrible face. Hairy and rough and sunburned and feral. Staring in at us with such anger and hunger. It was more than Brother Bartholomew and I could stand. We are great sufferers—did I mention that?—great sufferers. We fell down in one of our fraternal swoons. Eww. Mew. When we awoke, Father was dead. The room had been ransacked and a paper with 'THE SIGN OF NINE' written on it was left upon my father's chest."

"Hmm… Yes…" said Holmes, tapping his lips with scholarly gravity. "From what you say, it is possible the man entered the room and murdered your father while you and Bartholomew were unconscious. Still… I think natural causes are more likely. You see, though the human liver can fail at any time, such episodes are more common in moments of stress or great excitement."

"That is the *heart*, Holmes."

"The sight of his dreaded antagonist must have been too great a strain to bear. Your father suffered a sudden liver attack—"

"God damn it."

"—and bore the secret to his grave. Tragic."

"And more than a bit inconvenient," Mary added, narrowing her eyes at our host.

If Thaddeus realized just how much blame lay beneath her words… well, I think he didn't, for he failed to burst into tears. Instead, he simply agreed. "Oh! Mew! *Dashed* inconvenient. But Father had showed me where he'd hidden the pearl goblet, so I claimed it and announced my intention to send it to Miss Morstan. Mother was horrified to be separated from the treasure, and Bartholomew objected. He said to willingly send treasure away would be more than Mother could stand. She would die, he said. Hew! Preposterous! He did not want me to send so much as a single pearl. But, of course, I did."

"And how did your mother take the news?" Holmes asked.

"She *did* die," said Thaddeus, with a sad shake of his head. "Brother Bartholomew was furious with me. Ah-hew. But how could that be anything more than a coincidence? I have heard it is common for people to die soon after their spouse. Isn't that true?"

Holmes and I shared a pained look. If Mrs. Sholto was indeed a greed demon, sustaining herself by a connection to a great treasure, it was entirely possible that Thaddeus's unselfish act may have severed that connection and doomed her. Then again, neither Holmes nor I were overly eager to voice that particular theory.

"Sure," said Holmes. "That sounds true."

"For years we could not find that treasure. Ah-mew!" Thaddeus complained. "I was forced to support poor Miss Morstan using only a single pearl per year. Brother Bartholomew stayed in our ancestral home, Pondicherry Lodge, but I fled here to escape his fury, and to await the day the treasure was discovered. And now—mew, hew—at last, it has been!"

"Where's my share?" said Mary Morstan.

"It is all with Brother Bartholomew. We must plan the

best way to encourage him to surrender your half."

"Oh, here's my *plan*," Mary growled. "We drive round there tonight and tell him to hand it over, right now!"

Thaddeus threw a hand to his chest. "Madam! Do you propose I rob my own brother?"

"Er... no," I said, though I imagined that was exactly what she was proposing. "I think Miss Morstan is only suggesting that there is no benefit to delay. And would not a direct and honest approach be best?"

"But so forceful! Hew!" Thaddeus said. Yet then he tilted his bulbous little head to one side and added, "Still... Miss Morstan has a point. Conflict is not in my dear brother's nature. He was never as—mew, mew, mew—as masterful as I."

"*Really?*" I found myself asking, before I could choke it back.

He turned defiant eyes on me and sniffed, "Yes, really! Hew! You will see! Hew! Yes! I am now convinced: Miss Morstan is entirely correct. Why shy from the inevitable? We must be bold! We must drive there right now and make our case. Miss Morstan, can you accompany me?"

She made a face, as if this were the most foolish question she'd heard in some time, and said, "I suppose."

"Very good! Now... mew... if your escorts feel the hour is too late, I would be happy to—"

"No, that's all right," said Holmes, brightly. "I want to see how it turns out. Right, Watson? Of course we'll come."

"Oh..." said Thaddeus, a moment's disappointment

playing across his doughy features. Yet, to credit the man, he recovered instantly. He reached for an ostentatious brass bell that lay beside his pile of cushions and gave it two clangorous shakes. "*Khitmutgar! Khitmutgar!* Bring my hat! We are off on an adventure!"

5

HAD I THOUGHT I WAS PART OF A STRANGE GROUP, EARLIER in the evening? Ah, the benefit of hindsight. As we rolled away from Thaddeus Sholto's house, I knew better.

It had taken the old *khitmutgar* and Williams the boxer roughly a quarter of an hour to disassemble their master's suspicious hookah and reassemble it in Sholto's carriage. Thaddeus apologized for his weakness, but assured us that he was incapable of being separated from his "comforts" for long.

Well did I believe it. Within minutes the interior atmosphere of the carriage had become nearly intolerable. Whenever Thaddeus Sholto went more than a dozen breaths without a puff from his hookah, he became visibly weakened and—strange to say it—even floppier than normal.

Oh, and another thing: Holmes now had the second strangest hat of our little gang. Thaddeus rarely went outside, he said. Especially at night, for his ears got cold. He was a great sufferer—had he mentioned that? Yet he had a special hat for just such occasions. It was rabbit skin, he said.

What he should have said was that it was two rabbits. Two unfortunate rabbits that had been caught, murdered, inexpertly hollowed out, and sewn into a peaked monstrosity that just managed to cover Thaddeus Sholto's bizarre head. One rabbit had been gray, the other brown. Very little work had been done on them; they were mostly intact. Their stiff little legs shook up and down as the carriage bounced along. Their hollow eye-sockets stared at me, begging a sympathy that I certainly granted, though I suspect they failed to appreciate it. Both rabbits' ears had been hacked away, inverted and sewn to their sides to make little flaps that hung down over Thaddeus's own ears, to keep away the night's chill. What an horrific sight he made, sitting across from me, holding his hookah-stem in one hand, absentmindedly stroking one soft rabbit-ear flap with the other, telling us all about his beloved brother.

Holmes sat beside him. I had hoped Mary Morstan might sit beside Thaddeus—a privilege I'm sure he'd long dreamed of—yet Holmes still seemed to hope that romance might bloom between her and me, and resisted every attempt to place Mary and Thaddeus together.

"Holmes, why don't you sit near me?" I suggested.

"No. You sit with Mary."

"I sat with Miss Morstan on the way here. Perhaps she could sit next to Mr. Sholto, so that you and I might confer."

"But, no. She needs to sit with you!"

"Really, Holmes? Why?"

"Because I want to sit next to Mr. Sholto."

"Oh, do you? And why is that?"

"Well… um… because I want to try the hookah!"

"You *what*?"

"Yes! I've always considered buying one, you know. Yet I did not wish to do so until I'd tried one out. Mr. Sholto, I don't suppose you'd mind?"

"Oh, no! Mew! Wonderful things, really. And so underappreciated. Hew. I warn you, though: it's strong stuff! Oh dear, strong indeed…"

And suddenly I realized this was not a battle I minded losing. Let Thaddeus sit with Mary another day; tonight was for finer sports. Tonight was for watching Holmes try to keep a straight face while sucking on a methane hookah. It's funny the little rewards adventuring brings.

How well I remember his look of dread as the mouthpiece neared his lips, the whiteness of his face and the beads of sweat that stood out upon his brow. With fondness, I recall that his initial reaction to that first puff was not his expression—oh, how well he mastered himself— but a trembling spasm that started in his stomach and ran out to all four limbs. Then the coughing and retching took over. Thaddeus seemed rather hurt by this, until Holmes insisted that he simply was not used to the hookah, but he liked it very well. Yes. Yes. It was forceful yet mellow with a fruity initial bite but a woody undertone with just a hint of… was that nutmeg?

Personally, I suspected it was swamp gas.

"Holmes you look ill," I said. "Come here and let me examine you. Miss Morstan, I'm sorry to inconvenience you, but if you'd be so kind as to switch places with—"

"No! Nonsense! You stay right there!"

"Holmes, are you sure?"

"Of course I am."

"Because you look rather unwell."

"I'm fine. And Miss Morstan must stay where she is, because… because… I haven't finished my hookah!"

"Oh? And you intend to?"

"Well, yes, I… I'm enjoying it, you see. Thaddeus, if you'd be so kind…"

One thing I will never fault Holmes for is his conviction. By God, he sat there the whole trip chatting with Thaddeus about the finer points of smoking, taking puffs from the hookah and occasionally opening the carriage door to spew still-smoking toast-and-soup vomit all over the street.

"Brother Bartholomew found the treasure by a simple application of maths," Thaddeus told us, as Holmes decorated the cobblestones for the third time. "Yes. Hew. You see an external measurement of Pondicherry Lodge revealed the house to be seventy-four feet high, but by measuring the floors, Brother Bartholomew found he could only account for seventy of them."

"Wait a minute now," I cried. "Your family's home is *seventy-four feet high*?

Thaddeus nodded. "Mew. But you see, the key was that Brother Bartholomew could not account for the extra four feet. We knew it could not be under the house, for I did not even include the fifty-two feet of cellar in my initial figure—"

"A hundred and twenty-six vertical feet? Your house is more than twelve stories tall?"

"Oh no. Only seven."

"Some of them must be of preposterous height, then."

"Larger than the house I am in now," Thaddeus confirmed, "but that is my only basis for comparison. Now, do you want to hear about the missing four feet or not?"

Mary gave me a vicious jab in the ribs with her elbow and insisted, "We *do*."

"Brother Bartholomew realized that the extra four feet could only be accounted for at the top of the house. Hew. Now that is funny, for the attic has always been his particular haunt, ever since he was a child and Father put him in charge of the alchemical laboratory we used to make Mother's perfume."

"Tell me, Thaddeus, did your mother's 'perfume' smell anything like your hookah smoke?"

"Ha! Hew! Why would it?" Thaddeus scoffed, but then pursed his lips and added, "Although, now that you mention it…"

"That is because—" I began, but a perfectly savage kick from Mary Morstan turned my sentence into a surprised yelp, followed by a number of words I ought not put to paper.

"The extra four feet?" she reminded us.

"Hmmm. Hew. Yes. Brother Bartholomew and I made a number of excavations in and around the house over the years. But it was only when he broke through the attic ceiling that he found—"

"My treasure!" Mary crowed.

"Well, *our* treasure, yes," said Thaddeus, his face showing the first signs of worry that Actual Mary Morstan might not be the same as Poetry-Journal Mary Morstan.

"Let's go get it!"

Rubbing my shin, I reminded her, "We are currently driving around in the middle of the night on *exactly that errand*, madam."

That quieted her a bit. Of course it could not calm Holmes's terrible noises. Coughing. Occasional vomiting. Deep belly gurgles worse than those he made on the occasions when he drank proper poison. Yet, since no amount of intestinal discomfort actually slows a carriage, we soon arrived at Pondicherry Lodge.

Good *God*.

The thing was monstrous. I'm sure only the fact it stood within a little hollow kept it from being one of England's most famous eyesores. If it had been on a hill, it would have dominated Upper Norwood and I'm sure been the subject of endless local debate. She was seventy-four feet tall and there wasn't a straight line in her. It was as if her architect had said, "Look the important thing is that it's huge. If it happens to go off to the left a bit, then to the right, then lean precariously forward for a while as if it's just going to tip over and fall on whoever is in the driveway, I find that perfectly acceptable. Now, build the thing." Pondicherry Lodge would have been quite grand if someone had taken the time to straighten her. Instead, someone had taken the time to rifle her. Her grounds were dotted with innumerable pits, where one or the other of the Sholto brothers had dug looking for the Agra treasure. In fact, even the exterior walls of the old house had been breached in several locations, leaving holes that looked like artillery hits. There must also have been some notion that the base of a tree would be a fine place to hide a treasure, for every single one had been undermined to such an extent that they leaned at precarious angles.

A blast of pale moonlight threw angular shadows across the house's irregular lines and did a fine job of pointing out: "Hello, I just wanted you nice people to realize you are about to head into a place that is not normal."

Yes, thank you, moon.

Thaddeus put on his most determined face, strode to the porch as gallantly as his little legs would allow, and gave the massive oak door a masterful pounding.

Splat, *splat*, *splat*, went his doughy little hand, so feebly that only those right next to him might have a chance of hearing it.

Luckily, there was a bell.

The man who opened the door was something like Williams, but nowhere near as subtle. If Williams was the former lightweight champion of England, this fellow must have fought in the yak-weight division. Apparently, it was a family habit to select the help solely from the ranks of England's most hardened ex-boxers. He cracked open the door and exclaimed, "Why, Master Thaddeus! What are you doing here at this hour?"

"That is no concern of yours, McMurdo!" our host

thundered, insofar as a pile of shapeless white skin could thunder. "We have business with Brother Bartholomew; admit us at once!"

"Right, but… it *is* my concern, since I take my orders from Master Bartholomew, and he's asleep at the moment, and I'm supposed to keep him safe and undisturbed, and you've shown up in the middle of the night with three strangers. You see what it looks like from where I'm standing, Master Thaddeus?"

Apparently, he did, for he wilted a little. Holmes, however, stepped boldly past him, waving one finger in the air and proclaiming, "Not all strangers, McMurdo! You may have forgotten me, but I'll wager you've not forgot that cross-punch I landed under your chin, eh?"

It rather seemed McMurdo had forgotten them both. He narrowed his eyes at Holmes and muttered, "Yeah… we call those 'uppercuts'." Then, with a gasp of recognition, he sprang back from the door and cried, "By God's holy balls! It's you! *The Whirling Fisticuffsman!*"

"The what?" I asked Holmes.

He gave me a prideful beam and said, "Did I not mention, Watson? I may have dabbled in amateur boxing for a time."

"That can't have gone well."

"What do you mean? I retired undefeated!"

"Why would anybody retire if they were still undefeated?" I wondered, but McMurdo illuminated me.

"I do remember that uppercut! It were the strangest thing. Hardly felt like nothing at all—"

"*Hey!*"

"—but it took me right up, off me feet. Way up. Ten, maybe fifteen feet above the crowd. Then with no warning, it dropped me down amongst the screamin' mob and the barker called the fight. Why, the Whirling Fisticuffsman musta taken ten or twelve men down like that! But where's that big moustache you used to have? And how'd you grow your teeth back?"

I slapped a palm to my brow. My own knowledge of Holmes's habits painted the rest of the picture. "So, you had disguised yourself…"

"…as a common Irish working boxer!" Holmes confirmed. "And let me tell you, it was my funnest disguise ever. Except the moustache kept falling off whenever I got punched in the face. Still, I had a fine time, trying my luck in 'the fancy'. Who knows how far I could have got if the fellows hadn't got rather afraid of me and started drawing official attention to my unique fighting style."

"And this is why someone retires undefeated, one supposes?"

"And hides in a cellar for two months, hoping he won't be burned for witchcraft. Yes. But I'm sure McMurdo won't keep us standing about in the cold now, eh?"

"Well," said the big man, "I prob'ly *couldn't*."

"Exactly!" said Holmes, giving McMurdo a companionable pat on the shoulder as he strode past. "Now, where would I find this Master Bartholomew of yours?"

"He's likely up in the—"

FISHGUT WAREHOUSE

Recently De-Loused and with Twenty Per-Cent Fewer Rodents.

MARVEL AT

the **DUBLIN DESTROYER**

the **CORK CRUSHER**

the **DINGLE DANDY**

Don't be the Only Gentleman or Lady in your Social Circle who has not seen First Hand the Awe and Majesty of this One of a Kind Pugilist. His Fists like Two Meat Pies Filled with Bees. His Arms like Charybdis of Greek Legend. His Facial Hair like that of other Men, but More so. Miss this Bout and Risk being the Embarrassment of Your Community.

PUNCHER of FACES
SWINGER of ARMS

The Proud Proprietor of Fishgut Ware-House, H. Fishgut, Proudly Invites You to Experience an Evening of Profound Pounding, Fantastical Fighting, Superlative Sweating, and Bleeding that is Beyond Belief.
Fun for the Whole Family.

the

Whirling

Fisticuffsman

It's you! The Whirling
Fisticuffsman!

But Bartholomew Sholto's hulking bodyguard was cut off by a strange sound. It started quite soft, from far above us, but grew louder as we listened.

"Aaaaaaaaaaaaaaaaaaahhhhhhhh!" Thud, thud, thud, thud, thud. *Pant*, *pant*. "Aaaaaaaaaaaaaaahhhhhhhh!" Thud, thud, thud, thud, thud. *Pant*, *pant*. "Aaaaaaaaaaaaaaahhhhhhhh!"

And so on, and so on, as a rather round lady in her early seventies made a panicked sort of progress down the stairs towards us, from the shadowed heights of Pondicherry Lodge, all the way to the well-lit foyer at the bottom. As she reached us, sweat-slicked, breathless and still attempting to scream, McMurdo laid a concerned hand on her shoulder and asked, "Why, Mrs. Bernstone! Whatever can the matter be?"

"It's Master Bartholome— Oh God… Master Barth— Oh, for Christ's sake! Oh, that's one tall goddamn house! It's Master Bartholomew!"

"What about him?"

"Well he's been locked up in that laboratory all day, hasn't he? I tried to get him to come down to bed, I did. Said it was late and hadn't he better come back to his nice pile of cushions and have a hookah and a lie-down? But there was no answer! And I looked through the keyhole— God help me—and there's something wrong with him! Terribly *wrong*! Oh, Christ, but the house is tall! Get me a glass of water, won't you?"

Holmes struck a heroic pose and declared, "Seems as if we've come just in time, eh, Watson?"

I wilted. "Really? All those stairs?"

"Come on, man! The game is afoot!"

If I had somewhat rebounded from my pathetic state of that morning, the long slog up all those stairs undid my progress. We went up the elegant, curving staircase to a smart-looking landing, on the floor that held all the family bedrooms, I think. The floor above that was slightly more threadbare—servants and storage, perhaps. The next floor was composed of a single room: the massive vault where Mrs. Sholto had lived for many years, in an atmosphere of pure "perfume". From there, a rickety wooden staircase led up to the floor above, the alchemical workshop where the chemicals were mixed to keep the more unusual Sholtos alive and well. Nobody answered my knock at the chemical-stained old door, nor my repeated attempts to call Bartholomew by name. I tried the handle, but found the door locked. Deeming that whatever tactics served nosey servants might serve a gentleman as well, I put my eye to the keyhole.

"Good God, Holmes!"

There, propped in his chair in a circle of flickering candlelight, sat Bartholomew Sholto.

Or what was left of him, poor fellow.

He must have been Thaddeus's twin, for if Bartholomew had been well and moving, I'd have had a hard time telling the one from the other. But he had practically melted into his chair, in a relaxation so profound that a wad of wet clay would have had trouble matching it. His neck was invisible, his head squashed down into his body so completely that they looked like one. His arm dangled off the chair's armrest as if it might be boneless, composed of white rubber. He stared straight at the keyhole with a broad, welcoming smile, somewhat spoiled by the fact that the left side of his face sagged so badly that his teeth seemed to be pouring towards the floor.

Oh, and also: he was dead.

"Get Mrs. Bernstone up here, immediately!" I cried.

From below came the sound of the old housekeeper, calling, "Are you *kidding*?"

McMurdo arrived at the top of the stairs, puffing and panting. "What's wrong?" he asked.

"It's Bartholomew! I fear the worst. I must get in to see if we can help him, or at least determine what has happened, but the door is locked. I thought Mrs. Bernstone might have a key."

"Maybe," said the old fighter, "but the only key I know of for sure is the one Bartholomew keeps."

"Damn!" I cried. "That means it's probably in there with him. We've got to find a way to—"

From behind me came a flash of purple light, an ear-piercing shriek, and the gentle sound of lock parts clattering to the floor.

"No, we are in luck," said Holmes. "The lock has exploded."

"What? Why? How?" McMurdo cried.

Holmes gave him a friendly smile. "Likely a booby-trap, don't you think?"

"Possibly," I said, giving Holmes a warning look. "Come on, I want to see what happened in there."

The most apparent thing, I had already guessed: murder. Bartholomew Sholto had no pulse, no breath, and his body was cool. Rigor mortis had not set in, but I suspected it never would; Bartholomew's body felt like a rubber bladder full of water. Whatever had killed him seemed to have liquefied his innards, while leaving his skin intact. Exactly what chemical or poison could do that, I had no idea, but as to how the agent had been administered, that much was clear: a jagged thorn protruded from the back of his neck. It was made of a substance rather like a compromise between wood and bone. As I knelt to examine it, Holmes drifted up behind me and said, in a quiet whisper, "I wouldn't touch that, if I were you."

"But, what is it, Holmes?"

"Most likely *not* a healthy dose of vitamins and minerals, don't you think?"

"But look at the material of this thorn! Doesn't it seem… unusual?"

"More than that, Watson. I suspect it is otherworldly. Look at the state of the man; he's practically juice. And let us remember: the other otherworldly poisons we have seen all have a tendency to liquefy things."

"Well, yes," I admitted, thinking back to the venom Grimesby Roylott had used on his stepdaughter (and also the back of my favorite jacket). Oh, and there was the unknown agent that had caused Eduardo Lucas's torso to melt to stinking brown sauce. "But this man has not liquefied nearly to the extent of the other cases we have known."

"He probably would have, if he'd been *boring*," said Holmes. "Yet remember: this man was half demon. The poison was not so potent against his interesting half."

"So then, this—" I flopped the rubbery, juice-filled arm of Bartholomew Sholto back and forth "—this would be a *mild* reaction?"

"And perhaps you'd better not get any of that toxin on yourself, eh? Leave it, Watson. There have got to be other clues about."

It was an understatement such as only Holmes could craft. Dear reader, can I possibly describe the number of things that were wrong in that room? It might well be easier to describe the items that weren't completely abnormal. The chair. The desk. The wallpaper. The rug. The door.

Oh, wait… the door had recently been demon-blasted.

Other than that, the room was singular. It was large, taking up the entire floor above Mrs. Sholto's vault. Each wall had one or two windows with heavy iron frames. These had been corroded shut by the miasma of vapors— both odorous and odious—that seeped forth from the collection of aged and leaky chemical tanks arranged about the walls. A coal-powered steam engine lay at the center of a room, connected to a gigantic leather bellows which was piped—by means of snaking rubber tubes—to some of the nearby gas tanks. Doubtless, this was how Mother's "perfume" was pumped to the floor below. On the desk before Bartholomew lay a piece of paper with "THE SIGN OF NINE" scrawled on it. As the paper was fresh and uncreased, I believed it to have been a recent addition—

probably left by the murderer. The desk also held a map of the house and grounds of Pondicherry Lodge, covered with red X's marking places where the Agra treasure had been sought and missed.

Also notable was the place where the Agra treasure had been found. Two stepladders stood beneath a hole in the ceiling, which had been hacked open using pickaxes, shovels, and no great art. The tools lay covered in plaster dust by the feet of the stepladders which—judging by the footprints in the dust—had seen a great deal of traffic in the last day or so. Climbing one of them, I stuck my head through the hole and up into the secret chamber where the Agra treasure had lain.

It hardly seemed a worthy hiding place for such a precious item; unfinished walls led up to bare rafters and the dusty underside of Pondicherry Lodge's roof. There was an access hatch leading out onto the roof, which—given the locked door and the corroded window frames—I instantly assumed to be the route of ingress for Bartholomew's murderer. My own skills as a tracker were slight, yet the particulars of the situation were so plain—and so bizarre— that I could hardly fail to read them. I called Holmes up into the little attic to show him what I had found.

"See this large, rectangular area where there is no dust? I think that is where the Agra treasure sat!"

"Unless somebody with huge, box-shaped feet came in here and took exactly one step, I'd say you are correct," Holmes agreed.

"And look here, between the hatch in the roof and the

area where the treasure lay. What do you make of that?"

The footprints were peculiar in the extreme. One set seemed to be that of a man; the tread of an average shoe or boot (my lack of skill did not permit me to determine which) on the left side was alternated with a queer, round impression on the right. I deemed that he must have lost that right leg at some point and been fitted with a peg.

Yet his tracks were not as unique as the ones beside them.

"Is that... a bear?" Holmes wondered.

"If so, a very small one, I should think."

The tracks had a narrow heel, and a wide, splayed foot with distinct scratch marks both in front of each toe and behind the heel. They were about the size of a child's foot but definitely not the shape that might be left by any child I'd ever met. Come to think of it, not any bear, either.

"Holmes... I'm no naturalist, but... is there such a thing as a bear with a claw behind its heel?"

"I don't know... Ah! The South-German back-clawed black bear! Yes, *Ursus germanicus back-scratchicus*—"

"You're making that up."

"Well, probably."

The claw-footed little fellow seemed to have spent quite some time near the hatch in the roof, working an old rope and pulley attached to one of the beams. He'd also gone near the treasure, where he and peg-leg had left distinct drag marks, pulling it from the center of the room to the pulley. Most tellingly, there was a set of footprints from the hatch to the hole down into the chemical workshop.

Looking down through the hole, one had a clear view of Bartholomew's desk.

"I'm no expert, Holmes, but as I read it the little bear-like fellow got in through that hatch, came over here, shot Bartholomew as he sat at his desk, then went back to the hatch, let in his one-legged compatriot, the two of them used the rope and tackle to lower the Agra treasure down the side of the house and escaped the way they'd come in."

"Er… *why* is there a rope and tackle here, Watson?"

I shrugged. "The mechanism is certainly old. I doubt the thief climbed up here and installed it. Probably that's how Major Sholto got the treasure up here in the first place. Egad! There's no hatch to the room below! Just imagine: whenever John Sholto needed funds, he must have had to scale the outside of his own house and sneak treasure out!"

"The old fellow didn't look very spry, even in that picture," Holmes laughed. "I imagine he didn't do it very often."

"No. No, probably he deposited a fair amount in a bank or made some other investment before he secreted the main body of the treasure up here."

Our investigation was cut short by the breathless arrival of Mrs. Bernstone, Mary Morstan and Thaddeus Sholto. It seems the old housekeeper had responded to our initial summons of some fifteen minutes earlier, but her arrival had been much delayed by Thaddeus's insistence that he come too. Mrs. Bernstone had therefore enlisted the help of Miss Morstan to drag her former master and his hookah up four flights of stairs.

"You needed me?" she called breathlessly, from the room below.

"Oh… not anymore, Mrs. Bernstone," I shouted back. "We wanted to ask if you had a key to this room, but we made our own way in."

"Bastards! I'll kill yeh!"

"We're very sorry, Mrs. Bernstone."

Any further threats to life and limb that might have been delivered by the sweating septuagenarian were cut short by a horrible cry from Thaddeus.

"No-no-no-mew-hew-no-mew! Brother Bartholomew! What has happened?"

Holmes gave me a pained look and climbed back down one of the stepladders. "I am so sorry, my new friend, but it seems somebody has broken in here, murdered your brother, and stolen the Agra treasure."

"Noooooooooooo! Rhaaaaaaaaaaaaaaaaargh!"

This latter, of course, was from Mary Morstan who was not well pleased to hear she'd just spent the entire evening traipsing all over London with a gang of utter weirdos, only to have the treasure she'd been promised pulled out from beneath her very nose. For an instant I feared she was going to snatch up Thaddeus Sholto and throw him across the room.

As for Thaddeus, all the bravery he had mustered to please Mary disappeared in an instant. The death of his brother had him perfectly overwrought. And why not? With his father and mother gone too, he was the sole surviving member of his family. Indeed, there was every likelihood he was the only surviving member of his *species* and now quite alone in the world. He wailed over his brother, fretted that the murderer might come back for him as well, and opined that—given his well-known feud with the late Bartholomew—he might be suspected of his brother's death.

Bernstone and McMurdo had no shortage of theories as to what had happened and it was dashed difficult to keep them from completely ruining the crime scene. Therefore, I insisted the discussion be moved downstairs—drawing a hard look from Mrs. Bernstone. After some moments' herding and cajoling, our assembly was at last returned to the ground floor. There, I left Holmes alone with the rabble for a few minutes, hoping to scout the grounds for signs of where the thieves had accessed the roof.

"Well?" asked Holmes when I returned some minutes later. "Any luck, Watson?"

"Right below the hoist there's a rather large dent in the flowerbed. It seems they dropped the precious Agra treasure at least part of the way. I found tracks from both peg-leg and little-bear. I think they went across the grounds in a north-east direction, but I'm not very good at this sort of thing. I've no idea where they've gone or how much of a start they've got on us. I don't think there's much I can do to find them."

"Ha! I'm sure *I* might be of service," said Holmes, with a mischievous smile.

"Holmes! No magic!"

"Try to extend me some credit, won't you?" he

grumbled. "That is not what I was going to propose."

"Oh?"

"I happen to know a more Watson-friendly expedient. Have you ever heard of Sherman's Menagerie?"

"I don't believe so."

"Well it's a very impressive place and old Sherman owes me a favor or two. You go there and tell him Warlock Holmes needs somebody tracked. He'll set you up."

"Capital! Now we just need to find a way to extricate ourselves from—"

"Already done," said Holmes, merrily. "Thaddeus wants to report the murder and burglary to the police."

"Wise, I should think."

"And Mary wants everybody arrested."

"Predictable."

"And I thought perhaps we should divide our forces. McMurdo will take you and Miss Morstan in Bartholomew's carriage. Drop Mary off at home, go see Sherman and hurry back here."

"What will you do, Holmes?"

"I shall go with Thaddeus to the police. I know most of them, so I'll do my best to make sure someone competent and sympathetic handles the case. Then I'll escort them back here and show them what you've discovered. As soon as you bring the tracker, we'll see if we can't beat Scotland Yard to our man. Sound good?"

It sounded *uncharacteristically* good. I stared at Holmes with growing suspicion. He'd been surprisingly competent today. Why? Knowing him as I did, I realized that what others often mistook for stupidity on Holmes's part was frequently simple distraction. Old men's minds will wander, after all, and Holmes was in excess of two hundred and fifty years of age. In truth, his depth of knowledge was colossal and he had managed on his own for longer than I could wrap my mind around. But still… why this sudden burst of competence? Did he have some reason to care greatly about the Sholtos? About Mary Morstan?

And then, I realized: it was probably *me*. He was making up for me. I was nearly at the limit of my strength and my mind was perhaps not as sharp as it might be, given the state I'd been in when the affair began. Was Holmes putting forth unusual focus and extra effort because I couldn't? As I stared up at him, trying to fathom his motivations, he said, "Oh, and by the way: have fun dropping Mary off! *Row-rowl!*"

"What do you mean, '*row-rowl*'?"

"*Rowr!*"

"Don't do that with your eyebrows, Holmes."

"*Ha-rowr!*"

"All right. I'm leaving."

6

THE JOURNEY BACK TO MARY MORSTAN'S EMPLOYERS'
home in Lower Camberwell was not the romantic retreat
Holmes seemed to hope it would be. For the better part
of the ride I slept on the seat across from Mary, while she
fumed. She left me in no doubt that this made me a very
poor escort and nothing like a gentleman, either.

I didn't care.

Despite the fact that we arrived in the pre-dawn hours,
both Mr. and Mrs. Cecil Forrester met us at the door.

"Oh look, Cecil," said Mrs. Forrester through a
clenched smile, "this fine gentleman is *returning* Mary to
us. I do hope everything is all right."

"Yes," her husband agreed, through a similarly
strained grin. "We had rather… um… *feared* that some
twist of fortune might preclude the possibility that young
Mary might ever return to us! Ha! Ha-ha!"

Poor fellow. I decided to show the light of hope to the
Forresters.

"Indeed, your fears were not far off," I said. "It seems
that Mary is heir to a fortune large enough that it would be

absolutely preposterous for her to continue in her capacity as governess."

"Really?" said Mrs. Forrester, tears of hope forming in her eyes.

"Unfortunately, we arrived to claim it just a few hours after the treasure in question was stolen."

"Noooooooo!"

"Yet hope remains. Scotland Yard and the great consulting detective, Warlock Holmes, are on the case. If fortune is with us, I may be bringing news to you soon."

"Oh God! Is there anything we can do to help? Anything? *Anything!*"

"At this moment, nothing, but allow me to return to my duties. Farewell, Mr. and Mrs. Forrester and… good luck to us all."

I slept again as McMurdo drove us to the address Holmes had given: 3 Pinchin Lane, a taxidermist's down near the river at Lambeth. Just as Holmes had promised, over the third establishment on the right was a sign that read SHERMAN'S MENAGERIE. In the window was a stuffed weasel, holding a stuffed rabbit. It was unclear whether the two were meant to be fighting or… *courting*. Whatever the nature of their discourse, old Mr. Sherman seemed to have framed it as a moment of profound ferocity. Teeth were bared, claws were brandished and he had replaced both animals' eyes with red glass marbles that practically glowed as the dawn's light fell across them.

I gave a knock. Then another. Then a rather loud third. I knew it was impolite at this early hour, but Holmes had insisted it was necessary. Finally a bleary-looking, white-haired gentleman slid open an upper window and shouted, "Bugger off! I told yeh, I don't do 'umans! Wait a moment... Who're you?"

"Not who you expected, clearly. I am a friend of Warlock Holmes. We need to track a murderer and he said you are the man to see."

"Warlock 'olmes, eh?" Sherman said and gave a grunt of... I don't know... grudging respect? "Best come in."

I waited as an alarming number of bolts and chains were slid free on the other side of the battered wooden door. Finally, it cracked open a pinch, emitting that special musk that only two hundred dead animals and half a hundred live ones are capable of producing. As he beckoned me inside, Sherman said, "Mind you don't let the timber wolf out. 'E's a bugger to chase down in the morning."

"Timber wolf?" I wondered, but my conviction that this must surely be the strangest member of Sherman's Menagerie did not survive more than five feet inside the door. The walls were lined with cages of unfortunate animals and the shelves with displays of even less-fortunate ones. Or so I thought. I was just regarding a strange composition of a badger about to eat a stuffed mouse, when Sherman mentioned, over his shoulder, "Mind that badger; she bites."

"But isn't she—"

In an instant, the badger dropped the stuffed mouse and made a sudden grab for my moustache. I cried out and lunged back, nearly tipping a puma's cage over, which may have made matters a great deal worse.

"People don't give 'em much credit," Sherman grumbled, "but badgers is one o' nature's most clever ambush-predators."

"So it would seem."

"Now leave the nice gentleman alone, Mrs. Scruffers, or I'll have to kill yeh and stuff yeh for real. And who wants that, eh? Now then... where'd I put that demon...?"

"What? *Demon?* No, no, no! I am here for a tracking dog!"

"Then you'll be wanting Old Toby," said Sherman, jerking one thumb at a stuffed dog on the shelf above his shop counter, "but you're about seven months late. Broke me 'eart when Toby went, it did. But never you mind. Mr. Warlock 'olmes left a demon in my care and said he might require the bugger's services someday. Well, today's the day, that's what I say! Ah! 'Ere we are!"

Mr. Sherman produced a large wooden crate that shook and rattled as he placed it on the counter. He carefully slid back two latches on the side, reached in with an iron poker and fished around until he had retrieved one end of a tattered leather lead.

"'Ere you go," he said, holding it out to me. "That's 'is leash. Don't let go of it. Ever. For any reason. He'll mind you so long as you're holding it, but drop it an' God 'elp us all."

With deep trepidation, I peeped around the side and into the dark confines of the crate. The thing that peered out at me was completely alien. It had four legs, though the term "spiny little spike-stabbers" might be a more apt description. It also had four eyes, although not in the usual place. They were luminous yellow blobs slung just beneath its jaw. The jaw itself was composed of a number of finger-like "teeth" that opened out to either side. The entire creature was covered in chitinous armor plates— black, but with all the colors of the rainbow shining in subtle iridescence, like a beetle. I'd have said it was an exoskeleton, were it not for the ropy strands of tangled purplish musculature that protruded from inside the creature and attached to various plates. So... a hybrid endo-exoskeleton, semi-insectoid physiology and... well look: the important thing was he was staring up at me with a brand of playful curiosity that made it plain he was wondering what I tasted like.

"We calls 'im Bix," Sherman told me.

"*Bix?* What kind of a name is that?"

Sherman shrugged. "Most of the other one-syllable sounds was taken. As I said, he'll mind you when you've got the leash in hand. And it's safe to tie 'im up, long as it's real secure, like; he won't go nowhere. But just don't let anything get near 'im unless you want it eaten. Now good day to yeh."

"What? No! You can't expect me to just go wandering the streets of London with a monster on a leash."

"Better'n off-leash."

"That is not my point, sir, and I believe you know it! Think of how it will look!"

"I don't care!" Sherman thundered. "Warlock 'olmes drops this bugger off and then I don't see hide nor hair of him for years! Never a 'how's that insect/demon/dog doing, eh?' Now Bix's got his uses, I'll warrant that. Better nose than even Old Toby had. Pretty good for scarin' away beggar kids, too. But enough is enough! Out!"

"But I can't very well—"

"*Out!*"

Desperately, my eyes flew all about the shop, searching for something—anything—I might use to disguise the hideous Bix. It had to be roughly his size, and something that wouldn't seem out of place on a leash. Really, there was only one choice.

"Toby! I want to buy Toby!"

"Eh?"

"You're a taxidermist, aren't you? Sell me that stuffed dog!"

"That's me best friend! He ain't for sale!"

"It's just a dead dog!"

"Oi! Toby were family! I'm a lonely man! Look about! See many kids runnin' around, do yeh?"

"Twenty pounds!"

"What?"

"I'll give you twenty pounds for that stuffed dog."

"Fifty!"

"How dare you!"

"Toby's family and the price is fifty!"

"That is robbery, sir!"

"Fifty pounds, or get out!"

"But I… Argh! Very well! But you have to throw in some string and lend me a pair of scissors!" I said, beginning a subtle exploration of my left ear. In our early adventures, Holmes had somehow magicked a significant quantity of cash into my aural canal. He'd warned me there was a finite amount in there, and only to use it in cases of emergency—which this certainly was—but I hated having to dig around in my ear for funds almost as much as I hated the circumstance that had necessitated it.

Twenty minutes later, I emerged from the alley behind Sherman's Menagerie, leading New Toby. Original Toby was now naught but a sad little pile of sawdust stuffing and sticks beside Mr. Sherman's suspicious boxes of… whatever it is taxidermists keep in dark alleys. Still, Original Toby had served his purpose. I had what I needed: the poor old mutt's hide, which—through the liberal application of twine—had been stretched over Bix's armor plates.

"All right, listen here," I hissed at him, as we stepped out into the street, "until further notice, your name is Toby. You are a perfectly average dog and I expect you to act like it. Is that clear?"

"SKRAX!" Bix shouted.

"Well that's not a normal doggie noise, now is it? Not helpful, 'Toby'! I don't suppose there's another sound you could—"

"STRAAAAAAAAAAAAAAAAAB-RAAAAB-BAAAABLE! XXRAAAAAAH!"

"Brilliant. Thank you."

What could I do but adopt the pose of the well-to-do dog owner. I pushed my hat back, thrust my nose to the stratosphere and held my leash arm straight ahead of me at shoulder level. *Look at the gentleman* said my supercilious posture; *feel no need to examine his pet.* If I had any illusions as to how well my guise was working, I kept them only until McMurdo saw me approaching the carriage.

"Awwwww! What the *hell?*"

"What are you complaining about?" I sniffed. "I'm the one who has to sit with him. Now please, just get us back to Pondicherry Lodge, won't you?"

Upon my arrival at Pondicherry Lodge, I was surprised to find the place deserted. I had no idea what to do next, so I tied "Toby" up in the grounds and sat in the drawing room to wait for Holmes. I don't think I'd been there for more than two or three minutes before I was fast asleep.

I was wakened some hours later by the sound of my new pet greeting my old friend.

"SKRAX! SKRAX! SKRAX!"

This was followed by Holmes's happy voice, saying, "Toby? Why, hullo, old boy! I haven't seen you in a dog's age! Did you miss me? Did you?"

"SKRAX! SKRAX!"

"Ha ha! Down, boy! Down! What did we say about jumping up?"

"SKRAX!"

"Wait… *Bix?* Aaaaaigh! By the twelve gods! Look what you've done to Toby!"

"SKRAX! SKRAX!"

"Bad Bix! Very bad!"

I was out the door in a shot, waving my arms over my head and shouting, "Holmes! It's all right! Don't damage him, Holmes! We need the disguise!"

To say Warlock was pleased by the state of his old dog friend—or the clothing of his old demonic one—would be to strain the truth. Nevertheless, I convinced him that any misfortunes suffered by Old Toby were only the fault of nature, and any subsequent indignities must be laid at my door. Bix was entirely innocent.

"Ugh," said Holmes, when I'd finished. "It sounds as if your morning was nearly as tiresome as my own."

"Whatever do you mean, Holmes? And does it have anything to do with the fact there's nobody here?"

"Hmm. The underlying cause, I fear," he sighed. "We went to the local police station to report Bartholomew's death. The matter was complicated, however, by the fact that the sergeant was being visited by one of Scotland Yard's detective inspectors, Mr. Athelney Jones."

"Athelney? What an unfortunate name. I don't think we know the man, do we?"

"Only by reputation."

"Which is?" I prompted.

"That he does not care for *my* reputation," said Holmes, with a shake of his head. "Moreover, he is spoken of as an inspector whose impressive number of solved cases is somewhat buoyed by his disregard for whether or not he's got the right fellow."

"Oh dear…"

"Quite. I'm afraid Thaddeus was first to be arrested. Jones was very interested in his and his brother's well-known difference of opinion about what ought to be done with their large fortune. Oh, he cried and meowed and made just terrible noises!"

"But, Holmes, we've got to help him!" I cried. "His hookah! I'm not sure he can survive without it!"

"Calm yourself, Watson, it's already taken care of. I forged a prescription and convinced Jones it was a medicinal hookah. I'm not sure how much my forgery looked like the actual article, but even if it makes it back to the doctor who supposedly issued it—one John Watson of Baker Street—I hope my story will not be contradicted."

"Well done, Holmes!" I cried.

"Thank you, Watson. Sadly, it was my only victory. Oh! Except for one other minor point: Mary got her wish!"

"Eh?"

"When she said she wanted everybody arrested."

"What? Everybody?"

"Down to the scullery maid, I fear," said Holmes. "You see, we protested to Jones that Thaddeus Sholto was perhaps a bit too frail to scale the side of a seventy-foot house unaided, and zap his brother in the back of the head with a blowgun. Sadly, Athelney Jones is one who can see conspiracy in every corner. More to the point, he also saw the pulley in the attic and reasoned that someone might easily have winched Thaddeus up there. He began looking for likely individuals and... well, I'm afraid he cast a bit of a wide net. Oh! That reminds me: is McMurdo here? McMurdo, can you hear me?"

Of course he could. One does not have two strangers in one's inexplicably empty place of employment with a demon on a leash, then fail to eavesdrop. The big prizefighter emerged sheepishly from behind a garden shed and said, "Yes, sir?"

"Sorry to say it, old man, but you're under arrest for murder. Do be a lamb and surrender yourself at the police station, won't you?"

McMurdo made a strangled little noise and ducked back behind the shed.

"No, no, no!" said Holmes, clucking his tongue. "I wouldn't run! I really wouldn't. Jones's case is coming apart faster than he can weave it together and Watson and I have every intention of bringing the actual culprit in soon. Fear not, McMurdo, and tell the rest of our friends the same; your stay is likely to be a short one. That said, I suppose we should begin the sad task of chasing the murderers down."

"Sad?" I wondered. "Why sad?"

"If you had to spend the morning leading one of your old friends around the streets of London dressed in the skin of one of your other old friends, do you not think you might get a bit melancholy?"

7

MELANCHOLY? HA! IN TWENTY MINUTES, HOLMES WAS perfectly joyful.

Though he gave a few tuts and a smattering of what–is–the–world–coming–to sighs as we led Bix to the spot where the treasure had left its dent upon the flowerbed, Holmes quickly warmed to the chase. When we showed our ill-concealed demon one of the peculiar, bear-like footprints, he gave an excited "SKRAX! SKRAX!" and set off on a straight line for the garden wall.

"He's got something, Watson!" Holmes enthused. "Quick now! Quick! Get after him, Bix!"

We burst out onto the lane and from there the little dog-clad abomination led us on a merry chase! We took a strange circuitous route through Lambeth, down around the Oval by way of twisting side streets and onto Kennington Lane. It seems our quarry had taken the less traveled paths—much to my relief. I'm sure we would have had merry hell pushing through peak traffic with our curious little pet, but the luck of fools was with us: it happened to be Sunday. The more pious Londoners were still in church. So... let us say...

three percent of the population. Happily, most of the other ninety-seven percent were having a lie-in and were not out and about to bother us. Well… the *humans*, anyway.

As we turned away from Kennington Lane towards the bend in the river, one of the local four-legged chiefs came to challenge the newcomer. He was a large German Shepherd and veteran of more than a few alleyway disagreements. One fang had been broken off—presumably in some canine unfortunate. One eye was crossed by a scar, which had left it milky and white. He had a territory to protect. He was boss. More than that, he was a shepherd, by God, and someone was astray. He stepped out in front of us and gave a deep basso, "Warf! Warf! Warf!"

To which Toby/Bix replied, "SKREEEXHA-KAIGH-KAI-BREEEEEEGAI I! RABBBLE!"

At this point, the grizzled old war-boss of not-quite-Kennington Lane decided, *You know… it's a free country, right? I'm clearly in the wrong here and… well… enjoy your day.*

Thus we were free to continue down Bond Street and Miles Street, with Holmes and Bix sharing rather a happy mood. I suppose neither of them got out enough. Probably a fine treat for the pair of them. Yet where Miles Street turns into Knight's Place, it all went sour. For the first time, Bix faltered. He stopped. He turned a circle. He wandered half a dozen feet up Knight's Place to our right, but then doubled back and went just as far up our left. Just as I was about to voice my despair to Holmes, Bix got rather excited. He ran into the center of the street, took a moment to give off a violent vibration that shook the nearby windows—signifying exactly what, I shall never know—then "skraxed" enthusiastically and bounded off towards Nine Elms, with Holmes and I racing along behind.

"Must be close now, eh, Watson? I say! Look at the little bugger go!"

Bix pulled up short just outside Broderick and Nelson's Timber Yard and began running in excited circles around a huge, steaming barrel of fresh creosote.

"Um… all right… What do you suppose that means, Holmes?"

My friend shrugged. "Perhaps the murderers have hidden themselves in creosote?"

"If so, they have already met a fate far worse than the courts would have offered them. No, it can't be that. There must be something I am missing…" I racked my brain for a few moments, then snapped my fingers. "Ah! Perhaps one of the murderers happened to *step* in some creosote at Pondicherry Lodge! Maybe Bix never was following the criminals, but has been tracking the smell of creosote all along! That would explain why he became confused at the Knight's Place crossing! If someone wheeled this barrel across our quarry's path, would Bix not follow the stronger scent?"

Holmes gave me a look of pity, as if I were a very simple child and sometimes things must be explained to me slowly and clearly. "He isn't following their *scent*, Watson. He is following their *essence*—the very identity of them."

"Preposterous, Holmes. That is not how tracking is accomplished."

"Oh? And tell me, oh master of deduction: when you were putting that disguise on Bix, did you happen to find a nose?"

"Er... now that you mention it... *no*. I mean, aside from the one I was tying onto him, of course."

"So there must be some other explanation for his behavior, don't you think?"

"I cannot fathom what it might be," I said.

Then again, I did not have to. The missing motive was—at that very moment—elaborated upon by Bix himself. He reared up on his two back spike-legs, extended a hidden row of blade-like spines from his front ones, violently scythed the top off the barrel, then ran forward and dunked his head into the black, tarry liquid.

"Awwwwwwww! Poor little fellow! He was *thirsty*! That was all!" said Holmes. "Did Watson forget to feed you? *Did he?*"

I was forced to admit: I rather had.

Bix was, by then, shoulder deep in creosote and had attracted no small amount of attention from the local workmen. Being Sunday, there were few of them about, yet I did notice one particularly surly example approaching me with an expression on his face that strongly implied he might recently have been the owner of one barrel of fresh creosote and that he'd just love to hear any explanation I might have.

I cleared my throat. "Ah. Well. Good morning. My... um... *dog* was thirsty and... I probably should have mentioned this before, but… how much do you want for the creosote?"

The man raised his eyebrows.

"And the barrel, of course."

Behind me, Bix finally succeeded in overturning his new treasure, sending a splash of pungent black liquid all across what was left of his disguise and a good proportion of the lumberyard, too. Apparently rolling about in creosote-soaked sawdust was just as important to Bix's mental well-being as drinking it was to his physical.

"And the cleanup. And the act of just… not mentioning this to anybody. Ten pounds, I should think. Yes? Ten sound fair?"

"Twenty."

"God damn it! Fine! Here! Holmes, grab Old Toby, won't you? We've got to track down our murderers before the little bastard bankrupts us!"

As we backtracked to Knight's Place—and our actual trail—Holmes and Bix seemed mightily pleased with themselves. Bix was refreshed and renewed. Holmes started humming a little walk-along song. To my horror, it was Beethoven's "Ode to Joy"—an uncomfortable reminder of yesterday. Though I should have been concerned with the memory of thousands of demons focusing their attention on my delicious little world, what really bothered me most was the reminder that Holmes intended to dismiss me as his companion—that this was to be our last adventure together. How I hoped Holmes might forget the whole thing. He forgot a lot of things, didn't he? And he looked perfectly satisfied with his creosote-soaked monster and the fresh Sunday air. He even began to sing the words to "Ode to Joy". Not the proper ones, of course, but just whatever his happy little mind concocted.

> I am going out tonight!
> I'm going to fight the min-o-taur!
> I don't think that I'll survive
> But, who knows? Maybe I'll get far.
> He's got those hooves and
> He's got those horns and
> All that I have is
> This big gun.
> I will fight the min-o-taur! And
> I expect that
> I'll have fun!

And off we went, down Belmont Place and Prince's Street. Despite my companions' mood, I was suffering serious misgivings. Not only about my fate with Holmes, but with the attention of my fellow Londoners. Bix's disguise, you see, had not fared well. I mean, in some ways it was better. It was somewhat harder to tell which parts of "Toby" were dog and which were demon, now that it was all covered in thick, sticky tar-derivative. For a few moments, Holmes and I could be said to resemble nothing more than two gentleman friends who had just dipped their dog in creosote and were now out enjoying a fine morning's walk. Yet the tar-sodden fur of

Original Toby was now too heavy for the string I'd used to tie it in place. Some bits of twine worked themselves loose and others began fraying. Significant portions of Original Toby began to slough away from New Toby. So significant, in fact, that Holmes and I could soon be said to resemble two gentleman friends who had just *boiled* their dog in creosote and were now out enjoying a fine morning's walk while the old fellow fell apart.

People were beginning to notice. People were beginning to point and stare. A few of them were even beginning to follow us, trying to comprehend exactly what they were looking at. To my great horror, two of them were police constables. Not any that Holmes or I knew personally, though I wasn't convinced that would help in any case—not if we were caught in possession of a demon and roughly one-sixth of a trusty old hound.

The only comfort was this: we'd gone as far as we could. As we came down to the end of Broad Street, Bix/Toby led us towards an old building at the edge of the river. It bore a sign that read: MORDECAI SMITH—BOATS TO HIRE BY THE HOUR OR DAY. By "boats" Mr. Smith must have meant "one scabby little dinghy", for that was all that was moored to the pier. Then again, our quarry may well have taken his finer boat. And how were we to pursue them on the Thames?

How indeed, for at that moment, one of the two constables approached and called, "Hexcuse me, gentlemen! Just hwhat do you think you're doin' hwith that *beast*?"

We had no chance to answer, for Bix—either alarmed by the proximity of so many unfamiliar people, or annoyed to have been called "beast"—reared up on his hind legs, extended his demon-blades, clawed the air before the policeman's face and hissed, "SHEEEERAXXAH!" The blades slashed away the last of my twine and Original Toby's sad, tar-soaked hide slid free from Bix's front half and slopped down onto the cobblestones.

To say the crowd looked a bit surprised may be something of an understatement.

"No!" I cried, lunging forward. "Toby! Or... Bix! No!"

But Holmes was faster. In a clear, commanding voice, he called out, "Bix! Go home!" There was a resounding boom and a generous explosion of swirling purple smoke. When it cleared, there was nothing left of Bix/Toby but a smear of creosote upon the street. As I knew Holmes and his ways, it was not hard for me to imagine that at that same moment, just a few miles off, there was probably a matching explosion underneath the shop counter of Sherman's Menagerie, as Bix returned to his accustomed dwelling and Sherman returned to Holmes's servitude.

The crowd of onlookers stared in disbelief. One of the constables began slowly moving his whistle up towards his quivering lip. I had no idea what to do.

Holmes had. Though I had been with him for the last few years, preventing exactly this sort of public exposure, Holmes had a long and clumsy history before

SHEEEERAXXAH!

my arrival. I ought to have known this was not the first time he had been caught out. And—as his facility as a liar was truly inspired—I should also have known he'd have a ready fix.

"Tah-dah!" he cried, sweeping off his goofy paper hat and dropping into a deep bow. As he straightened, he flipped the hat onto the pavement, open side up, and added, "Now how about some applause? And don't forget to show your appreciation for Johnny Magnificent—street magician extraordinaire!"

Egad, it was brash.

But it was also *perfect*. It was that hat that did it. I'm sure the present multitude would have challenged the notion that this was nothing but a parlor trick if it were not for the hat sitting there, offering to relieve them of their hard-earned shillings. Instead the crowd began a general muttering and rolling-of-the-eyes, as if to say, "Oh, please! Think that's worth tuppence, do you? The old disappearing-demon-dressed-as-a-dog routine? You'll have to do a bit better than that. Why, we could all see the creosote! Everyone knows that's how it's done. It's all down to the creosote. Um... *somehow*..."

The single voice of dissension belonged to one of the constables, who dropped three battered coppers into Holmes's paper chapeau and breathed, "Amazin'! Bloody *amazin'*, that was!"

"Thank you, sir," said Holmes, with a smile.

I think I held my breath the entire time it took the crowd to disperse. Only when they were gone did I dare to let it out in a combined explosion/exclamation. "Oh, by God, that was a close one!"

Holmes raised an eyebrow, brushed a non-existent speck of dust off one of his sleeves and said, "Not particularly."

8

IF I THOUGHT MORDECAI SMITH'S BOAT RENTAL establishment looked a bit rundown and disregarded, I should have perhaps saved that assessment for my first view of Mrs. Smith. It seems that she was expected to mind the shop and mind the little ones and mind anything that was at all important while her old man ran about getting up to… whatever it was disreputable tradesmen got up to of an early Sunday afternoon.

She looked as if she'd had about enough of it.

She came at our second knock, swinging open the door to reveal a tousle-headed six-year-old standing beside her who looked as if he'd just done something perfectly horrible to her laundry. "C'n I help you gentlemen?" she asked, in the tone of one who absolutely does not care if they can help you.

"Ha ha! Maybe you can. Maybe," said Holmes. He was wearing his friendly-as-you-like face, for I'd been coaching him on the brief walk to the door. We were not here to make any accusations, I had said, nor scare anybody. We wanted to be amiable. Harmless. We were here to charm information, nothing more. Holmes took a breath, forced his smile even wider and said, "But first you must tell me: who's this charming young nipper?"

"That's Jack. Right little bastard today, let me tell you."

"Ha ha!" said Holmes. "Come here, Jack! Come over here and tell me: is there anything you would like?"

The little boy shuffled forward warily, wiped his nose on one sleeve and shrugged. "Like a shilling, I guess."

"Nothing you'd like better?"

"Like *two* shillings. And maybe you'd better hand 'em over, or I'll tell everyone you 'sploded a demon in front of our shop."

"Ha ha! Um…"

I found that I quite agreed with Mrs. Smith's opinion of her son. He *was* a right little bastard. I stared at him levelly for a second, then said, "The policeman gave us three coppers; you can have those."

"Fine," he said. "Whatever."

The bribe delivered, he scuttled off to finish destroying the family's laundry. Mrs. Smith turned her eyes back to Holmes and me and wondered, "Anything *real* I can help you with?"

"We were hoping to speak with your husband about renting a boat," I said.

"Well, you're out of luck, for he's gone in it. Won't be back until the wee hours of tomorrow morning, from what I hear. Of course, there's the dinghy. You can have that. But you might not want it, unless your plans is for a good

Sunday drownin'. That's all the boats I got, nowadays."

"You used to have more?" I asked.

"Oh yes! Three steam launches for daily hire—and a good business we did with 'em, too. But then Jim—that's me eldest—he convinces his father that the latest thing is them steam boys, so shouldn't we sell all three of those slow old things we got and get one fast one. And Mordecai— bein' a damned fool—does it!"

My heart sank. Steam boys. Why did it have to be steam boys? Or, as they preferred the appellation, Steem Boyz. And they did tend to insist that—even when spoken— they could hear if you were spelling it the "correct" way or not. They were the bane of the Thames, and that was saying something.

The River Thames is London's foremost avenue of traffic and trade, filled with innumerable barges and scows, ferrying goods from the ports to the city and back. Yet, in this, the forty-seventh year of Victoria's reign, the thing that most dominated the Thames was the steam launch. In the time of my grandfather, they'd been naught but a curiosity, occasionally exploding when something predictable occurred to their early-model boilers. But as the years moved on they became cheaper, better, less likely to disappear in a scalding puff of vapor, and evermore quick and nimble.

So, of course, it wasn't long until a certain class of young sailor emerged, who wondered just exactly how quick and nimble they could be made to be. Boat-tuners. Steem Boyz. Gangs of useless thugs who slouched along both banks of the Thames in packs, wearing extra-baggy canvas sailor's trousers and turning their caps around backwards. One could find them lined up outside certain taverns at all hours, their launches parked in shining rows. Occasionally they'd all pile out onto the docks at once and stoke up all their boilers at the same time, just to see which one made the most smoke. They were numerous. They were devoid of tact or taste. They were convinced they were the fastest thing on the water.

And the most infuriating thing about them?

They were *right*.

So my odds of tracking Mordecai Smith's boat might be decent. My odds of catching it, out on the river... somewhat worse. At least I could gather information.

"Just the one boat, then? What was her name? *Galloper* wasn't it?"

"What? No! The *Aurora*!"

"Ah, yes. That was it. The black one with two red streaks. Black funnel with a white band."

"No, no, no," Mrs. Smith corrected me—just as I'd hoped she might. "Bright blue! Chromed-out funnel—a great big wide one. She's got the names of all the fellows who designed her bits painted all over her. The boiler's done by the Mugen brothers in Portsmouth and her rudder and keel by that nice Mr. Nismo, from just down the way. They've painted a muzzy-haired lad on one side, making a sort of odd sign with his hand and sayin' 'Wozza!' And there's a little plaque stuck on the back, what says 'Me other ride's your sister'. God help me, but that's the sort of thing that makes all the sailor boys laugh."

Despite the affront to decency and taste, I could not be better pleased. If that didn't help me pick the *Aurora* out of the crowd, nothing would.

"And you say you don't expect your husband until tomorrow morning?"

"Yeah. Two gentlemen hired 'im to carry them out to one of them rather suspicious steamers at the mouth of the Thames. So the boat's off at the tuner's today and they're all gonna meet up tonight and God knows where me husband and me boy and the two gentlemen have got to."

"I think I know one of the gentlemen you're speaking of. Had a peg-leg, right? Name was Miller, I think."

"Yeah, one of 'em had a peg and a big bush of hair. The other fellow, though! Short as a child and all wrapped up in that black cloak so no one could see 'im. Scared the hell out of the cats, he did! As to the name, I couldn't tell you. Oh! But it's right here, in the rental register. Let's see… Signed as Michael Falsename. But then, don't they all?"

"Any luggage?"

"Just one big iron chest, but they took it with 'em."

"Any idea which tuner has the *Aurora*?"

"It might be any of 'em."

"Thank you, Mrs. Smith; you've been most helpful. Holmes, shall we?"

9

I STOOD IN OUR SITTING ROOM, EYEING MY OPPONENT. I did my utmost to keep my expression stern, but thoughtful—an I'm-an-important-man-who-is-used-to-getting-my-way-and-I-will-not-be-out-negotiated kind of face. I drew a nonchalant breath and said, "Twenty heads of cabbage."

"Nah. It's not worff it."

"Oh, *come on*, Wiggles!"

"I don't want to."

"I have a perfectly good description of the boat. And everybody knows the rats all listen to you. You could have thousands of them swarming every boat-tuner in London in less than an hour. It should be easy to find!"

"Yeah, but it's a Steem Boyz boat, though, eh?"

"So?"

"So what's your description? Here, let me guess… It's some garish color."

"Well, yes, but—"

"And it's got a huge chrome funnel, thick enough to drop a cow down."

"Erm… again, yes, but—"

"And it's got a bunch of names painted on the side of it, what ain't the name of the boat or the man what owns her. And there's probably some little joke on the back what says somefing 'orrible about girls, right?"

"What? How did you know?"

"Because they all do! That's every single one of 'em! And if you fink I'm gonna set half the rats in London huntin' around to find some Steem Boyz ride what looks like every other Steem Boyz ride, for just twenty heads of cabbage, you might want to think again! And here's where you might want to start your cogitations: wif forty heads of cabbage, aged free days!"

"You actually *want* it spoiled?"

"Don't start fermentin' until it's spoiled does it? Forty heads. Free days. Half in advance."

I put my hands on my hips. "Now you're just being ridiculous. How could I possibly pay you that, unless I'd bought twenty heads of cabbage three days ago?"

"Not my problem. Shoulda thought of that free days ago."

"Fine. Forty heads. I'll start aging them today and pay you in three days."

"All right. I'll be back in free days."

"Wiggles, no! I need you now. The murderer is going to escape tonight and I need to know where his boat is hidden *before* he sets off in it."

Wiggles gave me a lopsided, somewhat predatory smile. "Oh, I see," he said. "This is one of them work-you-today-and-pay-you-next-week-if-I-remember sort of deals, is it?"

"How dare you, sir?" I thundered. Not that it was customary to call street urchins who could transform themselves into rats "sir" but he had me riled. "Do you doubt my character, or are you simply saying that to insult me? I am a gentleman, sir, and I pay my debts!"

"Oh yeah. Well… *some* gentlemen do, I guess."

"You know me, Wiggles."

"I do," he said, snapping me a little salute, "and that's the only reason I'd consider acceptin' the job for the low price of sixty heads of cabbage, paid in free days' time, with the understandin' that if you don't cough up, me an' some of the boys is gonna sneak in here while you're asleep and chew all your boots to shreds."

"Please, Wiggles, please! You've got to help me," I said, shooting a nervous glance towards Holmes's room, where he puttered with his alchemical devices, humming a little tune. "Holmes is talking about ending our partnership. I need to prove my usefulness. Do you understand?"

There are many that say that, when speaking to a friend, honesty is always the best policy—that a man can never do better than stating what he wants and why he wants it.

Do you know who says that?

Bad bargainers.

Wiggles's smile widened. "Well *now* I understand. Tell you what: sixty heads of cabbage, aged free days, two bushels of floppy carrots, your word that Mrs. Hudson won't lock the rubbish bins for the next two weeks and I'll be taking whatever you've got left in that brandy bottle wif me when I go."

"Oh, you furry little bastard!"

Wiggles shrugged and turned for the door.

"Fine! Fine!" I cried, as the last shreds of my dignity dissipated into thin air. "You win. But you had better be able to pinpoint the *Aurora* for me before dusk tonight."

"Easy," said Wiggles, swinging open my front door and popping on his ragged cap. "Have it in two hours, I bet." He started out, but then stopped himself with an exclamation of happy remembrance. A slight detour brought him within snatching distance of the bureau, from which he gleefully lifted my brandy bottle. As he left 221B, he gave me a smirk that preserved little doubt as to his low opinion of my character. And I left him with some parting words that showed he was absolutely right.

"*I hope a cat gets you!*"

At least my next group of friends treated me better.

Not *at first*, of course.

From behind his desk in the darkest, most-forgotten corner of Scotland Yard, Lestrade raised an eyebrow at me. "Let me get this straight, Dr. Watson... You want me to *blockade* the Thames?"

"Exactly."

Vladislav Lestrade turned to Torg Grogsson and gave him the sort of incredulous head-shake that was intended more as a question than a statement. The question being, of course, "Has Dr. Watson's fragile grasp on reality finally given way?"

Grogsson gave a dispassionate sort of shrug, designed to communicate, "Yeah. Probably."

"Well, if not that," I grumbled, "then at least you must find any suspicious freighters near the mouth of the Thames and stop them from putting to sea tonight."

"I could do that," said Lestrade, "But first, let me just swat every single midge in Scotland. That will be easier, as I think there may be fewer of them."

I fumed. Fortunately, Grogsson chose that moment to play the rarest of his roles—the voice of reason.

"Why?" he asked.

"Because Holmes and I have a strong lead on the murderer of Bartholomew Sholto. He's stolen a great treasure and means to spirit it away tonight, by way of a boat called the *Aurora*, to some unknown freighter. Wiggles located the launch and examined her to see if the treasure was already on board; it was not. I went round and spoke to the owner of the jetty she's docked at—Mr. Edelbrock. He says he expects the *Aurora*'s owner to retrieve her tonight. But *only* her owner. My guess is that he is picking up his passengers and their cargo on the water, and by then it will be too late. If we can't catch them on land, we can't catch them at all."

"Why?" said Grogsson, again.

"Because she's a highly tuned craft—she's owned by one of the Steem Boyz."

I don't think I have ever given Torg Grogsson a finer

present than that single sentence.

"Gwwwaaaaar! Gwaaaaaaah! Steem Boyz! Yaaaaaaaah!" he cried, then rose and shattered Lestrade's desk with a single punch. All eyes turned—both criminal and constable alike. Scotland Yard got strangely quiet. Vladislav Lestrade gave a look of extreme annoyance as the two battered halves of his desk fell in on themselves—a look aimed not at Grogsson, but at me.

"Thank you, Dr. Watson."

"What did I do?"

"Steem Boyz! Yaaaaaaaaaah! We can beat them!" Grogsson roared.

Lestrade put one hand to his brow and said, "I think I would have preferred it if you could have mentioned this particular challenge to my colleague in a less public area. Ideally an open field, where there was nothing expensive lying about."

"Well I didn't know," I said, with some annoyance. "Why does Grogsson care about the Steem Boyz, anyway?"

Lestrade sighed. "The force has long since come to recognize its weakness against tuned steam launches. The Thames has become a perfect highway for smuggling, for though we attempt to intercept the launches as they land, they travel faster than we can get word up or down the shore. And while they are afloat, there is little we can do. Grogsson is the most successful at dealing with them. He has personally sunk three high-speed launches."

"How?"

"By throwing rocks from the shore."

"Egad!"

"Hmm. Yes," said Lestrade. "He's practically as good as a cannon. Still, it is not an ideal solution. All the barge captains are afraid of getting hit by a stray rock as the launches dodge between them, so if any of them see Grogsson on the shore, they tend to drop anchor to wait it out. Traffic on the Thames has been brought to a standstill twice. And even when Grogsson does hit a launch, the result is less than satisfactory. They're built for speed, not toughness, so there tends to be little left of them and nothing left of their crews, who—let us recall—have not been found guilty of any crime. And, of course, any evidence that they were currently engaged in one tends to end up at the bottom of the Thames. Suffice to say, this particular method of enforcement has not proved popular with the London populace."

"One supposes not," I agreed.

"Hgraaaah! *Long arm!*" Grogsson cheered, picking up one half of Lestrade's former desk and smashing it to bits on the floor. Carefully cataloged case files splashed across the carpet. Lestrade favored me with yet another look.

"By God, he's worked up," I noted. "Is he bragging about his arms now?"

"He is suggesting a solution," said Lestrade. "My fellow detective inspector is of the opinion that we should make use of Scotland Yard's newest method for countering the Steem Boyz. Why don't you both come with me—far from this desk I used to love—and I will show you."

* * *

She was exactly as you'd expect: a good idea but a secret, poorly kept.

Lestrade led me to a secret berth on the Westminster wharf, partitioned on the landward side by a fence and guardhouse and on the river by a shoddily constructed wooden framework, hung with old sailcloth. Behind this semi-concealing screen of oh-what-could-the-police-possibly-be-hiding-back-there-I-wonder lay the latest addition to Scotland Yard's arsenal: *Long Arm*.

She was long, sleek and low. Her sides were painted plain black with a single white stripe, and her deck was simple varnished wood. These were modest colors, even dowdy, designed to say, "Oh look: a boat like grandfather would approve of. Feel free to ignore it." Yet the black was a bit *too* black—shiny and slick. The varnish upon her deck gleamed more than it ought and every plank was flawlessly flush and straight. If these giveaways were too subtle, one had only to look at her power plant—a shining silver monstrosity with a funnel so wide, any Steem Boy who saw her must flush with envy. Lestrade must have seen me raise an eyebrow, for he said, "Yes. We know. Not as understated as we would like. Sadly, the boiler and funnel could only be done in nickel, with polished brass strapping, because nickel is the best at being... er... you know..." He faltered.

So I volunteered, "Shiny and awesome?"

"Yaaaaaaaaaaaah!" Grogsson confirmed.

"Look, this will work. She is fitted with all the latest technology," Lestrade assured me. "Stepped hull, to keep drag as low as possible. The boiler is custom designed by the head of Cambridge's mechanical engineering department—their first female department head, Mercedes Dinan. The propeller is by the Korean genius Soobaru Hankook."

Indeed, I could see their names painted on the side of the hull in subtle charcoal-gray, hardly visible against the black hull. Clearly the defining aspect of Scotland Yard's campaign against the Steem Boyz was a secret desire to *be* Steem Boyz. They even had the requisite gender slight, though this had been executed with the Yard's typical misunderstanding of youth culture. A polished plaque at the back of the boat read, I WISH GIRLS WOULD TALK TO ME.

"What do you think?" Lestrade asked, eager—I could tell—for me to fawn over her.

"Is there anything that marks her out as a police boat?" I asked. "Anything other than her failure to be hot pink, I mean?"

"That green lantern."

"Remove it," I said. "And make her ready. I shall be back with Holmes as quickly as I can. It's getting dark and I don't know what hour our quarry will take to the water, but I know this: tonight, I will show Holmes my worth. The murderers of Bartholomew Sholto will face justice. And *Long Arm* will best the *Aurora*."

According to later reports, Grogsson's cry of joy could be heard as far away as Brighton.

10

THE NIGHT WAS DARK, BECAUSE... WELL... NIGHTS ARE.

The air was moist and cold for so early in the season. Great tendrils of fog reached out across the Thames, turning her into a moonlit ribbon of vapor. I could hear the lapping of water against *Long Arm*'s side, though the fog was so dense I could not see the ripples. Holmes sat with me at the bow, staring across the Thames with that still, tense focus he could gather at times like these. Towards the stern stood an entire elite team of coal-stokers. That is to say: Grogsson with his shirt off. But really, I cannot imagine the five-man crew that could possibly have bested him. Just ahead of him sat Lestrade, fussing over the cluster of expensive gauges that told him how hot the fire was, how hot the boiler water was, how fast we were going, and how likely we were to explode. Beside him, at the wheel, stood Inspector Stanley Hopkins. After all, if he were to be one of us, this was the sort of night he needed to be involved in.

Grogsson tipped another shovelful of coal into the furnace. I winced to see it. If we wished to move off at a moment's notice we had to keep steam up, but the boiler was large, and that made our furnace hungry. *Long Arm* was designed for speed, not longevity. To sit for so many hours, just waiting for our prey to move, was sapping our limited coal supply. Holmes must have noticed my anxiety, for he asked, "See anything, Watson?"

I raised my binoculars. Did I see anything? Of course. Rather a lot of fog. I could just make out the lights of Wilhelm Edelbrock's Oversized Coal-Chute-atorium on the far bank. Through the grimy windows, I could make out occasional movement. But was it old Edelbrock, or our quarry? At this distance, I had no hope of telling. We had a spy on that side of the river, but what if he'd fallen asleep? Or smelled some irresistible butcher's scraps and taken off for a quick meal?

I should have had more faith in him. As I peered through the binoculars, a scarlet flare arched up into the sky, turning the surrounding fog into a glowing pink haze.

Then a green flare.

Then a yellow one.

"Wiggles's signal!" Holmes cried.

"You don't think you two might have picked something a bit more subtle?" I complained.

"It's done the job, Watson," Holmes countered. "We saw them, didn't we?"

"Yes. Everybody did," I said, as two purple rockets flew into the air, followed by another red one. "Unless the *Aurora* is crewed by colossal fools, I imagine they now know something is afoot."

Yet Holmes had no answer except to cry, "Oh, pretty! Blue one!"

"Damn it," I muttered. "Grogsson, Lestrade, how long?"

"Hrragh!" said Grogsson, heaving a massive scoop of coal into the furnace. He swung the door closed, locking in the heat.

Lestrade stared down at his collection of dials. "Temperature is good… We're boiling… Pressure is coming up…"

"So we can *go*?" I urged.

"No, no. The turbine needs to come up to speed, once we have pressure, that is."

"Turbine? What is that? Do you mean those long metal sticks that go 'chuff-chuff'?"

"Pistons?" Lestrade laughed. "*Pistons?* Ha! We might as well row. Perhaps pistons are good enough for your average Steem poseur, but we've got something better. Listen to this!"

He triumphantly threw one of his levers forward. A slow, grinding noise emerged from the cylindrical casing, just in front of the boiler. Aaaaaaand…

That was about all.

"What is it doing?" I asked.

Lestrade shrugged. "It has a fairly heavy flywheel. It will take some time to come up to speed."

"But, but… I can't even see the *Aurora*!" I complained. "If she knows we're coming, she might disappear into the fog on the far side of the river! Get this useless tub moving!"

Grogsson gave an angry snort and for just a moment I feared I was going to end my days floating in the Thames with a coal-shovel dent in my skull. But Holmes gave my arm a calming pat and said, "I'm sure our official friends know what they're doing, Watson. See? I can hear the turbine getting faster, can't you?"

He was right. The slow grind had been replaced by a rhythmic *scrape-scrape-scrape*, which grew in speed as he spoke, to a constant blather of white noise. I looked eagerly down at the fog-shrouded waters and observed, "We still aren't moving."

"Of course not," said Lestrade. "The clutch is disengaged. The turbine is connected to the boiler, but not the propeller screw."

"Well can we connect them?"

"Very nearly. Is everybody ready?"

Hopkins gave a grim nod and tightened both hands on the wheel. Grogsson smiled and crouched down behind the furnace. Holmes reached forward and grasped one of the wires that stretched along the perimeter of the bow.

"Here we go," said Lestrade, and tipped a second lever forward. *Long Arm* gave a tortured, mechanical shriek, and leapt forward. So did my feet, which were placed firmly on her deck. My head and body, which sort of *weren't*, sort of *didn't*. My legs were out from under me in an instant. If I'd been standing near the stern, I'm sure I would have gone into the water. Instead, I found myself bouncing over the deck as *Long Arm* sped by beneath me. Indeed, the entire craft might have gone by and left me gasping in the Thames, were it not for the turbine-casing that slammed into me and equalized our momentum.

"Ow! Ow! It's hot!" I cried.

"Hmm. Yes. I believe the term '*steam*' has been mentioned once or twice," said Lestrade, failing to keep a tinge of satisfaction from his voice.

Struggling to my knees and away from the searing-hot machinery, I peeked out over the gunwale. There was little doubt we were moving now. Fog rolled off the bow as we shot through the water. How wide the river had always seemed to me, and how daunting a chore to cross it. Yet at our current pace it seemed as if it might be an all-too-easily accomplished task.

"*Turn!*" I shouted.

"Yes. Probably a good idea," Holmes agreed. "Hard to port, Hopkins."

The diminutive inspector swung the wheel and we heeled left, sending a wall of spray up on our starboard. I nearly lost my footing again. By God, when had boats become so *good*? *Long Arm* turned her nose downstream. Holmes was beaming, as was Grogsson of course. Hopkins—standing at the wheel of such a marvel—how could he not smile as well? Even the perpetually dour visage of Vladislav Lestrade cracked into a grin and, despite my crop of fresh bruises, I'm sure mine did as well.

What a night!

What a ride!

As I reflected on the wonder of it, we burst forth from

a fog bank into the clear, cold air of the London night. Holmes jabbed one finger straight out in front of us and cried, "There she is! The *Aurora*!"

She was just steaming out of the other side of the clear patch we'd steamed into. She must have been well over two hundred yards ahead of us, but in the naked moonlight we caught a glimpse of her gaudy blue hull and her "Wozza!" cartoon. Wiggles's signal had clearly not gone unnoticed, for we could just make out two figures on her stern, feverishly shoving coal into her furnace. That queer clarity of sound over water brought the *chuff-chuff-chuff* of her pistons to our ears. Later testimony would bear out present observation that the *Aurora* was a worthy adversary. She had a reputation as a proper flier.

Nothing like *Long Arm*, though. Even at that first glance before she disappeared into the fog, it was clear: we had the better of her.

"Quick, lads! Into that fog bank!" I howled.

Grogsson wrenched open the furnace door and heaved two shovels of coal in. I heard the whoosh–whoosh as the flames kicked higher and felt our pace increase. Had I called this craft a useless tub just a few minutes before? Shame on me. Had I doubted the value of a steam turbine? Double shame. Why, in that moment, I could have turned about and kissed the thing.

Which would have scalded my lips *right off…*

But you know what I mean.

In hardly more than a minute, we were plunging into the fog. Ahead of us, I could just make out the bobbing yellow lamp that swung from the *Aurora*'s stern and the orange glow of her furnace. I raised the binoculars to see if I could make out any more, but no. The problem was not distance, but fog. All I achieved was to narrow my focus, much more than I ought.

"Probably turn again," Holmes advised, "so we don't hit that big gray thing."

"Hit what?" Hopkins asked, but then added, "Aaaaaaaugh!" and spun the wheel hard to port again.

Lestrade cursed in Romanian and pulled first this lever and then that one, disengaging the prop, selecting reverse, and re-engaging. Our wake turned to churning froth as the screw clawed backwards against the not–insignificant forward momentum of our craft.

"What in…? What is that?" I cried out, as the gray wall of fog before us solidified into a gray wall of wood. Though our course was changing and our pace slowing, it was still a near-run thing. We came so close I might have reached out over the starboard rail and touched it.

It was a barge.

In fact, it was one of three barges being towed in a line in the middle of the night by a nondescript tugboat running with no lights. I don't think it was a coincidence that the tug and all three of the barges she pulled had been painted the exact color of London's famous fog.

Grogsson stuck his chin out at her and opined, "Smug'lar, I bet."

"Hmm. What do you think she's hauling?" Holmes wondered.

Hopkins gave a low whistle. "Whatever it is, she's got a lot of it."

"Never mind!" I shouted. "Just get around her!"

As we rounded the bow of the tug, *Innsmouth*, a gray face with a mat of gray hair topped with a battered gray fisherman's cap popped up over the rail to stare at us. I will swear there was something wrong with the man—that the skin was *too* gray, that his eyes were not simply yellowed by age and bad living, but may have been slightly luminous. I shook my fist at him as we passed and called, "Do you realize how lucky you just got, you little bastard? On any other night, I'm sure this boat full of policemen and paranormal investigators would be very interested in finding out what you were up to! Do you hear me? *Any other night!*"

As we no longer had sight of the *Aurora*, we had no choice but to point our nose straight downstream and pour on speed. Grogsson went to work in earnest, shoveling pile after pile of our precious coal to the furnace.

"Careful," Lestrade called back to him. "Don't melt her."

Before we even cleared the fog bank, I could see innumerable possible targets. London had no shortage of lights, both on the water and the shore. But which was the *Aurora*? I half feared she'd backed off steam in the fog and simply let us shoot by, or lain to close to shore to make herself invisible against the multitude of moored watercraft. But no. As Holmes and I scanned the thousands of lights, I saw one yellow one suddenly dip and disappear.

"There!" I yelled. "She just threw her lantern overboard. Ha! Poorly timed, Mordecai Smith. We're back on you now!"

And so we were. Perhaps she might do without her lantern, but since the *Aurora*'s furnace opened towards the rear of the craft, they could not hide the orange glow of her fires. And as fast as she was, we were faster. At Greenwich, her furnace was nothing more than a dim light in the distance. By the time we reached Blackwall we could see her crew clearly.

"Look at that fellow stagger about," I shouted to Holmes, pointing. "That's our peg-leg, I bet."

Holmes nodded. "And a fairly big box he's got with him, too. Can you see what he's doing with it?"

I could not, even with the binoculars. "No. He's gone to the other side of the boiler; I've lost sight of him."

"Look at the little fellow, though," Holmes laughed. "He doesn't look like he's very pleased to see us, eh?"

No indeed. He was crouched down behind the stern, wrapped in a black cloak. I could make out some of his face; his skin was very dark and his eyes darker still. When the *Aurora* steamed into a patch of moonlight, I got a good look at him, staring back at us with an expression that—even at this distance—could never be mistaken for friendly. Just behind him, a pair of men labored with shovels, piling every lump of coal they could find into the howling orange furnace. Their family resemblance was unmistakable: Mordecai and James Smith, probably regretting the day they'd sold off all three of their serviceable launches to get one really fast one.

The *Aurora* had left the main flow of the river by then, hugging the southern bank. Finally, with Barking Level on our one side and the Plumstead Marshes on the other, we drew within four boat lengths. It was then that the smallest member of their crew jumped up on the stern and threw off his cloak.

"What the hell is that?" Hopkins cried.

The little figure who rose to challenge us was… well… not *quite* a tree. His skin was brown and knotted—more like wood or bark than hide. His eyes were black angry circles. He stretched both arms out towards us and pointed horrible, thorny fingers in our direction.

There was a little pop.

A second later, something whizzed past me.

"Get down!" I cried to Holmes.

But he only laughed in joy and pointed at our diminutive assailant. "Watson! Fingers! He's shooting his *fingers* at us!"

There was a further *pop pop* followed by two little whizzes. Whatever else, he was an accurate little bugger.

"Look out, Holmes!"

"But… does it hurt, do you think? Do they grow back? Or if he shoots too many, will he never be able to play piano again? Or—"

"Holmes, remember what one of those fingers did to Bartholomew Sholto?"

"Oh! Right. Best do something, eh?"

I already had the Webley out of my pocket and braced

against the wire that stretched across our prow. The boat bumped and shuddered through the waves, but I had him fairly steadily in my sights. I didn't want to kill anybody. In fact, I didn't even want to make the noise of a shot, but what choice did I have? I squeezed the trigger and felt the pistol buck against my hand. Did I hit him? Did I see that bullet knock a chip out of his shoulder? I'll never know for sure.

Because Holmes—in moments of great stress or distraction—had a tendency to forget our desire for anonymity. Despite the presence of the Smiths, of Hopkins and any number of observers on shore, he threw both hands to the sky and cried, "Azazel! Attend me!"

Three bolts of purple hellfire materialized behind him and flew in howling arcs towards the *Aurora*. The first struck the little tree-man in the center of the chest and blasted straight through him. Poor little fellow. I mean, yes, he'd just been trying to murder me, but I could not help but feel a pang of sympathy as he crumpled forward and splashed into the Thames. Oh, and he had one important property that distinguished him from wood: he didn't float. The second bolt struck the *Aurora*'s stern, just above the waterline. It must have exited through the bottom of her hull, for the water on her starboard side flashed bright purple and she listed towards it. The final bolt struck the *Aurora*'s boiler, which proved exactly how far modern launches had improved by not exploding. A great plume of steam gushed up into the air as the motive force of the *Aurora*'s chrome heart vented uselessly skyward.

"Ha!" I cried. "We've got her now! Lestrade, try to

lower our speed won't you, or we'll run right into her. Hopkins, bring us a bit... um... port? I can't remember. That way."

I pointed the way I wished to go. (And to my credit— yes, it was port.) Yet the boat failed to respond.

"Hopkins? Can you bring her that way?"

"Uh... no. Don't think I can't. Er... think I can..."

With growing dread, I turned. At the wheel stood Hopkins. He'd grown quite pale. He seemed unsteady on his feet. He had a look of confusion upon his face and a four-inch wood-like splinter protruding from the center of his forehead.

"*Oh!*" cried Holmes and I together.

Holmes leaned in towards Hopkins, spread his hands and said, "Now, stay calm. Stay still. Let's assess the situation and see if there's anything we can do to—"

Hopkins was just beginning to nod his agreement, when a great retching noise burst forth from between his lips.

Followed by a huge gout of vomit.

Followed by all his internal organs.

When it was finally done, Stanley Hopkins gave us a relieved look, reached up and wiped his mouth with his sleeve, then tipped forward and fell apart into a great burst of chunky juice, with bones in it.

"Oh, *come on*, Hopkins!" Holmes complained. "How am I supposed to fix *that*? There is a bloody limit you know, and I fear you've passed it. Oh, by the twelve gods... Look at this mess... You've got yourself all over my shoes, too." He shook his head and turned to me. "Well, now I suppose it's even more important to change your destiny, eh, Watson? I don't think your handy-dandy walking doom-sponge is going to be able to absorb much more punishment on your behalf."

"Wait! Holmes! Is Inspector Hopkins *still* soul-bound to me?"

"Well... until about twelve seconds ago. Did you think it was mere coincidence that you've come to no harm these past weeks, despite putting yourself in harm's way over and over, and making terrible decisions, and failing to have even the slightest care for self-preservation? Oh, speaking of which... should one of us be at the wheel?"

He wasn't wrong. Despite Lestrade's efforts to slow us, we were in real danger of colliding with the *Aurora* or running aground. The reedy bank was very near us now. We'd entered the Plumstead waste, where the land sloped towards the Thames so gently and had so much standing water on its surface that it was the matter of some debate where the ground ended and the river began. Still, I was in no mood to find out. With a yelp, I rose and splashed through the puddle of Hopkins to grab the wheel. I flung it left just in time. The stricken *Aurora* slid past on our right.

"We've overshot her!" Lestrade called.

"No trouble," I shouted back. I kept the boat turning in a wide arc, out towards the middle of the river, then briefly upstream, then back towards the southern bank again. It was just what we'd needed, as taking her round in a circle bled off all our excess speed. If the *Aurora* had still been seaworthy, it would have left us at a great disadvantage. Yet the concern was academic; *Aurora* wasn't going anywhere. Indeed, Mordecai Smith now only had two options where to stop his boat: the Plumstead bank or the bottom of the river.

He selected the former.

As we looped *Long Arm* around to intercept at a safer pace, the *Aurora* brushed through the reeds and beached on the muddy shore. Both Smiths threw up their arms and shouted their intent to come along quietly and make no fuss. Not so their one remaining passenger. He waved his fist at us and cried, "You may have got Tonga, you ruddy bastards, but you'll never get me!"

Abandoning the huge iron treasure chest, he charged the full length of the *Aurora* and leapt from her bow. What a jump! He sailed over the nearest patch of reeds and landed heavily in the swampy mud just beyond.

So heavily in fact that he drove his good leg deep into the soggy morass. His peg-leg fared even worse. He was up to his hip, tipped violently to his right. He gave a couple of experimental tugs to see if he could free himself.

When that didn't work, he began feeling about on the surface of the mud for any plants within reach that were well-enough rooted so he could pull himself free.

When *that* didn't work, he amended his earlier statement.

"Actually… could you…? Could you come and get me?"

11

WE ALL KNEW WHERE WE'D EVENTUALLY END UP:
Scotland Yard. Yet even the two of our number who
worked there had no desire to show their faces until they
could present a satisfactory explanation for the murder of
Bartholomew Sholto and the fate of the Agra treasure.

Oh, and somebody was likely to wonder where Hopkins
had gone.

We needed friendly ground and time to regroup. We
needed 221B Baker Street.

Lestrade hid *Long Arm* and—by extension—the
slowly thickening mortal remains of Stanley Hopkins.

Holmes conveyed Mordecai and James Smith back to
their home and used magic to do something really horrible
to their memories of the evening. Ask them about how
their boat wound up stranded in the Plumstead Marshes
with a hole blown through the bottom and you were likely
to get a sweet tale of a flower girl with a heart of gold, or
half-comprehensible mumbles about little gray men from
the moon, but I shouldn't hold out much expectation to
hear any useful truths.

Grogsson stomped halfway across town with the iron treasure box on one shoulder and our trussed-up, one-legged prisoner on the other.

And I made tea.

We set our prisoner on one of our overstuffed chairs and pulled his gag off. This had been a necessary precaution as the man had not come quietly. He'd been glad of our assistance in extricating him from the bog, but once that was accomplished he'd given us nothing but trouble. He'd twice tried to jump over the side of our boat—once actually making it into the water. As he was fully dressed, with his hands cuffed before him, his attempt to swim to shore had been somewhat… underwhelming. Certainly he would have drowned if we had not all heaved a collective sigh, pulled *Long Arm* around in a wide circle, drawn up beside him and watched him thrash for a few minutes, before asking, "So… how's that working for you? Still pleased with our masterful escape plan, are we?"

No sooner had we made landfall than he began screaming to anyone who would listen that we were not real police officers but kidnappers. That he was a loyal subject of the Crown who was being absconded with for dark, unchristian purposes.

Hence the gag. And one may well believe we made sure he was trussed up pretty well before we removed it. No sooner had we pulled it away than he began howling that this was mistreatment, and that he had rights.

"So did Bartholomew Sholto," Lestrade said, kneeling down in front of him. "So did Inspector Hopkins."

"I don't know nothing about that!" our prisoner insisted. "I've never met them in my life."

"Well, I for one believe him," said Lestrade. "I propose we let him go."

"Really?" the prisoner asked eagerly.

"No. Idiot. Now make things as easy on yourself as you can, eh? Why don't we start with your name?"

"I told you: it's Queen Bloody Victoria!" he yelled. Which was a lie. The first time we'd asked he'd said Robin Hood.

"Right, that's it," said Holmes, stepping forward and cracking his knuckles. "This is getting us nowhere. Time to use magic."

"Holmes, no!" I protested. "You don't think you've done quite enough of that today? Remember sending 'Toby' home? Perhaps it's time to give conventional methods a chance, don't you think?"

"But I'm tired, Watson. I want toast and soup and a lie-down. This is going to take forever. We can't even get this fellow's *name*."

"It's Jonathan Small," I said.

"Eh? How do you know?" said Holmes and Lestrade and Grogsson and—with an unmistakable look of horror— Jonathan Small.

"We know Major John Sholto was terrified of a one-legged white man, and that this fear was associated with the Agra treasure. We likewise know that the treasure was associated with the sign of nine—and that this sign was left with both Bartholomew and Major John Sholto following their deaths. Mary Morstan brought us one of her father's old papers, a map labeled with 'THE SIGN OF NINE' and signed by four persons. Recall, however, that Agra is in India. Three of the signatories had traditional Indian names and are fairly likely to be dark-skinned. Only one of the names on that list sounds like it might be English—and that the owner of that name is most likely to be white. Therefore the balance of probability…" I indicated our prisoner. "Jonathan Small."

He gave me an angry sneer and growled, "You think you know so much, eh? Well we'll see how far you get!"

"Ha!" crowed Holmes. "You don't know who you're dealing with! John Watson has the best talent for deduction that I have ever encountered. He has just determined your name. In a minute more, he'll have deduced how you are connected with the Agra treasure, how Morstan and Sholto came to know you, how you came to know a little demon finger-sniper, how Sholto got the treasure, the nature and location of the other three signatories to 'the sign of nine' map, and what 'the sign of nine' truly means! Ha!"

I think I must have cleared my throat one time more than I should, or shuffled my feet a bit too conspicuously.

"What's the matter?" said Holmes, looking over at me.

"Well, I mean… that's a lot of questions, isn't it? And we haven't actually got all that many clues, so…"

"So… five minutes, then?"

"No, Holmes, I think it is likely to take—"

"An hour?"

"Significantly longer than that! Why, if the whole truth

is ever known, I think it would only be with—"

But I had lost my chance. Holmes locked eyes first with Grogsson, then Lestrade. The three of them all said, "Magic."

"Oh, *come on*!" I protested.

"No. Magic," said Holmes, reaching out his right palm towards Lestrade. "Everybody, join hands."

Lestrade took Holmes's hand, then reached out for Grogsson's. Grogsson reached out for mine, but I crossed my arms and declared, "I refuse! We must not be cavalier with the fate of the world! I will not—"

"We might need Watson's powers of deduction," said Holmes. "Grogsson, get him."

"Don't you d— Aaaaaieeeeee!" I howled as Grogsson grabbed me by the back of my jacket and hoisted me into the air. I'm sure I would have had more opinions to offer if I'd been given the chance. I wasn't. Holmes gave a satisfied nod, licked his left index finger, and thrust it deep into Jonathan Small's right ear. For just an instant, Small looked as if he might like to protest as vociferously as me.

But only for an instant.

Suddenly, Baker Street was gone. There was a flash of nothing.

Then we were standing on a village green. It was morning, or early afternoon. Directly in front of us was a picturesque bench-swing, hung from a sturdy oak. On the bench was a young lady in a Sunday dress, a mass of blond curls bouncing beneath her bonnet. She was smiling at the lad on the other side of the bench—a love-struck country fop if ever I saw one. He was fawning over her, saying, "Oh, Molly! Molly, Molly, oh! Say you'll be mine! Oh, you'll make me the happiest man alive. So happy, we could be! Happy, happy, happy, oh!"

"Hey!" Grogsson yelled. "Where we?"

The answer came from our prisoner who glanced around in utter amazement and gasped, "Pershore! We're in Pershore! By God, that's Molly! The love of my life!"

"Ha!" said Holmes, pointing at the lad on the swing. "That's *you*?"

"Hmm. Doubtful," I said. "That man does not resemble Mr. Small."

Even as I said it, a second young man jumped from behind the oak tree and threw a pistol into the first man's lap. "An honorable duel!" he announced, then drew his own pistol and blasted swing-boy straight in the face.

"Oh!" cried Holmes and Lestrade.

"Eeeeeeeeeeeeeeeeeeeeeeee!" opined Molly, staring with horror at all the bits of blood and skin that had come to rest on the forward portion of her bouncing curls.

"Now, *that* looks like Mr. Small," I noted, pointing at the triumphant murderer.

"So what if it is?" our prisoner protested. "I was young! I was in love! He was my rival! Any man would have done the same!"

"Pretty sure I wouldn't. How about you, Torg?" said Holmes, removing his finger from Small's ear and dropping Lestrade's hand. As nobody disappeared or faded out of the memory and back to the real world, it seemed safe for Lestrade to reclaim his hand from Grogsson and for Grogsson to drop me into the nearest hedge.

"No!" said Grogsson. "Fight with on-ur!"

"I did!" Small protested.

"Hmm… no," said Holmes. "Murder, I should think."

"Sure. Easily. Murder," Lestrade agreed.

Grogsson nudged him with his elbow and urged, "Write dis down."

"Oh! Yes. Yes, of course," said Lestrade, patting his pockets in search of his notebook and pencil. "I mean… I'm not sure another man's dreamscape is admissible in court, but better safe than sorry."

Jonathan Small crossed his arms and complained, "Well have it your way, then. You coppers always do. I'll admit there was some debate over whether the duel was fair. In the end, there was nothing for it but to take the Queen's shillin' and head out with the Third Buffs, what was bound for India."

"Fun!" said Holmes. "Let's go there now."

There was a sickening sort of lurch and Pershore was gone. The air was suddenly hot and dry, dusty. The call of strange insects filled the air. Before us lay a cluster of tents around a flagpole. The Union flag hung limp, for there was no breeze at all. Behind us the ground sloped down to a huge river of brownish-yellow water.

"So this is India?" I said. "Well it's better than Afghanistan at any rate."

"Why bless me!" Jonathan Small cried. "We must be back in—" But he stopped suddenly and a look of horror crossed his face. "Wait! No! We don't have to watch this part. We can go."

From behind us came the faint sound of somebody calling, in a thick Scottish brogue, "Private Small, ye daft! Get out of the water!"

To answer it came a gruff laugh and an already familiar Worcestershire drawl. "Sergeant Holder, you great coward! Why don't you get in? Afraid I'll splash you?"

The voices issued from a little bend in the river, well obscured by scrub. Our little party set off to see what we could see. Small didn't want to go, but Grogsson grabbed him by the shirt and dragged him. As we went he gave a little cough and began to sheepishly explain, "Well, India's rather hot, you see. So… er… well, one day I thought I'd take a little swim in the Ganges."

Yet any explanation that might have been forthcoming was rather overshadowed—or no: foreshadowed—by Sergeant Holder's remonstration, "There's crocodiles, ye great numpty! Don't y'see 'em?"

"Oh! Oh! Crocodiles!" replied the mocking voice of younger-Small. "Maybe I should just wet m'nappy and run back to m—"

There was a sudden snapping noise, followed by a great deal of screaming.

Even as we ran, the four of us were shaking our heads at the remarkable imbecility of our prisoner. He had the good grace to color from the hair on his head to the tips of his toes. We at last crested a little rise and looked down into a small shallow inlet that presented a rather predictable sight: young

Jonathan Small thrashing in a widening pool of red water. At his side floated a crocodile with its snout pointed skywards, happily chewing on Small's disembodied right leg. The time Young Small gained while it took the beast to eat his lower extremity might have been enough to make it to shore, if his progress was not rather hampered by the fact he was now hopping through Ganges mud. To worsen matters, a second crocodile was closing in with a look on his face that very much resembled the reptilian equivalent of "Well, would you look at this? Stupid *and* wounded! Must be my lucky day."

The only unexpected part of the tableau was Sergeant Holder. He was surprisingly slight, a wiry little fellow who looked like he might weigh no more than 130 pounds soaking wet. And he *was* soaking wet. He was waist-deep in the Ganges, unarmed, racing the crocodiles to his injured comrade.

By God, I will never know what inspires bravery like that.

The two men reached each other and the wounded Small threw his arms around Holder. Holder whipped round and began dragging Small back towards land, looking over his shoulder at every chance to see how they were doing.

Not well.

The crocodiles were very close by the time they reached the shore. But here is the thing: crocodiles can go on shore. They might be a bit slower than in the water, but not so slow as a 130-pound sergeant, dragging a 190-pound wounded man.

"Well, we can probably go, eh?" present-day Jonathan Small suggested. "I mean, you lads know how I lost my leg, so…"

But how could we turn away from such drama? As the two men struggled up the muddy bank, Holder glanced over his shoulder one final time, then back to Small with an expression of pain and remorse.

"It's no good!" he said. "They're too close. I'm sorry, I have to leave you!"

A look of grim resolve broke across Young Small's face. He gave a heavy sigh, as if he knew what he must do, but dreaded the duty.

He planted his remaining leg firmly in the mud, grabbed the smaller man by his belt and the front of his shirt, hoisted him up into the air over his head, and threw him, screaming, to the crocodiles. As the two massive reptiles fought over who got the larger half, Small turned and hopped up the bank, shouting that there had been a terrible accident.

"Small," said Holmes, with a shake of his head. "Poor form."

"Yes," Lestrade agreed. "I think that is very nearly the *exact definition* of poor form."

"I was about to get eaten by a crocodile!" Small protested. "Any man would have done the same."

"I hope you are wrong," I said. "I'm not sure you are, but I hope so."

Grogsson gave Lestrade the elbow again. "Dat's two. Write it down."

"Oh, right you are," said Lestrade, and began scratching away.

"You know something, Holmes," I whispered, as Small leaned in over Lestrade's notebook to be sure he was being fairly treated, "I am astonished how forthcoming Mr. Small has become."

"Yes," said Holmes, beaming. "It's a little trick I learned from a play. Catch a fellow off guard, use a bit of magic, show him scenes from his own life, and he just can't help himself! He'll narrate the entire thing, both the good and ill."

"You learned this from a play, you say?"

"Yes, Charles Dickens showed me. Amazing fellow. Smart as… well… smart as the Dickens, actually. Before you came along, I had to use this trick rather a lot. Probably will after you're gone, I suppose."

I frowned. "Stop saying that, Holmes. I am not going anywhere."

"No. You are," said Holmes, with an air of great sadness. "Really, Watson, I've given it a lot of thought and I'm afraid you must. You've got yourself so worked up over Irene Adler, and so poisoned with Persian mummy that there is simply no chance you'll survive if you remain. Why, you're so doomed you've killed Hopkins three times and there's still no appreciable drop in your doom level. I will be very sad to see you go, but imagine how sad I'd be if I got you killed! No, no. It must be avoided."

"Ah, but you forget, Holmes: I do not have to leave

221B Baker Street unless I want to. And I do not want to. I am staying."

"No. You aren't. I've got it all worked out. But come on, Watson! Don't make us sad! Try to enjoy our last adventure together, eh? Let's get back to our play. For your viewing enjoyment, Dr. Watson, Warlock Holmes proudly presents: *A Christmas Carol*!"

As he said it, the scene wavered and shifted again.

Now we stood in a broad tent, with the sun beating down on the canvas. Around us lay nine or ten men. Soldiers. Sick ones. Foreign deployments and bad habits always take their toll; the place stank of typhoid and malaria. On a cot before us lay the young Jonathan Small, with a bitter expression on his face, staring up at an officer.

"Look, I told you before, Major. I did all I could, but it were no good! I couldn't save him!"

"I know what you told me, Small. But a few of the village boys tell a somewhat different story."

"You know these Mohammedans, sir. You know what passes for truth with their like, eh?"

"Yes," said the major, slowly. "Unfortunately for you, Small, I know them perfectly well. And I think I *do* understand their value of truth."

If the major's gaze was a bit cold, Jonathan Small was not about to be outdone. He squinted up at his commanding officer with perfect malevolence. "No matter," he said. "I don't see what you could do about it. It's my word against... well... practically *nobody*'s, really."

The major gave a grim smile. "You're right, I'm sure.

There's no military court that's going to hang one of our own on the word of an Indian child. It's too bad. John Holder was a good man. And yet, Small, that's not to say there's *nothing* I can do."

"What do you mean?"

"You've got one leg, no particular skills and a black mark on your character. Why would the army wish to keep you?"

"You can't do that!" Young Small protested.

"I have already filed my recommendation," said the major. "You're out, Small. You're being invalided."

"No!"

"If I had any sense of justice, I'd let you rot as a beggar in a Bombay gutter. Luckily for you, Small, there's still one purpose you might serve. Abelwhite? Step forward."

From behind us came a weedy sort of man, clutching a Bible to his chest. At first I assumed that he was an army chaplain, for he had the book and the requisite expression of someone who thought they knew everything and were being very generous when they spouted it at you. Yet his clothes told a different story. He was a civilian—a businessman, unless I missed my guess—and rather wealthy.

"Mr. Abelwhite here runs an indigo plantation. It's fairly isolated and—what with all the muttering that's going about—the general's staff feel he might be a bit safer with a few tough British lads about. And God help me, Small, I'll say this much for you: you're tough as they come. And you aren't afraid to hurt a man, are you?"

Young Jonathan Small gave a look that left little doubt he'd just added another man to the list of people he wouldn't mind hurting. Abelwhite leaned forward, gave the Bible a little shake and said, "You have erred, Private Small, yet with hard work and diligent repentance, who is to say you may not yet be saved? Why, if you can help me bring the word of the lord to the local savages, oh what a penance that would be!"

Small gave a bitter look, which drew a smile from the major. "You're a civilian now, Small, so I cannot order you to take the job," he said. "But I can tell you this: you're an awfully long way from home and I don't think there are many other men who would employ you in these parts. Word gets about, you know?"

Holmes gave a tour-guide's smile and announced, "Next stop: the plantation!"

And with a blur and a fuzz, that's where we stood. Abelwhite's indigo fields stretched off in all directions, dominated by a sprawling, stately plantation house. Dozens of laborers bent to their tasks. It must have been harvest time, for they all had bushels of indigo strapped to their backs as they stooped to gather more. The nearest worker was using his bushel as armor against the efforts of younger Jonathan Small, who sat astride a horse belaboring the poor man with a whip.

"I see you, you coolie bastard!" young Jonathan Small howled. "I see what you're doin'! Slowing down a-purpose, are you?"

We all turned to look with unveiled disdain at present-day Small, who spluttered, "Hey now! I'd just lost me leg, you know, and found meself trapped in a far-off land! I was only tryin' to make meself feel better. Any man would—"

"Yes, yes," we all told him. "*Any man would do the same.*"

"I don't know if anybody's told you, Mr. Small," said Holmes, "but you have a very dim view of our species."

Personally, I was willing to lay some of the blame on the shoulders of Abelwhite for allowing such abuses. Yet I was in error. At that moment he came bobbing through the indigo, shouting, "No, no, Mr. Small! You mustn't *whip* them! Where did you find that? Who gave this man a whip? I thought I'd been very clear!"

Young Small shrugged. "Found it in the shed. Need it to do my job, sir."

"No you don't!" Abelwhite hissed and looked about with a nervousness his wide-brimmed hat could not hide. "Things are bad enough, Small! Morale is low! And I've heard quite enough muttering about how we treat these fellows without you charging about whipping everybody for no reason. Now, give me that and get inside."

"But m'day's not done, sir."

"Yes it is! Get inside!"

"You oughtn't to go easy on them, sir," said Young Small.

"Ha! And I was right, too!" cried Older Small. "For, do you know what happened next?"

The scene around us fuzzed, just slightly. We stood in exactly the same place, but now smoke and flames poured from the windows of the plantation house and the air was alive with screams. Screams of joy, of triumph, of fear and of pain—disparate emotions given the same voice.

"The Great Mutiny," said Small, with an air of satisfaction. "The little brown bastards rose up all over the place."

"Can't imagine what drove them to it," I muttered.

Nobody worked the fields now, but a quick look around showed us young Jonathan Small—shirtless and with dripping wet hair—coming up a path from the nearby river, looking confused. A man on a horse flashed by us and up to Small.

"Hey, look! It's old Dawson!" our version of Jonathan Small said. "Bloody great fool, he was."

Dawson pulled up just beside the younger Small and shouted, "John! John, we've got to get out of here!"

"What's happened?"

"Word just came in—the whole countryside is in open rebellion! The instant the natives heard, they were on us. They got to the tools, the machetes, rakes and spades. Catherine and the girls… they didn't survive, nor Mr. Abelwhite. It's just you and me now. Look, the barn is on fire, but some of the horses got out. See if you can catch one. You've got no chance if you can't get a horse."

Young Jonathan Small nodded at the wisdom of this advice, reached up, grabbed Dawson by the shirt, and pulled him from the saddle. He made sure Dawson landed heavily on his head.

Lestrade paused, notebook halfway up and wondered,

"What do you think, Torg? Should we count that one?"

Torg hesitated. Dawson gave a pained groan and reached up, feebly trying to catch Small's trouser leg and stop him from mounting. Small turned and gave Dawson a savage kick. There was a resounding *tunk* as his wooden leg connected with the side of Dawson's skull. Dawson sank to the mud, senseless.

"Yeh," Grogsson decided. "Dat's free."

"I was about to be murdered by rampaging heathens!" Jonathan Small protested. "Any man w—"

"Look, just save it, all right?" said Holmes. "You killed your friend and you got your horsey. Now, where are you off to?"

"Oh, ho! You see, now that's where it gets interesting," said Small. "Because now, I'm off to the fortress at Agra."

12

"THE FORTRESS AT AGRA" WAS SOMETHING OF A MISNOMER.

What the British high command probably ought to have called it was the "hey-remember-when-we-took-over-that-crumbling-old-fortress-then-built-a-shiny-great-modern-section-but-neglected-to-cart-off-the-old-wreck-it's-connected-to" at Agra.

Which is to say that the British Army's lack of architectural foresight somewhat complicated matters, once the Great Mutiny began.

Agra being the only fortified camp for miles around, hundreds of British soldiers and civilians flocked there as soon as things went wrong. In some ways, it was a good choice. There was a well-stocked armory at Agra, ample food, and reasonable medical support. The fort commanded a strategic bend in the river and was well defended on... let us say... two and a half sides. Those portions might have bested a modern army.

It was the other side and a half that was the problem. Over the years the fort had gone through many iterations and most of these had simply been cobbled on to the ruins of what came before. A wiser, less budget-minded army would have cleared the old section away. But no, we'd left it. Which was to say that—on any given foggy night—there were dozens of entrances into the old, decrepit portion of the fortress that might be crept into. They were so far from the section where the troops and civilians lodged—so well hidden by bent and crumbling corridors—that half a regiment of enemy troops might easily get in and live undetected for a week or two. Then, at their leisure, they could pop into the modern portion and slit every sleeping throat they found. Thus—though cannons were at a premium—three of the fort's finest guns were aimed not to the outside, but the inside, loaded with canister shot and trained down the three main corridors where the old section met the new. The fort's command had no illusions: if there were to be an infantry charge that overwhelmed their garrison, it would come not from without the fort, but from within. Combine this with the fact that the Indian allies upon whom all depended looked just the same to British eyes as the Indian rebels... well... it was hard to get a good night's sleep at Agra.

It was into this cauldron of uncertainty that a wretched, rag-clad, one-legged man stumbled one night. To the commanding officers' horror, he made it across the river, past the few sentries, through one of the doorless doorways in the old section of the fort, and all the way to the garrison. Really, the only thing that salvaged the situation was that when he hove into view of three startled guards who tossed away their cards and went scrambling for their rifles, the tattered specter threw up both hands and declared, "Wait! Hold your fire! I'm an Englishman! I need help! I've lost m'leg!"

Though, as they sprang forward to offer medical aid, he did demur and clarify, "Well, my *wooden* one…"

"Looks like you had a bit of an adventure getting here," Holmes observed, to present-day Small.

"I'll say. Lord only knows how many of those mutinous buggers I had to kill before I finally made it safe."

"Curses!" said Lestrade, throwing down his notebook. "Now the whole count is just rubbish."

Yet Grogsson was unwilling to give up this great new game. "Just count da ones we see," he urged.

Lestrade gave a grumbly little sigh. "Very well."

"So, anyway," said Holmes, "you murdered and murdered and murdered and finally made your way here. Then what?"

"Well, they found out I had military experience," said Small. "Now, I might not have told them exactly *how much*, but as it were a bit of a situation they gave me a uniform and a rifle and welcomed me back into the fold. Ah! They were fine days. I even made a bit of a name for m'self. See, we found out there was this camp of rebels out near Shahgunge. And I were ready to get some of me own back, so I talked the colonel into giving me a company of men for a night attack and—by God—we gave 'em what for! Oh! Let's see that part! Please, can we see that part?"

"No," said Holmes. "I don't like you. We're skipping right past it."

Sure enough, there we stood amongst the garrison at Agra, as happy soldiers recounted their adventures while their jealous-eyed fellows listened. It had been the only successful mission in weeks, so everybody gathered around young Jonathan Small to slap him on the back and pour another drink down him.

And oh, the look on older Jonathan Small's face as he watched… He must have relived that night over and over a thousand times in his memory: the hour a universally hated man was loved. How he must have longed to return to this exact moment. Now he beheld it once more, but with the knowledge that such joy would never be his again. I felt a deep swell of sympathy for him.

Then again, he was just a *crazy murderer*.

And there was something else… My eye kept traveling to one fellow standing on the outskirts of the gathering. He pulled aside several members of the successful sortie, one by one, and spoke with them in guarded whispers, often gesturing towards Jonathan Small. He was a native, a nervous-looking sort of man with dark circles around his eyes. Very dark. The sort of circles that made you want to spend years befriending him, just to build up the kind of rapport that eventually allows you to ask, "Say, I've always wanted to know: is that your natural coloring, or do you just *never sleep?*"

My curiosity about the fellow kept growing, until I realized I had a rather felicitous way of finding out more about him. I elbowed Jonathan Small and asked, "Who's that?"

"Ah!" he cried. "Mahomet Singh! He is my brother—the man who nearly saved me, who nearly turned my life's fortunes around."

"And," I whispered to Holmes, "one of the other signatories to Arthur Morstan's 'sign of nine' map."

To Jonathan Small I said, "He seems to be taking something of an interest in you."

"That makes sense," Small admitted. "He knew all about me by that fateful night—the one that changed everything."

"Oh!" cried Holmes. "Fateful night? Let's go there!"

The world fuzzed and blurred around us once more. We found ourselves standing in a small guardroom, with an open doorway that looked out over a rain-swollen river. Once there had been a door, but now there was nothing left of it save a few rotted planks and one rusty iron hinge that still clung to the wall. In the feeble moonlight I could see gray rain falling onto gray water, from which thick gray mists arose. A finer night for an ambush I could hardly imagine.

In the room with us stood young Jonathan Small, leaning on his rifle and looking out across the river. Mahomet Singh was there as well, and another Indian fellow whom I did not recognize. The third fellow constantly shifted his weight from one foot to the other, and his eyes betrayed such nervousness that it was hard to believe he hadn't already wet his trousers.

"What are you doing?" Holmes asked.

Small shrugged. "Well, it had become clear that a single sentry was not enough to hold a door. It was too easy to overpower a lone guard—and silently, too—as I had proved when I got in."

"I hope you didn't hurt him too badly," said Holmes.

"Oh… er… well…"

"Four," said Grogsson. Lestrade scribbled a note.

"Look, the point is," said Small, "we needed more guards. But there weren't enough soldiers. And which of the natives could we trust? So we started putting one British private with a rifle at every door, and two unarmed natives. Harder to sneak up on three than on one, eh? Of course we knew you can't hold an entrance against a determined enemy with only one rifle. If a door was attacked, the sentry was a dead man. But the hope was that in the time it took to overwhelm all three guards, one of them might fire the rifle and warn the garrison."

"Hmm," I noted. "Bleak."

"Aye," said Small, "but that was not to be my fate. Just watch."

So we did. There stood young Jonathan Small with a cigarette paper in one hand and a rifle in the other. He had a tobacco pouch on his belt but—here's the rub—no third hand to get the tobacco out of the pouch and into the paper. He gave his two Indian comrades a distrustful look. Should he chance it? No. Dutifully Young Small turned his attention back to his job, rifle in hand, eyes constantly scanning the river. For a minute. Maybe two. But he still had that empty cigarette paper in one hand. He looked down at it almost hungrily, then cast a suspicious glance at his native companions. No! Duty! Eyes across the river!

But then... slowly... eyes back to his empty cigarette. Because caution is its own reward. But then, so is tobacco. And at what point does caution become folly? With a final sigh, Jonathan Small leaned his rifle against the wall and reached for his pouch.

In an instant, the unnamed third man pounced upon Small's rifle, snatched it up, and ran into the crumbling bowels of the fort. As he passed me, I could see his eyes were squeezed shut in desperate horror, with the hint of tears at the corners. He made it through the doorway and halfway down the corridor, before he ran face first into a wall and fell over with a cry.

A split-second later, Mahomet Singh reached into the folds of his tunic and produced a "pistol" which he leveled at young Jonathan Small's chest. "Freeze where you are, sahib!" he croaked. "I have a *gun*! And it is *loaded*! And it is *not carved of wood*! And I will shoot you if you try anything and I will not even cry because I am a bad, bad man, just like you!"

I rolled my eyes at the feebleness of his deception. Modern-day Small blushed. Small the Younger was taken in entirely. He gasped and threw his hands up, sending a plume of tobacco into the wall behind him. Mahomet Singh seemed relieved his gambit was proceeding so well. He paused to wipe a great slick of terror sweat from his brow. The other fellow crept cautiously back into the room, sporting a bloody nose. He made a vague attempt to point Small's rifle at him but it was clear his heart wasn't in it.

Young Small, whose terror-widened eyes had been

taking the whole situation in, offered the observation, "If you shoot me, the noise will bring the garrison. Then we'll all be dead. You can't do it. You can't take the fort."

"What? No, no. I am not trying to take the fort, sahib. Why would I do that? I am a Sikh. It would be greatly against my own interests. Besides, it is very difficult for my people to do bad things. We know we're not supposed to, you see, and it makes us feel very…"

But he realized what he was saying, gave a gasp, waggled his fake gun at Small's chest and insisted, "But I will, though! I will kill you, *so hard*! Bang! That's what it will sound like!"

It was plain that Young Small was entirely confused. "Er… so… what do you want?" he wondered.

"I want to make you rich."

"Eh? Why?"

"Listen to me, sahib. Listen. What do you intend to do after the mutiny?"

"Probably just… stay in the army, I guess."

"But, sahib, as everybody knows: you are not *in* the army."

"Yes, but they might let me stick around, don't you think?"

Mahomet shook his head. "It is not their way."

"Then I'll go back to England."

"How? Have you money for the journey? Have you any prospects waiting for you there? I only ask because you have several times told the fellows around here that you do not."

Young Small growled. Singh retreated a step and spluttered, "But I can give you that! Listen to my tale, sahib. In the north there is a rajah—very rich, very rich—he has always been loyal to the British, but he would shed no tears, I think, if all of you were slain. So what did he do when the mutiny broke out? Should he aid the British, knowing that if his countrymen triumphed, they would treat him as a traitor? Aid his countrymen, knowing the British would do the same? No. He has stayed out of it, waiting to see who wins. To safeguard his position, he has divided his treasure. All of his gold and silver remains in the north, with his countrymen. If they should triumph, he is still a wealthy man. All his gems and his true treasure, he has sent to British territory, so that if they triumph he still is wealthy. That treasure is coming here, tonight. He has an agent—a false merchant who uses the name Achmet. We have devised that his guide will be my foster-brother, Dost Akbar. He is bringing Achmet to this very door, within the hour. Achmet—oh, it pains me to say it—Achmet must die this night."

"Oh," said Young Small, as if someone had just invited him to a Christmas party. "You want me to help you kill him? Is that it?"

The young man holding Small's rifle burst into tears. "I *really* don't want to do it!"

Mahomet Singh nodded vigorously and said, "My people are not comfortable with... well... *murder*."

"It's hard to even say it," his tearful companion confirmed.

"Now, there is one item in the treasure chest which must

be destroyed," said Singh. "But what will happen to the rest of the treasure, though, eh? Do you see what I am saying?"

"I think I do," said Young Small. Every trace of fear was gone from his features now, replaced by cocksure bravado. "So… you, me, this fellow here, and your foster-brother, eh? That's four of us. So, I'll do it. No problem. So long as I get a full quarter-share of the treasure!"

Out of the corner of my eye I saw Singh's companion silently mouth, "Only a *quarter*?"

"Um, sure! A quarter. Whatever you say, sahib," said Singh. "But you must swear loyalty to us. You must swear to keep our secret and to let us destroy the black heart of that treasure. Look: here is paper and pen, sahib. My brotherhood calls itself 'nine'. You must write the number '9' on this paper and sign your name beneath, to show you are one of us!"

"All right," said Small. He scratched away for a few seconds, then stood back, beaming.

Singh looked over his shoulder. He gave a frustrated sigh. "That is the number '6'."

"Is it?" said Young Small, looking somewhat chastened. "I'm sorry. I… uh… I always was all right with my letters, but numbers is another thing, you know? Six… nine… It's hard to remember if the bumpy part goes on the top or the bottom. Right?"

"It's the top," said Singh.

"Sure. Sure. Sorry about that."

Small crumpled up the sheet of paper and threw it onto the little fire that burned in one corner of the guardroom.

Mahomet Singh handed him another sheet of paper and Small scratched away for a moment. When he was done, Singh looked over and said, "That is a capital 'P'."

"Argh! But you said the bumpy part goes on top!"

"Yes, but the other side of the top."

"Goddamn it!" Small roared. He crumpled up the second sheet and threw it into the fire.

With trembling hands, Singh held another sheet of paper out towards Small.

"Careful," he said. "This is my last piece."

"Well, it's hard!"

From the corner of the room, Singh's companion suggested, "Perhaps, if sahib is better with letters, he could write 'the sign of nine' instead of… you know… that shape we use as the sign that means nine."

"Could you do that?" Singh wondered.

"O'course I could!"

"Good, then. All right. Do that."

Jonathan Small bent to his task one final time. When he was done, Mahomet Singh heaved a deep sigh of relief and said, "Good. You are one of us now, Jonathan Small. You are our brother. This is my partner, Abdullah Khan, and we are glad to have you with us."

"So glad!" said Khan, handing Small his rifle back. "Oh my God, *so glad*!"

But Small looked down at his rifle with disdain. "No good," he said. "A shot's the signal that will bring the garrison. Here, we'll use this…"

He went to the fire, rummaged in a bag of cooking

supplies for a moment, then came up with a long, serrated bread knife. He held it up for his companions' approval. In the firelight, it gleamed a dull, ominous orange. Mahomet Singh grew very pale.

"I am so glad I don't have to do it," Abdullah Khan said. "That fellow can have as many diamonds as he *wants*!"

There was nothing left to do but wait. After about half an hour, the sound of labored breathing came to the ears of the three conspirators. They all sprang up and made ready. Through the doorway, Small could just make out the shapes of two figures, struggling along the wet riverbank. Between them they bore a chest made of heavy, filigreed iron.

Whispering as loud as he could, Singh challenged them. "Who goes there?"

"Dost Akbar," one of the figures said. "I am here with the merchant, Achmet."

"Good, good! Come inside."

The two men hauled the chest past Small, dropped it in the middle of the guardroom, and stood panting, brushing the rain from their clothes.

"Ah, thank you," said the merchant Achmet. "And who is this fellow?"

"One of the soldiers, Jonathan Small," Singh said. "He is here to convey you directly to the colonel."

"Very good."

Everybody stood about for a minute.

"Go on…" Singh urged. "Conduct our friend to the… you know… *colonel*…"

"Eh?" said Small. "Oh! Yeah. Right."

He then laid a savage kick against the side of the merchant's knee that broke it in a single blow. As it sagged sideways, the old man drew a breath to scream, but Jonathan Small clapped his left hand over Achmet's mouth. With his right he reached back, withdrew the bread knife from the back of his waistband and plunged it through his victim's throat. Dost Akbar's eyes went wide with horror and revulsion. Mahomet Singh gave his foster-brother a little nod, as if to say, "You see? I told you I'd find the man we needed." Abdullah Khan lost all veneer of self-control and began to sob loudly.

"Which, I believe, would make five," said Lestrade, jotting a quick note.

"Dat was a good one," Grogsson opined.

"Quick," said Singh, "put him in the corner, where he can't be seen from the door. The chest is locked; he must have a key somewhere."

The four conspirators rifled through their victim's pockets, but found no key.

"Bastard probably swallowed it for safekeeping," Young Small opined. "Well, it won't work!"

With that, he plunged the bread knife into Achmet's torso and began sawing.

"*Bloody hell!*" cried Dost Akbar, Mahomet Singh, Abdullah Khan, Warlock Holmes, Vladislav Lestrade, and myself.

"Any man woulda done the same!" present-day Small shouted.

"You da worst," Grogsson told him.

Though he was a small man, Abdullah Khan nevertheless managed to produce about two gallons of vomit, along with a fresh burst of tears.

Young Jonathan Small sat digging about in Achmet's abdominal cavity for a few minutes—squeezing this bit of intestine, poking at the organs, looking for the key—until Dost Akbar at last said, "Ah! Here it is! In his turban."

"Huh," said Small. "Shoulda thought of that. Oh well! Let's see what we got, eh?"

Three of the men—for Abdullah Khan was still... *occupied*—crowded round the chest. The lock yielded to the key. The lid swung open. And...

Just...

By God...

It was like something out of a children's book about pirates. Or dragons. Or some finance minister's greedy, secret dream.

There was the golden cup, with six huge pearls embedded in it. It rested atop a mountain of gems. There must have been hundreds. And the *size* of them! Some were only gem-sized, of course, but a number were simply preposterous. The Hope Diamond, the Star of India, the Black Prince's Ruby—each of these might find a home within that chest of wonders, but none of them could command pride of place. This was a treasure the like of which the world had never seen.

So it rather surprised me when Mahomet Singh and Dost Akbar began piling it unceremoniously onto the floor. They continued for some minutes, digging about in the wealth of ages with mounting anxiety, until Singh at last gave a cry of triumph.

"Here it is, my brothers! We have done it!" He pulled forth his treasure to display to his confederates.

"Oh dear…" said Holmes.

In Mahomet Singh's upraised hand sat a blackened iron disc. The coin. The relic of greed. One of the nine fetishes that had the power to command the wills of men.

"This is it!" Singh cried. "The source of our unhappiness! This is why the foreigners come to our land! Let us destroy it, my brothers, and be rid of them forever!"

"I don't know…" said Dost Akbar, dolefully. "We may have to destroy the Hieroform as well."

"Then so we shall! So we shall!" said Singh. "But that is a work for another night and it does not lessen this victory. Quick! Abdullah! Get the tools; there is not much time!"

From the corner of the room, Abdullah Khan fetched a rag-wrapped bundle. He unrolled it in the center of the floor to reveal a battered set of blacksmith's tools. Mahomet Singh did not hesitate. He grabbed up a metal chisel and a heavy hammer. He placed the coin on a flagstone, positioned the chisel in its center and brought the hammer down as hard as he could. The chisel sparked and rang, but left no mark upon the surface of the coin. The second blow fared no better. The third cracked the flagstone beneath.

"Too much noise!" Akbar hissed.

"And yet we cannot fail," Singh insisted. He took the

coin to the little fire in the corner of the room and threw it in. From the pile of tools he selected a small bellows and a few lumps of coal. He arranged the coal just over the coin and began working the bellows feverishly. In the few minutes it took the coal to burn down, Abdullah hurried over with a small anvil and a wedge, designed to separate hot metals. With tongs, he withdrew the coin from the fire. It smoked a great deal more than I thought it ought to, but did not glow. Sure enough, when he placed it on the anvil and struck it with wedge and hammer, no mark could be seen upon its surface.

They made a pretty good dent in the anvil, though.

"Noise!" Akbar hissed.

"I don't care!" Singh shot back. "It does not matter if we are taken! It does not matter if we are killed!"

"Eh?" said Jonathan Small, looking up from a slightly-more-than-a-quarter-share-sized pile of gems he'd been making. "Yes it does!"

"We must destroy it!" Singh insisted.

But Akbar shook his head. "You are not going to. Look at it, my brother, look. It is clear we do not have the art. Your efforts may serve to bring the fury of the white man down upon us, but it is clear it cannot serve to destroy this wicked coin. We must find another way."

Mahomet Singh looked as perfectly heartbroken as I have ever seen a man. Finally, though, he nodded his assent.

"Quickly!" said Akbar. "Everyone! We must hide what we have done. Is the room ready?"

"What room?" Small wanted to know.

"Just down the corridor, in a room with a ruined wall," said Khan. "We have dug a hole in the floor to hide Achmet's body. Perhaps there is room for the treasure as well. When the mutiny is over, we can return to claim what we wish—and to destroy the coin. Until that day, we must do our best to hide our crime and to discover a way to break the spell that curses our efforts."

"What? But I want my diamonds *now*!" Small protested.

"Oh yes?" said Singh. "And how do you intend to explain them to your fellow soldiers? You shall have your prize, sahib, but not until it is safe to take."

The four conspirators busied themselves piling treasure back into the iron chest. Yet, as they did, a strange thing began to occur to the body of Achmet.

He opened his eyes.

He sat slightly upwards—as much as his severed abdominal muscles would allow.

He pointed one finger forward; at what, I cannot say.

And he let loose a great sigh. A thick, whitish green vapor escaped between his gray lips. Though none of the living men was looking in Achmet's direction, Dost Akbar and Abdullah Khan made faces of distaste. Apparently, even in this atmosphere of murder and vomit, the change in smell was apparent.

"Ah," said Holmes. "I should have guessed it. There she is."

"She?" Lestrade wondered.

"The entity that would become known as Mrs. Sholto," said Holmes. "A greed demon, drawn strongly hither. And is it any wonder? Look at the size of that treasure. See the fresh murder that has been done in its name? And in the presence of the black coin, no less—a magical focus so potent, it represents and controls mankind's collective desire for wealth. How could she not have felt its call?"

"*That's* Mrs. Sholto?" I asked, pointing at the reeking mist.

"That's her right now," said Holmes, with a shrug, "but it may be some years before Sholto arrives to claim the treasure. If she spends the interim thriving off the power of the black coin, who knows what she'll look like by the time he gets here?"

The corpse of Achmet closed his eyes and sagged back to rest. The stinking fog began creeping towards the Agra treasure. Tendril by tendril, it seeped into the chest. Yet, if the four conspirators noticed it, they paid no heed. Only Jonathan Small wrinkled his nose and complained, "By God, that corpse stinks!"

"We must hide it, sahib! We must hide the treasure!"

"All right, but not in the same hole, yeah?" said Young Small. "I don't want dead-guy juice all over my diamonds."

Older Small shook his head. "I shoulda known. The whole situation smelled damned rotten, and it went damned rotten."

And suddenly, with a quick blast of buzzy-fuzz, we stood in the fort's open courtyard. There before us were the four conspirators, bound in chains. Khan looked tearful; Akbar looked fearful; Singh looked like exactly what he was—a man who had come so close to achieving a holy purpose, only to have it crumble to nothing at the last minute. Small looked defiant. On a raised platform before them sat the regimental colonel, two majors, and an angry-looking fellow in a turban.

"How do you explain it, Small?" the colonel asked.

"Don't know what you're talking about, sir, with all due respect."

The colonel bristled. He pointed a finger at the Indian man on the platform with him and said, "This is Mr. Sanjja. He is here to meet the merchant, Achmet Ras, who was last seen in the company of a guide named Dost Akbar. Mr. Sanjja saw them approach this fort by way of the riverbank last night. Do you still claim to know nothing?"

"Sorry, sir. It just don't ring any bells."

"Well that's a funny thing, Small, because we checked the guardroom where you were posted last night. Do you know what we found? Some missing blacksmith's tools, a tear-soaked pile of vomit, and one rather impressive bloodstain. Still not ringing any bells?"

"Perhaps somebody tripped, sir."

"Hmm. Yes, perhaps. And all their blood came out. So much blood, in fact, that it wasn't hard for us to follow the trail of it to a shallow grave just two rooms down. But perhaps somebody tripped, sustained a fatal wound, then had the courtesy to drag themselves to a pre-dug shallow grave and bury themselves, to spare us the cleanup?"

"Anything's possible, sir."

"And here's a funny thing—what with our limited laundry capabilities—a few of the boys couldn't help but notice one or two little spots of blood on your uniform this morning."

"It's been a rough week, sir."

"And we seem to have acquired an entire extra person in the night. None other than Dost Akbar, who was traveling with the murdered merchant. Hello, Mr. Dost Akbar! Do you have any idea what happened to Achmet Ras?"

Akbar shook his head, sheepishly.

The turbaned fellow next to the governor leaned forward and said, "Unacceptable, I fear. I am very interested to know about the last moments of my cousin and… uh… his belongings."

"Look, we haven't got time for this," the colonel spat. "I told you, I've got a caravan of refugees and supplies coming in from Cawnpore. They'll never make it unless we send a relief force to retrieve them. I am sorry, but this is simply not the matter of the day! What do you think, gentlemen, have you heard enough?"

The two majors nodded, then drew close to the colonel to discuss the specifics of their judgment. It took less than a minute to reach agreement. The colonel waved them aside and proclaimed, "Dost Akbar, Mahomet Singh and Abdullah Khan: you have committed a crime of a most serious nature in a time of war. You are hereby sentenced to life imprisonment."

The three men shuffled their feet and looked down.

Then again, if there was anything surprising about the sentence, it was its leniency.

"Private Jonathan Small," the colonel continued, "you are a British citizen and soldier; your conduct has been most disappointing. Furthermore—as it is clear you were responsible for the actual killing—I hereby sentence you to die for your crimes. May God have mercy upon your soul!"

"Hey now!" Small protested. "Nobody saw nothing! You can't prove I—"

But the colonel cut him off. "There is blood up to your elbows. Good day."

"Any man woulda done the same!" cried Young Small and present-day Small together.

"A pity," said Holmes. "And so, they killed you?"

"No," said present-day Small. "I guess a few of the lads who remembered what I'd done at Shahgunge had a word with the colonel. Got my sentence reduced to life, just like the others'. We spent the rest of the mutiny at Agra, then some time in Madras, and finally off to a prison colony on Blair Island. And that, gentlemen, *that* is where my fortunes took their second great turn."

13

BLAIR ISLAND IS A LITTLE NOTHING OF A PLACE IN THE Andaman chain, far off the coast of India in the Bay of Bengal. As a prison, it had only one thing to recommend it: it was remote. Any prisoner who was not capable of swimming two hundred miles or so, or of secretly constructing an ocean-worthy craft with several weeks of stores on board, had little chance of seeing mainland civilization ever again.

That is not to say it was the *worst* place Jonathan Small could have ended up. As we fuzzed in, I have to say I was rather taken with the bracing sea air, the beauty of her swaying palms and the boundless expanse of blue sky. Also, I'm told the fact that none of the natives seemed to put much stock in the idea of clothing did contribute to the island's popularity amongst the British military staff.

Yet, these natives had proved to be less gullible than those in other parts of the world. They suffered only as much contact as they absolutely had to with the occupying foreigners. Indeed, farther up the island chain, they had a not-undeserved reputation for spearing and eating any sailors who had the misfortune of being shipwrecked there. It may seem cruel, but to give credit where credit is due: they were one of the few people our ships had reached that did not find themselves quickly placed both beneath our flag and our sailors.

Port Blair was the exception. As the prison was yet in the early stages of its construction, most of the inmates were kept chained in a large, palm-frond-topped lean-to, but released during the day to gather food and materials to build the colony. Those who showed any familiarity with the British way of life were treated much better. A number of them—Small included—had little huts at the base of the hills. Blair Island was a prison to Small only in that he was not allowed to leave it. I think if the colonel at Agra had realized he was sentencing Jonathan Small to life in a private hut in a tropical paradise, he might have been more than a little put out.

In fact, I think he might have been jealous.

Yet this did not stop Small complaining about his treatment as he showed us the cabin where he had spent his days, the officers' mess where he served refreshments, and the little infirmary where he worked. It seems he'd acquired some medical skills in his year on the island, which allowed him to be of some help in dispensing drugs for Dr. Somerton, the army surgeon. This in turn allowed him to purloin no small quantity of said drugs, which he put to any number of dubious uses. Most prominently: trading with the local soldiers and officers in exchange for items and favors to make his life easier. But the thing he really gained was information.

In the evenings, Dr. Somerton, the officers, the sailors who ran the docks and a few civilians would gather to play cards in the infirmary. Small would sit in Somerton's office, filling bottles, writing out forms and ordering replacements for the supplies he'd just stolen. Often he would listen to the players' talk. And that is the scene we entered. Small in the office, busy with his thievery and eavesdropping, while seven men sat playing a card game of hideous complexity. The deck they used was gigantic and seemed to be composed of cards from several traditions: the familiar fifty-two-card deck, but also tarot cards and a few symbols that reminded one of mah-jong. It was one of those games with several rounds of betting, of discarding and re-drawing, maneuvering for advantage with an opponent's discarded cards, and battling the shifting vicissitudes of luck.

Or, no… not luck… *cheating*.

There was entirely too much conversation for there not to be agreed-upon little codes about what one was holding or thinking of discarding. Too many funny little gestures that tended to be repeated. Too many raised eyebrows and answering smiles. It was clear the air was abuzz with secret language. Just as clear: the civilians spoke it fluently. The officers did not.

We watched for a few moments, trying to glean the obtuse and intricate rules, until—with a final burst of laughter and moans, a quaffing of final brandies and flicking of final cigars—the game broke up. The civilians rose. Dr. Somerton excused himself. Two officers remained.

I knew them.

One, I had seen in a painting. Major Sholto was younger, to be sure, less worn by care and his own misdeeds. Yet that shabby brand of martial splendor I'd noted in his portrait attended him already.

The other was less familiar. Yet, if one noted the general grayness of his form and character—that bitter unfriendliness of bearing and the pinched grimace of a man who thought the world owed him more than it was delivering—there could be no question. He was certainly related to Mary Morstan. He sat with his head in his hands, staring down at the table with horrible anger.

John Sholto picked up a stub of cigar from the ashtray, took an exploratory puff and said, "That last hand, Artie… What the hell was that? Couldn't you see he was building a hangman's bridge? You just kept betting."

"Of course I saw what he was building! I'm not a fool! But I knew I could beat him!"

"Well… you didn't."

"But I had fours! Nobody was holding fours! I knew I could get them all. I had the four of diamonds, the four of cups, the four of fives and the lotus blossom four. All I had to do was stay in the game until someone dropped a four and I'd have had him!"

"Four of spades came by, didn't it?"

"And I grabbed it up! Yet no sooner did I have it in my hand than I realized I never did have the four of fives…"

"Oh! No, Artie, not again!"

"I'd been holding the *bloody five of fours*! They look exactly alike!"

"Not quite."

"Well, they've got those same twenty dots on them, don't they? I mean... I dropped it as soon as I could and started looking for that last card to get my five-of-a-kind, but..."

Major Sholto gave a grim smile. "How bad is it?"

"All the way! I'm done!" said Morstan, throwing up his arms. "I thought I could save myself, you know? Win back all that money I was supposed to have been sending home! So I just kept throwing more and more in. I've nothing now. Less than nothing. How am I going to pay back those marks I was betting at the end?"

Sholto shrugged. "Well, don't look at me. I passed the point of no return last week. I'll be out of the army in a month; I'll have to sell my commission to cover my debts."

"Then I suppose I'll see you back in England, for I think that is my only course now, too," Morstan said.

At this point, the two men were interrupted by the sound of the closing office door. They looked up in annoyance to have their secret shame intruded upon.

There stood Young Small, with a mischievous gleam in his eye. "Oh," he said. "So sorry, sirs, I thought the game was done."

"It is, Small, it is," said Morstan. "Yes, I'm afraid the game is well and truly done."

"But you know, I'm glad to catch the two of you," said

Small, "for I've got a question about the army. Policy and procedures and such."

"Tomorrow, damn it," Sholto barked. "Can't you see we're busy?"

"Oh, but it's just a small thing," said Small, struggling to keep the smile off his lips. "I wanted to know who to report hidden treasure to."

Sholto's eyes brightened just a shade. Morstan's did not. He waved his hand dismissively and mumbled, "The regional exchequer. They handle all that sort of thing. I'll help you write a letter tomorrow if you want, but Major Sholto is right: leave us alone."

Sholto's hand gripped his friend's shoulder with sudden earnestness. "Oh, but, Captain… are you sure? We've got time, haven't we?"

"Time? What time have we left?"

"God damn it, Artie! Aren't you *curious*? Don't you wish to know about this hidden treasure?"

"Not really. Go away, Small."

"You don't think it might be *amusing* to find out how much it is? And… er… *where* it is? And how many people know about it?"

"Not particula— Ow!"

Major Sholto's grip was now so tight it looked as if he might crush Morstan's clavicle. He stared down with wide eyes and a smile so broad and tense it looked as if he'd eaten three pounds of large decorative rocks and was now attempting to pass them. As Morstan looked up, his countenance made it plain that he had no energy for this.

Yet his friend appeared most earnest, so he sighed and said, "All right. What is it, Small? Find a shiny pebble, did you?"

"Several, actually," Small said, with a smile. "I don't know if you've heard what got me sent here, but the three Sikhs and I were sent down for the 'possible' murder of a merchant. His cousin said that merchant had been in possession of a great treasure at the time, but of course we didn't know anything about that. But... well... now we've been on this island for a while and probably nobody's too worked up about that merchant anymore... I thought, maybe if we *did* remember something about a treasure, perhaps we could exchange the information for our release."

Morstan shook his head. "I shouldn't think so. The charge is murder, Small. Do you think the Crown will so easily forget such a serious—"

"The treasure's worth at least half a million."

Several eyebrows in the room went up. Mine included, for I knew it to be a gross underestimate of the Agra treasure's true worth. Half a million? Please. You'd be wrong to trade that iron box and its contents for the Crown Jewels. Sholto looked excited. Morstan thoughtful. After a time, Morstan said, "You may have a point, Small. The sheer value of such a contribution might make the Crown forget much. I'm not sure if it would get all four of you off, but just you... perhaps. I tell you what, I'll write the exchequer a note tomorrow—"

"What? Exchequer? No, no, no, Artie! Think of what

you're saying!" Sholto cried. "What good would that do? Why, even if Private Small here could secure his freedom, even if he could get freedom for all his friends, where would they be? All that money would disappear into Her Majesty's vaults. Private Small would still have no prospects. Think: might there not be a better way for us to help?"

"What do you mean?" Morstan asked.

"I mean, if what Small says about the value of the treasure is true, why, that's enough for more than just a pardon. That's enough for a *boat*. That's enough for a one-way ticket off this island for whoever thinks they might want to go—for new papers and new names and a fresh start. All Small would need is a confederate who could come and go from the island freely."

Morstan sniffed. "Well, good luck finding one! This island is—"

Sholto slapped him across the face and peered down at his friend with pure fury. Morstan looked up in shock and indignation for about half a second, before realization lit his features and he cried out, "Oh! Oh! *We* could be his confederates!"

"Hey now," said Small, finally letting his hidden smile burst forth, "*there's* an interesting idea."

"I think we might imagine a scenario," said Sholto carefully, "wherein one of us goes to confirm the treasure is real. If so, I'm sure release might be secured one of these nights for Private Small. Just think: half a million, split three ways—"

"No!" Small insisted. "Six ways! The Sikhs are my brothers and I swore an oath. I think I could talk them into going sixes, but whatever deal we strike has got to end with me and my brothers on a boat with our cut. I gave my solemn vow!"

"Awwwww," said Holmes to me and present-day Jonathan Small. "Now that is nice. You see? An unexpected vein of loyalty to brighten a character stained by disrepute. Nobody is irredeemable, I always say!"

"That's one interpretation," I said. "But here's mine: Jonathan Small had no intention of giving up five-sixths of the Agra treasure. Yet, if he could secure his freedom and a boat so cheaply, that would be more than worthwhile. As long as he made sure he was at sea before he murdered the three Sikhs, he could be reasonably sure he'd keep their share."

"But that's horrible!" said Holmes. "And besides, it would be three to one; they'd overpower him."

"They might," I agreed, "if he hadn't spent a few years stealing drugs from Dr. Somerton. I imagine, just following dinner one night, the three Sikhs might find themselves feeling rather drowsy."

Present-day Jonathan Small crossed his arms over his chest and mumbled, "Any man would have done the same."

Holmes's mouth dropped open. "Oh, well! Grogsson is right about you, Mr. Small. You are absolutely the worst!"

"Except he can't have managed to pull it off," I noted, "because when this story began, he didn't have the Agra treasure, did he?"

Small made a horrible face and nodded. "You guessed it. I talked to the others. Singh agreed, so long as he got to keep the black coin. The other two were just glad of a way off the island. Of course, Morstan and Sholto weren't about to throw away what was left of their careers unless they knew the treasure was real. I didn't want to let them do it, but they swore up and down they'd be true to us. In the end we made a deal: the Sikhs and I would make a map to the treasure and we'd trade this for a full confession of our escape plan, signed by Morstan and Sholto. Then one of them would go to Agra, confirm the treasure was there and send a boat for us. We'd all go pick up the treasure together."

"Even better," I scoffed. "Once off the island, with all five others on a boat in the middle of the Bay of Bengal, with a pocket full of sedatives, you could be pretty sure you'd end up with the whole treasure, couldn't you?"

"I might have. Me and Singh and Khan and Akbar made that map in good faith. I wrote 'the sign of nine' at the bottom and we all signed our names."

"I've seen it," I told him. "It was in the possession of Arthur Morstan, and subsequently his daughter."

Small shrugged, "He musta got it from Sholto, then. For Sholto were the one who did us wrong."

Just a small leap forward in time brought us to the two officers, leaning in over their massive deck of cards. Morstan cut the deck, flipped the cards in his hand upward and cried out, "Yes! The ace of aces!"

"Well, an impressive-*sounding* card," Sholto said, "but let us remember that the value of ace is one."

"Oh."

Now it was Sholto's turn to cut. Was it my imagination, or was there just a flick of the wrist as he palmed the cards? Had he forced the draw? It seemed he hardly had to look at the card in his hand before he declared. "Bad luck, Artie! It's the twelve of cards, I'm afraid. Looks like I'll be the one to go to Agra. Don't worry though, I'm sure I'll be bringing back good news."

Present-day Small frowned. "The first sign of trouble came the morning after Sholto left. I'd tucked the confession he and Morstan had signed into my shirt and slept with it overnight, while I tried to think of where to hide it. When I woke, it had dissolved into a gooey mess of nothing. Seems like it was trick paper, made with gelatin in the pulp. I was furious of course, but Morstan seemed as surprised as I was. That's what made me really worry. Sure enough, a few weeks later, a letter comes. Says the treasure wasn't there—either I was lying or someone else had found it. After that, nothing. Sholto should have come back but he didn't. Instead, a few months later, we got word he'd left the army. Apparently some rich uncle nobody knew he'd had left him a pretty sizeable fortune in jewels.

"Now, with Morstan deep in debt and holding on to his commission by the skin of his teeth, it took him years to find out where Sholto had gone. At last he got word that Sholto had bought a huge house in London. He wrote and demanded to know why Sholto had betrayed him. Morstan don't know it, but I saw Sholto's return letter before Morstan himself did. Sholto promised Morstan half the treasure, and all Morstan had to do was make sure me and the Sikhs was dead, then come to London and claim his share."

"Why didn't he?" I wondered.

Small shrugged. "Probably didn't want to risk facing a firing squad until he were damned sure he was going to get his half of the treasure. Took a little holiday to London and never come back. From what I can gather, Sholto did him in as soon as he saw him."

"I know something of the matter," I said. "And I am forced to agree. So you must have had a very long wait for your revenge. But how did you ever make it off the island?"

"I thought I never would. Until I met Tonga."

"Oh! Oh!" said Holmes. "Watch this!"

Blur. Fuzz.

We were standing just behind the infirmary. It was a drizzly sort of day, and we were watching a somewhat older and more careworn Jonathan Small peeping out of the back door to talk to a small deputation of Andaman natives. One of them wore an ornate headband, decorated with beading and a few sprigs of feathers and clearly meant to say, "I know you're not one of us, but do you think hats like this happen by accident? No. A lot of effort went in, and it looks like it denotes social importance, yeah? So, probably talk to the guy with the hat."

Their language was strange to me. Small had picked up a smattering of the local tongue and the man who came to deal with him had learned some English. Yet, though the words were a laborious mixture of the two languages, one of the benefits of stealing another man's memories is that the underlying meanings are clear.

"They said you wanted to talk to me?" said Small.

The head of the native deputation nodded. "It is said you know much of the white man's medicines and poisons."

"Yes, I suppose that's what is said. What of it?"

The islander looked around to be sure they wouldn't be overheard and asked, "Do you know of a way to kill a spirit?"

"A what?"

"A spirit. Have you heard our word 'Tonga'? It means... how should I say...? It means to take revenge against somebody who has not really done you any wrong."

Small smiled. "Is that why you fellows sometimes shoot a poisoned dart or two at us English?"

"No," said the native, icily. "That is something different. Tonga is... Well, let us say you find a gourd. A nice one, perfect and round and you are very pleased with it. You put it somewhere for safekeeping, but forget where. You are upset you cannot find it. Then you see a neighbor with a perfect round gourd and you are angry that he has found your secret hiding spot. So, you beat him to death with a rock, pick up the gourd and head back to your hut. On the way, you walk past your favorite napping tree and catch sight of *your* gourd. That is Tonga."

"And... what? You want me to stop that sort of thing from happening?" Small asked.

"No. On this island, there is a spirit. He is like a person, but different. Very small, and made of hard material. We try to avoid him because he is… how would you English say…? Ah! Just the *worst*. He is very much the embodiment of the idea of Tonga. Last night he came into one of our huts where we kept the bottles of the whiskey we had traded from the English. He drank them all and now he is very sick. Maybe he will die. Maybe he will wake up. We do not know. But we know this much: if he wakes up he is going to kill and kill and kill for no reason. So… um… do you think you could find a way for him *not to*?"

"Huh…" said Small. "Sounds interesting. Bring 'im in."

With a blur and a fuzz, we were watching Jonathan Small betray the natives by nursing Tonga back to health. Of course I'd only seen him by moonlight before, as he fired his fingers at Holmes and me (and notably, at Hopkins), but it was unmistakably him. His skin was of a hard, bark-like material and his feet displayed the strange backward toe-claw that had made its mark in the secret attic at Pondicherry Lodge.

He was more than just hung over; he was positively poisoned—our terrestrial brews being utterly alien to his other-dimensional physiology. Yet over the next few days, Small dutifully brought him water and yams. He covered the little fellow up when he shivered and uncovered him when he sweated. Since the little blighter spoke only in utterly nonsensical clicks and rattles, their conversation was somewhat one-sided. Small bitterly recounted his misadventures with the Sikhs, the treasure, and the officers who had betrayed them.

And strangely, I think *that's* what saved Tonga. He leaned in with such interest whenever Small spoke of what he wanted to do to those that had let him down, that I got the distinct feeling that what was really keeping the little fellow going was that he was hearing the story of a group of individuals who needed to have some Tonga practiced on them.

Sure enough, by noon on the fourth day the queer little man was gone. Younger Small seemed saddened by it—as if the prospect of facing life alone on the island without his little vengeance-friend was particularly burdensome. If so, he did not have to bear it long. Two nights later there came a click, click, click at the door to Small's hut. Small swung it open to find Tonga standing just outside.

"Oh, hello. What do you want?"

The little man made no answer, just turned and trudged away over the sandy soil. Jonathan Small watched him for a moment, brow furrowed, then followed. Over the sand they went, across the moonlit camp, past the stockade where Small's three Indian "brothers" still languished. He spared them nary a glance as he passed, but left them to their fate. As Tonga and Small neared the shore, Small saw two skeletons lying in pools of rancid liquid; one was wearing the remnants of simple robes, the other a soldier's uniform.

"Your doing?" Small asked his tiny companion.

Tonga beamed back at him for a moment, then pointed down the beach. An angular shape jutted out into the water. Small gasped and started running. Sure enough, it was one of the natives' canoes. Next to it lay one of the natives. He was nothing but bones and disgusting juice, but the ornate beaded headband that drooped down over the skull left no doubt as to whose canoe we were looking at.

Small turned back to Tonga and said, "So, you got that chief fellow back for tryin' to get me to kill you, eh?"

Tonga put his thorny hands on his hips and gave a proud nod.

"Good on you!"

The canoe was well stocked with yams, coconuts, and gourds filled with drinking water: all that was needed. Yet, if it seemed Jonathan Small's journey to freedom was about to commence, there was one more errand left.

A little farther down the beach lay a man—a Pashtun, by his dress. He was propped up against the base of one of the palms that grew nearest to the sea, snoring gently. When he saw the man, Young Small's face hardened into a mask of rage.

"Oh dear," I said. "Any man would have done the same, I suppose?"

"Well look here," present-day Small protested, as his younger self began to stalk, silently, down the beach, "that man were a vile Pathan who never missed an opportunity to have a kick at me. Made me life miserable whenever he could. And besides, what if he were to wake up, eh? What if he should see me heading out to sea?"

Lestrade paused with his pencil just above a page of his notebook and mused, "Hmmm. It's been a while. What number is this?"

But Grogsson grunted, "Quiet! Torg want to see."

The man must have been one of the garrison, for he had a rifle beside him and a long knife tucked through his belt. Small had no weapon at all and it was clear from the way he was looking about that he wanted one. Finding none, he stopped just a few paces from his sleeping victim and began fiddling about with something on his right leg.

"Oh no," I said, breathlessly. "You aren't going to…"

"Yep," said Holmes. "He is."

By the light of the moon, we could see the asymmetrical form of Jonathan Small raise his false leg up over his head and battle-hop the last few paces to his foe. The sound must have woken the poor fellow up, for we saw him jerk in surprise just an instant before Small brought the heavy prosthetic down and cracked his skull.

Then he cracked it a second time.

And a third.

And six or seven more after that.

Holmes shook his head and tutted, "Unnecessary, Small."

Grogsson jabbed a finger towards the murder scene and said, "Look! What he do now?"

Small was hunched over the body. He withdrew the long knife from his victim's belt, then bent over the man's legs, hacking and sawing away. Present-day Small colored and said, "Well, you see, Tonga had done a fine job with the yams and water, but… nothing with any *protein*, really…"

"You're going to cut that man up and take him along to eat him?" I cried.

413

"I just took the leg muscles," Small protested, but as his previous self wandered back past us, whistling a jaunty little tune, a small item tucked into his belt made a liar of him.

"Cor blimey," said present-day Small, scratching at his head. "Now, why'd I take his face?"

"For use as a clever disguise, one assumes?" I said.

He snapped his fingers. "That was it! It's funny what we remember and what we forget, eh?"

"Now look here, Small," I said, in my sternest tone, "I just want to make my position clear, right now. Whatever Scotland Yard chooses to do with you for all these crimes, you bloody deserve it."

He gave me an ungenerous look.

As Young Small approached the stolen canoe, Tonga applauded his recent performance and beamed with joy. If he had hoped he'd chosen the right human companion— the man who most embodied the spirit of Tonga-ism—he now knew he could not have picked a finer.

Holmes gave a little sigh and wondered, "So that's it, eh? You sailed back to London?"

"What, in that?" Small scoffed, pointing at the little canoe. "We'd never have made it. Especially as I weren't much of a navigator. The only thing I knew of it was I'd heard to follow the sun."

"The sun?" I said. "The sun that rises in the east and sets in the west and would just have you blithering back and forth until you ran out of food and water?"

"That sounds about right," Small admitted. "Ten days

we tossed about, with nary a sight of land. At last we was picked up by a boat of Malay pilgrims, heading for Jeddah. But we still had no money, so it was some time before I could get us to Egypt. From there to Italy, then Germany, then France, and finally home."

"Oh yes, let's," said Holmes.

Blur. Fuzz.

We were standing outside one of the lower-story windows of Pondicherry Lodge, looking in over Young Small's shoulders at the aged figure of John Sholto, who had called his children to his side, to hear his dying words.

"Oh, look!" said Holmes. "There's Thaddeus. *Hello, Thaddeus!* By Jove, I'd nearly forgotten about him. I suppose we'd better finish up and get him out of police custody, before he perishes of air inhalation."

We could not hear what Sholto was saying to his children, but we did see the fateful moment when he looked to the window and beheld the face of the man he'd betrayed. The glass could not block the volume of his final scream of horror. We saw his children follow his gaze and swoon in sudden fright. Egad, they were so doughy and frail, it was hard to imagine a more natural action for them. Jonathan Small scrabbled at the window, desperate to find a way in, to kill his foe. Yet, fate would cheat him. Even as we watched, the face of John Sholto began to stiffen.

"Oh yes, I'd forgotten about this bit," said Holmes. "What did you say it was, Watson? Heart attack?"

"I did, but... but see how he clutches down low there, on his right side?" I pursed my lips and watched in professional incredulity a moment, before deciding, "You know, I may actually owe you an apology, Holmes. I think what we might be seeing is the first known *liver* attack."

"Well done, Major Sholto!" Holmes cheered. "Always a pioneer!"

"I don't understand," I mumbled. "What could…? Perhaps… No… Ah! Perhaps a burst aneurysm of the hepatic artery? Is that what I'm looking at?"

However, I must admit that my academic curiosity proved to be somewhat… well… academic. An instant later, Young Small tore open the window and rushed to his fallen foe. By God, how he raged when he saw that vengeance had been stolen from him. How he cursed fate and any divine entities that might have a hand therein. He went to the desk, swept up a pen, wrote "THE SIGN OF NINE" on a piece of paper, and flung it violently at Major Sholto's corpse.

Well… in as much as one can violently fling paper. It just sort of fluttered at him. It would have been an impotent gesture at the best of times, but the fact that its recipient was already dead just lent it that special *je ne sais quoi*. Grogsson barked out a great laugh. Present-day Small rounded on him and for just a moment I thought he was about to punch Torg Grogsson. Which—now that I come to put it to paper—would have been a right and fitting end for someone who had displayed so very little self-control all the long years of his life. Instead, he stood fuming while the younger version of himself helplessly searched the room for any clue as to where his lost treasure might reside.

Clearly he found none, for a quick series of blur-fuzzes showed him sneaking in by night to dig futile holes in the grounds and indeed, the walls, of Pondicherry Lodge. Sometimes he would lift a window latch and roam the corridors by night, peeking here and probing there. Sometimes he would gaze malevolently down at the sleeping form of Bartholomew Sholto, his face a mask of rage. Yet his efforts came to naught.

Until, finally, we were standing outside the drawing-room window of an early evening. Within stood Bartholomew Sholto, excitedly slurping at a hookah much like his brother's. Between hyperventilative puffs, he was loudly exclaiming to his butler and McMurdo how he'd found the treasure. He didn't have it yet, but he was sure he'd guessed it right! Why else was the house four feet taller than it needed to be? Why else was there a rusted old pulley at the corner of the roof? The butler and bodyguard seemed unconvinced. Apparently they'd heard such wild theories before, and seen them come to naught. Yet Bartholomew Sholto's excitement was mirrored in one other set of eyes. Outside the drawing-room window— opened just a crack—huddled the figure of Jonathan Small. He looked as if he was only just keeping himself from crying out in triumph.

One blur and fuzz later, we found ourselves standing beside the drooping figure of Bartholomew Sholto as the life waned from him. Looking up through the hole in his ceiling to the secret attic above, we could just see Jonathan Small entering through the roof. Little Tonga was grasping at his friend's sleeve and pointing happily down towards Bartholomew.

"Hang on," I said. "We've skipped an important bit. Mr. Small, did you direct Tonga to kill that man?"

Lestrade raised his notebook expectantly, but present-day Small shook his head. "Nah. Probably would have if I'd thought about it, but Bartholomew had never done Tonga wrong, so…"

"Ah yes," I said. "*Tonga*."

"Yep. Tonga just Tonga-ed him. Right in the neck."

"And thus, I think, our story is complete," I reflected.

With a final buzz and blur, we found ourselves once more in the sitting room of 221B Baker Street. Our bodies were in the same position as we'd left them. Grogsson, shocked by the sudden change in position, dropped me on my rear. Holmes let go of Lestrade's hand, withdrew his finger from Jonathan Small's ear, and dropped into a low bow.

"Ladies and gentlemen, this has been *A Christmas Carol*, by Charles Dickens and Warlock Holmes! Thank you for attending this evening's performance!"

14

IT DID NOT TAKE JONATHAN SMALL LONG TO REALIZE HOW badly he had erred. "Erm… they're going to hang me, aren't they?" he said.

"Oh absolutely," said Lestrade. "The British criminal justice system has been greatly relaxed over the last few decades. Nevertheless, the number and severity of your crimes demands nothing less. Then again, if it is any consolation—" Lestrade gave a wide, fang-y smile "—any justice system would have done the same."

"Another case brought to successful conclusion," said Holmes. "Well, nearly… I suppose we must reclaim the black coin. I think Mahomet Singh was correct: it must be destroyed. Oh, and we've got to tell Mary she's rich. Oh, and save Thaddeus from the police. Oh, and break the news about Hopkins. Oh, and clean the Hopkins-goo off *Long Arm*. Oh, and—"

"Holmes, one thing at a time," I urged.

"Treasure first!" Grogsson insisted.

"There is no key," Lestrade complained. "I found no weapon and no key on Mr. Small's person."

Small gave a defiant snort and said, "Bottom of the Thames! Take that!"

I had to smile. A suspicion that had been growing in my mind began to mature into a certainty. You see, I had beheld the stunning grandeur of the Agra treasure in Mr. Small's memory. I had seen the weight of that iron chest as Grogsson hauled it across town. This much my senses had presented me, but do you know what they hadn't? A rattle. A shake. A single sound. An iron chest, filled with precious gems, being manhandled by Torg Grogsson, ought to make a little noise, oughtn't it? When we'd first caught sight of Jonathan Small, he'd been partially hidden behind the boiler of the *Aurora*, performing some action we could not quite make out.

I now suspected I knew. It was something about the pride he put into the words *bottom of the Thames*. A uniquely ungenerous thought came to me. I am to this day ashamed of it, but I have always endeavored to write the truth in these pages, even when it does not reflect well upon me.

"I'm sure that feeble old latch cannot stop Grogsson," I said. "But you know… shouldn't Mary Morstan be present when we open it? She has a vested interest, after all."

Why did I want to look on Mary Morstan when her hopes crumbled? Distasteful as I found her, I had to admit she had done me no harm. To wish to be there to gloat at her misfortune was one of the meanest impulses I have ever had. Rather *Tonga* of me, really. But I didn't care. By God, all I wanted in that moment was to see her face when that empty chest was opened.

"Perhaps that would be for the best," said Holmes, with just a hint of sadness in his tone. "Lestrade and I will conduct Mr. Small to Scotland Yard and report the resolution of this case. Since Grogsson has rather an unfortunate habit of always telling the truth, it might be a good idea if he were off on some other errand while we tell the official story. Torg, why don't you take the treasure and accompany Watson to see Miss Morstan? Then you can join us at Scotland Yard."

"M'kay," said Grogsson, who never needed much urging to stomp about London with a whacking great treasure on his back.

Thus agreed, we rose to leave. As we walked to the door, Holmes held his hand out to me to shake, and said, "Watson, it has been a grand privilege to share these adventures with you. I shall miss you terribly."

"What? No, no, no, Holmes! Our adventures are not at an end!"

"Well... they are."

"No! I do not consent to leave your company, and the bargain you struck on the day we met precludes you forcing my hand."

"As I said before, Watson, it has already been taken care of."

"Don't be ridiculous, Holmes! We shall discuss this when I come back."

"That's just the thing, Watson. You aren't coming back. Not really. So... farewell, my friend."

As we stepped out into Baker Street I held the

conviction that my good friend Warlock Holmes was barking mad.

Which he was. But he was something else, besides.

He was right.

This is how it all played out.

Jonathan Small escaped the gallows. It would seem that magic-induced dream sequences are not admissible in a British court. There were three recent deaths to explain, but Lestrade's testimony exonerated Mr. Small on all counts. The death of Major John Sholto had been a medical accident, and even if Jonathan Small's sudden appearance had played a part, it could hardly have been by design, and had hastened the victim's passing by only a few moments. The death of Bartholomew Sholto had come at the hand of Tonga. Well... at the *finger* of Tonga. If we had been in possession of Tonga's remains, the thing would have caused no end of uproar. But as these were missing, the story was plain: a small, brown-skinned individual Jonathan Small had picked up in the Andaman Islands had been firing poison darts every which way. In this age of empire and xenophobia, there was no difficulty convincing the judge of this.

Corroborating evidence was found upon the body... er... well, the *remains* of Inspector Hopkins. A second thorn, identical to the one that had struck down Bartholomew Sholto, was found lodged in his skull. Scotland Yard could mourn Stanley Hopkins as a fallen hero—struck down in the noble pursuit of duty. And really, wasn't that about the best outcome that could be hoped for him? The expectation that he was going to actually solve a case had been seeming ever more remote.

Thaddeus Sholto was freed from custody in the nick of time, as his medicinal hookah had run out of vapor. Though his jailers were certainly glad of this, due to the smell, they could not help but notice Thaddeus's rapidly declining health. By the time Holmes reached him, he was positively green. He was spirited home with all haste and quickly recovered. Solid fellow, he took the news that the Agra treasure had been lost (which indeed, proved to be the case) with a stiff upper lip. Well... actually, a doughy, wobbly upper lip, but one that behaved admirably, nonetheless. Rather than wallow in defeat, Thaddeus modified his brother's hookah into an underwater breathing device and made repeated dives into the Thames in an attempt to recover any missing gems. He did find a few and—to his great credit—surrendered every other one to Mary Morstan. He even attempted to file a patent as the inventor of the "methane-enriched-oxygen underwater breathing aid machine, Mk1", though—as this was as vile to the average underwater adventurer as it was toxic—I have not heard the patent was granted.

The black coin stayed, for a time, at the bottom of London's great river. Any upswing in the value of trade upon the Thames, as well as the level of violence and greed associated with the pursuit of that commerce, may very well be ascribed to coincidence.

Or it might not.

Yet, the final dénouement of this tale does not rest with Jonathan Small. Not with his treasure. Not with his victims.

That honor—that rather dubious honor—goes to me.

I was at the very end of my endurance. I was shaking. Had it been only the morning before that I'd begun my quest across South London with a demon on a leash? How long had it been since I'd slept? Considering my recent habit of poisoning my body, my blood, and my slumber with shredded Xantharaxes, how long since I had really *slept*? I had every intention of returning to Baker Street as soon as I could, falling into my bed and letting slumber take me. If I slept for three days, it would not have surprised me. In fact, it would have delighted me. Yet, there was one thing I must do first. A petty thing. An unkind thing.

And I relished it.

It was morning by the time Grogsson and I finally knocked upon the door of Mr. and Mrs. Cecil Forrester. The instant I announced my name to their butler, he was shoved bodily aside by the couple themselves.

"Ah! Dr. Watson," Mrs. Forrester said, "how eager we have been to see you again. And this must be… er…"

"This is Detective Inspector Torg Grogsson, of Scotland Yard," I told her. "We have brought the case to its conclusion and retrieved this item from Bartholomew Sholto's murderer. As Miss Morstan is entitled to half its contents, we thought we would unseal it in her presence."

"Yes! Oh, by God, yes! Come into the sitting room, won't you?"

I had a pang of guilt. Not only was I abusing Mary Morstan, I was crushing the hopes of Mr. and Mrs. Forrester to be rid of her, and that, at least, I regretted.

Hardly ten minutes later, we found ourselves sitting comfortably, provided with steaming cups of tea while Mrs. Forrester bustled Mary downstairs to hear our tale.

She didn't care for it.

As we recounted the previous night's adventure—the chase along the Thames and the capture of Jonathan Small—Mr. and Mrs. Forrester sat in rapt attention. They tried to get Mary to do the same. When I came to the unfortunate end of Stanley Hopkins, Mrs. Forrester said, "Isn't it sad, Mary? Why, he gave his life to help you!"

"Yes," said Mary. "Sad." Yet her expression left little doubt that her words were false. He'd been a policeman, after all. That had been his job. And whenever Mary did her job to everyone's satisfaction, she did not feel quite so much need to boast of it, did she?

I smiled. Strange, the thrill I felt to be here, delivering her just deserts to her.

"And this," I said, indicating the iron chest, "is what the villain had in his possession. It exactly matches the description and size of the treasure chest stolen from Bartholomew Sholto at Pondicherry Lodge, on the occasion of his murder."

Now Mary was interested. She leaned forward in her chair.

"It has yet to be opened and we found no key," I said, "but I think that will present no great difficulty. Inspector Grogsson? If you would be so kind…"

"Eh?" said Grogsson, then, "Oh." He reached down, closed one hand around the ancient iron lock and gave a squeeze and twist. There was the quick squeal of deforming metal, then the pop-and-tinkle of latch and lock parts that knew when they were bested.

"Ladies and gentlemen, may I present the Agra treasure!" I said, and flipped the lid open.

There was nothing. The Forresters' faces fell. Mary Morstan's expression resolved into one of unalloyed hate. She locked her eyes on mine.

"Oh dear, it seems Jonathan Small elected to give the treasure to the Thames rather than allow it to fall into the hands of the men he knew would catch him," I said. "And yet I am glad of it. Had you become the inheritor of a treasure so great, Miss Morstan, you would have been forever beyond my reach."

Mr. and Mrs. Forrester exchanged surprised but hopeful looks. Mary looked completely shocked, though this did not seem to ameliorate her anger. In fact, I think it redoubled it. My own hand flew to my mouth, and I stammered, "Oh! No. Excuse me. I did not mean to say that last part. What I meant to say was…"

What I meant to say was something along the lines of "Ha ha, that's what you get" but I was never to have the chance.

Mary rose, pointed one finger straight in my face and declared, "Then I thank God it is gone, for I wish nothing ever to come between us!"

Then she recoiled with a look of horror and muttered, "No. Wait… What I meant was: you're an ass!"

"And you are a terrible person," I told her, "and I want

to kiss you, right in the middle of your awful, awful face."

She slapped me. Hard. Yet I think there was a fierce joy in it, for both of us. Even as I turned back to rebuke her for it, she grabbed a fistful of my hair and pulled my lips down onto hers. I kissed her with a ferocity that I had no idea I owned, then used the free corner of my mouth to say, "Unhand me, madam! Mmnf. I can never be happy if we are parted! I can only be at peace when I'm with you!"

Which—I realized, to my horror—was true. My distaste for Mary Morstan had in no way lessened. Yet, what did it matter? I had infinitely more respect for Violet Hunter. And a perfect fascination with Irene Adler. Yet, what did that matter, either? Mary Morstan was now my core and my center. My place of rest. My home. The reward for all my battles. The fact that she was a vile harpy was immaterial.

"Let's get married, you useless cad!" she growled.

"Damn it! I wanted to be the one to ask!"

"Haw!" Grogsson laughed, pointing one mocking finger at me. "Watson kiss, kiss!"

Mary tore open the front of my shirt, sending two of my buttons clattering across the Forresters' sitting-room floor, then lunged back in to renew her affections.

"Woah!" Grogsson noted. "Okay… Watson *kiss, kiss!*"

"The library!" Mrs. Forrester cried, springing to her feet. "I've just realized: Inspector Grogsson has never been shown the library."

Grogsson and her husband exchanged puzzled looks.

"But…"

Right in the middle of your awful,
awful face.

"*Right now, Cecil!*"

"Yes! All right! The library!"

The three of them beat a hasty retreat, Mrs. Forrester pointing out certain aspects of the architecture that had never been to her taste, you know, but the house was so old and the features were original, so had she any right to change them? She made sure to close the door behind her.

Mary kissed my face and neck, pausing only to gasp, "I don't understand what's happening!"

Neither did I. I struggled to pull my mind back from the present situation—to observe it dispassionately and deduce the reason. By God, who was I in that moment? What was happening to me? I had to recover my power of reason! I had to...

And, I had it.

"Oh no!" I cried, running my hand over Mary's thigh. "*Holmes!*"

"What about him?" Mary asked between kisses.

"He wanted me gone and I said I wouldn't go. So what did he do? Don't you see? *He bound our souls together so I'd leave of my own accord!*"

Such ideas were strange to Mary. She stared up at me for a moment, parsing my words, searching for understanding. Then she shook her head. "No. I don't care," she decided, and began tugging at my belt.

"Warlock Holmes!" I screamed, shaking my fist in what I thought might be roughly the direction of Baker Street. "Warlock Holmes, you blighter! You bastard! I'll kill you!"

ACKNOWLEDGMENTS

I ACKNOWLEDGE THE SUPERIORITY OF DILETTANTE Chocolates' peppermint truffle cremes over all other candies. I'm going to eat this whole Costco-sized bag, puke it up, then eat that whole other bag.

Thanks again to the usual gang of misfits who made this book a book. To Sam and Sam, Miranda, Sean and Hayley. Without you guys making me a real-live published author, I'd have no cred to back up my insufferable snootiness.

To that Arthur guy: hey, didn't your version of Toby live? Ha! Now I've even surpassed you as a dog-murderer! Eat it, Doyle!

ABOUT THE AUTHOR

GABRIEL DENNING LIVES IN LAS VEGAS WITH HIS WIFE AND two daughters. Oh, and a dog. And millions of micro-organisms. He's a twenty-year veteran of Orlando Theatersports, Seattle Theatersports, Jet City Improv and has finally figured out to write some of that stuff down. His first novel, *Warlock Holmes: A Study in Brimstone*, was published in 2016, and the *Booklist* review said "Mashup fans will be eagerly awaiting more", which is why he wrote the sequels.